The 'Be

S

Book 1

Crime and Suffering

ISBN: 978-1-916732-40-7

A copy of this book is deposited with the British Library.

Published By: -

i2i PUBLISHING

i2i Publishing. Manchester.

www.i2i.publishing.co.uk

Contents

Preface

The 'Behind the Scenes' Series

Between 2005 and 2015, I lived and worked in South-East Asia. Gradually, I became aware of aspects of society which crossed over into corruption, criminality and poverty, especially the people trafficking behind the facade of the popular tourist paradises. Also, many of these activities were not only long-standing practices, but their continuation was being facilitated, often to the benefit of people in the institutions whose stated role was to stop them from happening in the first place.

My intrigue in how this contradiction worked led me to asking questions in areas that most people were careful to avoid. In turn, I became involved in more detailed research as I learnt more and more about how these activities really worked.

When I left the region, I began to write and since then, I have had many books published in Swedish. As my writing developed, I decided to try and tell the stories that interested me using the novel as my writing tool.

One of those books, *Unter Floden* (*Under the Surface*), was written to tell the story of the people I met and got to know in Laos, Cambodia and Thailand, in the ten years I was there. Next, I wrote a follow-up called *Tiggar Pojken* (*The Begging Boy)* which continued the story. I then wrote *Sista Farden* (*The Last Trip)* which completed the story told in all the books.

When I decided to publish my books in English, I agreed with Lionel Ross, the publisher and proprietor of i2ipublishing.co.uk to split *Unter Floden* into two parts: the first half of the book would become *Crime and Suffering*; the second half would now become *Bodies for Sale*. *The Begging Boy* would be re-named, *Rich and Poor* and *The Last Trip* would be re-named

Changing Identities. We decided to package all four books under the series title of *Behind the Scenes.*

The books tell the story of members of the Hmong people of Laos that were working with the CIA during the Vietnam War. After the war ended, the Hmong, an indigenous ethnic group originally from south China, were often subject to persecution and not afforded the opportunities provided to everyone else.

Just to survive, in the face of crushing poverty, many members of the tribe found themselves drawn into or forced into the questionable and often illegal activity that underpinned much of society in the region.

The tribe and their plight always interested me. Indeed, I met many of the people who have formed the basis for the four books in the *Behind the Scenes* series.

The books can be described as fiction based on fact and are an exposé of the main aspects of criminality often seen in the region, including the trafficking of people, prostitution and the smuggling of guns, drugs and products of all types.

Most of this activity is underpinned by corruption often carried out in various ways by people within official institutions ironically, in existence to protect the people they are supposed to represent, not to take advantage of them. All the books make reference to these activities and their participants.

It took me four years to write the *Behind the Scenes* series. The story has not been an easy one to tell and for some, will be difficult to read.

I hope you enjoy this first book in the *Behind the Scenes* series.

Staffan Nordstrand
Stockholm 2024

Chapter 1

Tiger Cage

It was early morning in the small village of Tat Kuang. The mist lifted over the jungle-clad mountains. Prim, still wearing her nightdress, stood outside her family's hut, for once, awake before the rooster. She stretched and welcomed the day, feeling the soil between her toes. Looking up, she saw the birds wheeling aimlessly through the air. In the courtyard, the village dogs lay, sprawling untidily. One yawned, stood up, stretched, took a look around and then returned to rest on the terracotta-coloured ground. All was silent, except for the gentle tinkle of the brook, down in the long valley. The thunder from the B-52s and their bombs had long since died away. But the traces remained, along with a deprived Hmong-people. Prim's paternal and maternal grandparents, who experienced the Vietnam War, were still fast asleep. They lived in the village as well, along with their black and ever-playful pot-bellied pigs.

Prim shut her eyes and inhaled the scents that could only be found in the morning breeze from the mountains. She felt elated, curious as to what the day would bring. Remembering her grandmother's words that you should make the most of every day, she was not so sure. It was difficult when you had to go to school. She wanted to have time for herself. She wanted to be a grown-up. While she stood there, in the cool mountain air, the people around the yard started to wake up. She left the rest of the morning to them and returned to the hut to start the day.

*

The houses in Tat Kuang lay alongside the main thoroughfare, Phothisarat Road, which led on into Luang Prabang, the second largest city in Laos. The city was about thirty kilometres away. Getting there took about one hour on that rough and winding road. Life in the village was simple and uncomplicated. Most people lived off the land. They raised animals, generally pigs, whose meat was easy to sell to Thailand. When the villagers came home after the day's toil, they washed themselves in the communal water vat, a public bath centrally situated for everyone to use. This had been the daily practice for generations. The women always cleaned themselves before the men and after they bathed, the villagers returned to their respective homes. Prim's family did just as they always had done. They went home and made a fire, out by the road. On its flames, they cooked their supper. This evening, just like all the others, it consisted of chicken and vegetables.

Prim was the oldest of two siblings; she was born in 1984 and her brother Pom arrived two years later. Prim's father, Fang, came from the village of Pak Mong, another thirty kilometres further north while her mother, Lu, came from the village of Pak Ou, just north of Luang Prabang.

The family's house, a hut with earthen floor, was constructed directly on the ground and was built on a wooden framework of bamboo poles. These were driven down into the earth and bound together from the ground up to the eaves, which were not much higher than the height of a person. The walls and the roof were rendered watertight and draught-proof on the outside with bast and large leaves, a building technology that dated back to the fifteenth century. Only a bast wall on a simple wooden frame separated the kitchen from the room where everybody in the family slept.

With the exception of Lu's brother, who lived in the village Muang Nan, eighty kilometres south of Luang Prabang, Prim's relatives all lived in the adjacent huts. Why her uncle did not live close to the rest of the family, nobody knew for sure, but neither was anyone particularly keen on staying in contact with him. Apparently, he was involved in some slightly shady business. He was always smartly dressed and had a nice car as well. Probably, the relatives' suspicion originated from jealousy.

Every night, when Prim came home from school, her first task was to help her baby brother wash himself and then to play with him for a while until her parents had gathered the family around the fire for supper. Her maternal and paternal grandparents always sat with them as well. When they had grilled the meat and vegetables, with darkness falling on the village, Prim loved to listen to the old people's stories about the past and how they lived, about the war, the famine, the poverty, the communism and the corruption.

*

This particular evening, it was Prim's maternal grandfather who started. Anant had been born in 1944 in the village of Vieng Xai, close to the Vietnamese border. He had experienced the war at close range.

"Please, Grandpa," asked Prim, "tell us about things you've experienced and how you met grandma! Pom and I would like to know."

"Of course I can," he replied. "But I believe a few people here will have to turn a deaf ear. They've probably heard it all before."

"Oh yes, Anant," Prim's father, Fang, said. "We probably have, but it's always possible there will be some things you haven't already mentioned."

"Yes, that might be the case," Anant confirmed.

The campfire they sat around spread a comforting light, visible even to those few cars that passed by.

"Grandpa," said Prim, "I'd really like to hear your stories."

Songchai, Prim's paternal grandfather, smiled. He had been born in the same year as Anant, in Luang Prabang and had similar experiences. The city was about one hundred kilometres from the borders of the surrounding countries; China to the north, Vietnam to the east, Burma to the west and Thailand to the south.

"Okay then," began Anant, "what the hell!"

"No cursing!" grandma May cut in instantly.

"But should I tell the children? In that case, they have to be tough enough to hear the truth," he cautioned.

"Yes, but you could leave some details out, couldn't you?" she said.

"We live in an evil world and that's the way it should be portrayed, without beating around the bush. But if there hadn't been so much damned bombing, we would never have found each other, would we?" he reminded her.

May, Prim's maternal grandmother, had been born in 1945 in the village of Muang Khoun near the Vietnamese border while Mak, Prim's paternal grandmother, was born a year later in the village of Viang Vien some eighty kilometres south of Luang Prabang.

"Yes, I suppose it was the war that brought us together," agreed May.

"Really?" exclaimed Fang. "I thought it was love!"

"No," said grandpa, "that came later."

"If it ever comes at all," Fang said, a touch of acid in his voice.

"Grandpa, don´t forget me. I want to know" said Prim.

"No, I would never forget you, Prim," he assured her. "It's just that I have to prepare myself; to remind myself of the feeling of the caves of the village of Vieng Xai, caves in which we were forced to live and die."

"What do you mean, die?" Prim wondered.

"Well, I'll tell you," he continued. "It's important that people your age get to understand our background. Those of us who belong to the proud and independent Hmong people, living mostly up here in the mountain districts, immigrated in vast numbers to Laos at the beginning of the twentieth century, because in southern China, they didn't like us and the Chinese treated us very badly."

"You've never been this specific before," said Fang.

"No, but it's about time that I was," grandpa replied. "Don't you think all our grandchildren should know about their origins? And, of course, it's a subject I like to talk about, so please allow me to go on."

Fang nodded his assent and Anant continued.

"In the highlands, we have cleared and scorched the croplands. As you know, Fang, we have been clever at cultivating opium. All that was ended by the French, along with the government of that time. Despite that, many of our people still grow it, in secret locations high in the mountains. Back then, there was always a war going on somewhere. If there was no war in our country, there was a conflict in the countries around us, like the Indochina War where our people fought on the French side. During the civil war, I joined the secret forces, the 'Secret Army', led by General Vang Pao. This was in '62, the same year your father was born. It was necessary."

"Why?" asked Prim.

"Well, so that the communists wouldn't take over," grandpa replied. "Although that's what ended up happening anyway, but we did try to stop them back then. In Sam Thong, there was a large union of Hmongs. We were trained by the CIA, American special agents and their helpers from the Thai army, who had a secret base in Long Cheng."

"Well, I'm going to bed," grandma said and turned towards grandpa, "but first, we have to bring in the piglets."

They were tiny, fat black Vietnamese pot-bellied pigs. They were running friskily about beneath the evening sky. It would be another year before it was time for them to be slaughtered.

Prim's family was not the only one sitting by the roadside eating food cooked over an open fire. The whole village sat near them, trailing alongside the road. This was not always safe. Some of the people that drove past had only recently obtained their driver's license. Driving lessons were out of the question. If you could start the car and drive around a gravel area outside a police station, it would suffice. The policemen who issued the licenses were not the least interested in a candidate's driving skills. The only thing that concerned them was the sum one could pay them. This was the case all over Laos. If the license itself cost seventy thousand kip, barely eleven dollars, there would be yet another payment of twenty thousand kip to bribe the police. And bribes were taken at all levels.

At that moment, the only people left by the fire were Anant, Fang, Lu, Pom and Prim. Grandpa had been silent for a while. Should he tell them everything, or spare them some of the details? He decided to tell all. His audience was old enough to handle the truth. There were risks in spreading his tale too widely, but the children here learned at young age to keep quiet about what was said within the family. So grandpa continued.

"I was in the Secret Army for twelve years. It's a wonder that I'm still alive, really. It's partly thanks to grandma," he said.

"Why is that?" asked Prim.

"Well, now I'm curious too," added Fang.

"As we both know, you have quite a lot to tell as well, Fang," grandpa pointed out.

"Yes, of course, but I was just a child when the war was at its worst. We can talk about that later," Fang replied.

"Anyhow, those twelve years were tough," grandpa continued. "The US had an influence on everything we did. It was their war, but our hell. Much of it took place around grandma's village, Muang Khoun, where we often hid in the giant pots that still stand out in the fields. The whole area, with all its villages and small towns, had been occupied by the North Vietnamese. Every long valley and every mountain peak was controlled by them. We waged a full-on guerrilla war, with air support from the US and with food bombing from Air America. In general, all employees in that company were agents. The whole operation was kept confidential by the US armed forces. Neither the American nor the European public knew anything about what was going on up there in northern Laos. All eyes were fixed on Vietnam."

"Why did you fight, Grandpa?" asked Prim.

"For we Hmongs, the communists were our enemies and we were ready to die for our cause," grandpa confirmed. "Most of us did die in the battles over there. Even now, I feel as if I can still smell all the dead bodies each time I return to visit grandma's relatives. But the worst memories are those of my relatives and friends."

"You pulled through," said Fang.

"Yes, but wouldn't you like to know how I did that? If it hadn't been for May, I would have been just one more piece of meat torn to shreds by the dogs, just like the rest of them."

"What happened, Grandpa?" Prim asked again.

"It was towards the end of the long war up there," he replied after pausing and taking a deep breath. "We had lost almost the whole of our army and were severely weakened in spite of the support from the US and their bombing, which sometimes hit some of us as well as our enemies. Those Yankees sat comfortably, high up in the sky in their B-52s, releasing their waves of bombs while we, the guerrilla soldiers, were down below hiding in the jungle. To our opponents, the jungle was not an unfamiliar place but to make it worse, they were clever and cunning strategists. And of course, you shouldn't underestimate the help they got from China and the Soviet Union.

"It took place on a night when we felt that things were quite calm. Our guerrilla group, fifteen of us, plus two American advisers, was suddenly detected as we made our way from Phonsavan to the smaller village of Nong Pet. We believed that Nong Pet would be safe at night since the village was more or less shot up. According to our observer, the only person left there was an old woman and her dog. We avoided the road and kept to the shadows. It was scary. We knew the moon might expose us at any given moment. Before we arrived, a corporal, Paton, said we should circle the village to ensure we were not taken unawares by the commies; he told us that the neighbourhood was absolutely swarming with them. So, covered by the dark and our camouflage, our faces were painted black and our bodies covered with nets where we had attached twigs and leaves, we crawled ahead slowly.

"The problem was that the commies had their own plan: not to linger in the village after carrying out the massacre there, but to stay hidden just outside. With one of the Americans, I kept one metre behind Paton, who had taken the lead position. It was deathly silent; you could hear nothing but your own breathing. Suddenly, Paton fell to his knees. He froze for a couple of seconds, before wheezing in an effort to speak. He had crawled over a Vietnamese, who had dug himself in. We could see that Patton's throat had been pierced, from the front right through to the back of the neck by something that appeared to be a sharp bamboo pole. When Paton fell backwards, all hell broke loose. We were caught in the midst of their hiding place and couldn't get out. The commies managed to kill seven of us. How many did we shoot? I still don't know as it was dark. We just kept firing away until the magazines in our sub-machine guns emptied. Of course, they didn't want to kill us all immediately;

we might yield information, you know. But for most of us, being killed would've been a better deal," Anant concluded.

"That's enough for me," said Lu, "I'll take Pom with me and leave you now. Otherwise, I won't be able to sleep tonight. And you, Prim, you are to come soon."

"But now that Grandpa is telling his story, I'd like to listen," Prim responded.

"I'll bring Prim with me, when Anant has grown weary of telling his stories," said Fang.

"Stories? Surely you can tell that this is fact and not fiction!" Anant exclaimed angrily.

"I'm sorry, of course," replied Fang.

"Your father learned how to use guns when he was twelve," Anant continued, "something he'd like to forget. But that's the way it was."

"Don't you start, Anant, keep to your own stuff. Soon enough, Prim will get to hear about my adolescence," said Fang.

"Yes, well anyhow, we were captured," Anant said. "We had stepped into a hornets' nest, you know. We only had ourselves to blame, I suppose. Come morning, it became clear that there were about one hundred of them close by, so our informer had probably missed out on some crucial details. He didn't get to make any more mistakes and get any more of us killed, since he himself was killed shortly afterwards. The next day, we were transported in a lorry back towards Phonsavan, which was hell on earth. It was from there that we had started our hazardous mission. The whole valley was filled with dead Vietnamese. During just the last two months, almost a thousand men had lost their lives. Since they were now in control of the valley, they could risk using the vehicle. We were finally thrown off the lorry by the lake Nong Nam Nyan, where the Vietnamese had a camp."

"But didn't you have to hide the bodies of the dead first, before you were taken away?" asked Fang.

"No, not hide them. We had to undress them and remove their dog-tags, that's all," Anant confirmed.

"Why?" Fang asked again.

"To hide their origins; it was the best thing for them. In any case, I was happy that I wasn't an American. They usually killed us off pretty quickly, but since there were two Americans in our group, the commies became suspicious and the six of us who had survived ended up in the same shit as the Americans. Even now, I still dream about it. There we were, lying in the dust. Nobody was allowed to get up or move. We could only lie there, still, beneath the burning sun with guards all around us and not a drop of water. An officer arrived later that morning and didn't say a word. We lay silent, looking at each other, realising that the first of us to open his mouth would end up dead. Nothing happened, until suddenly, the silence was shattered. Our friend, Soy had received a heavy blow. One of the soldiers had lifted his rifle and using the butt, struck down as hard as he could on Soy's right hand. We could see how it was smashed. His fingers curled upwards. The pain meant that Soy could not keep silent, so he received another heavy blow with the same rifle butt, now to his mouth. This time, he didn't scream. He just wheezed and whimpered and only those of us close by could hear him. He started to shake and then he went into shock.

"All of us were ordered to get up. I tried, together with an American called Nick, to help Soy to his feet, but it was impossible. We couldn't get a good enough grip on him and Soy was incapable of helping out. It would have been easier for us to grab him under the arms, but the Vietnamese wouldn't allow it. They said that they would take him to a hospital at the camp. We were led to our destination.

"'Down to the lake!' yelled the officer and off we went, slowly.

"'Out on the jetty!' he yelled again and we had no idea what was going on until we reached the jetty at the shore of Nong Nam Nyam. Then we understood. Out there, at the furthest point on the jetty, stood a couple of commies, who had hoisted up a part of the jetty's floor. It looked like a lid. We were terrified. Were they just going to let us drown?" Anant paused.

"Anant," said Fang. "Please, there's no need for you to go into all the details; it might be a bit much for Prim."

"No, not at all," said Prim. "I've heard a lot of it before from other people. We've even talked about it at school. But I've never heard it from Grandpa before and that makes a huge difference. I'd like you to go on, Grandpa."

"Alright, then I will," said her grandfather. "We went out to the edge of the jetty and stopped at the hole in the jetty floor. Nick told his pal, Tom, that it was a 'tiger cage'. I didn't really know what he meant by that term. It proved to be an almost completely submerged bamboo structure under the jetty. They would make us go down into the cage and then shut us in, dropping the lid they were holding up. They were not planning on drowning us, or at least, not yet, just on keeping us there until it was time to fetch us if we hadn't actually drowned as a result of our injuries or exhaustion. When we entered our underwater cage, it became clear that we couldn't touch the bottom with our feet. To keep our heads above the water, we were forced to hold onto the walls of the cage. It was made of strong bamboo poles, with enough space between them to enable us to stick our hands through and in this way, keep our chins above the water. Nick instructed us, 'Get your arms all as far as possible through the poles, far enough to hook yourself in place if you fall asleep. That'll keep you from drowning.' We did as he said and that's why I still have this on my forearm."

Her grandfather showed her a scar: one and a half inches wide and four inches long.

"After the first night, we were already in a very bad way," he continued. "Tom and Nick were suffering from a severe stomach bug. The bacteria in the foul water were more dangerous for them than they were for us. You could say that those of us who lived around here had a built-in resistance, while those from elsewhere easily ran into problems. Those affected had to receive medication and water so that they didn't die from dehydration.

"The sun had just risen when we noticed that there was something going on at the beach. Through the openings between the poles of the cage and the boards of the jetty, we could see the Vietnamese approaching, dragging Soy with them. His upper body was naked and bloody all over; he appeared to be totally lifeless. We told each other, 'He's dead; they've killed him.'

"Those communist pigs had tied his wrists together and were using a rope to drag him out onto the jetty. We had assumed they would hoist the lid and throw him down, but instead, they just dragged him there and left him lying on the lid above us. At the same time, we were enduring the stench of the excrement from Nick and Tom, who insisted on apologising and excusing themselves, although they couldn't be blamed for becoming ill. Above us, we could see our half-dead comrade bleeding from his eyes, nose, mouth and from a deep wound on his forehead. His hands were wrecked as well. One could only guess as to what they'd done to him. We tried to speak with him, but he could not communicate at all. All we could hear was his heavy breathing, accompanied by the sound of his blood dripping down into the cage. Soy died after a couple of hours. It was the best thing that could have happened to him, really.

"We wondered who would be next. They dragged Soy away from the lid and just let him lie where they happened to drop him. We were horrified, but, as I mentioned earlier, I was glad that I wasn't an American. It became clear that they hadn't decided which one of us they should pick next. It ended up being Nick. Everyone inside clung along the walls of that two metre cage. It wasn't hard for them to grab one of us; it was like fishing at a restaurant, just pick your prey and pull it up.

"Two Vietnamese took hold of Nick's arms. I think he tried to make himself as heavy as possible, for when they sensed that he wasn't cooperating, they began to beat him furiously with their sticks to make him yield. Then, it was almost as if he sprang up out of the enclosure and fell down hard onto the jetty. They grabbed hold of his forearms and dragged him until he got to his feet by himself and began walking, following them down the jetty.

"This was the last we ever saw of him. And we were lucky not to hear much more, due to the ear-splitting noise of the B-52s, which were carpet bombing vast areas of northern Laos without a break. But between the falling bombs, which inflicted vast, gaping wounds on the land, we could still hear Nick screaming in fear and pain.

"We could only imagine what they were doing to him. One of their methods for making a prisoner talk was to bind open his mouth and then draw a big workshop file over his teeth. It was a horrific method they had learnt from the Russians and was far more effective than pulling out the teeth one by one. It always made the prisoner speak."

"Good grief, Grandpa, how terrible!" exclaimed Prim.

Then, she heard her mother calling out, "That's enough, Prim, get inside and let Dad and Grandpa talk about their old memories by themselves! You've been up far too long as it is!"

Reluctantly, Prim retired to the hut.

*

Fang sat quietly, admiring his father-in-law. Although his own father had also fought the communists, it was usually Anant's stories that aroused his interest.

Prim had gone in to Lu. She washed her hands and cleaned her teeth using a sort of face-cloth which she wiped over them. Then, she took a blanket and lay down quite close to mum's and dad's bedding. She rested her head just inside the wall, facing the area where grandpa and dad sat talking. Absorbed by her grandfather's story, Prim struggled to sleep. She knew that if she said anything about it to Lu, she would never again be allowed to sit together with them and hear their tales. For the moment, it was best to be quiet and pretend to be asleep. Nevertheless, Prim was listening intently.

Lu sat with Prim and talked to her for a while, caressing her back. Then, she left her daughter, convinced that Prim would soon be asleep.

Back outside, the discussions continued.

"It's quite peculiar," Fang said, "Nowadays, we live side by side and even marry into one another's families."

"Yes," said Anant, "but that's the way it's always been, hasn't it? Alright, I'll go on if you want."

"Yes I do," Fang confirmed, "although I've been trying to forget what happened back then for a long time. It will always stay with me, though. How could it not, when so many of our soldiers were slain during those battles that when we just twelve years old, we had to learn how to kill the enemy?"

"Yes, you were born in '62, so you were truly hurled into the war," Anant said.

Prim had never heard this before and immediately, she was wide awake. She inched closer to the thin wall, close enough to feel the heat from the fire still burning out there, on the other side. The fire was necessary. At that time of year, the temperature usually dropped at night to eleven degrees, sometimes twelve, but it was not unknown for it to fall as far as freezing. To keep warm during the night was crucial, either by heat from the fire or from the bodies of other family members.

Tat Kuang, their village, had been badly damaged during the war, but not to the same extent as the villages of any of Prim's grandparents. For this, Prim felt grateful. Somehow, it gave her the feeling that it was safer in Tat Kuang, even though twenty years had passed since the war had ended. There was, however, always something reminiscent of the war. If it wasn't grandpa's stories, it was all those sea-shell clad edges alongside the paths and walkways and the signs everywhere warning 'Danger!! Mines!'

Unexploded ordnance was still found in such quantities in these areas. Around sixty children were either killed or seriously injured each year. As a result, Prim and her friends had become pretty hardened, enough to kill yet another Vietnamese, if you were to believe their games in school.

"But we can return to my experiences later," said Fang. "How did things turn out after what you've just described, Anant? And when does May come into the picture? I've always assumed you two met a long time after you'd been wounded."

"No, that's not correct. May nursed me, healed my wounds and hid me in the caves up at my native district around the village of Vieng Xai," Anant explained.

"Hold on!" Fang exclaimed. "Let's return to that later. Tell me what happened in Nong Nam Nyam."

Anant continued his story. Now, both Fang and Prim remained silent, each listening intently from either side of the wall.

"It probably didn't take the commies many hours to get what they wanted out of Nick. I have to tell you, all that rubbish they show in the films about the Vietnam War and how the Americans keep quiet during interrogation is nonsense. Nobody in the world could resist the torture they were subjected to. You talked. Yes, you even confessed things you didn't know the first thing about and this was understood by everybody who dealt in torture. The Vietnamese had a knack for making their prisoners speak. There was an old trick that was pulled on one of us, but I will come back to that later on. Anyhow, we never saw Nick again and I've always thought he's still lying there, somewhere north of that lake, even though people have looked for his remains and other clues as to his whereabouts and never come up with a thing." Anant was silent for a moment.

Then, he continued.

"During that afternoon, two of our group couldn't cope anymore. They succumbed. They remained hanging by their arms for the rest of the time we were there which was three to five days, I guess. I'm not sure. I've still got lapses in my memory."

"But what about you? Did you remain in that tiger cage?" Fang asked.

"Yes, we did and that was lucky because suddenly, the Vietnamese had no time for us. We survived those days in the cage thanks to an intense rainfall, which offered us drinkable water; the water we were up to our necks in was too contaminated to drink. And after that, there was a hellish pressure from the Americans and the whole area came under an intense aerial bombardment. The Vietnamese suffered a great many casualties and were about to abandon the camp. When a couple of Vietnamese came running out onto the jetty, I released the cage-wall I was hanging onto and made for the side nearest the shore. I assumed that those lifting the lid would be standing facing the other way and that they would grab the first man they saw on the other side of the cage from where I now was. That turned out to be Tom. They disappeared with him, but soon returned and opened the roof of the cage once more. That very second, I dived down beneath the surface towards the floor of the cage. I couldn't see anything, but I heard an intense whistling through the water, which I realised was the sound of their bullets. I found myself a short distance behind one of my comrades and succeeded in holding on in such a way that he ended up hanging over me. Then, I felt an intense pain in my face, as if it had been torn off. Instinctively, I let go and started to float up towards the surface."

"What happened?" asked Fang.

Prim lay behind the wall lay, listening breathlessly. She had never heard these things before.

"Why, the commies were shooting us, executing us. But the thing was that they were under such stress that they made a poor job of it. They thought that I was dead as well. I wasn't, obviously, but I had been hit and severely wounded. A bullet had gone straight through my mouth, in through one cheek and out the other; a small, discreet hole on the way in and a larger, uglier one on the way out. That's why I look the way I do, but this you know already. Another bullet smashed my cheekbone while several others hit my right arm, which I was using to hold my comrade's waist. If I hadn't been so focussed on my own survival, there's no doubt I would have died too.

"I kept myself under the surface for a while, but eventually, I heaved myself up on the jetty and staggered towards the shore. Luckily enough, everybody had gone and later, our people found me lying on the beach when they arrived to secure the area. I heard someone calling out that I was alive and I made an effort to show that he was right. I only just managed it because I was so weak. Our comrades saw to it that I got a comfortable transport to some sort of assembly point for wounded soldiers. There were a few Americans there, but no sign of either Tom or Nick.

"Some of us were transported to my native district, Vieng Xai. Along the route, I saw some bodies that had been burned and twisted from napalm. The village was completely burnt out. In the mountains surrounding the village, there were several hundred caves. They say that the Vietnamese were clever at living in caves, but so were we. Nowadays, the Tham Xieng Muang-cave is one of our best-known caverns. Being two hundred metres long, it's our deepest. Back then, it contained a secret hospital that had been established for some time. I was taken there and nursed by a couple of female soldiers, hospital personnel. This is where your mother-in-law enters the story: one of those soldiers was May, you see. As you know, Fang, there were a total of about twenty-three thousand people sheltered in all the caves in this area during the war. In the caves, we had not only the hospital: there were conference rooms, factories for the production of weapons and tools, conduits, schools."

Prim had heard and read about those caves up at grandpa's village. She knew where they were, but there remained a great deal of mystery surrounding them. If you didn't know where the entrances were, it was almost impossible to find them. It is not until now, in recent years, that some of them had become available for tourists to see.

"May and I lived a soldier's life for six months down there in those caves, but there were many who lived in them for several years," Anant carried on.

"It's remarkable that you managed to live down there for such a long time," said Fang. "We only ever took shelter in them during the bombing raids, when the Vietnamese were too close."

"Yeah, we certainly had a tough choice back then. It was hard to know what to do. Now, we know how badly things went for those who stayed on the surface, but we also know the fate of those the commies found inside the caves. They were blasted and buried alive," Anant confirmed sadly.

Prim was ready to sleep now, but was unable to. She couldn't stop brooding about what had taken place in grandpa's caves during that horrible period.

"It still amazes me, you know," Prim heard Fang say from the other side of the wall, "when I see the tools my parents and you others made from the remains of the bombs that had been dropped; spades, pickaxes and pots and pans. To say nothing of all those bombs that did not detonate, from which you made weapons, using the powder for detonating and in the hospitals to stop minor haemorrhages by cauterising open wounds. That kind of cave manufacturing would be a sight for the world to see. But now, Anant, I think I'd better leave you and go to my family. Why don't you stay awhile and warm yourself by the fire; it will go out before long."

Pom slept like a log, but Prim was still awake. She heard her dad coming in and looking around the hut in search of his blanket. Locating it, he wrapped himself up in it and tiptoed towards his bedding. On his way, he happened to wake-up Lu, half on purpose.

Chapter 2

Pigs and Whiskey

Fang and Lu led ordinary lives under the same conditions as so many others, neither better nor worse. But during hard times, the sort of ill-fortune which might befall anyone, Lu could get some help from Surachai her brother, six years her senior.

Fang had fallen madly in love with Lu the moment he first met her. Lu was about to meet a female friend and was on her way from Pak Ou, by the Mekong River close to Tat Kuang, to catch one of the boats frequenting the Mekong from Luang Prabang to Ban Xieng. Unfortunately, the regular boat had broken down and the repairs would not begin for another week, once new parts had arrived.

Fang's father, Songchai, owned an old river boat, on which he had transported a great variety of goods, among other things, old weapons which he had sold expensively to arms dealers. He knew where the arms caches left over from the war were located. This was how he had supported his family. Nowadays, however, it was passenger traffic that was his main business, so the old man was quick off the mark in offering paid trips between the jetties. Fang was the boat's helmsman and the first day Lu was a passenger, their romance began. Fang was twenty-one at the time and Lu was nineteen.

Fang was completely taken with the young woman. She was so beautiful and shapely that to his eyes, she had no match, not even in the magazines he occasionally found in the shops. Her beautiful black hair was long, reaching almost all the way down to her lower back and bound in a ponytail. Lu's nose and cheekbones told him that she was one of the proud people. She wore a thin blouse made of fine, white silk and a pair of slacks which were not too revealing. Nevertheless, Fang stared, longing for a glimpse of more.

When Lu disembarked on the other side of the Mekong River, Fang decided not to leave the beach at Ban Xieng until she returned. He knew she would come back to the beach later that evening, because she had asked Fang's friend, who took payment on the boat, how late the boat made the return trip to Luang Prabang. So, Fang waited. He gave his friend instructions, too.

"Even if you have to come back here empty from Prabang. When you see my signal, just do it! I need to meet that girl, properly!" he had said.

"You're out of your mind!" his friend exclaimed, laughing. "Don't you know; she's already married and has at least seven children? Her husband will kill you!"

This observation was just to pull Fang's leg and Fang knew it.

Sure enough, Lu returned before evening. Because the crossing didn't take long, Fang had almost no time to speak to her. The butterflies swirling in his stomach made it difficult to say anything at all.

"When will you be crossing again?" he asked her.

"In about a month," Lu replied.

"Does it really have to be a whole month before I get to see you again?" he inquired.

"Yes," Lu replied, smiling.

"I'll be waiting," Fang confirmed.

On the eastern shore of the Mekong River, where it joined up with the Nam Khan, lay Luang Prabang. Along the roadside, the local people built a low wall. From openings in this wall, steps led down to the beach.

You could count up to fifty riverboats down at the beach, all of the same kind as the one owned by Fang's family. But only ten of those were working; most of them lay long abandoned.

No one chose to bathe in the Mekong: it was oily and full of garbage of every description. Only the neighborhood dogs moved around along its shores. The path was up on Khem Khong Street, the town's main street, which ran along the river from one end of Luang Prabang to the other.

*

No more than a few days had passed before Fang spotted Lu again. She had not come to cross the river, however, but rather to go for a stroll with a couple of friends. Fang was fortunate as he had been ordered to sit on the wall up by the road. His assignment that day was to keep a tally of the number of passengers and from up there, he had a vantage point over the beach and any passengers travelling with each boat. If there was one way in which the fare-takers cheated their employers, it was by misrepresenting the number of passengers.

Fang was just as surprised as Lu when they caught sight of each other. As she approached him, he thought Lu was like an ethereal vision. He had not been able to think of anything but her since their first encounter. For Lu, it had been the same. Lu's girlfriends noticed immediately that something was up when they passed Fang. Lu smiled and looked into his eyes as she said hello.

This time, Fang knew what to do. He would not waste this opportunity. And yet, somehow, he did. Later that very day, he found out where Lu lived and went there. He was anxious to avoid being seen; all he hoped for was to catch sight of her again, at a distance. Fang was madly in love. He wanted to make contact but was afraid of making a fool of himself. Eventually, he departed without having achieved anything.

The next day, he decided to return to Lu's house. This time, he was hell-bent on making contact. Fang went up to the hut in Pak Ou, shouted hello and waited. There was no answer.

Then, he circled the hut and entered the small courtyard around which her family's huts were located. Outside one of the huts sat a couple of old women who had just slaughtered a hen for supper. He asked if they knew of Lu and where he might find her. The old folks looked at each other and smiled.

"Well, you'll find her down along the road. She's gone to fetch some pigs," they told him.

Fang set out on the road in the direction pointed out by the old women. After half an hour's walking, he spotted Lu with two pigs leashed on strings, as if she were out walking a couple of dogs. She smiled warmly at Fang. It was a pleasant surprise to see him. Fang told her that he had come to meet her and that the old women in the courtyard had been kind enough to point him in the right direction.

"You mean my mother and my aunt," Lu said. "Then you've already met a part of my family."

Fang was not stupid. He understood that Lu's mother had liked him straight away. If she had not, she would not have shown him where to find her daughter. It could not be the case that the old woman wanted to get rid of her daughter, to throw her at the first boy that came along, could it? In fact, Lu herself had decided to escape the squalor she lived in as soon as possible, to get away from the filth, the earthen floors, the perpetually stinking village and all the demands from everybody.

They sauntered on with the pigs, slowly, ensuring that it would take a long while to get back. Lu mentioned her younger brother, who never made himself useful. She always had to be the one to take care of everything, from chopping wood, to cooking, to helping out with the slaughter of the animals. She was also the one who ended up cleaning the house. This meant that there was very little time for leisure. Lu's older brother Surachai had left home at an early age; and what he was into, Lu did not really want to discuss. But later, she would tell Fang that

Surachai made a lot of money and that it was not through rice or slaughter but by selling old weapons, like Songchai, Fang's father. Probably, it involved narcotics as well. That was the only way he could pay for the car and that house he lived in.

Anant, Surachai's father, thought that he had taught his son to keep a low profile, but that was not the way things had turned out.

*

It took only a few months of intense dating before Fang and Lu had set their hearts on a life together. There was a flame between them. They would never allow it to die down and that was what they promised one another when they married six months later.

Their wedding night turned out the way wedding nights often do with the couple falling asleep with exhaustion, too drunk to have sex. This was definitely the case on Fang's part. His cousins and Lu's brother, Surachai, had done their best to render it impossible for him to be a good lover that night. There had been a lot more than just one glass of Mekong whiskey too many. Drinking too much of the stuff could have a serious effect and that was what Fang had done.

He definitely did not think about sex that night and neither did Lu. But this was of little consequence as they had started having sex with each other within two weeks of their initial stroll with the pigs along the road at Pak Ou. Lu suspected that she was pregnant although she decided not to mention anything to Fang until she was certain. She was right. When it arrived, the baby would be called Prim.

The party was held at a small hotel in the village. Their room was very plain, but it gave Fang and Lu the opportunity to sleep in a bed together for the first time. But Fang missed out on the whole thing: he slept sitting upright on the edge of the bed. Every time he risked lying down, the whole room began to spin, forcing him to sit straight back up again. He did not want to throw up on his wedding night. But that had probably been for the best, because when Lu woke up in the morning, her husband was still sitting on the bedside half asleep.

"You really missed out on something," she told him.

She tried to make him turn around. It took him a while, not unlike those occasions when you turn and find that all the details in the room do not appear in their proper place until some minutes later. When Fang's gaze stopped, he realised his mistake. There was Lu, lying on her side facing him, naked.

His eyes took in her silk-brown body. He placed a hand on her hip and caressed her gently up over her chest, beneath her arm. She rolled over on her back, so that Fang should not miss out on touching her breasts properly.

Fang caressed her firm bosom and allowed his fingers to play over them. Lu told him to get inside her and he tried but failed to get an erection.

"I'll help you," she said soothingly.

She tried but was unsuccessful. Fang pressed himself on top of her and tried to enter her anyway.

Suddenly, he felt his nausea getting the better of him.

"I've got to get up!" he said, panicking.

Fang dashed into the toilet to vomit, but nothing came, just the terrible feeling that came with being so hungover. He knew he would regret what was happening for the rest of the day, if not longer.

"It's okay," Lu said, "we will marry just once, you know, so there will only be the one hangover like this one."

Fang agreed.

Chapter 3

Grandpa's Business

Prim was still awake. She could feel the warmth radiating through the wall from the fire on the other side, where grandpa was probably sitting and sleeping. Two years after Prim had arrived, Pom had come into the world.

Fang and Lu had an active and fulfilling sex life. They often seized the opportunity when they were alone out in the fields or when the children were sleeping. This time, however, Prim was awake and she could hear that her father was willing once more.

She was soon to turn twelve and she looked just like her mother. Her breasts had started to show and she could feel her body pinching at the seams, but it had not yet begun to scream out its rage at emerging from its chrysalis as it entered into adulthood. All of this was soon to come.

Tomorrow, Sunday, Prim was supposed to go with Songchai, her grandfather, to Luang Prabang and shop at the weekend market. All sorts of things made by the local population would be on sale: textiles, watches and merchandise 'imported' — or rather smuggled — from China. The street Sisavang Vong ran through the whole town, as did the market which was open until late. That was why it was also known as the night market. Items of every conceivable form were being sold.

*

When Prim woke next morning, the sun had begun to warm the earth and the roosters had already crowed, bidding the morning welcome. No doubt there was something peculiar about the roosters of the village: none of them had the courtesy to wait until seven o'clock to begin crowing. Instead, they set about their racket at four or five in the morning.

It was a beautiful time of year, giving a clear morning view over the mountains. The sunbeams filtered down through the palm leaves and coconuts, large and distended, forming clusters that were to be harvested and sold at the market. Mak, Prim's grandma, was busy packing nuts onto the lorry's small loading platform. It was mostly the sparse tourists who bought opened coconuts, prizing them for their sweet coconut water and coconut meat.

Songchai, Prim's maternal grandfather, was always up to something. Mak said that this was what had drawn them together: the excitement and the drama. Prim liked being together with her maternal grandfather just as much as with her paternal grandfather: it was a good combination. Songchai was always at work upon some clandestine businesses or seizing an opportunity to cash in on unexpected incidents, just as he had been on the spot when the ferry had broken down, or if someone got into difficulties and had to borrow money. When such things happened, Songchai would be there offering his help (and charging for it, of course).

This morning, Prim was tired. How long had she lain awake? Probably until midnight. She had fallen asleep before the fire went out and she had not heard grandpa leaving his spot. In the morning, she had not been woken up by the roosters; not by all the noise outside and not by her mother's incessant shouting. It was Pom that had woken her up.

"Prim, get up now!" he urged.

"I'm too tired. Let me be!" Prim replied.

"You've got to get up. Grandpa's leaving soon. You know he won't be waiting if you dawdle," Pom emphasised.

Pom decided to do something that he was certain would rouse Prim from her bed. He went off and got a small bucket of water. He knew that everyone in the hut would be angry with him, because it was not good to dampen the earthen floor. But this morning, he didn't give a damn. He was determined to get Prim up and he knew that she hated what he was about to do. Pom carried the bucket to Prim's bedding and poured the water over her. Then, he ran off as fast as his legs could carry him.

"Pom!" Prim cried out in a high screech, "I'll get you for this!"

She shot to her feet, angry as a bear, but even through her rage, she could not keep a straight face.

"I'll get even with you when I catch you! I swear, you'll get such a beating and so much water over you that you'll never forget it!" she threatened him.

Now Prim was on her feet, at least. Pom, however, was already far from the village and would not return until he was certain Prim had left with grandpa. He knew she would make sure to tan his hide if she succeeded in catching him, but come evening, she would probably have forgotten the morning's incident.

"Prim, come on!" Songchai shouted. "Everything is packed and it's time to hit the road."

It did not take long to get to the town, but as usual, grandpa had other plans.

"I'll have to take a little detour," he said.

"Why is that?" Prim asked.

"I have to meet some friends down at the Nam Ming River. I'll just talk with them for a short while and then we'll continue on," he explained

"Okay," Prim replied.

*

After an interminable drive along a badly kept, muddy and narrow road, where it was impossible to travel faster than twenty miles per hour, they arrived at Nam Ming. The river was at a level a few metres lower than the road and fifty metres from its edge. A rather brushy green open space separated the road from the river. Songchai stopped the car and got out. Prim could see that there were a couple of men down at a longboat which they had pulled up onto the muddy beach. Songchai waved at them as they caught sight of each other, but said nothing as he walked down towards them. It was easy enough for Prim to hear what they were saying as the river valley was quiet and she was downwind of them.

"That sure took a long time!" grandpa began. She looked over the men who she was sure, even from this distance, were unfamiliar.

"What have you been doing?" he asked them.

Prim listened intently; being with grandpa was always an adventure.

"The terrain up at the caves was more troublesome than we anticipated. A section of the cave had collapsed," one of the men said.

"Did you find what we were looking for?" Songchai asked.

"Yes," one of them replied and lifted a blanket covering something on the boat.

Songchai bent down and picked up an object that looked like a handgun.

"Did it all look like this?" he asked.

"No, a lot of it was in bad shape. But there were a great number of Russian-made landmines and we suspect this cache is a big one. We need to dig down deeper, but that might be risky," the man confirmed.

"Fine," Songchai said. "Prim and I are going to the market today. We never met here today, okay? We'll see each other tomorrow. Till then, I'll get in touch with some buyers who I think may be interested. We may well have to transport the goods by boat, down the Mekong."

Songchai came back to the truck and Prim pretended to have heard nothing. Smart in some ways, grandpa suffered from the same stupidity as the rest of his generation: he assumed that children didn't understand anything. What a mistake that was. Prim soaked up everything like a sponge. Even before they had set out, she had worked out that what grandpa was up to was hazardous. She had heard grandma warning him, but he had just laughed and changed the subject.

Now, they were on the road again. Prim was worried that they would be late for the market, but grandpa kept track of time. There was no point in getting there before eleven o'clock because there would be no customers until two or three in the afternoon. There would be plenty of time for them to deliver the coconuts.

"Grandpa, I'd like to look around at all the things put up for sale, meet some friends but above all, walk around with you," she said.

"Why, yes of course," Songchai replied.

They entered Luang Prabang and turned right onto Kitsarat.

"But why are you taking this road?" Prim asked.

"I'll just drive a bit on to Wisunarat; we can park there and then walk through the monks' temple park. That way, we don't have to park near the market street," Songchai explained.

"But the truck is full of coconuts, Grandpa!" Prim reminded him.

"Oh yes, that's right!" he replied. It was clear he had his mind on other matters. "I nearly forgot. Alright, we'll drive around, unload the coconuts quickly at the market and then I'll park the truck. I've got to run an errand though, so I'll have to leave you alone for a while."

Now, Prim began to worry about what grandpa was up to. He had been anxious since the meeting with the men at the riverside. And now, he wasn't following his usual routine with the coconuts. Was he just going to leave them?

"We unload them here; that'll be easiest. I'll open the lid in the back and we'll just let them all roll off," he said.

"Okay," Prim answered.

No sooner said than done, all the coconuts were rolled off in one go. It was clear that grandpa was in a hurry.

"Prim, stay here, close by. I'll be back in an hour," he told her.

Songchai parked the truck and ran off into Phu Si Park. The park sloped fairly steeply upwards. At its summit lay a monks' temple. This was where he was heading. It was now clear that Songchai had a different reason for the outing than the one he had given Prim.

*

When Songchai returned after two hours, he behaved as if nothing had happened.

"How are you, Prim? Have you looked around, found anything of interest?" he inquired.

"Yes," Prim answered, somewhat sulkily. "I had time for almost everything since you never showed up. Where have you been, Grandpa?"

"Why, I was just up there chatting with some people I know and also, the monks," he confirmed.

"About what?" Prim asked.

"Oh, nothing special," he replied, furtively. It was obvious he was lying to Prim.

The fact was that Songchai did not want her to know more than that. His business was not for children and the more so, given her uncle Surachai had also attended the meeting, the subject of which had been the smuggling of weapons.

Surachai, Prim's mother's brother and Songchai, Prim's father's father, had found one another at an early stage of Fang and Lu's relationship. The men were two of a kind and shared similar interests, a union of an older and a younger generation. There were differences, however: Surachai was also involved in the transport of animals of some sort. As Prim understood it, the animals were sensitive to light, since they could not be transported during daytime. As usual, Prim's powers of perception had been underestimated.

Even if the two men were similar, Prim did not care much for her uncle. And it sometimes seemed as if Surachai did not like his sister's kids, either. It was as if he was jealous of them. But Songchai, whatever his lies, cared deeply for his son's children. It was a proud grandfather who walked along, hand in hand with his grandchild. As they strolled, Prim thought that if only she had a few coins, she might have bought something for herself. Her pockets were empty, however.

Songchai was thinking about his arms cache: how large could it be? What sort of weapons were there? Who could help out with the digging and the transport? Just who could be trusted? These were all difficult questions, as the entire venture was absolutely forbidden, of course. If the arms cache was large, it was probably best to involve the police and bring along some men from the military as well. Why stop at bribing them? It was probably best to invite them to join in and help excavate the cache. Given the amount of money the weapons could bring on the black market, they would probably want to help out with the digging as well. Songchai was going to organize the digging up of the weapons and the transportation, while Surachai would arrange everything with the buyers. Would the delivery of the goods take place on this side of the border, or on the other? These were crucial questions demanding swift answers.

The easiest and most frequently used route for the smuggling of goods like these had always been via Thailand, perhaps due to the avenues for transportation and corruption being so well-developed in that country.

Songchai had a lot on his mind and so had Surachai on his account. Surachai had gone to Vientiane, the capital, to meet potential buyers. In the city, the arms dealers were almost interchangeable with the drug dealers, the human traffickers and the gangsters, the Mafia.

Now, it was almost the afternoon, but grandpa was so preoccupied with his planning that Prim had to remind him it was time to eat.

"I'm hungry, Grandpa," she said.

"Yes, of course, it's about time for some food," Songchai replied and turned off towards Sakkarin Street. "Let's go to my favourite place."

"Yes!" Prim replied, glad that they would visit a real restaurant and not some small street-kitchen.

The place grandpa was talking about was called Tamnak Lao. It was a plain restaurant, where the town's workers could get a cheap beer and a bite. It was a shabby place, with the tables set right at the back of the premises and the kitchen facing the street. This was often the case so that the smell of the cooking would not be overwhelming for the customers eating in the restaurant. This way, all the cooking would be carried out in the street and the smells would disperse outside not inside.

"Order your favourite dish and I'll have the same," he instructed her.

"Yes, Grandpa, I'll have the chicken casserole with ginger and rice," Prim replied.

"We'll have lemon water to drink," Songchai confirmed.

It was turning out to be quite a cosy trip and that was really all that Prim had wanted: to have some fun with grandpa and get a chance to spend some time alone with him. The food was carried in. Prim, who had been sitting and wondering, asked, "Grandpa, what is it that you do, exactly?"

Songchai looked inquiringly at Prim.

"Well, what are you thinking about?" he asked her.

"You were gone for a good while today and it was a bit boring," she observed.

Songchai was relieved. He had braced himself to answer a very different question, a question probing the way he really made his money, something he didn't want to discuss.

"Prim, we have to finish our meals now and go home a bit earlier than usual today. We cannot stay in town till the evening. I have quite a few things to potter with at home and it's rather important," he told her.

Songchai was an expert at avoiding questions and if he said it was time to go, it was time to go. Prim had been hoping that they would not be returning to Tat Kuang before the evening. If they would get home before dinner, Prim would have to help out with all the preparations for the coming week.

The truck was parked on the other side of Luang Prabang. The small town, however, was not wider than eight hundred metres, as it was situated between the Mekong River and the Nam Khan. The two of them walked at a fast pace. Grandpa appeared to be under stress. When the truck came into view, Prim saw there were some people standing by it.

"Wait here, Prim. I have to speak with those people. Sit down there on the bench by the side of the street," he instructed her.

"Hurry up, Grandpa! I don't want to just sit here and wait," she replied.

Songchai walked towards the truck and it was easy to see that he was upset about something. Prim heard him talking loudly to the men standing by the truck.

"You shouldn't be here!" he urged them.

Then, Prim could not hear anything more. She could just see arms gesticulating violently, until grandpa called out to her, "Come on, let's go."

Prim went to the car and settled herself at grandpa's side. Then, they took off, heading for home. For a long while, they remained silent, until Prim asked, "Grandpa, who were those people you spoke with before we drove away?"

"Nobody in particular," he replied.

"Oh yes they were. I could see you were angry with them. It was something, Grandpa. And down by the boat, today, I saw you holding a pistol. What were you talking about?" she insisted.

"Prim, you oughtn't to be so nosy! And what you have seen: you never saw!" he stated.

"But I did, for sure! I really did see it!" she replied.

"Yes, yes, but I mean you can never tell anyone, not even grandma or daddy or mommy. You've got to promise me that, or else I can't let you go with me again," he said.

But Songchai had already decided to never bring any of the children again; they saw and heard too much. Although he was an old man, he knew what was going on. He was vigorous and focused. However, when it came to children, he was naive.

It took almost an hour and a half to drive home to Tat Kuang along the winding and badly kept roads on the heights outside Luang Prabang.

Chapter 4

Drunk Driver

It was almost evening by the time Prim and Songchai made it back to the village, but darkness had yet to fall. At this time of the year, the sun set at about half past six. Since the sun dictated the time of day, you could never claim that you had missed supper or that you didn't know what time it was.

Coming home at this hour meant Prim would have to help out with Pom. Prim thought Pom was big enough to look after himself, but this was what her mum wanted. Nevertheless, Prim still had a bone to pick with him after the morning's incident.

"Prim," Lu said, "if you don't take care of Pom, you'll get to bring in the pigs and then to go to grandma for rice and to carry in water."

Usually, it was dad who would fetch the pigs, but tonight he was away. He would be home later if there was no fog over the mountains; if there was, he would not return until tomorrow. Surrounded by the evening fog, you could barely see three metres in front of you. It was not uncommon for the fog to prevent driving over the mountains.

Yesterday, it had been Fang's job to light the fire; tonight it was Anant's, Lu's father. The ash was still warm and the firewood dry, so it was easy enough: Anant turned the ash over and before long, out of the remaining embers, the evening fire grew, ready for cooking and as a place to gather together. A peaceful Sunday had passed for the residents of the village and now it was time for most of them to light their fires, cook their supper and relax. But Lu had a feeling that this would not turn out to be just a regular Sunday evening. Fang was not home and being alone at home with the children was not something she was fond of. Or was it rather the case that Lu disliked Fang being away because it meant she had to go to bed alone? She was not used to sleeping without Fang. It felt wrong and somehow, unsafe.

Pom was out in the yard and the others were going about their evening chores and would come out later. Lu called out to Pom, since she understood that Prim was not nearby.

"Pom, what are you doing?" she said.

"I'm playing with the cats," Pom shouted back.

There were always cats in the yard, chiefly for one practical reason: rats. Lu was satisfied with her son's answer and continued to prepare the simple supper.

Prim tried to gather the pigs, which was easier said than done. They did everything they could to avoid getting captured. But the chore was not that difficult to achieve and it was a fun task as the little, black pigs were so cute.

*

Pom had a favourite cat called Nam, which meant water and the cat was called this because he liked water. In addition, he had a dog called Long, which meant lost. Pom always had to fetch Long when the dog failed to find his way home. Long was not in the yard: it was likely that the dog had forgotten it was time for supper. Pom carried on playing with Nam.

The yard was not separated from the road by anything except the edge of a ditch, about a foot high. Not many cars passed here, mostly oxcarts. The huts were situated just a few feet from the road. Nam bounced away spiritedly with Pom hot on his tail, laughing. Nam was frisky, just like a young cat should be. He sneaked quickly in between two huts and on out onto the road.

It was just at that point that the car that was not expected to come, driven by a driver that ought not to have been behind the wheel, influenced by Mekong whiskey, which was the done thing after a Sunday out with the relatives, came along. The cops were not interested in enforcing breathalyser tests. If anyone tried such a thing, they would probably overload the whole of Lao's police force, since there were not many sober drivers on Sundays. In addition, not many policemen used their official cars or motorcycles. But if there was a way of using the scheme to bring some cash into the policemen's pockets, checkpoints would have been set up without delay. They would work a little differently, however, with the driver driving into the checkpoint, paying a fine and driving off, leaving everyone happy.

This particular driver, who could not tell day from night, caught sight of something happening in front of the car. From the light of the headlights, it looked like a cat and a boy. Next, there was a thud, the car wobbled slightly and he drove on. By the side of the road, life stopped and everything went silent. The only thing that moved was the weak light of grandpa's fire, illuminating the narrow gravel path outside the hut. For a few seconds, the cat, Nam, stood perfectly still, then it carried on. Pom was lying on the far edge of the ditch on the other side of the road, only a few metres from his mother. But Lu had heard nothing.

The fire that grandpa had started now spread its light over the road, but did not reach Pom, as he was lying in the shadow of the ditch's edge. With his face turned downwards and covered by his beautiful black hair, it was hard to see him in the dark.

"Go and see what Pom's doing!" Lu told Prim, who had returned after successfully gathering in the pigs.

Reluctantly, Prim went out in the yard and called out to Pom. Hearing no response, she went on towards the road and then she called down towards the hen house. There was no answer.

"Pom, answer me this instant and quit hiding! Mummy wants you to come!" she shouted.

Silence.

"Alright, I will only look in one more place and then you've got to tell me if I'm getting warm!" she continued.

Not a sound. Prim went back into the hut.

"Mummy, I don't know where Pom is and he doesn't answer when I call out for him," Prim confirmed.

"He was playing with the cats. He's probably just up to some mischief and will be back soon enough," Lu replied.

When she had prepared the supper, everybody gathered around the fire. Pom was still missing.

"This is odd," Lu said and started to call out to Pom.

By now, the others had begun to get worried too. Both grandfathers and grandmothers called out and went looking.

Several neighbours joined in to help out. They tried to ease the family's fears, "He has probably just gone over to visit someone," one of them called out.

"No," Lu said, "he never leaves the yard. There's something wrong. Something is wrong! I know it." She had a horrible feeling.

Three hours later — the time was somewhere between ten and eleven — everyone in the village was joined in the search for Pom. Lu was afraid and in tears. Prim was still calling out after her brother, promising never to hit him or be angry with him for pouring water over her, if only he would show himself.

The women of the family gathered inside the hut and the neighbours gathered outside, while the men continued looking long into the night. Nobody, however, thought to look at the edge of the ditch. Prim and Lu were sitting close together holding each other and crying. They were trying to comfort one another, telling each other that the men who had gone out looking would come back soon with Pom and that everything would be back to normal.

The men returned, empty-handed. They had searched high and low, in all the hiding-places they could think of. They had asked all the people they saw, but nobody knew anything. Lu started crying loudly and called out to Fang, but he wasn't around and had no idea what was happening at home. By now, Lu was crying so hard she was shaking. Prim was so scared that she began to vomit. A couple of women came into the hut and gave both of them a drink prepared according to an old recipe which had been handed down through the generations and which included, among other ingredients, opium. It made Prim and Lu fall asleep.

Out in the yard, the village elders sat gathered together. There were Songchai, Mak, Anant and May. Not many words were spoken. They were just sitting, waiting.

*

At sunrise, they heard Long begin to bark. One of the men went to have a look at what the dog was barking at. When he got close enough to Long, who was standing by the ditch, he stood, paralysed. He turned around and looked Anant straight in the eyes. Anant understood instantly. He had seen that kind of look before. Anant got to his feet in silence and walked up to the man, who was pointing to the edge of the ditch. Anant took a deep breath and turned around.

Calling to Songchai, he said, "You must come, over here."

The old men crouched down over Pom and checked him. The boy was cold. Songchai and Anant looked at each other in silence. Then, they helped one another to turn little Pom over and to carry him, ever so carefully, to the yard, where they laid him down with all the dignity possible, when it is a child that had died.

In one blow, sorrow engulfed the village. Lu and Prim were awakened by the lamenting and crying. They went out into the morning. When Lu saw what was lying there, on the ground nearly thirty feet from her, she lost control. She screamed. When she fell, she was still holding onto Prim, who was trying to hold her mother up. But Lu was too heavy and Prim had to drop to her knees in order to hold her. Both of them were crying uncontrollably and continued to cry as Songchai and Anant led them back across the yard.

For the remainder of the day, Lu was not capable of rational thought. Some of the older women from the village sat with her, together with a couple of monks. Prim was with her maternal grandmother and spent the day talking about Pom. Grandma said that the grief would be eased by a lot of talking about the person who had died. This was her experience since the war and wisdom gained through age.

"And I was so angry with Pom yesterday." Prim said, sobbing.

"Yes, that's the way things are, Prim, you never know when it's time," grandma said.

Grandma Mak went in to see May. She was worried about what would happen when Fang returned. How were they to go about telling him the terrible news?

"We'll leave that to the men," May told her. "They'll watch out for him coming home."

As Fang finally approached, Anant and Songchai stood waiting five hundred metres outside the village.

"How are we going to let him know?" Songchai asked.

"I haven't got the faintest idea. I've experienced quite a number of deaths, but I've never been in this particular situation," Anant replied.

The two men, both hardened war-veterans, were holding each other and crying when Fang caught sight of them.

"What's wrong with you?" Fang exclaimed. "What's happened? What is it? Why are you crying? Tell me!"

"Fang," Songchai said to his son, "it's Pom. He was hit by a car last night and we found him dead."

"What are you telling me? My Pom?" Fang exclaimed.

Everybody around them fell silent.

Fang said nothing. He just walked towards his hut. He did not notice the rehearsal of the funeral music by the funeral piper, playing the bamboo-pipes. The men stood looking after him as he walked with heavy steps past the drummer. Fang did not look into the yard or ask where his son was. He presumed that everyone was in the hut. And there was Lu, dissolved into tears and the monks, the old women and the members of the funeral committee. They were all proficient at dealing with grief, but it was to no avail.

The funeral committee had been set up after Pom had been found. Despite Fang not being home, they were obliged to begin the work needed for Pom's ascension. Out in the yard, as well as inside the hut, everything was already prepared. Pom was lying there, all dressed up in a plain open casket, with all the accessories needed to make his journey to his ancestors as easy as possible. For company, he had received one of the roosters that crowed at the wrong times. This was an important element of the Hmong culture: the rooster was believed to show the soul the road to its ancestors, with whom it was to live in the other world. During the journey, the soul took refuge in the shade of the rooster's wing if it was too warm, or under its tail-feathers if it was raining. The rooster became the guide of the soul during the three-day long journey. The funeral ceremony had already begun and it was important that all elements were in place so that Pom's soul would get off to a good start. All his best toys were there, his tools, food, money and clothes. Fang opened the door to the hut. First, he saw Pom, then Lu. When their eyes met, Lu threw herself at him, then she screamed, hit him in the face and kicked him. She was like a wild beast. Fang had never before seen such behaviour from his wife.

The monks and the old ladies made a desperate attempt to stop her. Eventually, the alderman of the committee managed to restrain Lu and calm her down a little.

Fang was now kneeling and begging her forgiveness.

"Forgive me, forgive me, Lu! Forgive me, Pom!"

"I will never forgive you!" Lu yelled out again and again, louder and louder. "I will never forgive you! You, go to hell! I don't want to see you, ever again!"

The monks were trying to subdue her, but to no avail. One of them brought Fang out into the yard. The funeral was to take place at the sunset of the third day and Fang was needed for helping out with the preparations. It was important that the necessary items were sacrificed, for all the people present as well as for Pom's ascension.

After the funeral, things were no longer the same as before. Prim cried a lot, together with Lu and they talked about Pom as if he were still among them. Fang, however, found himself excluded and was forced to grieve in solitude.

*

For the family, it was as if time stood still. A couple of months passed since they had buried Pom.

When Fang thought that Lu might be ready to speak with him, he approached her.

"Lu, I miss you," he said.

"Well, I don't miss you," she replied harshly.

"We haven't talked with each other for two months, now. Don't you believe that I miss Pom too?" he continued.

"No! Actually, I don't! I don't believe anything you say!" Lu responded, still distraught.

The thin walls of the hut spilled their quarrel all over the yard.

"No, Fang," she continued. "As a matter of fact, I don't believe you're mourning the way I am. You're too self-centred. While I'm in bed with my grief, you sometimes come home drunk and try to fuck me. Don't you understand that I can't and I don't want to! I only want to be with Prim and my sorrow."

"But please Lu, I want to be a part of it. Don't leave me out!" he implored her.

"You've always been on the outside. Look at us! What are we? Look at our situation! We are still living in a hut by the roadside in the outskirts of the village, a downright dangerous location. If I had any sense, I wouldn't have given birth to a child in this environment. If you'd been home, this would never have happened!" Lu claimed with bitterness in her voice.

"You can't blame me for all of it!" Fang said.

"Where were you, really?" Lu asked. "And was it really so bloody foggy that you couldn't make your way home? Or was it you that was so bloody foggy that you couldn't find your way home?" Lu spat the words out at him.

Prim was outside, but she did not want to come in any longer. She turned around and went to her maternal grandfather. Hopefully, he would tell her some war stories. The fact that her paternal grandfather, Songchai and her father, Fang, belonged to the same family was clear in the way their egotism revealed itself. While all the other relatives were in mourning, Songchai and Surachai were busy dealing in weapons. They did not spend many days mourning for Pom. They had no time for it and Prim liked them less for it. Prim's maternal grandfather, on the other hand, mourned for Pom to such an extent that he fell ill. Prim remembered that her maternal grandmother had told her you could die from grief.

Fang was coming home late and drunk so Lu thought it more suitable that he should sleep with the pigs, instead of in the hut. Prim felt her father's pain and found her mother's approach very hard on him.

Fang was making pathetic attempts to approach Lu, but he was not welcome. She did not want him around at all. She yelled and threw things at him. She told him he had ruined their life.

"What's more," Lu said, "I believe you're seeing someone else."

"No, that's totally wrong! You're all I have!" he tried to assure her.

"Why don't you come home at nights? And why do you keep on drinking?" Lu asked him again.

"I'm mourning," Fang said, now crying.

"That is a hell of a way to mourn," Lu observed.

Prim thought that Lu was being too harsh on her father and could not refrain from saying it out loud. Lu's response took her by surprise.

"It's none of your business! You're too little and should keep your opinions to yourself! Damn you. You shouldn't stick your nose into our marriage!" she said to her daughter.

"What marriage?" Prim answered back, precociously.

Before she knew it, she had received a slap in the face, one that left a crimson mark on her cheek alongside the painful sting. She ran out into the yard to her maternal grandmother, who was sitting by her husband's bedding. Grandpa felt that everything was going downhill. He said that all that had been in the family before Pom's death was gone. Gone, too, were the evenings by the fire when the family had once gathered to eat supper together.

Chapter 5

Dangerous Bar Job

All at once, Lu's life had changed and she was no longer the same person. At the age of thirty-two, she had turned bitter, mean and dismissive towards everyone and everything. Fang was not the only one being pushed away. The same fate was suffered by Prim, as well as both her mother's and her father's parents, once beloved relatives whose presence in the yard was now a source of constant anguish to Lu. As a result of all the quarrels, Prim's spirits sank further and further.

One day, Fang walked up to Prim and put his arms around her.

"Prim, this is going nowhere. I can't stay with Mummy anymore. I've packed my stuff and I'm moving out today," he told her.

"No, Daddy!" Prim began to cry and held him hard. "You can't. Daddy, you mustn't move away! I love you!"

"But Prim," he continued, "you're big enough to understand this. It's no use. I can't be kept hanging on and still not be a part of anything."

"But what about me? Can't you take me with you?" she asked.

"No, that wouldn't work," he confirmed.

"But Daddy, I don't want to stay here with Mummy. It's not just you she's mean to!" she revealed.

"Prim, I first have to decide where to be. Then, you can come and visit me," Fang tried to reassure her.

"No, I want to come with you now!" she insisted.

"It's not possible," he said again.

Fang fetched his case. It was only half full, yet it contained all his personal belongings. Everything else, which was jointly owned, had to be left behind. He did not say goodbye to anyone but Prim. Fang had lost his son and his wife, a woman he had loved more than anything on Earth, but who had become estranged after Pom's death. He had lost his family. Nevertheless, there was Prim and he had made up his mind to try to stay in contact with her. Time would tell. When he walked away, he felt totally empty.

It was not until much later that Prim learned he had met another woman and moved to the north of Thailand.

Prim became lonely and her days tedious. It seemed as if everybody became irritated by her presence. She tried to take part in all the duties, but it didn't help.

"I've got to get a job," Lu announced one day. "I will try to get one at one of those new tourist bars in Luang Prabang. I'll have to work until late, but it'll mean good money."

"But Mummy," Prim said, "how are you going to get home, if you're working late?"

"Oh, it'll sort itself out," Lu said, without a thought as to what Prim was supposed to do during her lonely evenings in the hut where she would be left alone if Lu wasn't there.

*

Lu managed to get a job as a waitress at Night Stalls, a restaurant with a bar on Kitsarat Street. It had just opened and drew many tourists who were interested in the young girls working there, girls that did not mind earning a bit extra as so called 'room guides', another name for a prostitute. And depending on their customers' inclinations, all kinds of sexual activities were demanded and on offer. What they made working at the bar, was not much. But working as a room guide, at best, a girl could make in three days what it would take a month to make from any other job. Therefore, the owners kept an eye on what the girls made through contacts they made at their bar. Through those contacts, they could demand their share of the profit.

When the owner of Night Stalls saw Lu entering his office to apply for a job, he began to get excited. This one would no doubt draw in the customers. Lu would have been both shocked and surprised if she knew what he was thinking.

Lu got started immediately and felt satisfied with the salary she was to get. Never before had she been paid for her work. It felt liberating to be able to make money for herself and to be able to do what she felt like. Right away, she struck up a good relationship with two of the other girls at the bar, Tim and Som. After just a couple of days, Som told Lu how she could make extra money by going off with some lonely guest. Lu couldn't believe her ears.

"Never," she said. "I would never do such a thing. How can you, alone with a guest! I can't believe that you're willing to take the risk!"

"Oh, it's not dangerous," Som replied. "Why not do it this way? Why should you go out and meet somebody at a bar instead and then end up in bed with him? It is better this way, isn't it? To have a good time now and then, get good food, get sex and get paid. Rather that, than get fucked by the local guys and suffer the indignity of being called a whore afterwards and not getting as much as a penny for it."

"Well, I see your point," Lu said, but decided to keep clear of that part of the job.

During the evenings after work, there were often problems getting home. It could take almost two hours for her to reach the village after she left the bar. In order to get to the bus stop, she had to walk down the dark road to the sports field. Sometimes, however, she was given a lift by someone she knew who was going in the same direction.

This particular evening, it was Lu's turn to clean up after closing time and she had worked later than usual. Tired, she was plodding slowly toward the bus stop. A car stopped beside her and Lu looked up, startled.

"Oh, it's you!" Lu said.

"Yes, I just wanted to ask you if you wanted a ride. I'll drive you home," the driver replied.

It was Lu's boss. She realised that this was a lucky break and she got in.

"How are you doing, Lu?" he asked.

"Fine, thank you," she replied.

"Are you happy with the job?" he continued.

"Yes, very," she said.

Soon, they were on the dark, badly kept road leading away from Luang Prabang. The bar-owner slowed down the car, bringing it to a stop on the side of the road.

"How happy are you, Lu?" he inquired.

"I don't understand," Lu said, confused.

"I'll explain," he said and laid his hand upon Lu's knee in order to bring it up between her thighs. "I'm wondering how grateful you are for the job I've given you?"

"Get your hands off me!" Lu yelled, just as he grabbed hold of her blouse with his other hand, slid it in and held her breast.

"I want to fuck you; don't you get it?" he stated.

"But I don't want you!" Lu said pushing him away.

He grabbed hold of her again. This time, he had both his hands on her breasts inside the shredded blouse, but Lu was busy trying to open the car-door. She threw herself out. Her boss remained in the car while she ran into the bushes to hide. It would have been difficult for him to pursue her in the dark.

Lu sat and hid, silent and afraid.

"You'll be back tomorrow, you hear! And you are not going to say a peep about this, otherwise you're for it!" she heard him calling out.

He roared off in a hurry.

Lu waited a while before leaving her hiding place. She soon heard the bus approaching, went out onto the road and waved it down. The driver recognised her and stopped by the roadside.

"What the hell have you been up to?" he exclaimed as she got up into the bus.

"Nothing. I got caught on a banister," Lu lied as she sat down in the nearest seat.

What a stroke of luck it was that the bus had passed by just at that moment. At home, Prim was already asleep. Lu felt terribly alone and stayed up for a while, brooding about what had happened. She thought about the number of times she had been forced to deal with horny boys as they tried to grope her during her school years, when everyone was curious about sex. But she had never experienced this in her adult life, though. It was frightening!

Before Lu went to sleep, she decided to go back to work because she actually enjoyed the job, the money and the new opportunities that the money provided. But she was not going to be one of those who charged for sex. She would never become a hooker.

Restless, Lu fell asleep.

Chapter 6

Profitable Plan

There was a great deal of activity out in the yard. Lu's father-in-law, Songchai, had maintained his practice of running guns. There were a lot of people involved, which made it a risky business. But for now, the village had become his headquarters.

It was in the caves up in Ban Na Sala that they had found the vast caches which demanded thorough organisation if the opportunities the guns offered were to be realised. There were Russian and Chinese pistols, submachine guns, hand grenades and landmines in such quantity that if the weapons were to fall into the wrong hands, they might influence the outcome of a new war. That was the reason for the total prohibition on appropriating and doing business involving such weapons.

Any caches that were discovered were to be immediately reported to the police or the military authorities. But Songchai was into making money. What he actually then did with all his cash, nobody knew. He lived the life of a poor farmer up in the mountains, the Laotian counterpart to the archetypal old Sicilian Mafiosi, the men who sat beneath their lemon trees looking plain and poor, but who actually controlled everything in the little island and beyond, all the way to New York. Just like them, Songchai ruled in the background.

Besides Songchai, there was Surachai - always tagging along whenever there was a whiff of money - and a cop, Tatchacon, as well as two others, Suteluck and Pooi who worked in administrative support for the police. None of them felt any remorse over what they were intending to do.

*

Songchai began to outline the plan.

"Surachai, when do we need to deliver the goods? And to which place?" he asked.

"To Khao Nong Kon, southeast of Bangkok. We have a month," Surachai replied.

"Why there?" Tatchacon asked. "And just who's buying?"

"I don't know," replied Surachai, "but I believe the weapons are bound for somewhere in Africa. I don't care who the buyers are. We'll get half the payment when we get over the border to Khemmarat and the rest on delivery. The guys making the deal are playing it safe and don't want to mess about."

"So, they'll pay us the rest at our final destination on Thailand's coast?" Suteluck asked.

He was a major. He knew the small village well.

"Sure. These goods are a lot bulkier than narcotics," replied Pooi, who in his military role, served as a captain. "Drugs are easier to move about."

"What do you mean." Surachai said.

"Why, you know. They let pigs swallow condoms holding the drugs and when they reach the slaughterhouses in northern Thailand, the pigs' bellies are opened up and the drugs are taken out," Pooi explained.

"Did you know that Songchai?" Suteluck asked.

"I thought everybody did." Pooi said. "But it isn't just weapons and drugs that get smuggled over the borders. There's counterfeit stuff, young girls, you know."

"Enough of that." Songchai cut him short. "Here's the plan. Some friends of mine, farmers in Pok Mong, will help us bring the merchandise down to Ben Houa Keng and hide it there, until we get the river boats up to Ban Pak-Ou. Servicemen will help out with the transport and the loading of the boats. It won't look suspicious since they'll be using military vehicles for the move from the warehouse to the boats. I'll get five of the bigger riverboats. If we raise the floorboards, we'll have room for plenty of weapons on board. And, if we were to be stopped, there will be some passengers sitting in the boats looking annoyed."

Songchai turned to Pooi and Tatchacon.

"It won't take more than five or six days to get the stuff delivered, but there are some difficulties along the way, like the Sanakham border control," he continued. "We will certainly not drive through it. That would be far too dangerous! But we are going to pass by it and that might mean trouble, too. So your job is to make sure that the authorities there turn a blind eye when we show up."

"How far do we have to get?" Surachai asked, sounding worried, although, as usual, he was keen on a quick buck.

"All the way down to Ban Na Muang," Songchai confirmed.

"But damn it! That's down towards Cambodia!" Surachai exclaimed.

"That's the best crossing," Pooi told him. "We should be able to pack everything into a container standing ready in Khemmarat, on the outskirts of town. From there, an established forwarding agent will take care of the container and escort it to its final destination. Surachai and I will travel down as tourists and be there when it arrives."

"I have fixed things with the peasants from the valley. They will be on the boats." Songchai added. "Their only condition was that they would be home again for the rice harvest. I've promised them that and it'll pay off. They trust me."

"We have to get started tomorrow," Suteluck pointed out. "The trickiest part is the landmines. Songchai, have you really thought this through properly? Have you considered everything that might go wrong? It's a journey of almost a thousand kilometres on the Mekong, you know."

"What can happen? Suteluck and Pooi will keep a check on everything along the Mekong. Tatchacon will keep in touch with the police on the journey and at the border controls. What's more, young man, you are not to question my planning. We have spoken before about this," Songchai responded.

"And the trucking service?" Surachai wondered.

"He will not take the goods across the border. We'll fix that. We'll reload them from boat to container on the Thai side. They are driving within their borders and won't question anything. As I'm sure you understand, it's one of our own guys in Thailand who'll be behind the wheel."

"Okay," Surachai replied, content with the answer.

"It's about time that we got moving," Tatchacon said. "I have to be home in fairly good time. It's already twelve o'clock and everything seems to be under control."

"Yes," Pooi answered. "We'll ride with you back to Luang Prabang."

"Then it's agreed," Songchai said. "See you tomorrow."

*

In the car, the police officer and the military men began discussing alternative plans. They thought the old fart was making too much at their expense.

Songchai was a sly old fox and could tell that something was wrong. "We have to be vigilant," he told Surachai. "We've worked with Tatchacon, Pooi and Suteluck for a while, but there is a lot of money at stake here. I think we've got to be prepared for them being disloyal to us."

Surachai agreed. Being involved in organized crime, he knew that life could be cut short. Even amongst gangsters, there were rules and if you broke them, you were endangering your life.

On the way home, there was a lot going on inside Surachai's head. He was the one that had fixed the buyers: wasn't that the most important part? He had been involved in transports before and had good contacts in that area as well. Smuggling Rolex copies, Lacoste clothes and Nike shoes from China to Laos and Thailand was bread and butter to him. On one occasion, he had helped out with taking young girls, the most lucrative contraband of all, from Laos to Thailand.

It took some time for Surachai to get home. The road south between Tat Kuang and Muang Nan was bad, to say the least and the huts along the way were situated just by the roadside meaning that you had to drive carefully. Surachai's house was not just another hut with one part for cooking and keeping animals and another for sleeping. No, this was a proper house, raised on poles, like the houses down in the lowlands. It was practical. The car could be parked beneath the house and there was no lack of storage space. Surachai had all the comforts he could want: TV, radio, car, couch, chairs and table and a bedroom with a big bed and a proper kitchen. He was on his way up. He never intended to live in squalor again. In the meantime, he kept himself busy with several girls, all of them younger than himself, of course.

Now there was this golden opportunity to climb another step on the ladder. He intended to keep close to Songchai, learn the old man's routines, uncover his weaknesses and get rid of him when the time was right. He did not have a lot of time, a couple of weeks at most, because after that, he had to take care of the delivery, up until they arrived in Ban Na Muang and the border crossing to Khemmarat.

Surachai drove the car in under the house and went up to the anteroom. His plan was to look over some maps of the areas they would pass through. Some places he knew, but there were many others that could involve danger for the transport and the people travelling with it.

Deftly, he navigated in the dark, up to the lamp in the kitchen that would shed its light over almost the whole house. When he turned it on, he heard a sound from the bedroom, a weak whimper.

"Who's there?" he asked, his voice loud in the night.

"It's me, Ta," came the reply.

She was one of his lovers and during the evening, she had been gripped by the urge to go to his house and wait for him in hope of a romantic interlude.

"What the fuck are you doing here, Ta? You've got to go home. I want to be by myself tonight," Surachai said angrily.

"But please, Surachai," Ta cooed.

"No, it's not possible. You have to come back some other time," he insisted.

"There won't be another time," Ta said sulkily as she left.

Surachai got the maps and laid them out on the kitchen table. Where had Songchai decided that they would stop for the night and sleep? Or was his idea that they would travel non-stop? Where were they supposed to take breaks, fill up with fuel and to fill up with water? What if something were to go wrong? There were parts of the Mekong that were dangerous, with boulders hidden just beneath the surface and strong currents where a miscalculation could cost lives. Surachai was certain the old man had thought out a great deal of things which he hadn't bothered to mention.

Surachai traced the stretch of the Mekong River with his finger from their starting point to their final destination. He felt that they should be able to reach Sanakham, the frontier station to Thailand, during the first day. It would be perfect to get provisions and water in Ban Pak Ton. They might well reach Ban Paksa on the second day and then they would arrive in Ban Na Muang on the third day, a hellish journey, but a safe one for smugglers.

He let his finger rest at Don Tan, slightly more than fifty kilometres north of Ban Na Muang, a small, unguarded village with perhaps a hundred inhabitants, situated on the Thai side. Wouldn't it be better to stop there? They could reload onto trucks and then travel by road through Thailand down to the final coastal destination. He knew a couple of smugglers living in Ban Naphan, not very far from Don Tan, but on the Lao side of the Mekong. Might that work?

Exhausted by all these thoughts and plans, Surachai went to bed. He fell asleep instantly.

Meanwhile, the others had arrived at their home village, but stayed in the car, talking.

"I think we should wait one day and run through alternative plans," Tatchacon said to Pooi and Suteluck.

"Yes," Pooi answered, "but if we are to come up with a new plan, we have to get rid of Songchai and then what about the lad?"

"I don't think he will pose a problem. I expect he will be pleased," Tatchacon replied. "If we agree, I'll get in touch with Songchai tomorrow morning and tell him we can't start just then and we have to put off the departure one more day. Let's meet tomorrow and discuss this through properly and then we'll take the necessary measures. Pooi, I think it's best to meet at your place tomorrow morning."

All three of them lived in the outskirts of Luang Prabang towards Ban Aen. Pooi lived somewhat more quietly than the others, in a quarter of the town where a lot of police officers and military had made their homes, almost like a village of its own. The residences had been erected during the eighties and were more like houses than huts. All of the residents were bachelors. Most of the accompanying women were bought.

*

The night had been rather chilly. One of Pooi's morning routines involved a moment of leaning against the wall of the house in some sunny spot. He was still sitting there when Suteluck showed up.

"We'll wait with the tea until Tatchacon gets here," Pooi suggested.

"Yes, let's," Suteluck agreed.

No one came, however. They waited for an hour, then for another.

"We can't wait any longer," Suteluck said eventually. "Let's go over to Tatchacon's. If he's changed his mind, we have to get up to the caves and start work."

"Yes, but it's not like him to keep us waiting like this," Suteluck said.

The two servicemen, who were well known in the village, were saluting left, right and centre on their way towards Tatchacon's house. They refrained from speaking to one another about their plans, afraid that someone might overhear them.

When they arrived at Tatchacon's house, Suteluck called out. Nobody answered. Pooi picked up a stick and knocked on the wall. Again, they heard nothing.

"What the heck!" Pooi exclaimed. "Isn't he home?"

Suteluck walked up to the door and knocked once more. It was still silent. He pushed against it and it opened.

"Unlocked," he said.

Stepping quietly through the silent house, Suteluck went on to Tatchacon's bedroom, which was plainly decorated, with just a bed and a small bedside table. There was nothing on the walls other than a layer of white paint, which here and there, had begun peeling from the old teakwood that lay under it. The sun filtered in through a venetian blind, hung up in a glassless window to prevent scrutiny.

Tatchacon was lying very still in his bed. Suteluck laid his hand upon Tatchacon's shoulder, then cried out. His friend was cold and lifeless.

Pooi came in quickly.

"What is it?" he said

"He's dead," Suteluck said. "And look at him!"

"What the fuck has happened?" Pooi exclaimed as he turned Tatchacon over.

It looked as if Tatchacon had put up a fight, wrestling with someone in the bed, but had not been able to fight off a cardiac arrest.

"And this should happen right now!" Pooi continued. "What are we going to do? Should we inform the police? Did anyone see us entering the house?"

"No, I don't think so. Let's leave him be and take care of it later on. But it's a mess. We'll just tidy up a bit and lay something over him," Suteluck confirmed.

"We'll be back, old mate," they said to Tatchacon, who was no longer among them.

Outside the house, they looked around to make sure no one had seen them enter it. Back on the road, they trudged in silence, pale and with laboured strides, away from Tatchacon's house, as if they had merely passed by without entering it.

"Where to?" Pooi asked.

"We could go to my place. But we have to drive up to Songchai and tell him what's happened," Suteluck said.

They walked on until they reached Suteluck's car and drove off to Songchai without exchanging another word.

Chapter 7

Gulu's Bar

That morning, life in the village started even earlier than usual. Perhaps what Prim's dad had said so many times was correct: the roosters really did belong in a cuckoo's nest, since they couldn't keep track of time.

Prim was woken by all the sounds of the village, the clattering, the dogs barking, the cars and the loud gossip. There was nothing to do but to get up and put the bedding straight, without waking up her mother. This was easier nowadays since there were just the two of them occupying the same space that had once been occupied by four. But with the fall in numbers came not just silence and loss but the chill of the night as well, with fewer people helping each other to keep warm.

Prim went out and did her morning routine. She arranged for the fire to catch on, blowing on the embers and setting tiny, dried sticks in place. She managed to get it started using the same methods that had always been used, methods shown to her by her mother's father. For now, when grandpa was ill, it was up to Prim to fix the fire. She put on a kettle with water and while it was boiling, she went to see to the pigs and the chicken run. When Prim was crossing the yard, a car entered, going so fast that she had to jump to the side. She glared wide-eyed at the two men inside the car. They looked even more scared than she was. Prim went on to the chickens, picked up a couple of eggs and went back to the hut and the fire, now burning.

"Mummy, rise and shine! I've boiled some water for tea and I'm putting on some eggs," she shouted through the door.

"I'm coming," Lu replied. "I'm so terribly tired. I came home late last night. I must sleep just a little more."

Lu was lying with her arms around her knees, almost in a foetal position, the way she had been lying all night. She was still scared by what had taken place on her way home. Most of all, she wanted to speak about it with someone; up until now, she had just been lying awake brooding.

Again, Lu fell asleep. Prim ate her breakfast and got ready, putting on the blue skirt and the white blouse that all the schoolgirls wore. While she was drinking her tea, she overheard a loud conversation between her paternal grandfather and the men that had arrived in the car. It was unpleasant to hear yelling and screaming between adults. Nowadays, it was quite common to see strange people in the yard and the conversations were often not friendly, the way they had been before, when her father lived at home.

Prim and Lu had no contact with the others anymore. It was as if everybody felt that it was their fault that Pom had died and Fang had taken off. Several of the villagers saw Lu as a failed woman, for not being able to keep her family together.

Prim shouted to Lu, "Bye, bye, I'm off!"

Lu stayed in bed and listened to all the noise, to the voices that came in through the thin walls, just listening and thinking about what had come of the family.

*

When Lu finally rose, it was late morning. Prim had long since gone and the fire was almost out. The tea Prim had left for her was cold and the eggs were probably boiled into hard little balls. Lu did not want breakfast anyway. She only wanted to put her clothes straight in order to leave as soon as possible. The gossip was already going around in the village about Lu working in a bar, a whore-bar, as they put it. Only the worst would do as a subject for local gossip. If there was nothing sensational, there was nothing to talk about.

Lu picked up the blouse she had worn the previous night and looked at it. Several buttons were missing. Only one man had full access to her body: Fang. The fact that someone else had groped her breasts made her feel sick. Before Lu got dressed, she grabbed a flannel and washed her breasts meticulously, wiping away the sensation of dirty hands on them.

She looked around carefully as she left the hut, sneaked around the corner and vanished down the road towards the city. She did not want anything to do with the toil and grind of the yard. She was enough of a burden herself and she wanted to get away as soon as possible. She didn't want to see May, who might just as well have been on the side of the village hags, too spineless to defend her.

It would take until midday for her to get there, assuming someone came to pick her up, a car or a motorcycle. Today, it would be a three-wheeled motorcycle lorry and it would take longer than usual. The old man driving appeared to be half-blind. He did not see the potholes in the road and to play it safe, he drove extra slowly. Finally reaching Luang Prabang, she thanked the old man and began walking towards the home of her colleague, Tim.

Tim lived in a simple one-room apartment on Phu Vao, a cross-street to the right at the post office. With the mongrels barking about her, as she walked towards Tim's apartment, Lu mulled over whether she should tell her friend what had happened. She knew that Tim had a different moral code from hers, but also that she probably would listen to what Lu had to say.

When Lu reached the apartment, she knocked carefully. Shuffling feet approached the door, which eventually opened.

"Hey Lu. Come in," Tim greeted her.

Lu entered the small apartment. The room was square and perhaps four metres long. A door in the corner led out to the rear. To her left, there was a bed. The dirty walls were damaged by mould and were painted in a green-blue colour, probably dating back to when the house had been built. It felt cooped-up and stuffy. On some nails on the wall, clothes were hanging and on the filthy floor, there was a pile of shoes and slippers. A solitary chair stood by a table, hardly bigger than the radio standing upon it. Lu asked herself how Tim could live in such a poky hole, even her own hut was better.

"Why the visit?" Tim asked.

"What have you been up to? You look like shit," Lu said. She did not swear regularly, but this time, it was justified.

"Would you like some tea? Have a seat on the bed while I fix it," Tim said.

She stole away through the small door facing the rear, where she had her cooking facilities outdoors on a platform. While Tim was out, Lu sat on the bed, reflecting on what was around her. There were no sheets and no pillow. It was very much like the bedding Lu slept on herself, but with two differences: above the bed there was a lamp that cast a red light and upon the bed was a thick bedspread, almost like a fur coat but woven from threads in red, green and blue. Lu looked down to the floor by the bed. She saw condom wrappers but she pretended not to notice them as Tim came back.

"Here's your tea," Tim said sitting down on the broken chair. "Well, as you can see, I'm living here among my stuff."

"So I see," Lu replied.

"Lu, what's up?" Tim asked once more.

"I came here because I needed to talk to somebody. Something unpleasant happened after closing time, yesterday," Lu explained.

"Was Gulu at it again, trying to do you, was he?" Tim asked. "He's out of his wits; thinks he can fuck us for free. That bastard sees it as an extra bonus. If he was a good lover, it would be okay, I guess, but he's lousy and just wants to show that he's in charge."

"Yes, he has offered me a ride home many times, after closing up the place. But he has never groped me before. Not until yesterday, after closing time," Lu revealed.

Lu continued to fill her in on what had happened and added, "I was totally shocked. I didn't think he would do what he did."

"He just grabs what he wants and if you're to keep on working at the bar, you'd better start delivering. And that means some extra money to him, as well as your having to please him now and then," Tim confirmed

"I'll quit the bar and go looking for a job at a restaurant or a hotel somewhere else," Lu said.

"Lu, there's no difference," Tim began to explain. "I've worked at most of the bars in this city and they're all the same. If the girls in the bar don't offer their services, the bar doesn't get many customers. But if there are beautiful and young-looking girls who happen to be friendly towards the customers and give extra services for money, the bar gets crowded with tourists, men with money ready to pay. And Lu, plenty of those men are so drunk they can't even perform. You get them back to their hotel room and they're too wasted for sex."

"You've got to be out of your mind!" Lu said.

"I'm sorry, Lu, but that's just the way it is. Hell, you can make a month's pay just by being extra nice. I've been in this business for three years now and look at me and Som! What do you think, are we looking terrible?" Tim asked.

"Yes," Lu said laughing, "take a look at yourself in the mirror. You do look terrible!"

Tim replied, "Yes, I made a mistake last night. I went along with a guest and he wanted to go on to other bars. He paid for everything while I was supposed to be his guide in the city. There were a lot of drinks. When we parted, I got a bundle of bank notes for my services and he got me a taxi to take me home. If I had walked on my own, I would never have made it back. I was too damned pissed. He was a nice guy, actually, from Norway I think, or maybe it was Sweden. I can't remember. He was chatting away about snow and polar bears. He was probably a bit bonkers. He was going to show up tonight again, he said."

"What do you do with the money?" Lu asked her friend. "You certainly don't spend much on this place."

"No, I send as much as I can to my son and to my mother who's taking care of him in Vientiane. I put some away so that eventually, I'll be able to get out of here," Tim explained.

"Tim, what do you think I should do? Lu asked again. "Should I go and have a talk with Gulu to see what mood he's in today?"

"Yes, your only risk is that he might throw you out and that's not the worst thing that could happen," Tim said.

"I'd better do it before the bar opens, then," Lu replied. "I'll take off now, so you'll have some time to get yourself into shape. I think it'll take a while."

*

On her way to the bar, Lu spoke quietly to herself. She had been hoping for some comfort and support from Tim, but instead, her friend had all but come to Gulu's defence. Her attitude seemed to be to question why Lu should enjoy privileges that no one else had. Everyone in the bar seized the opportunity to make extra money and Gulu had expected Lu to deliver. It wouldn't be easy to get empathy out of Tim. She just had to choose the right way to put things.

Lu went up to Gulu's office where she knew he would be working. As usual, at this time in the day, he was sitting counting the previous day's takings. Lu knocked and Gulu yelled "Come in."

Lu knew the yell was not because he was angry, but because he wanted his voice to carry, so she went in.

"Why are you here?" Gulu asked, surprised. "You don't start until later on!"

"Well, that's right, but bearing in mind what happened yesterday, I wanted to talk with you," Lu said.

"Lu, I really made a fool of myself and I'd really like to apologise," Gulu said, much to Lu's surprise.

During the early morning, Gulu had learned that Surachai, the gangster, was Lu's brother and that Songchai of Pak Mong, the old warrior, was her father-in-law and these were men he didn't want any trouble with. One thing he didn't know was that Lu had hardly any contact with her brother and that the old man was living a life quite apart from her own. If Lu got into trouble, they would probably say that she only had herself to blame; if you play with matches you can get your fingers burnt.

"I ruined your blouse. If you'll find a new one that you like, I'll pay for it. Are you okay with that?" he asked her.

"Yes, absolutely," Lu answered, astonished by the fact that Gulu was apologising to her.

He went up to her and took her by the hand.

"So, we have an agreement? No hard feelings?" he said and kissed her hand lightly.

"Go down and start arranging the table settings and prepare for the evening. I think we're in for a busy night," he continued.

Lu walked away and closed the door, wondering briefly whether or not the man was a psychopath. She allowed the thought to drift away deciding to be happy that things had worked out so well. She had been expecting the very opposite. Evening came and so did all the girls who worked in the bar.

It was rather weird at the bars because at first, nothing was going on. The staff would be all there, standing, attentive, all spruced up, their make-up as perfect as they could get it. The customers would not arrive until after eleven or twelve. Then, it would be like all hell had broken loose with everybody wanting everything at the same time. That was the case this particular Friday night.

Prim knew that mummy would not be back until late, or early, depending on how you looked at it. Lu was not usually worried about her daughter, so she took the evening as it came. How she was to get home was an issue to be dealt with later.

It did not take many minutes for Tim, Som and the others to find some guys who wanted more than just to hang around the bar drinking with the girls.

Tim told Lu, "Damn it, seize the opportunity now! These guys are okay and will probably pay well."

"No!" Lu replied harshly.

"But Lu, you need a man to screw you. You haven't had anyone for a long time and that has to be a real drag," Tim said.

"Tim, please Tim, don't go on about it, not here and not now. You do whatever you want and I'll do what I want," Lu said.

"Alright, okay," Tim said. "I hear you."

That night, Lu had to work hard. The girls were hanging around at the bar drinking whatever the guys were buying, while Lu and a few others got to serve, smile, clear the tables of the food plates and dirty cocktail glasses on the counter, smile again, go to the toilet and grab the hose and flush out a lot of things that weren't pee and then return with yet another smile.

Chapter 8

Eventful Party

It had just turned two in the morning and it was finally time to close the bar. Gulu was about to leave when one of the guests, part of a gang of four, approached him.

"You, you're the one who owns this bar, aren't you?" the man said.

"Yes," Gulu answered. "What do you want?"

Gulu was not scared of tourists acting tough, the sort who believed their money meant they owned the city and who took it for granted that the poor people of Laos would be at their beck and call. The guys were intoxicated but not so much that they couldn't behave decently.

"My name is Fredrik and this is Kjell. We're from Sweden. This is Will and this is Frank."

Frank and Will were from the US and were in Laos to work. Fredrik and Kjell were there on a short vacation. All four of them were staying at the same hotel and had become acquainted at the hotel bar a few days earlier. The chemistry between them was good and they had spent a couple of days together.

Fredrik and Kjell were in the computer business and had been to Hong Kong for a computer fair. They had some time on their hands and had left their colleagues in Hong Kong, taken off for Bangkok and then onward to Luang Prabang, an idea they had been discussing since their departure from Stockholm.

Their families were completely in the dark about what they were up to. They had told their colleagues that they had to go and see some suppliers in Bangkok, while in reality, they had gone to Laos for a week of partying, to have a good time on their own. Since both of them spent plenty of time around the world on various assignments, no one suspected they might be lying.

Will and Frank were in a very different line of business, one that had to do with dead people. They were working for the American Defence Department, the cooperative organisation Joint POW/MIA Accounting Command, or JPAC and CILHI, whose mission was to seek, find and bring home the mortal remains of fallen American soldiers and there were still plenty of these in Vietnam and Laos, whose remains had never been found. If the remains were tracked down, they would be taken home. So Will and Frank were, in effect, head hunters and were paid for what they found. They were not exactly on a vacation, but they had decided to take a few days off together with the Swedes. The men were all about the same age and had similar interests: motorcycling and sailing. That night, they had two reasons to celebrate: Fredrik was turning forty and this was to be their last night together. They had planned some serious partying. Fredrik's celebration of his fortieth birthday back home would be a very different affair.

"I'll invite you to an after-party!" Fredrik said to Kjell.

"It'll never work; we'll get in trouble with the neighbours in the adjacent rooms," Kjell replied.

"Nah, I'll fix things. I'll rent this bar for the night and make sure that the owner locks out all the guests except the four of us. All the staff will serve just us, in every way," Fredrik said.

"In every way?" Kjell asked with a knowing smile.

"Yes," Fredrik answered.

*

Having started his conversation with Gulu, Fredrik continued, "Are you interested in renting out the bar to us for the rest of the night? Shall we say until eight o'clock tomorrow morning?"

"Sure," Gulu answered, immediately seeing a business opportunity. "I'll just check with my staff and then I'll get back to you with the price."

"Great," Fredrik said and gave the thumbs up to the others to show them that there probably was a green light for the night's party.

Gulu brought some of the staff up to his office and informed them that they were to work until eight o'clock the following morning and that this was an order. Then, he returned to speak to Fredrik.

"I want three thousand dollars for the staff, a thousand for the premises and four thousand for everything you'll be drinking and eating and for the mess you'll be leaving. If you're interested, we'll pull the folding walls shut and ask the other guests to leave."

"It's a deal," Fredrik replied, pulling out a bundle of notes which he began counting while the bar personnel stood watching. Eight thousand, that was more than most people with a regular income made in three years.

*

Gulu did precisely what he had promised: he threw everybody out and locked up. The four men were now the only guests. The staff consisted of eight women, one man behind the bar and another two women in the kitchen.

Kjell let out a whoop of joy. Being a guest at a party like this was a first for him.

"We want beer, more food up on the counter and the ladies close, so that we can touch them," Fredrik said loudly.

Lu did everything she could to avoid leaving the kitchen during the night, but even from there, she could not avoid hearing and seeing everything that was going on. Tim was drunk, dancing on the counter to the loud music. The other girls were sitting with the guys, who were watching Tim's wild dancing while they ate. The guys did not know where to start, whether to stare at Tim and cheer her on, or to eat, or to engage in some heavy petting with whichever girl was sitting closest.

Som was serving from the opposite side of the bar. Kjell was helping Som make the drinks and succeeded in undoing the tiny piece of cloth covering her bosom. He was alternating between tasting the drinks and her small firm breasts.

"God damn, Fredrik, this was an awesome idea!" he cheered. "She's hot and has everything in the right place. This is far better than hanging around some hotel in Hong Kong!"

Kjell had placed himself behind Som. She was moving her backside towards his crotch with a gyrating motion. Kjell grabbed her hips from behind and pulled her hard against his erection. It was still inside his trousers, but not for long, he hoped. Som had to understand that he wanted more.

Kjell was forty-four, married with two children, a boy and a girl. The boy was fifteen and the girl nineteen, Som's age. At the family dinner table back home, he would denounce all such behaviour and demonstrate in every way that he found prostitution abhorrent.

"These girls are not much older than my daughter!" he would exclaim.

But that was at home. This was a very different place, where he could do things he was to forget on the way home, just as Som would forget him as well, hopefully.

Tim's dancing became more and more risqué. After a while, Will got up on the counter as well, to dance with her, fondling and stroking her enthusiastically. They were dancing with their legs wrapped around one another's thighs, sliding rhythmically to the beat.

Frank grabbed two of the girls and went off. They were going to have a nice time in the hotel room, he said.

Fredrik was totally absorbed by Tim and Will's dancing on the counter. He couldn't decide whether to look at Tim's naked body winding itself around Will's, or to concentrate on the incessant kisses over his own fat body from the girl on his left side, or the stroking between his legs from the girl on his right. Fredrik was silent, just toasting and drinking and eating whatever was on the counter closest to where he was perched, straddle-legged, upon the bar stool. When he laid his arms upon the counter, he was always preceded by his belly.

The girls stroking his body were getting no response. It was as if he were not there at all. They made a real effort, but this, Fredrik took for granted. He was the CEO of his company, lived at an expensive villa in the outskirts of Stockholm and did all he could to make the family understand he was a good family man. Whenever he arrived at a hotel in Asia, he would rent a whore and he often went to that part of the world on business. This was a perfect night, but they would never talk about it again once they had left Laos and Luang Prabang.

Fredrik told the girl who was stroking him between his legs to try to get him hard, "You'll get ten dollars extra if you give me a blow job," he said.

He remained on the bar stool straddle-legged, the same position he had been holding all night. She slid down with an experienced motion between the wall of the counter and Fredrik's legs and began to please him. Tim was naked on the counter in front of him and another girl was working rhythmically between his legs. Damn it, he was on his way to heaven!

At that point, the long counter finally got too crowded and the food and plates were barely saved when Will slipped down on his knees. Tim's legs ended up either side of him and Will, who was ready for sex, pulled her on top of him.

Kjell, meanwhile, was at it with Som.

"She wants some more money, is that okay, Fredrik?" Kjell asked, always in need of Fredrik's approval.

"It's okay," Fredrik answered absently, as if he really were not there at all.

Things didn't work out for Will. He grabbed hold of Tim's body too hard and she fell, almost flying over him toward the end of the counter. There, she lost her balance and fell further on to the floor. There was a chair beside her as she fell and Tim's head hit it's frame hard, hard enough that the blow was heard above the music. Everybody stopped short. Suddenly, the bar was silent.

"Tim!" Som called. "What happened?"

Kjell's fear turned him stone-cold sober at once and he found himself staring at Tim lying there, motionless. Will had a medical education from his army days. He walked up to Tim and turned her over so that she was lying on her side.

"She's breathing and she's got a pulse," he said. "She's okay, but she has to lie still. She'll probably have one hell of a concussion from hitting the chair."

Lu came out to help. Som and Kjell were standing there, staring. Fredrik had not moved an inch, but he had become irritated by the fact that the girl who was at work between his legs had stopped. She could forget about any extra money for that.

Will and Lu left Tim lying on the floor, but made her more comfortable.

"Let her be for a couple of hours," Will said, "and she will probably get better."

Will introduced himself to Lu, who he had not noticed until then.

"But now, I'll go back to the hotel," he said and turned to Fredrik.

"Thanks for tonight, Fredrik. I'm off. I think we're damn lucky that it's just concussion. If she'd died, we'd all have had one hell of a problem getting out of the country, that's for sure!"

It was a little overdue, but Kjell was finally thinking, imagining the implications if the girl had died. His immediate family, all his relatives and all his colleagues would have known what he had been up to.

"Yes," Fredrik replied, his tone matter-of-fact. "It's a shame that it should turn out like this." But he hid his irritation over Will's clumsiness.

At this juncture, the party was over. Will was heading for the door with Kjell in his wake, but at the last moment, Kjell turned and asked Som if she would like to continue the party with him, in private. He had not had enough.

"You know the price," Som told him.

"Sure," Kjell answered and the three of them left.

Fredrik remained at the bar. He had rented the place until eight o'clock and it was still only five. He wanted his money's worth. One of the girls was sitting by his side stroking his hand.

Lu was tidying up in the bar, keeping an eye on Tim who was still motionless down on the floor.

"Anyhow, it's lucky that it all ended up like this," Lu said to herself, quietly.

"I hear you saying something," Fredrik said.

"Yes, we got lucky; it could have been far worse," Lu said.

"Well, I think it ended badly enough. I've bought a package I never received," Fredrik complained, bitterly.

"I think you should get out of here now," Lu told him. "Take a hooker with you and get out, so I can clean up this place after you."

Fredrik slouched off with a girl on his arm.

Yes, Lu pondered on how it was a way to make a living, one of the oldest and most dangerous in the world.

Having made sure no one was left, she locked up, checked on Tim, who had fallen asleep, tidied up the scraps but left the glasses, grabbed a blanket and lay down on the floor beside Tim. She thought about Prim, who she knew would have cooked her own dinner, done her homework and gone to bed. She would wake up alone wondering where her mother could be. Well, that's the way it had to be today.

"Goodnight, Tim," Lu said and went to sleep.

*

It felt like only moments later that she was woken by the morning sun blazing into the smoke-reeked bar.

"Tim," she asked, "how do you feel?"

"I feel so damn dizzy," Tim replied. "I can't move my head. I think I'm going to throw up."

A moment later, she did precisely that. Lu was holding her head and began to get worried.

"What am I to do?" Tim said.

"Just lay still. It's important that you don't move. I'll help you," Lu said trying to reassure her.

While Lu was wiping up her friend's vomit, there was a knock on the bar door. It was Will. He called out to them when he saw that they were still on the premises.

"What do you want?" Lu asked.

"I just wanted to check that Tim is okay," he said.

"I'm coming," Lu said.

Will walked into the bar, seeing it in a very different light from the way it had appeared the previous night. He wondered about what he had been doing the night before. He thought about what booze could make you do.

"How is she?" he asked Lu.

"She threw up just a moment ago," she replied.

"Yes, that can come after bad concussion," he confirmed.

Lu felt reassured. Will knew what he was talking about, so she softened her attitude and became friendlier.

"Would you like some coffee?" she asked him.

"Yes please," he replied.

He seated himself at one of the tables rather than at the bar. He had had quite enough of that. Lu went out into the kitchen, brought the coffee and took a seat at the same table with her own cup of tea. The two of them looked over at Tim who was still lying down, her face pale.

"We can probably take her home in a while," Will said. "Do you live close by?"

"No, I live a bit outside the town. It takes me between one and two hours to get home. But Tim lives just fifteen minutes away," Lu confirmed.

"Okay, so we should be able to get her home quite soon," Will said.

Lu was sipping at her tea while she was looking at Will.

"How long will you be staying in Luang Prabang?" she asked him.

"I don't know. It depends. We have a lot of work to do and sometimes, it takes a while. We're not here as tourists, Frank and I. We're working. Fredrik and Kjell, on the other hand, are here on vacation. We don't really know each other; we just happened to meet here in town, at the hotel," he explained.

"But I got the impression you had all known each other for some time," Lu said.

"When you're partying, all boundaries get blurred," he replied, smiling.

"Yes, God knows," Lu commented.

"Fredrik and Kjell are in the computer business. Frank and I are working for the US government, the army, you could say. We're looking for the remains of American soldiers who went missing during the war here in Laos. You know, there was an enormous war fought here in this district and above all, up around Phonsavan. With help from the CIA, the Hmong people formed the Secret Army."

"Oh yes," replied Lu. "I know all about that. We are Hmong and my father was one of the fighters up there."

Will was surprised at how quickly and easily he had made contact with someone familiar with the district. His plan had been for he and Frank to get up to Phonsavan and try to make contact with some elderly people. With their help, they'd find their way to places of special interest. It was always a hassle, involving bribes, having to find and befriend the village alderman, who was in charge. If they could employ Lu, it would be advantageous and possibly even better, given her father's history.

"I don't have much contact with my father and what's more, he's seriously ill." Lu said. "But I can find someone else that can help you find your way. My mother is from the village of Muang Khoun. She has friends living in those districts that might interest you."

"That's good," Will said, draining his coffee.

Tim, still lying on the floor, woke up.

"Oh! Hell, I feel so damn dizzy!"

"You really ought to take it easy today," Will told her. "If I were you, I would go home and go to bed for the rest of the day and tomorrow as well."

"I think I'll do that," Tim said.

She got up carefully and sat down on the chair that was closest to her.

"Well, I'm off now," Will announced. "I have to find out what's happened to Frank. He's probably got a bit of an achy head today as well, I guess. When will we meet, Lu?"

"I'll be here tonight from seven, so you can come by. You'll have to see then if I have any information for you," Lu replied.

She wanted to get home. Soon, Prim wouldn't have seen her for twenty-four hours. She was bound to worry if her mother wasn't home when she returned from school. Lu decided to do something she only had done on special occasions before: she took a motorcycle taxi home to the village, a trip that set her back almost half a day's pay, but it was already nine o'clock in the morning and she had to get home quickly.

*

Back at home, a strange silence seemed to hover over the huts. A lot had happened recently. Lu walked up to her parents' hut and called in through the opening.

"What do you want?" spat May.

"I'd like to speak with Father," she answered.

"He's too tired to talk to you and he's sleeping, anyway," May replied.

Everybody still blamed Lu, her uselessness, as they put it. And Prim was treated just as badly. Lu went on to her own hut, hanging her head. She lay down to rest for a while, but she could not sleep. She was brooding on what had happened during the night.

Tim could have broken her neck in that fall, something that Will probably realised. What types they were, those Swedish guys: totally callous. Lu hoped they would get what was coming to them. As for Frank, who'd taken off and avoided everything at the end, he seemed to have luck on his side. Will, though, seemed like a nice guy.

Lu mulled over how she would be able to help him with what he needed. As she lay thinking, she recalled the story that Anant had related a couple of times, about those advisers who had been captured up in the village of Nong Pet and kept in that water cage up by lake Nong Nam Nyam. Wasn't that where they had disappeared?

Lu decided to stay home until Prim came back from school, so she would get an opportunity to speak to her. She wanted to see her daughter, but her conscience did not trouble her too much as Prim was big enough these days to take care of herself during the daytime.

Lu dozed off and woke to the sound of Prim entering the hut, mad as a hornet.

"Mummy! Where have you been? Don't you see that I've been worried? I could tell from your expression that something had happened the other night and your blouse was torn apart. What are you up to, really?" she demanded to know.

At first, Lu was quiet.

"I don't have to explain anything to you. It was just an accident," she replied.

"But why don't you come home at night, Mummy?" Prim asked her.

"Well, there was this other thing that I was going to tell you," Lu admitted.

Lu related what had happened, not the whole story, but the parts that were suitable for a child. What Lu did not know and did not care to know, was that Prim had come to learn a great deal during the past year. She was on her way to being a woman and understood plenty of what the adults around her were doing.

Lu got up, changed her clothes and told Prim that she was going back to town, back to her job.

"Job, at the whore-bar, you mean," said Prim, with a glimmer of contempt in her eyes.

That second, a blow landed on her cheek. She had received a slap which made the hut ring.

"What do you mean by that?" Lu asked.

"Everybody is talking about the place you are working at, everyone except you and they say that it's a whorehouse, a whore-bar!" Prim yelled to her mother.

Lu was shocked by Prim's directness.

"I'm sorry, you're right. That's what they call the bar, I know. But I'm not selling myself, Prim! I'm waiting on the guests and tidy up after others," Lu tried to reassure her.

"I don't give a shit what you do, just don't let it affect me! It's bloody revolting!" Prim came back at her.

"Prim, I have to leave now. I've got to be back at seven, so I need to take the bus and it will arrive soon. Go down and check the hen house and the pigs before you go to bed and we'll see each other tomorrow morning."

From this, Prim inferred that her mother would be home late or not until morning. Prim kindled the fire outside the hut, sat down by it in solitude and allowed her thoughts to wander to Pom, her maternal grandfather's evenings and all that was lost.

*

When Lu arrived at the bar, Gulu was already there. He had dashed to the bar after being informed of what had happened. He wanted to make sure that the police were not involved or that Tim had had to go to hospital. Getting onto the police radar would not be good for Gulu; he was an anonymous public figure and wanted it to stay that way.

The police and the local authorities knew about his business, of course, given they were customers, but it would not do if it got out that there had been accidents. That might cause customers to frequent other bars which would not be good for Gulu's business, as he used to remind everyone. They met down on the bar floor. Gulu had not had time to go up to his office yet, where he usually sat alone and called up one of the girls, when needed. For now, what he needed were facts.

"Lu, what happened? I understand that Tim can't work for a couple of days. You'll have to take her place," he said.

Lu was scared by this suggestion. She began by telling Gulu about the night and finished by begging him to be excused from selling liquor from the other side of the bar. On that side, Lu's role would be to sit with a guest, be extra nice and let him treat her to drinks and to prostitute herself. Some things, she could consider, the others, not.

That night turned out to be quite quiet and Gulu found the sales too low for his liking.

During the night, Gulu made it clear that everybody was to sell champagne and nothing else. They were to have a contest to see who could sell the most of it. In addition, the guests would have to pay for a couple of extra bottles if they wanted to take one of the girls to their hotel. From now on, Gulu demanded all the profit the girls made, like a fully-fledged pimp.

"Sell champagne," he said. "All the ladies like champagne and all the guys like to buy it for them and what's more, it'll make the cash roll in."

It was past ten o'clock when Will and Frank stepped into the bar. When she saw them coming, Lu was very relieved. She was sitting by herself, luckily and they caught sight of her immediately as they walked in. Frank greeted Som, his memory of her still fresh. Will had paid little attention to Som the previous night, except for her serving drinks in the nude. Frank was not the type of guy who would talk about what had happened yesterday, which was gone, feeling that it was better to look ahead. Lu met them and asked them to be seated at a table instead of at the bar.

"What would you like to drink?" she asked them.

"I think we had a little too much yesterday, so I'll have a Coke," Will said.

"The same for me," Frank added.

Lu went off to fetch the order and caught a glimpse of Som.

"You must sell other things too. Nobody can make a living off Coke," she said.

Lu pretended not to have heard, got a Coke for herself as well and sat down with her new friends.

"Lu, can you help us? You'll be paid for your trouble," Will said, getting straight to the point.

They talked in a low voice, so that the other guests would not hear them.

"We've got maps for the whole of northern Laos and all those districts ravaged by the Vietnamese. We've also got information about our people and where they were situated. We have to meet the people in the villages who might know something and guide us to the right places. You know both the language and the land," said Will.

"How much money are you making when you're working here at this shithole?" Frank asked.

"A hundred dollars a month," Lu replied.

"Damn, is that all. Does that include all types of services?" Frank said, a glint in his eye.

Lu realised he was joking.

"No, those are extra," she confirmed.

"Oh, that figures, since it turned out to be rather expensive yesterday," Frank said, smiling.

"How much would I get for helping you?" Lu asked.

"Well, about three hundred a month." Will said. "And if we're successful, you'll have work for at least three months ahead."

Lu calculated quickly and told them she wanted at least twelve hundred dollars for three months.

"Okay," Will replied immediately.

The maths was simple. Lu estimated that she made a hundred dollars for each month at the bar and multiplied by twelve, this was the equivalent of what she would now be getting in three months. That meant that if the job ended after three months, she would still get by the rest of the year without having to find more work. Will, Frank and Lu concluded the deal without anything written down: they trusted each other already.

"Fine," Lu told them. "I'll go up to Gulu and tell him that I'm quitting right now."

"You do that," Will said. "We'll wait and make sure that you get home sadly by cab. And tomorrow, we'll get together at the Merry Lao Swiss Hotel and start working."

*

That night, Lu arrived home earlier than expected. Prim, who had fallen asleep, woke up and was surprised at her mother's presence.

"What, is it you, Mummy?" she asked.

"Yes, it's me. Go back to sleep and we'll talk tomorrow," Lu replied. "I'll go out to sit down by the fire for a while. I can't sleep right now."

Lu was sitting, looking at all the stars. Up there was Pom, now a star himself.

"You're with us," she said, her voice low.

Prim, who had sneaked up and stood behind her mother, heard her words.

"Yes," Prim said, "he is always with us."

At that moment, their eyes met in the dark.

"Sit down," Lu said. "I've got a good deal to tell you about. You might as well hear it now, since you're awake."

This time, Prim got to hear everything, from the beginning to the end, with all the details about what had taken place at the bar the previous night. Lu excluded nothing: she accepted that Prim understood. Lu talked about the guests, the exploitation, the dangerous avenue to easy money. In turn, Prim told her mother what had happened at the village during recent evenings and nights: the strange visitors, the loud conversations, her wondering what grandpa Songchai was up to.

"Yes," Lu said, "Songchai has always been involved in businesses that we probably should keep clear of and the same goes for Surachai."

As they were sitting there out by the fire, there came another light that outshone the fire's glimmer. A car, driven slowly.

"Mummy, that's the car I told you about, the one that came onto the courtyard at high speed and it's the same people sitting inside."

Chapter 9

Caves and Caches

Pooi and Suteluck stopped the car in front of the hut and waited. When Songchai came out, they exchanged a few words through the window, the old man took a seat in the car and then, they were off.

"How did it turn out?" Songchai asked.

"It was a nice funeral," Suteluck replied. "Everything was well prepared for Tatchacon's journey to the other side. The whole village was there and naturally, everybody was wondering about the cause of his sudden death."

"Well, cardiac arrests can take you by surprise. He wasn't old though, just fifty-three. You've better be careful," Pooi said.

That night, the men were to drive up to Pok Mong. At dawn, they were supposed to meet some local farmers who would come along and help carry the merchandise out of the cave up in Ban Na Sala. They had fallen behind schedule, thanks to the recent events. Songchai had made the decision that Surachai was to take up Tatchacon's role, in addition to his existing one. This entailed Surachai making contact with his friends and gearing up the police along the road, a measure that probably would cost them extra in bribes. Surachai was coming to the meeting as well, but in his own car.

The road between Tat Kuang and Pok Mong stretched for about a hundred kilometres. In many places, it was barely passable and there was a risk of dense mist. They expected to arrive just before sunrise.

"I've made sure that the boats are rebuilt, so that we can bring as many weapons as possible," Songchai said. "I'm a bit worried that we might have some problems with the old landmines, but we have to take as many of them as we possibly can. They'll generate a huge profit."

"It's lucky the boats don't jog about, like cars do along these damn roads. Then, we'd probably become airborne," Pooi said, laughing.

Spirits were high during the car trip. Nothing in the behaviour of Pooi or Suteluck suggested that if Tatchacon had not died so suddenly, their plans would have been different.

*

One of Songchai's old friends and brothers-in-arms, Supot, was to wait for them at dawn. It had fallen to him to find the farmers that would dig and carry, men who were used to hard labour and willing to take risks for a price.

Supot was not just the big man of the village. He was also a war veteran and a scrap merchant. Many people had become scrap dealers after the war: it was almost impossible to cultivate the land, after all. Everywhere, there were scraps from various countries including Soviet tanks and parts from shot down American planes, torpedo bombs and cluster bombs. Each cluster bomb contained between six and seven hundred items the size of tennis balls and each of those was made up of two hundred and fifty steel pieces which between them, could spread destruction over an area of five thousand square metres with devastating effect. Supot gathered scrap and sold it in Thailand, among other places. The others in the village used it to make pots and pans, picks, spades and knives.

The old war veteran controlled most things in his domain, including what lay hidden in the caves. He would receive his allotted share of the profit, but did not want to participate in the actual trade as he knew that this might cost him dearly. According to chapters seventy one and seventy two in the martial law, the most severe law of all, you would get five years' imprisonment for dealing with weapons from these caches. If you got caught, there was every chance you would never escape Laos' prisons alive. You would die from disease and from lack of proper care long before you were released. But Songchai and his two cronies knew how to handle both the police and the military. After all, they were their friends. But even friends had to be paid: no bribe, then no friendship.

Pooi drove the car while Songchai and Suteluck slept. The high spirits of the first few hours had quickly given way to deadly boredom. He woke the others up as they drew closer to Pok Mong. If there was anyone who could orientate his way in the village, it was Songchai, no matter how thick the mist. It didn't take long for them to reach Supot's settlement. Supot welcomed them outside his hut, which was larger than the norm, comprising three parts: two separate bedrooms and a joint space which was like a kitchen. In the middle of the latter, a fire spread its warmth. Its smoke rose through a hole in the ceiling; that is, the smoke that wasn't trapped, left hovering about the room like a mist.

The men sat down around the fire and Supot's wife served a broth-like soup in bowls made from bomb heads. She had polished cartridges - sixty centimetre-long anti-aircraft rounds - which she used as vases on a small table upon which there were daily fruit sacrifices to Buddha. For the most part, she sold them to tourists who liked to have a cartridge upon the table in their home. While they guzzled down the soup noisily, they discussed the journey. This was a common way to encourage conversation.

"Have you been up to the caves in Ban Na Sala, like we discussed?" Songchai asked.

"Yes," Supot replied, "but it'll probably be harder than it sounded in your description. I do agree that it appears to be one of the largest caches. But it is also one of the most inaccessible."

"Tell me more!" Pooi said, then turned to Songchai. "You said you knew everything about this cache."

"Yes, but let Supot finish," Songchai urged him.

"We know that all these caves are almost inaccessible. If this had not been the case, they would never have been used as hiding places," Supot continued. "But the worst thing is that the Vietnamese used blasts to destroy parts of certain caves, with varying degrees of success. The cave that we want to clear out was partly destroyed by aerial bombardments aimed at targets close by. The main passage has caved in. There is a tunnel to the side, but it's too narrow to be used as a transport passage. So, no matter how we decide to do this, we still have to dig. I've been talking with some friends of mine in the village who usually work with aloe trees. Their market is doing badly for the moment, so they are more than willing to help out with the digging. We should get going today. Then, there's another problem: the mines. It would not be pleasant if someone stuck a spade in a mine. The whole mountain would probably go off and then some."

"It would be great if it would take Education Camp Seven with it," said Suteluck, who had been sitting silent for a while. "I've heard there are still political prisoners there."

"Yes, that's true," Pooi told him. "It wasn't so long ago that we learned Thongsouk Saysangkhi, our former vice minister, had died in that prison - excuse me, that 'educational establishment' - in 1998. And there are people that have been stuck there since '92 without trial, without pen or paper, without any way of communicating with the outside world. Add to that the thirty thousand or so men that the state eliminated, or confined to jail, for their opinions. No, damn it, this isn't the time to talk about that crap."

"Anyhow, we'll manage to get up to the cache," Supot said, resuming the more pertinent topic. "When we're on the site, we'll decide how we should go about it. Everything else is done and as you know, nobody will have seen anything; the police have already been paid."

"Great," Songchai said. "Then, there is just the question of where Surachai is at."

That very second, Surachai's car was heard braking outside the hut. He dashed in when he saw the others' car.

"Sorry I'm late. I overslept. I should've started earlier," he blurted out.

Surachai was lying, of course. He had stayed up almost all night, mulling over his plans and had finally come to a decision: somewhere along the road, he would lay his hands upon the cargo and make himself two million dollars richer. He had known the sly old fox and scrap dealer for some time and was well aware that Supot traded in plenty of things besides what was official. Drugs usually formed part of the supply as the Hmong could not make a living by selling aloe trees or aromatic wood to the Arab countries.

Surachai was not invited to take a seat, since it was already time to head for the caves where the arms were located.

"Will you drive in front of me and lead the way?" Surachai asked Supot. "Have you got spades in your car?"

"Yes, but first, we have to get hold of the guys that'll fix the lighting. We'll get electricity from the petrol generator on the back of the pick-up," Supot confirmed.

"Good thinking. It wouldn't do to use paraffin lamps inside of powder keg," Pooi said, laughing.

"Those are two guys we can rely on. And they're also willing to come along all the way down to Khemmarat," Supot added.

"Are you absolutely positive that we can trust them, Supot?" Songchai asked his old friend.

"Absolutely, they're among my most trusted assistants and they're used to risky assignments," Supot replied.

"There'll be seven of us. That should be enough, if everybody works. We'll know soon enough whether we need any more," Songchai said.

*

Having picked up their assistants, the cars headed for Ban Na Sala. Since they were not to go all the way to the village, the road over the mountains was the most suitable. It was the least busy and the huts were widely scattered, but it was almost impassable. The cave they were aiming for was situated between Ban Na Sala and Pok Mong. The closer they came to their destination, the more the tension increased inside the cars.

"Hell," Songchai said. "Something is wrong. I can't put my finger on it but I'm having this weird feeling."

"Take it easy now," Supot told him. "It's just your old nerves haunting your mind. Actually, old men like you and I should have got out of this kind of business a long time ago. There's too much tension. It could kill us."

"Maybe you're right," Songchai said. "Can you see the others behind us?"

"Yes, they've just reappeared after a sharp bend," Supot confirmed.

Along the road to the caves, it was easy to catch sight of someone driving after you, as clouds of dust rose around the cars despite their slow pace. No rain had fallen for a month. Songchai pulled out a map to check their whereabouts. Even though they knew where the caves were situated, it was easy to get lost.

"Supot, we should probably stop soon," Songchai said.

"Yes, there's a suitable place behind the crest. We can park the cars there in such a way that they won't get spotted," Supot pointed out.

Surachai was now hot on their tail. The exit road was perfect: a narrow channel cut into the jungle and its dense vegetation. The tall coconut palms offered perfect cover from above, while the ferns, the towering trees and the areca palms concealed the cars from all directions making it impossible to see what was hidden.

"We can load up here and work without interference," Songchai said. "We'll unload the cars and walk the last part; it's only a kilometre or so."

"Are the paths and the ground around here safe?" asked Pooi. "Those bloody Russian mines don't stop working. They've killed and maimed enough of us since the war ended."

"Yes, that's a real problem around here," Supot said. "As late as last week, one of my neighbours lost a leg when he was out clearing his land. You have to be careful."

"The two assistants will carry the generator," Songchai said. "Pooi and Suteluck will carry the spades. Surachai, you'll take the lamps, Supot will take the ropes and I'll take the maps and the first-aid-kit. Let's get going!"

"Walk slowly and pay attention!" Pooi told Songchai as they set out.

"I think it's for the best if I take the lead," Suteluck said. "I've got some experience of districts like these. We are not to spread out, that might be dangerous. Instead, we'll walk in a long line."

Pooi thought about all those bloody mines, many of which had been buried for a long time, some of them for twenty, even thirty years. This meant that nowadays, they were often impossible to spot. Besides there being mines hidden under ground, the entrances to the caves were also hard to find. They were always overgrown. Even if an entrance was cleared of bushes, it would be overgrown again within a month.

*

The seven men began walking slowly into the jungle, carrying their tools and other equipment. Quite soon, they were swallowed up by the greenery. After a few hundred metres, Suteluck halted and stood staring at a couple of furrows in the ground, created by the rainwater on its route from the hills to the valleys.

"Why have you stopped?" Pooi asked.

"Come and have a look," Suteluck replied.

When Pooi reached him, Suteluck asked him to look down in the furrow.

"There you go. We're in dangerous territory. We'd better go about this bloody carefully or none of us will get out of this place alive," he confirmed.

Down in the furrow, clearly visible, were three mines lying on their edges, just a metre apart, laid bare by the recurring bursts of rain, far deadlier than the king cobras that lived in the bush. Once Pooi had marked out the mines, they all passed by them carefully without taking their eyes off them for a moment.

"That sure was creepy," Suteluck said, "but anyhow, now we're aware that there are mines on the way."

They walked carefully, almost as if they were in slow motion. Nobody wanted to rush. Surachai was noticeably nervous and kept far behind the others, at a safe distance in case someone stepped on the wrong spot.

"It feels like I'm back in the places of my childhood, ten or twelve years old," he said, his voice loud enough to reach Suteluck in front of him. "I thought I'd managed to forget all of it. Only once in a while, the memories return. Their clarity differs from time to time, but this time, they are absolutely clear. It's as if I were back there all over again."

He paused, then spoke again.

"Do you hear what I'm saying, Suteluck?"

"Yeah, I hear you," Suteluck replied.

"We were just kids when we learned how to shoot the Vietnamese and how to lay mines. There were no adult soldiers left on our side. We had suffered enormous losses in these districts. The CIA taught us how to fight," Surachai said.

"I know. But it was not just us Hmong," Suteluck reminded him. "We should not forget all the volunteers from Thailand and the Yao people. Together, we made up an army of thirty thousand. And imagine, out of these, over ten thousand were Thai."

"But we were just kids. I can see it all again: my friends getting blown to bits by those fucking mines, or when they were shot by the trespassers," Surachai commented.

"We have to stay focused now. Don't dwell on the past. All of us have memories, but it's not necessary to speak of those horrors now. That's war for you, Surachai. Well, I can't keep on walking here listening to you," Suteluck said and walked quickly past the rest of the group, taking the lead again.

Songchai glowered at Surachai. There seemed to be something up between them. Was it jealousy? Or was it that Songchai knew Surachai too well and for that reason, was a little suspicious of him. Songchai was an old crook and Surachai was a young one. This meant that there were major differences in their working methods. Surachai never hesitated if violence was necessary for him to get money or power. He was ready to kill for his purposes. In addition, he was easier to read. Songchai knew more about strategy, power plays and cunning. He would never kill to achieve his aims. But he made sure that what needed to be done was done. In contrast to Surachai, Songchai's intentions were almost impossible to spot. Nobody could read what he was thinking.

"The cave entrance isn't far away now," Supot announced. "It's for the best to be extra careful and not stray from the line. When we get up there, Pooi, you need to bring one of the guys and clear the working area, so we can be sure that there's nothing lurking in the bush. Make sure that some fifty metres around the cave are cleared and that you broaden the path enough so those helping with the carrying won't end up in a mess!"

The vegetation grew denser and harder to pass through the closer they got to the cave. Suteluck's arms were exhausted from chopping through the thick jungle. It was hard to get your bearings, but Supot, the old war veteran, kept them headed in the right direction.

"This is extremely dangerous," Suteluck said. "We can't see what's ahead of us on the ground, whether it's mines or old stiffs."

Supot laughed, "If it's just old stiffs, we should be glad, because that means that any mine will have already gone off. We'll be there soon enough, now. I recognise that mountain crest up there. Yes, this must be the place."

"Where?" Pooi and Surachai said simultaneously, while the two men who were to help with the digging just stood looking at the others.

"This is where we have to chop our way through," Surachai said. "It's incredibly hard to find the entrance if you don't know where it is."

Pooi, Suteluck and the two men helped one another to chop away the bushes and thickets that concealed the entrance. They decided that Pooi should do an initial reconnaissance. He walked in through the entrance at a crouch as it was just a metre high, so he had to make use of his thigh muscles. A few steps in, he had to stop and look around. The corridor leading in was fifty centimetres wide, at most, but still a metre high. Ten metres further in, there was some sort of meeting place, a cavity where you could step aside and let another person pass. Pooi turned around and walked out again.

"What was it like?" Suteluck asked.

"Dark and cramped," Pooi said. They walked up to the rest of the group sitting a couple of metres from the entrance.

"I think I know how we need to go about this," Surachai said, "and I can tell you already that Songchai, Supot and I won't be going into the passages. It's far too tough for us. You'll have to do it. You've got young legs. We will help with everything on the outside. I suggest that you, Pooi and Songchai bring the lighting with you once you have connected the generator and after we've had a short rest. You are to take a look around and then tell us what's there and how we should get the cache out. We haven't got a lot of time, so a half hour's rest will have to do."

Songchai took a different view. When the break was over, he split up the workforce again.

"Change of plan," he said, resolutely. "Pooi, you and one of the hands are to help one another to clear the area of any possible mines. And, for the sake of safety, go back to the cars and clear the path so it'll be safe for the carriers. Surachai, Suteluck and Supot, you are to go into the passages. Can you manage it, Supot? You're the one who knows how the caves are structured, so it would make sense if you could join them."

"That's okay," Supot replied.

"The rest of us will stay here on the outside and arrange the electric cable that you'll need for the lighting. Is everything clear? Let's get going!" Songchai said.

*

It would prove hard for Supot to manoeuvre inside the passages, given his advanced age, but he was made of the right stuff. Surachai would also have difficulties. He was too big to walk around crouching for any length of time and on top of that, he was out of shape. For Suteluck, however, it was quite a different matter. Like all servicemen, he was fit and during his training, he had walked hundreds of kilometres in passages like these.

Pooi had eagerly anticipated entering the caves, but was unhappy with the assignment he had been allocated. He reconciled himself to do the clearing up as quickly as he could. Once he'd finished, he'd get to join the rest of them in the cave, where the fun would begin. The group split up and started their assignments.

"I'll go first and then you'll come after me, a couple of metres apart," Supot said, entering the passage.

He constantly talked with the men behind him, telling them what he could see so that they could visualise what was ahead.

"Make sure that we always have the electric cable with us so we won't have any problems with the lighting. If we can't see where we're going, any one of us could fall into a trap. If that happens, well, you won't like it, but you won't have long to complain about it either: you'll be pierced to death by sharp bamboo canes stuck into the ground a metre under the pit's cover. The more you struggle to free yourself, the deeper the canes will dig in. There's no getting out alive. We have to make sure to circle the traps," he explained.

"Okay," replied the others, now anxious after what Supot had just told them.

Plodding forth, in a crouching position, they got some twenty metres in. By then, they had passed three meeting places.

"This cave is said to be six hundred metres in all," Supot said."

Surachai, who was already feeling pain in one of his thighs, tightened his jaw and said nothing.

"I hope we have enough cable," Suteluck said, while pulling on the cable behind them.

When they had covered about a hundred metres and reached the first room, they decided to rest their legs. Surachai looked at Supot.

"It looks like you need to stretch out your legs for a while. Lie down on the table here and I'll massage your muscles. This table has been standing here since the war, so it can probably take your weight," he said.

"Gladly!" Supot replied.

When Surachai began to massage Supot's tensed muscles, he could sense how tired the old man was. The room they were in had been used as a hospital and an operating theatre during the war. It was plainly furnished. Further in, were a classroom, bedroom, kitchen, dining room and workshops for, among other things, the production of weapons. After a couple of minutes' massage, Supot was ready to go on. The old man was as eager as if he were just twenty-five again and the place was swarming with enemies. He got up from the table and resumed the lead.

"Crouch down!" he called out. "The passage gets lower here so the enemies would be lured in and get stuck. All the easier to kill them off. I suspect we'll have to dig it out. Otherwise, we won't be able to carry anything through this part. And watch out for the cylinders on the passage floor! They were used to poison the enemy. If you step through them, the rolls, which are covered in sharp metal plates, will start rotating against each other. They cut deep into your feet and legs. They used to be prepared with poison that got into your wounds. Your time was up if you didn't manage to get your leg amputated in time."

Supot led the others further in, as sure of his own guidance as he had been before.

"Is your thigh feeling better?" Surachai asked.

"Yes, no problem," Supot replied, although Surachai reckoned a bit too smugly about his agility. "Soon, we'll reach the next room. I suggest we take just a moment to stretch out and then go further as soon as we can. "

"It's weird," Suteluck said, "that the air supply is still working this well after all these years. I think we've gotten deeper down now, so we'd better watch out. We might get to a flooded tunnel. In that case, somebody will have to dive in to reach the passage on the other side. I really hope that won't be the case. We can't carry the boxes across the moats. The only way is to dig our way past them."

Surachai didn't think he would ever manage it. To dive down in a waterlogged passage, not more than a metre high and half a metre wide. He just couldn't do it. Meanwhile, it was starting to dawn on him that the pain in his thighs was becoming unbearable. A sense of panic begun to creep up on him. All he wanted to do was drop to his knees. But he was walking in the middle of the group, some hundred metres into an old war passage with earth all around them. There was no chance for him to stop, but the pain was terrible. He decided to try and cope until they arrived at the next room.

Supot pressed on, eager to forge ahead.

"I've arrived," he said a minute or so later, but Surachai's legs could not take it anymore. Suteluck, who was the last in line, had noticed that Surachai had run into difficulties, fallen to his knees and was dragging himself over the last few metres.

"What the fuck is this?" Supot said. "I thought you were in shape. This won't do. You'll have to stay here until you're feeling okay. Then you can walk or crawl back. I don't give a shit which. How about you, Suteluck, are you alright?"

"I'm okay. I've run many miles in passages before," he replied. "Grab the cable and let's move it."

"Hey Supot," Suteluck said, when they were part of the way into the third passage. "Didn't somebody say that there had been collapses in some places and that it might be difficult to find the cache?"

"Yes, that's right. We'll see soon enough," Supot confirmed, while entering a new room. "I think we're close now, it should come right after this room which looks like a workshop. But the question is, which of the passages should we take; two of them appear to go in opposite directions. Let's take the left one and hope for the best. If it's sloping downwards, it's the right passage. If not, we'll come back and take the other one."

"Okay, it's your call," Suteluck said.

"It seems to be sloping downwards," Supot said, after a few minutes' plodding.

"Wait, the cable is getting sluggish and heavy now," Suteluck told him. "One of us has to double back and install an extension lead in the room we've just passed. Otherwise, we'll run the risk of breaking the cable and then we might never get out of here. Let's do that. I'll stay here in the dark and you go back to the others and get help. You'll need someone with you if you're going to get more cable in and set up an extension lead."

Suteluck set off immediately. Old Supot could not keep still, but made his way back to the workshop room. Unable to see what he was touching, he could just make out that there were wooden boxes with soil on top. There had been a collapse around the boxes, but it would be impossible to assess the damage until Suteluck had fixed the arrangements with the cable and the lighting. Suteluck was swift. A combination of military discipline and willpower brought him back to the room where Surachai was waiting.

"You're back" he said, surprised. "Has anything happened?"

"No, not at all. It's just that the cable has become too heavy and we have to set up a splice for the lighting. How are you? Can you manage to get out now? You can walk behind me. That will make it easier. If you can't make it all the way, you can rest in the first room. From there, it's not far to the entrance."

"I'll try to hang on," Surachai replied, noticeably shaken. "I thought it wouldn't be a problem to be shut in like this, but I'm probably not the right guy for this kind of assignment."

When Suteluck disappeared into the passage and Surachai crouched down, he realised his legs still couldn't carry him. He dropped to his knees and began to call to Suteluck while he was crawling forward.

"Wait! I can't see! I can't do it!" he cried out.

"Yes, you can," Suteluck said, who was used to dealing with young men who had joined the army just to act macho. "You can always get out somehow. Just don't lie around in there getting in our way when we're coming back through. If I were you, I'd get out as soon as possible, before your relatives out there get to know what a coward you are."

*

When Suteluck got back to the others, Pooi and his helpers had just finished clearing a large area around the entrance and now they were busy clearing the path of any mines on the way down to the cars. So far, they had found three and disarmed them.

"What's it like inside?" Songchai asked. "Is it easy to get in and past all the obstacles?"

"It's working out according to plan," Suteluck answered. "We've only got one problem and that's Surachai, whose legs are exhausted."

"I'd have bet my life on it. When it gets tough, he becomes useless. He's got no staying power at all. We'll just let him be and see how it works out," Pooi said. "We have to get more cable in. I'm not sure there's enough of it and Supot's still there in one of the rooms."

"The cables are at the entrance, I can see that. But where's the extension lead?" Suteluck asked. "Isn't it there as well?"

"No, there's no extension lead here. We had to bring some spades instead, so we could dig if we had to."

"Alright, we'll just have to carry it. But where is it?" Suteluck said.

"If it's not here, it must still be in the car. I'll go and have a look," Songchai said.

Songchai went half-running down to the cars, aware that time was precious and that one of the group posed a problem. He was wary of scared tough guys. Next, he began by looking inside the cars, then around them. There was no extension lead. He was frustrated. Without it, they wouldn't be able to allocate power to more cables and lamps. Could they really have been so clumsy that they'd forgotten to bring it? Well, he'd just have to drive off and fetch it; he'd go back and tell the others he was leaving. They'd keep themselves busy broadening the passage where it got narrower and getting a splice to the lamp so that, at least, Supot might get a bit further in.

"There's no extension lead in the cars either," Songchai said, when he got back. "It looks like we've forgotten it. I'll have to go back and get one. In the meantime, dig out what has to be dug out. And tell the 'tough guy' inside to come out and help clearing out the mines, if he's got the guts. I'll be back soon."

*

Songchai dashed away. On his way down to the cars, he pondered the best course of action. Should he borrow an extension lead? If he did, there would be a lot of questions and he didn't want that. Should he go to Supot's house? No, too far. Go home? No, it would take far too much time. I'll drive down to Phonsavan and buy one, that's easiest, he decided. He drove fast. It was midday by now and his stomach had begun to rumble. It was probably the same for the others up in the cave.

Phonsavan was a fairly small place with just one road running through it, which later became the road to Vietnam and with more hotels than inhabitants. After the war, a great many Vietnamese remained in the area and it seemed that all of those who stayed set up either a hotel or a bar. You could hear Vietnamese spoken everywhere in the streets and at the markets.

Songchai couldn't stand his former enemies, but hunger was more powerful than hate, so he made a stop outside the Crater Bar. He ordered seven portions of chicken in ginger to takeaway. After he had bought the food, he went on to a workshop nearby that repaired everything from cars to houses. There, he bought a used extension lead. On his way out of the workshop, he had the feeling that someone was watching him. He stopped and turned around.

"Do we know each other?" he asked, looking carefully at the person walking towards him.

It was the woman who had been standing in the service department of the workshop.

"Yes, I think so. There's something familiar about the way you walk," the woman replied, now just a few metres away.

"Well, we've all got our own special walks," Songchai said.

"Oh yes," the woman agreed, "but yours is hard to forget. Do you remember me? Your name is Songchai, isn't it? I'm Nat and I've been living around here since the war."

Songchai was dumbfounded. He certainly remembered Nat. She had been a friend and lover during hard times, a long time ago. Their feelings had been mutual. Nowadays, of course, this was just a part of history and both of them were married with partners of their own.

"Nat, is it you? Is it really you?" he said.

"Yes, it's me. How are you doing? How come you're here?" she asked.

"I'm just passing through," Songchai lied. "I live in Pak Mong and have been to Nam Khan, at the border."

Suddenly, he realised that if there was anyone who knew where all the caves were and what they might contain, it would be Nat and her family.

"This really was a surprise," she said.

"You really have to excuse me, Nat," he said, "but I'm in a hurry and have to be home before evening. It was really nice meeting you again after all these years. Take care!"

Songchai noticed that she was disappointed with the way he had cut short the conversation, but useful as she might be, the fact that someone had recognised him made him anxious and he felt an urge to return to the others as soon as possible.

*

Up at the caves, the work was in full swing. Nothing had stopped just because of a missing extension lead. And during Songchai's absence, Supot had brought out some handguns, pistols and submachine guns. Not entire boxes, however, just a few items of each type so that their condition could be inspected. And, with a tremendous effort, Surachai had eventually managed to get out.

On his return, Sonchai announced, "I brought some food and an extension lead."

"Both things are most welcome," Pooi said.

Supot filled Songchai in on the situation with the cache.

"I think it's going to be quite difficult. We'll probably have to drive home towards evening and return early tomorrow morning. There's a lot of boxes and a couple of the walls have collapsed. My guess is that the fourth room could hold one hundred and fifty boxes of automatic weapons, if all the boxes are of the same size. In the fifth room, which I also managed to get to, there are about eighty boxes of pistols, plenty of ammunition and some fifty boxes of mines. Tomorrow, we'll get into the other rooms and take a look. It will be difficult to carry it all, but I guess we'll manage it."

"I see," Songchai said. "We'll do as you suggest and pack it in as soon as we've linked up all the power and hidden our machines. Supot, do you think it's okay for your guys to keep watch during the night?"

"Yes, we've talked about that already. It's decided then: all of us will be ready here at sunrise, tomorrow, including you, Surachai," Supot replied.

Chapter 10

Human Remains

It was to be a long drive back to Tat Kuang. Songchai was not good at driving in the dark these days, so he had to rest every other hour along the route. When he arrived back at the village, he behaved as if none of the day's clandestine activities had taken place. The hour was late and Lu was sitting with Prim at the fire, kindled by Prim after school. These days, it was not a regular occurrence for Songchai to approach them. Usually, he went directly to his hut without as much as a word to them. On this occasion, however, things were different.

"Hi there, how are you doing?" he asked.

Lu looked at him with surprise.

"Fine now, thanks, but it's been hell and you probably don't want to hear about it," she replied.

"No," he said. "I have enough of that to deal with myself. Let's focus on the positive stuff. Tell me about it. You first," he said to Prim. "I'll sit down here with you for a while."

"You do that. Well, Grandpa, I'm going to quit school and start working instead," Prim began.

"Alright," Songchai replied. He probably wasn't listening to what Prim was saying. If he had been, he would no doubt have told her off. And that had been Prim's intention. She wanted to check if her grandpa was really interested or if there were other reasons for his sudden interest.

"And how about you, Lu?" he continued. "Are you still at that bar in town?"

"No, I've quit and I will never work at a bar again," she responded.

At that moment, Lu grasped the opportunity to ask Songchai what he knew about the events up in the Phonsavan area during the war.

"I've landed a new job this morning. And since you've got the time, I'll tell you all about what I'll be doing and the people I'll be working with," she said.

"Yes, do so. I won't go to my hut for a while yet," he replied.

Songchai was still exhilarated by the events of the day and was having trouble relaxing. Sitting outdoors in the company of others for a while was just what he needed.

"What is it you've been doing lately?" Lu asked.

"Oh, nothing special. I've just been meeting some people I know, reliving old memories," he said, casually.

Lu thought he was lying, as ever.

"Lu, what was it you were about to tell me?" he asked.

"We've barely spoken since Fang moved out, you know," Lu started, "so I'm almost bursting from everything I've wanted to say. But tonight, I'll just mention the latest news, although there's a lot I'm wondering about." She paused. Continuing, she said, "Have you heard anything from Fang? Why aren't you trying to talk with Prim anymore? Why doesn't anyone in the village speak to us anymore? We'll let that rest for now. Let's talk about it later," she paused.

Restarting, she said, "The other night, my last night at the bar, I met some nice men. That is, I met them in the correct way. Their names are Will and Frank and they've been guests at the bar for a couple of nights. They're Americans and they work for an organisation called CILHI. Their work is to track down the remains of American soldiers who disappeared during the war. I believe that you and your old brothers-in-arms probably know something about this, since you fought side by side with the Americans, all the way from south of Luang Prabang up to the Vietnamese borders. If I'm not mistaken, you were involved in the fighting up in Vieng Xai, Ban Na Sala, Phonsavan and Sam Tai. You were probably at some other places as well. Anyhow, I suspect you and your friends know quite a lot about what happened."

"Well, it was such a long time ago, you know and you put away all the horrors," Songchai said, avoiding the question.

This was not the time. He did not want to get distracted from planning his activities. Also, he most certainly didn't want any Americans running around up in Ban Na Sala at this point.

"Lu, if you just hang on a couple of days, I'll find out what you'd like to know," he continued, "but I think the areas up there have been gone over with a fine-tooth comb for the bodies of servicemen, all of them returned to their countries by now. Yes, there were quite a number of volunteers and some of them had to go home in coffins. Then, there's another thing. It's a bit difficult for me to engage in this sort of thing. I made a vow, you see and it might get risky for me, if I break it."

"What was that about?" Prim asked, curious.

"You see, I was in the state's retraining camp for almost a year. They said it would be for just two weeks, but while I was released, there are still people sitting in those camps and they'll never get out of there. They let me out on several conditions, one of those being that I could never cooperate with foreign powers. As you know, we Hmong are especially suspected," he confirmed.

"But Songchai, I would be very happy if you would help us, help me, with some information. I'm going to meet them first thing tomorrow morning at Hotel Merry Lao Swiss, you know, in Luang Prabang. We've agreed that I'll be working for them for at least three months and I'll be making much more money than I could ever make at the bar. Also, from now on, I'll be working more normal hours, so I can spend more time with Prim," Lu explained.

"That sounds just fine," Songchai said and got up to leave Lu and Prim for the night. "Yeah, I'll get back to you about your questions. But you do know that you might end up in serious trouble, don't you? You mustn't forget that we're a minority and the government would be more than happy to get rid of us completely."

"What's he talking about, Mummy? Tell me more about these men and what you're going to do!" Prim said, looking worried.

"Prim, just remember Grandpa's words. It might get dangerous if informers find out that I'm helping foreigners, especially those two," Lu confirmed.

"Yes, I know. In school, I'm always hearing that I'm a Hmong and what terrible things we did during the war," Prim said.

"Well, we'll have that yoke around our necks for as long as we're living here," Lu said. "Thirty years ago, there were about thirty thousand Hmong living in this part of Laos, you know. Today, we're about three or four hundred. Since the war, we've been the poor people around here and the government have made sure that we won't be getting on in the world."

"Why is that?" Prim asked.

"Isn't it obvious? You've heard about it many times. We fought together with the US army against the communists. We picked the wrong side and we'll have to pay for it for as long as we live," Lu reminded Prim sadly.

"Mummy, I understand. I won't bring it up again," Prim said. "I'll never tell anybody what we're talking about, I promise. But can't you tell me, at least? Tell me about the Americans."

"Alright, I'll tell you," Lu said, giving in to her daughter.

Many months had passed since Lu had sat down and talked with Prim this way.

Lu told Prim about her discussion with Will and how they had agreed that Lu would work for him and Frank.

"They told me about their jobs and that they were on the lookout for two Americans who were working as military advisers in these districts during the war. Since we are Hmong, they think they might get some information through me as I can speak with the people here in our tongue, you know. I think the job seems exciting. I'm going to be well paid and it'll be fun," Lu explained.

"Mummy, will you be away a lot?" Prim asked.

"No, I won't and there'll be no working late nights," Lu replied, although she was not being entirely honest with Prim. At that time, she knew nothing about the working hours.

"Mummy, I should really like to know what Daddy is doing and where he is," Prim continued, changing the subject.

"Yes, I would too," said Lu. "But sometimes, it's better not to. I know that he's living in the north of Thailand, in Chiang Mai and that he's working with houses. He's some sort of estate agent, I think, but I'm not sure, Prim. Now, I think we'd better go to bed. I have to get up early tomorrow. It's my first proper workday on my new job and you have to get up for school. You go in and I'll come after."

Prim went into the hut and spread out her sleeping mat, a bast one. On it, she placed a buffalo hide and for a quilt, she used a thick blanket woven like a carpet. She never used a pillow and if she were forced to, she probably wouldn't have been able to sleep. Prim took the opportunity to arrange Lu's bedding as well, so it would be ready for her when she came in.

Lu remained sitting for a while, pondering on this and that, above all, how nice it was to get rid of the bar job. But she missed Som, Tim and the others, a feeling that would probably remain if she didn't make the effort to visit them from time to time. Tim could probably help her with her new job because she knew a lot about what happened up around Phonsavan, coming from a family who'd been living in that area for a long time.

"Mummy, come in now!" Prim called. "Your bedding is ready."

Lu let her thoughts go and went inside to bed.

"See you in the morning," she said and fell asleep right away.

That night, both of them slept well. Nothing could disturb them, not even the crowing rooster that started early, as ever and didn't let up for hours.

*

They slept until the sun began to warm up the walls and a pleasant, welcome warmth entered the hut.

Both Prim and Lu were lying there and thinking about the same thing: why should you have to get out of bed when it feels so good?

Lu was excited to get started on a fascinating new job. Suddenly, she startled from her snooze, remembering where she was and that the bus for Luang Prabang would soon depart.

"I have to get up really quick," she announced. "The sun's been up for a long time now and you'll be late for school!"

"I'm not going today," Prim told her.

"What are you saying?" Lu said, astonished.

"I don't want to go to school; I just don't," Prim replied, this time, in a louder voice.

"But Prim, you must go!" Lu insisted.

"No!" Prim yelled. "I hate school! I don't want to go there. Everybody is so bloody mean and they make fun of me all the time. They do mean things, they trick me, they tell me I'm just a damn mountain slut, that my family ought to leave and that we should keep to the mountains! They wonder why we didn't go with the Americans back to the US after the war like everybody else did."

"Prim, not now," Lu said.

"Whenever I need to talk about something, it's never the right time and now you've got this new job so you don't have to give a damn about me, as usual," Prim exclaimed, frustrated.

Lu was surprised. Outbursts from Prim were rare and this one seemed to have come from nowhere.

"It's not true that I don't care for you and what you do," Lu said, her voice growing louder as if in competition with her daughter's.

"You do too!" Prim yelled, even louder and kicked away her blanket so it smacked into the wall.

"Prim, could we please talk about this when I get home?" Lu said.

"No!" Prim yelled. "I don't give a damn about what you do, any more than you give a damn about what I do! Why don't you just run off to your bloody Americans?"

Lu was shocked. Naturally, she knew about the fits of temper some girls could experience during puberty, but she had not expected anything like this.

"Let's get this straight," Prim added. "I won't be going to school today!"

Despite the scene, Lu hurried to get dressed to get to Luang Prabang as soon as possible. While Lu was putting on her clothes, Prim was sitting in a corner cursing that her mother was leaving.

"I hope you'll disappear, you bloody hag," Prim said to herself quietly. "I'm planning to get away from this bloody place myself," she added, in a much louder voice, this time.

"Prim, please. We'll see each other tonight," Lu said.

She tried to approach her daughter, bending to kiss her on the forehead, but Prim turned her head away so that Lu could not reach her.

Lu left the hut, which was looking more like a shack with every passing day. There was no one to provide maintenance and Lu had lost interest in the residence a long time ago. She walked proudly along the road leading through Tat Kuang, her head high and her back straight. The villagers, standing along the road in their blue pyjama-style clothing and pointy hats, ready to go about their work, could say whatever they wanted behind her back. She had decided that she would never hack away at the dirt again.

She got lucky once more, if such a thing as luck exists. Or perhaps motorcycles and cars had simply become more common? After just a short while, a motorcyclist appeared and he gladly took Lu with him to Luang Prabang. She felt a little angry with Prim, for having almost spoiled the beginning of her day, but her thoughts quickly turned to Will, Frank and the forthcoming meeting that morning. Lu was so preoccupied by what the job would entail that she barely noticed that they had arrived in the centre of Luang Prabang.

"Thanks for the lift!" Lu said to the biker and trotted swiftly towards the hotel, almost an hour late.

*

Will and Frank, who were still sitting at breakfast, knew that the locals had different ideas about punctuality: they were never exactly on time, just roughly.

They were waiting patiently for Lu to arrive. The previous night, Frank had clarified who they were and what they were doing to the owner of the hotel and the staff, so they could come to an understanding. If they didn't, it would be better for them to move to another hotel, as Frank put it to the owner who had understood the message completely.

The receptionist looked up when she saw Lu walking in.

"Welcome," she said and smiled at Lu, who thanked her, surprised. "You are to go to the restaurant," she said and once again, Lu was astonished by her cordiality.

Will and Frank were the only guests sitting there.

"Good morning," Lu said and smiled at Frank who immediately got up to greet her. Will's reaction was slower, since he had been sitting with his back turned towards Lu as she entered the room.

"Hi Lu," he said, with a broad smile.

"Hi," Lu replied.

Will savoured how good looking she was but caught Frank's glance: his friend was telling him to forget about it.

"Have a seat, so we can go through all the details," Frank said. "Would you like something to eat? Have you had breakfast?"

"No," Lu replied. "I had to rush this morning, because I woke up too late and had a scene with my daughter, so there was no breakfast."

"Then we'll order something for you," Will said and went away towards the kitchen.

"Lu," Frank said, "We need to fill you in on the current situation."

"I'm listening," she said.

"We're working for an organisation called U.S. Army Central Identification Laboratory, Hawaii. Its acronym is CILHI," he added, sounding out the letters for her. "You can go on the internet and read about it later, if you want to."

While Frank was talking, Will had returned to his chair.

"I ordered some more coffee for us as well," he said.

"Fine," Frank said and continued. "There are several different teams of us, all working around the world in cooperation with local authorities to find the remains of American citizens. So, the authorities here in Luang Prabang know we're here and what we're looking for. We have their support. But it's still important that you keep everything that we talk about to yourself, because we don't want to have anything to do with the local newspapers. Those guys are always nosy."

"I see," said Lu.

"Normally, we bring the local civil servants with us when we're interviewing the locals, asking our way to places that we'd like to have a closer look at," Frank continued. "But we decided the other day, before we met you at the bar, that we should try another method this time. Officials always demand money under the table and the only thing they want is to stall the whole thing. But we're short of time and have to be very efficient, not just because we want to find the remains but because our visas here will only last for thirty days. Sure, we could get them extended. But since we have an employer with a tight budget, we're always running the risk of having to pay for the overtime ourselves. So we think our work might advance quicker with your help and our bosses at CILTHAI, a subdivision in Thailand, are ready to give it a try. Before we asked you to work for us, we found out a good deal about you and your family. We're aware that the work might get tough, since there are plenty of people in the districts we want to get into who don't like us or what we're doing. Most people there are Vietnamese and they've got their reasons for keeping us away from what we're looking for."

By now Lu had received her breakfast and Frank his fifth cup of coffee.

"We're looking for two advisors to the Hmong Secret Army, which operated in the district around Phonsavan and Nong Pet in June '69," Will said taking up the thread. "We know you're Hmong and we know what you've had to endure and still do. Since this might get you into trouble, we won't insist that you should go on working for us. You may leave whenever you like."

"I see," she said, "and I'm grateful, but I'd very much like to work with you. I don't want to go back to the bar-job."

"Okay then," said Frank. "I have to go and get some water. You two continue!"

"Lu, I understand that you know the dialects and some Vietnamese. How much do you know about those villages we've mentioned?" Will asked.

Lu was gazing at Will through her pitch black eyes and if this had not been a serious business meeting, Will would have tried to lead the conversation on a very different path.

"I know this district well," she said. "Both my parents and my parents-in-law fought there. We could also talk to Tim, that is, if she's survived." Lu smiled at Will. "Her father and her father's father were also there about that time. It's possible that she can take us to them. I can ask her."

"On a different topic, Fredrik and Kjell went back to Hong Kong this morning," Will said.

"I certainly won't miss them," she replied, in a matter-of-fact voice. The message was clear: don't talk about them.

Will backed off and returned to the discussion of their plans. Frank had taken the opportunity to visit the bathroom while he was off in search of water for the table.

"Well, it took a little longer than I thought it would," Frank said when he returned, "but I've got us a map of the area we're talking about. Lu, look here. Phonsavan isn't that large."

"No," Lu said, "but there are a lot of people living in the area. There are only a few roads, but there are thousands of paths. It might take some time. And most of them speak Vietnamese, but this you know already. There are not many Hmong about. Given that the roads are bad and it's quite far – it'll take two hours to travel up there – it might be a good idea to change to a hotel up in Phonsavan." As she said this, she realised what the consequence would be: Prim would have to be alone during the evenings.

"But I cannot be away from my daughter too much," she added, salvaging her conscience at the last moment.

"I see," Will said. "But how are we to go about it, then?"

"We always find a way," Frank told him.

"I'll talk with Prim and my mother to see if we can work something out," Lu said. "Perhaps, it would be enough if I were to stay in Phonsavan a couple of times a week. We'll see, I'll know more tomorrow."

"We could go up there early in the mornings and go back in the evenings," Will suggested.

"Hold on, let's wait until we see what comes out of our first meeting up there," Frank said to Will, who was eager to do anything to please Lu. "You have to bear in mind that it'll take four to five hours every day if we're to journey there and back."

Lu asked tentatively, "What do you know about those advisers that disappeared?"

"Their names were Tom Travis and Nick Anthony," Frank said. "They were twenty-three and twenty-six and came from Phoenix, Arizona. Their mission was to help our guys get in better positions against the North Vietnamese and to coordinate intelligence so our pilots knew about critical events on the ground. That's why we know they were in Nong Pet. We've also been told by our sources that they were in Phonsavan, but there, the traces disappear. We believe they were captured by the enemy and taken to a camp, but this we have to ferret out when we're up there."

"You never know, we might bump into a Vietnamese who was there and is prepared to talk about it," Will added. "But for now, I think we should go out for lunch. We've only been guzzling down coffee all morning and Lu, you're probably hungry."

"No, I'm fine," she replied. She had only just finished the breakfast Will had ordered for her.

"I can see it wouldn't take a lot to fill you up," Frank told her, "you're probably running on bird food!" The three of them laughed.

"But Lu, where should we go to get some decent local food?" Will asked.

"I've got a suggestion," Lu told him. What had sprung to her mind was Songchai's favourite place in Luang Prabang. "If we go for a stroll, I'll show you. You won't be disappointed, neither at the food nor the price."

They left the hotel and walked slowly towards Tamnak Lao Tree Elephant Café. Only a few tourists ventured inside, not because of the danger, but because the place looked just a little too local. Will and Frank stopped in the doorway and let Lu enter first. The staff greeted her cheerfully as she walked into the slightly shabby room. Lu said something in Lao, which made everybody look at Will and Frank with a smile.

"Come here. Be seated!" the owner greeted them.

"What should we have?" Frank asked Lu.

"If I may recommend something, I'd like to suggest the fried chicken and a cold Beerlao."

"That sounds tasty," Will said, looking contently at Lu.

"Great suggestion," Frank added. "It's true that I've barely eaten anything but chicken for a long time, but I've heard that you can cook them in a thousand ways. I hope this style of cooking will be the last variant! Are you having the same?" he asked Lu.

"No, I'm not so hungry! I'll have the salad with papaya, tomatoes, chilli and vegetables," she said.

"That sounds great as well. With a beer?" Will asked.

"I only drink water," Lu said, smiling.

"I've noticed that all the women I've met, except those working at the bars of course, do the same. Why is that?" Will asked.

"Women aren't supposed to drink. It's not considered nice," Lu replied. She went on, telling them about the establishment they were in. "This tiny restaurant is one of the oldest in Luang Prabang. The older men of the town come here for something to eat and a local beer."

"Good to know," Frank said, nodding to Will.

They fell silent for a while and watched the food being barbecued and boiled out on the pavement outside the actual serving room. The barbeque was astonishingly effective and before long, they were sitting with all their food on the table in front of them. The first beers had already gone down, so they ordered another round.

"The heat demands that you drink." Will said.

"But not beer," Lu filled in automatically. "For quenching your thirst, water is more effective."

The food looked delicious. Along with the chicken came a fresh salad, the leaves grown along the riverbank to the Mekong River, picked only minutes before being placed on the plate.

"Let's tuck in," Frank said. "Have you seen Tim and Som lately?" he asked, just to keep the conversation going.

"No," Lu answered. "They always work late and they probably have enough on their plates. I actually feel really bad for them. What can they do about it? They have no choice. To work in a bar and to act as a hooker every now and then, or to meet a guy that takes you to paradise. These are the only alternatives there are. There are no jobs. If you don't get one by fluke like I did, of course."

"Lu, after we have eaten, it's quite alright if you'd like to go home and wait for your daughter. Talk with her and your mother and get everything sorted before tomorrow. Then we can get going for real: we'll be going up to Phonsavan, to those areas we were looking at on the map and if we can, we'll meet some people and see how far we can get in our search for Tom and Nick.

"If you head home at this time of day, you'll have no problem catching the bus home, will you?" Frank asked.

"No, I won't. I'll do as you suggest," she said.

They all finished their food, greatly enjoying it.

"Lu, you go home now," Frank said. "Will and I will go and rest for a while at the hotel. We'll take it easy the rest of the day and write the report to our bosses in Hawaii."

It had already struck three in the afternoon and Lu felt that it had been a long and hard day, more demanding, in some ways, than the bar-job. Her head was filled with new impressions and lots of information. She felt tired all over.

"Yes, I think I'll leave you to your business now. I'd better start walking to the bus stop. Prim will probably get a shock, since this will be the first time I've been home this early for some time," she said.

*

Lu went straight to the bus-stop. A long, tedious and bumpy ride was awaiting her. The roads were worse than they'd been for a long time: the local road maintenance team didn't seem to work at all. The government's funds for maintenance had probably been submitted, but by the time they had been transferred to the community account, they had already been spent on other projects like the renovation of the chairman's house or office, for instance. In addition, if a road led up to one of the Hmong villages in the mountains, that road just stayed bad or got increasingly worse due to a total lack of maintenance.

Despite her early departure, by the time Lu got back to Tat Kuang, the sun was already sinking between the mountain peaks, spreading a red glow over all the village huts. The sunset looked mesmerising as she got off the bus. In the square, all the women were standing lined up, just as they did every other evening, to wash themselves in the public bath. Soon, it would be the turn of the men.

Lu did not like to wash herself together with the others: to stand naked and endure the looks of other women in the shower! No thanks! Both she and Prim always went down to a small brook that babbled through a densely overgrown area adjacent to the village. There they could stand naked and splash about as much as they liked without being disturbed. In the brook, they had made themselves a small stone tub in which they could sit down. Sometimes, Lu went there to be by herself for a while.

She walked into the yard, which lay silent. There was not a soul in sight. Nobody had prepared the fire that usually burned until night. The place was almost deserted, only the animals were there, running about. A strange feeling of solitude rose inside her as she approached her hut and opened the tiny door, as meticulously shut as it always was when nobody was home.

"Prim!" Lu called. "Prim, where are you?"

No answer. That was strange. Lu reckoned that Prim ought to be home, especially as she said she wasn't going to school. She went up to her mother's hut.

"Mother, have you seen Prim today?"

"No, I have not!" May snapped. "Don't you keep a check on the girl? You have to, at her age. You never know what might get into the head of a young girl. You have to watch out!"

"But what am I to do?" Lu said loudly to herself. This was typical of Prim! A scene that morning of historic proportions and now this, another form of revolt. What's wrong with the girl? Is she hell bent on ruining everything for me, on turning my conscience sour, when she knows that I need peace and quiet in order to work?

Inside the hut, Lu fetched a large blanket. Then, she kindled the fire. While the fire was catching on, she fetched a kettle of water for tea and a piece of chicken, although she was not hungry. She sat down and felt the pleasant warmth radiating just as it had done so many times before. Where could Prim be? She wrapped the blanket tighter around herself and fell asleep.

*

Lu was woken by the roosters crowing, at the wrong time as always. She rose and looked down the road and there she saw Prim walking home. Lu darted towards her like a bullet.

"So, you haven't forgotten where you live, after all?" she said.

"No," Prim answered self-assuredly, "I haven't. But why are you up this early?" she asked ironically.

"What do you think, young lady?" Lu said angrily. "Where have you been all night?"

"With a couple of friends," Prim replied.

"With a couple of friends! Do you have any idea what time it is? What have you been doing?" Lu said.

"Nothing special," Prim answered, annoyed by Lu's questions.

"How did you get back to the village?" Lu asked, now even angrier since her questions did not appear to bother Prim in the slightest. "You have to tell me where you've been and with whom, or else!"

Prim just looked at her and continued towards the hut.

"I'm tired," Prim said.

Enraged now, Lu grabbed hold of Prim's arm.

"Hold on. Now, you're going to tell me what you've been up to!" she said.

"Ouch, let me go! I told you that I haven't done anything special. It hurts, you bloody witch! Let me be!" Prim yelled and tore herself free from her mother's grip.

"If you keep on going on like this, I'll make sure that you'll end up with your father!" Lu threatened her.

"Do it, dammit! Then, at least I'll be rid of you!" Prim screamed.

Prim went into the hut, grabbed a blanket and lay herself down upon her bedding.

"No, no, my dear, you're to leave for school in about an hour. Sleep will have to wait until tonight," Lu said.

"I'm not going to school today! We're on leave, anyway. There's no school," Prim lied. "I'm staying at home."

"Then you can see to the chicken run and the pigs," Lu responded.

"I'll take care of that later on," Prim replied, sourly.

Lu felt completely shut out of Prim's life. It was painful.

"I'll be going up to Phonsavan today," Lu said, but it was too late. Prim was already asleep.

*

Prim had started to live a life of her own and Lu knew nothing about it. Prim's view of the matter was that her mother only had herself to blame. Lu understood nothing of what her daughter did or felt. How could she? She was never home, only thinking about herself. Even when she was home, she didn't listen to what Prim actually said, like that very morning before she'd gone back to Luang Prabang.

Prim had learned a thing or two which her school did not teach. The most interesting things were those her friends could teach her, especially the older ones and Prim was a swift learner. She had been together with some female friends in Luang Prabang. Together, they had gone to a party with some older guys who had later taken the girls to a club and then managed to get a hotel room where the party had continued. The night had just flown by as they drank beer and made out. For the first time, Prim had sensed that the guy she was with had something stiff between his legs. That was as far as it went, because before the guy could get his pants off, the hotel staff had realised what was going on and asked them to leave the hotel instantly and never to show their faces there again. Not only had the staff been disturbed, but several guests had been as well.

*

Lu left Prim to manage her day on her own. But first, she went to May to ask her to keep an eye on Prim. This, May promised to do, as reluctantly as Lu had expected.

Arriving back in Luang Prabang, Lu walked to the hotel where Will and Frank were staying. She had some time on her hands and it was nice to go for a stroll before it was time to travel again. When she got there, Frank was already standing by the car he had rented earlier that day.

"Hi, Lu! How are you this beautiful morning?" he asked.

"Oh, just fine thank you," Lu answered and smiled. This was the first time she had ever heard someone comment that a new day was beautiful. All days were, as everybody knew.

"Will's on his way," Frank said. "He's just a bit slow in the mornings. We said eight o'clock."

"But we don't follow a clock; we follow the sun. Or, if we want to get up really early, we follow the roosters," Lu said, laughing.

"What," said Frank, "to rise with the rooster? But then it's already seven o'clock!"

"No, not with our roosters. They wake up the villagers whenever it suits them," Lu told him, still laughing.

"It's lucky we're not living in your village, then. I think it's enough with all the cats in our neighbourhood, not to mention the dogs that bark all night. But maybe it wouldn't do Will any harm to try a rooster," Frank said, smiling. "Look, here he comes. Time to go."

"What?" said Will, peeking into the car. "Is it left-hand drive?"

"Sure, you knew that didn't you?" Frank said. "They drive on the same side as we do here."

"Of course, the commies feel comfortable with left-hand drive," said Will.

"I'll start at the wheel," announced Frank, "so you can take the back seat."

"What, why do I have to sit at the back?" asked Will, like a sulky child. "Is she to sit in the passenger seat? Yeah, yeah, I get it."

"No, I don't think you do. If you did, you wouldn't comment on it. I want Lu to sit in the passenger seat because she knows the district and that way, we won't have to sit with maps on our knees. It's just to make things easier and an excuse for me to have a beautiful woman by my side," Frank explained and smiled at Lu.

"I get it," Will said, "it'll be my turn on the way back, though." Everybody had a good laugh.

"It's lucky there aren't many cars or bikes on the road, because I'm not used to the local pace," Frank observed as he drove.

"You just have to drive slowly," Lu said.

"It's impossible to drive fast on these roads," Will said, as they pulled out onto Road 13 toward Ban Sèn, heading for the narrow and winding Road 7 which would take them all the way to Phonsavan.

What Lu didn't know was that way ahead of them was Songchai, who had chosen to take the same road. It was probably a good thing they didn't know each other's routes. Songchai didn't, under any circumstances, want to have curious people in the vicinity of his secrets.

"This is working out just fine," Frank said, already used to both the road and the car.

"Yeah," Will replied, "but I think I'll fasten my seatbelt anyhow. There are so many bends in the road that I'm bouncing from one side to the other. These roads must sure use up a lot of tyres."

"There's a reason why so many people go by motorcycle" Lu said. "You can get about much faster on a motorbike if you're alone. But it's dangerous. In Luang Prabang alone, there are twenty five serious accidents each month and ten to fifteen people get killed."

"Oh fuck," Will said, "then you shouldn't go by bike here."

"It's the same statistics throughout Asia," Frank said. "I believe that Phuket in Thailand has the highest number of motorcycle accidents. Over a hundred people get injured there each month. And about twenty or thirty of them get killed."

"No," Will said, "I believe that Saigon's numbers are even worse."

"It's possible," Frank said, "but it's fucking too many anyway."

The car dealt with all the bumps and bends as if it had anticipated them. Lu was just about to tell them about the waterfalls they were passing at Khouang-Si Falls, when Frank suddenly spoke.

"Just think about it," he said, "wherever you go in the world they've got views of waterfalls they like to sell to tourists and all of them get fooled by it. They jump on the buses just to see some water fall off the edge of a cliff. It's insane."

Will laughed and said "Yes, my wife and I, we always take the bus trips and often they include a stop at a waterfall."

Lu kept silent, but at the same time, she thought about how in their part of the country, they had the most beautiful ones, whatever anyone else said.

"Frank," she said, "if I should fall asleep, you are just to continue on Road 7, like I told you before. I slept poorly last night."

"Goodnight to our guide," Will said to Frank, in an ironic tone of voice.

Chapter 11

Mines, Guns and Bazookas

Surachai had covered a lot of ground on Road 7 and was almost at the exit to the mountains and the arms cache. The others were probably there already. He knew he was late. The sun had already been up for a while. He turned onto the dusty road. Pooi, Suteluck, Songchai, Supot and the two hands noticed a dust cloud rising up from the winding road below.

Despite Surachai's cockiness, he was physically broken after the last shift. He felt perfectly clear about one thing: he would never enter the cave again. He placed the blame squarely on his aching thigh muscles.

"Yes, yes," Pooi said, "You've got your reasons. But you've got to make sure you pull your weight later on or else, you're no use to us."

He was not mincing his words. Surachai felt fortunate that they were coming from Pooi and not from Songchai.

"Let's head up to the caves and get things ready. Today, we've got to get in deeper and start to carry out all that shit," Suteluck said.

Supot was already inside the cave entrance when the others were gathering outside.

"Stop, Supot," said Pooi. "First, we'll sort out the cables and the lighting. Suteluck, have you arranged for the transport down to Ban Houa Keng and the hiding place we'll use there while we wait to go on down to Ban Pak-Ou?"

"Everything is ready. They'll come on my call," Suteluck said.

"Then, we'll do a run-through before we get going, just to make sure that everything is perfectly clear," Songchai said, as ever, focusing on the details.

"But we are clear on everything," Surachai replied, eager to get cracking.

"Young man," Songchai said, "I have a few things to teach you: the first is to get in line. If you don't understand this, we'll all join in and make you understand. Do I make myself clear?" Songchai glanced at the others.

"You'd better toe the line, kid, or else you won't get old," Pooi clarified.

Surachai felt the anger and resentment to Songchai burn inside him. Songchai sensed the threat in the air, but let it be. There was a time for everything and soon enough, the time would be right to deal with Surachai.

He continued calmly, "Everything is ready with the boats and Suteluck has got an eye on what's necessary for the transport to Ban Houa Keng to make everything work as smoothly as possible. But I'm still a little unsure about the hiding place. Pooi, you've got to make sure everything is ready with the look-out."

"It's probably for the best that we guard the place ourselves during the night. That way, we won't just avoid paying for extra people but we'll also avoid the risk that they might squeal," Pooi replied.

"I think Pooi's right," said Supot. "We should probably stand watch ourselves, as well as doing the finishing work, packing the goods. It shouldn't be much of a problem. The night will be long and dark."

"Agreed. We've got to rethink and do more of the work ourselves," Songchai summed up.

"Let's get going," Suteluck said. "We haven't got all the time in the world. Look at the sky! It's getting darker and if we end up in the pouring rain, it will set us back even further. If water gets into the passages, it'll be difficult to get the arms boxes out."

"Has the road down to the parking area been cleared of mines?" Songchai asked.

"It's done," said Pooi. "Will you take the lead, Supot? You have a clear idea of where everything is down there, you know."

"Sure," Supot replied. "Pooi, let's bring out as much as we can manage. There's no point in anyone joining us. It's too small and cramped in there. We'll deal with the stuff that has to be dug out later on."

*

Supot and Pooi went crouching into the passage and made their way to the first room, where they organized the tools and cables that were to be taken into the next room.

"I've marked the spots where there are ground traps," Supot informed Pooi. "We need to fill the traps with dirt. We can't afford the risk of stepping down into them while carrying the weapons. I'll fill them up as we pass them."

After a few hundred metres, they arrived at the third room.

"You know which of these passages leads to the cache. Take the long cable, so you can cast a decent amount of light," Pooi said.

"Yesterday I was groping about the place in the dark, so it'll be interesting to see it properly, this time round," said Supot. "I'll go in now. You have to find a spot where you can hear what I'm saying."

"Alright," Pooi replied.

Before long, Supot was calling back through the passage. "There's more than I imagined yesterday: automatic weapons, pistols and loads of ammo in wooden boxes. I don't know how the hell we'll manage to carry out all this. Come and have a look!"

Pooi darted forward with crouching leaps.

"Dammit! We're in for one hell of a job!" he confirmed.

"That's for sure," said Supot. "But let's go on to the next cache. I wonder what it's like in the glow of a lamp. How much of my assessment yesterday was correct."

Pooi was just about to step into the next room when Supot cried out, "Stop, for God's sake! Look what's in front of your foot!"

Pooi stopped, petrified. He had been less than a second away from stepping on a mine.

"Are there more, or have we just had an overdose of luck?" he asked.

"Try to retrace your steps," Supot instructed. "Pooi, this is the first time I've been scared this shitless in ages."

"You? I was the one about to take the step," Pooi replied.

"Yes, but if you had done, none of us would've gotten out alive," Supot said.

"What do we do now?" Pooi asked. "We've got to arrange for clearing the place of mines. It's bad enough doing that outside. In a cave, it'll be even worse."

"You think! It can be done pretty quickly, though," Supot joked. "Come over here. I'll scout the passage to make sure there are no more mines in our way. In any case, now we can presume that nobody has been deeper down than this. Dammit, though! This isn't what we're supposed to be doing right now. Go back and tell them we need help, but avoid Surachai. He's no good for this sort of thing."

"I'll get Suteluck," Pooi said, crouching down to go back.

Outside, the others were waiting for the signal to start carrying, but it had been a long time coming. It was with a sigh of relief when eventually, they saw Pooi at the entrance to the cave.

"We need help," he said. "We've come across mines in the passages. Suteluck, you're going to have to come along and help us clear them out. We have no idea how many there are or where they're placed. We'll come back when we're done."

A few moments later, Pooi and Suteluck were on their way through the passage.

*

You had to be made of steel, in both body and mind, to cope with the knowledge that everything might blow up and turn black any moment with the earth engulfing your body. The dry taste of dirt forcing its way into your mouth and over your eyes, which you hadn't had time to close, unable to scream, move or breathe. The knowledge that you were on your way to the afterlife.

However, these men had what it took. They were aware that they alone drew the line and that was why the line was never drawn, with the exception of Surachai, at least. Everyone else had been through the worst life could throw at them. They had been shot or subjected to various forms of torture: they had been waterboarded; electrocuted through various parts of their bodies; had their nails torn out; been cut between the toes; been burned on the upper arms and in their armpits; had leeches placed on their bodies, to suck them dry until they died; had been left to stand with their feet in water, cold as ice, until their senses disappeared; had water dripping on the top of their heads until they broke; and been forced to watch their wives and daughters raped by the enemy and not just by one man but an entire platoon. Whatever their experiences had done to them, they were survivors. So what was a little fear in a cave passage? Suteluck and Pooi were fit and it didn't take them long to get to the room where Supot sat waiting.

"That was quick," he said. "I thought it would take longer."

"There's no dawdling here," Pooi replied. "We've don't have time for that."

They started with the mine they had detected at the beginning of the passage to the fourth room. Suteluck knelt down and felt carefully around it with his hands.

"It's an ugly motherfucker," he told the others, who were sitting unconcernedly, waiting for him to fix it so they could go on working. "But I'll get it up and disarm it."

Carefully, he lifted the mine out of the dirt.

"Damn, it's jammed!" he said. "It's virtually impossible to unscrew it. I'll just put it here at the side of the passage, by the wall. Bear it in mind when you're about to go in."

"Oh, thanks for the advice. I'd been planning to step on it a little, just for fun," Pooi said.

Gallows humour often helped to relieve the tension.

Suteluck got the lamp and directed its light forwards while he methodically scrutinised the passage leading to the larger arms cache.

"Here's another mine," he said after a while. "I'll get it up and place it next to the first one. I hope there's no more of them now. Clearing out mines drains your strength. Supot, come in and help me out with the lighting! Hold the lamp for me. I can't possibly dig effectively with just one hand."

"Sure," Supot said, "but there's no need to sound so grumpy."

"I'm the one digging for mines here. At this moment, your life is in my hands, so I'd better use both of them. By the way, what the fuck is Pooi doing?" he went on moodily.

"He's preparing to carry out the arms boxes and the ammo," Suteluck replied.

"I really hope he's careful. Fuck knows what might be hidden in this place," Pooi said.

Suteluck found four more mines along the way to the fifth room. He and Supot were between three or four hundred metres into the passages now. It took him more than an hour to defuse the mines. Afterwards, he felt utterly exhausted by the nervous strain. He had to retreat back to the fourth room and rest for an hour or so. He fell asleep instantly.

"We'll let him be," Pooi said. "In the meantime, I'll go into the passage to check out what's there."

It proved to be filled with the same type of boxes as they'd found in the previous room, but here, the roof had partly caved in. At a quick glance, the passage beyond appeared to be ruined and its depth was impossible for Pooi to assess. The presence of mines, however, was obvious.

Pooi went back to Supot.

"We'll bring a couple of these boxes with us," he said. "Then, we'll let the others step in. We need to put our feet up. And Supot, I think we'd better avoid digging out those boxes lying under the mess from where the cave collapsed. Also, we shouldn't dig our way into the passage leading to the next room. It wouldn't be very fortunate if a spade ended up halfway through a mine."

"You're probably right," Supot said.

Suteluck was still sleeping and they decided not to disturb him for a while to allow the tension in his body to loosen up.

"Alright," Supot said, "let's take a couple of boxes and get out."

*

Outside, the others were sitting and feeling idle. But this wouldn't last. Once Pooi and Supot got out, it would be the turn of the others to go into the passages.

Outside the cave, Surachai and Songchai sat talking with the two carriers.

"What the fuck are you doing, sitting here drowsing?" Pooi exclaimed when he reached the entrance to the cave. He would have preferred it if they had all been standing to attention, all set to start carrying.

"Well, you're certainly in a good mood," Songchai said.

"You're just loitering around, waiting while we do all the work!" Pooi said.

"Not at all," Songchai replied, "but we can't see through the earth to know where you're at and what you've got in your hands. We'll get going now if you would quit moaning."

"Yeah, yeah," Pooi said. "Supot is on his way behind me with a box as well. The smartest thing is probably to divide ourselves up into pairs in there: one pair to carry the boxes to one room and from there, the next pair can step in and carry to the next, until the goods are out. But I suggest that before we start, we eat and drink properly. That way, we'll cope better. Surachai, you'd better stay close to the entrance, so you can get out easily if you get into difficulties."

"That sounds fine. I can still feel some pain in the back of my thighs, but it'll probably be alright. I'll tell you if I run into problems," he said.

The men seated themselves round a pitched campsite without a fireplace. They didn't want any sign to the outside world that there was something going on up at the caves, so they had to make do with cold food washed down with fresh spring water. Pooi, meanwhile, found some time to rest after the ordeal inside the cave.

"I think we should keep going as long as possible. Inside, we can have the lights on tonight, but not outdoors because we might attract attention. We'll just have to grope our way in the dark. Are you okay with that?" said Pooi.

"Yes," everybody agreed.

They divided themselves up and began carrying out box after box of weapons and ammunition. It was sheer drudgery, but what is there that people won't do for money? They were toiling for hour after hour without a break and later in the evening, a hundred boxes had been carried out.

"It's weird," Songchai said. "These boxes have probably been lying here for decades, but they're still intact. It even says where they come from, so the buyers won't be disappointed."

"What kind of fucking war are they waging in Africa if they're buying ancient weapons like these?" Supot asked. "Although, I suppose I really don't care as long as they're paying for them."

"I guess they'll end up in various guerrilla groups," said Surachai, who had met the arms dealer. "He said they were bound for Africa but not where, precisely. Exactly how many wars are there actually going on in the world? Do any of you guys know?"

"About twenty big ones, for sure and a great number of small gangster wars," one of the carriers answered, a man who had been quiet up to now.

His name was Voratep and he came from Supot's village. Like Supot, Voratep was a war veteran and had experienced enough horror in his life. His family had been severely affected during the war. Being a Hmong, he had fought the North Vietnamese, of course, alongside CIA agents and had been stationed at the village of Nong Hét, just a couple of kilometres from the border with North Vietnam. He had brought his family with him, a very unwise decision. He had been on the receiving end of a communist attack late one evening, the kind of slow, quiet evening when nothing usually happened in the village.

The family had been sitting outdoors, as was the custom. They had no fireplace, since it would have been visible more than twenty kilometres away. Voratep had been away standing guard when the attack began. His family didn't have time to escape and his wife and his two daughters were captured by the enemy. They were not killed immediately, but were taken to the Vietnamese camp, where they had been abused in the cruellest and most grotesque manner. Both daughters had died following the rapes and the beatings. His wife had been released later on and had managed to get back, but had been in a bad way. Voratep had been able to see her and learn from her what had happened, but she had died from malnutrition and illness just a few days after her return.

Voratep's hatred for those who had done this to his family had never died. There were Vietnamese living in all the surrounding villages, including his own. If a new war were to break out, he would have had no qualms about using the weapons in these boxes against his neighbours.

"We should not talk about other peoples' wars now," Surachai said. "This is all going nicely. If we manage to continue at the same pace and keep working in the dark, we'll be done with all the boxes tonight, except those in the collapsed part of the cave."

"If you others can continue, Surachai and I will go down to Ben Houa Keng to see if we can get some help with the transport," Supot said, finally starting to feel the effects of all the hours of effort.

"But Surachai," Songchai said, "now that everything has gone so smoothly, couldn't we just as well take the cargo directly to Ban Pak-Ou ourselves? We'll take everything to the boats tomorrow night. That way, we'll avoid one round of reloading. Let's take a break and talk about it."

Supot called into the cave entrance to the man closest by, so that he could inform the others inside the cave that it was time for a meeting. When they had all emerged, they gathered around the spot where there would have been a fire, had it been safe to light one.

"We've been talking about taking all the goods directly down to Ban Pak-Ou and loading the boats tomorrow night," Songchai began. "It would cut the cost and that means more dough for us. More importantly, there would be fewer people knowing what we're up to."

"Yeah," Surachai objected, "but Pooi's and Suteluck's pals already know what's going on. If these guys don't get to take part, they'll know that they've missed a piece of the action and they'll be seriously pissed-off. If that happens, I really wouldn't like to be in your shoes."

"Wrong, kiddo," Pooi said, "that's not the way it works. They don't know what the goods are that are being transported. Their assignment is just to get a couple of drivers, put their arses in a truck each, pay them and make sure they get here. For all they know, they could just as well be moving marmalade."

"But when they get here, they'll find out what we're doing," Surachai said.

"Yes, that's for sure, but if they don't come, they'll never know what's being transported. You can rest assured, everything's under control. We just need to get another truck. Songchai, maybe you could drive off and borrow one. You certainly know enough people."

"It's possible," Songchai said. "Alright, how about it, then? Are we to work tonight and load the cars tomorrow morning? Maybe, we'll get time to rest during the day. Later that night, we'll take everything down to Ban Pak-Ou, load the boxes, eat and take off."

All of them agreed.

Songchai's mind turned to Nat, the woman he'd met in Phonsavan. She would gladly lend him a truck or vouch for him, so that he could borrow from someone else in the village. But it was too late in the evening now. If he showed up at Nat's at this hour, she would most likely think the old man had lost it and was trying to pick up where he'd left off so long ago. It was best to wait until tomorrow.

"We'll keep going and get out as much as we can," he said. "Then we'll stay overnight here. I'll go down to Phonsavan before sunrise and try to get a truck."

With that, it was time to carry boxes again.

"Look here," Voratep said to his companion, "those two last boxes we've got out."

"Yeah, what about them?"

"Can't you see it? They're bazookas."

Pooi overheard the conversation and approached them.

"What are you guys talking about?" he asked.

"Look," Voratep said. "They're bazookas. Are they also part of the deal?"

"I think so," Pooi replied, shooting Surachai a wondering glance. "Is that right. Are the bazookas sold?"

"Yes," Surachai replied.

"How can that be possible? You didn't even know they were here," Pooi pointed out.

"Well, the thing is, the arms dealer doesn't know he's bought them, but he'll have to pay extra for them whether he likes it or not," Surachai explained.

"Alright then, as long as you're sure he'll take them. If he doesn't, I can find a buyer for them, from Pakistan."

"Forget about it," Surachai said, hoping Songchai had not overheard what they were talking about.

"With that kind of weapon, you could shoot down a passenger plane flying at a low altitude," said Suteluck, who also had heard the conversation. "It's weird that there still are bazookas lying hidden here. They ought to be long gone, picked up by the army to be destroyed or used."

Suteluck didn't think it was right that weapons as powerful as these could fall into their hands, or into anyone else's, for that matter. But these were hard times and hard times meant money, even if it came from bazookas, had to come before morals.

The work went on without interruption during the late evening. It was easier to toil away in the coolness of the night. Inside the cave, the air was pleasant and slightly moist. Outside, it was bordering on chilly. The ground had turned cold, which in turn, gave rise to the frequent shroud of mist over the mountains. It was long into the night before Songchai announced that it was time to stop.

"Now we have enough," he shouted. "There's no point in carrying out more than we can transport."

"Yes, this will do. It wouldn't do to give the buyers more than they're paying for," Supot said.

"Of course not," Songchai replied, "but if we can deliver more, we'll get paid more, you nitwit."

"That's it, I'll just arrange my bed for the night," Pooi said. "I'm going to crash out. Nobody will need to rock my cradle tonight."

"Me too," Surachai agreed.

"I'll just lay myself down in the entrance to the cave," Suteluck said. "That ought to be just cool enough."

The others laid down round the arms boxes and before long, there came a sound capable of striking terror into any snake, rat or bird: a chorus of snores from seven deeply sleeping Lao men, who all looked equally vulnerable as they lay there.

Sleeping outdoors was not a new experience for any of them. They had been doing this since childhood. Having an arms box for a pillow was not completely unfamiliar either, even though it had been a while since any of them had rested his head on anything quite so lethal.

*

The remainder of the night passed quickly and soon, Songchai was up on his feet. He did his morning exercises in silence and stole away to carry out the next stage of his assignment, getting hold of an extra truck.

It was a beautiful morning. The sun rose over the mountains and dissolved the light mist in a silver-glimmering play of light. As Songchai walked down towards the vehicles, he was thinking about how breathtakingly each morning was born, to mature into the day and finally, once more, to be enclosed in darkness.

He took Supot's small pick-up and went straight onto Road 7. After forty or fifty minutes, he took a right onto the route to Phonsavan. As usual, the road dust did its job, warning him about the prospect of other cars, but there was no car in sight along Road 7. The only obstacles, apart from all the pits, were the animals from the farms, cute little black pigs. They looked like dwarf pigs but were, in fact, wild piglets and they were abundant both on and beside the road. Songchai was afraid of running them over. If he did, that might prove pricy. If pigs were hit, it was the driver's fault and owners were quick to demand damages. Songchai didn't have time to negotiate with some stubborn pig owner, so he was careful with the accelerator.

At the crossroads, just as he was about to turn right, a car came towards him. He slowed down and watched the car carefully as it passed by, afraid of being spotted. He was surprised to observe Lu was sitting in the passenger seat beside an unknown man, with yet another man in the back.

At this hour? he wondered. What the hell was she doing here? Why wasn't she at home with Prim?

Chapter 12

Important New Contact

At the same crossroads, inside the other car, a discussion was taking place.

"I thought we would be alone on the road at this hour," Will said from the back seat.

"No," Frank replied. "There's a lot of old codgers up this early, so it pays to watch out. You'd think it's dangerous enough with all the loose animals running about."

"Surely, you must be aware that everybody wakes up with the sun," Lu added, drowsily, "especially all the old men."

Will replied, laughing. "Yeah, I woke up without an alarm, so I see what you're getting at."

The previous day, Frank, Will and Lu had arrived in Phonsavan during the lunch hour and had accomplished little. They had stayed at a restaurant run by a couple of Vietnamese women. Oddly enough, the place had western dishes on the menu. There were pizzas, hamburgers and spaghetti in addition to the five pages of Lao food and six pages of Vietnamese dishes.

"It's all probably the same thing but just in different lingos," Will said. "But Frank, look at the walls! Now, I can see why there are hamburgers on the menu."

Lu had no clue what he was talking about.

"One of the women is probably living with an American," Will explained.

"Just the one," Frank replied, an eyebrow raised. "Not both of them?"

"No matter which, he's connected to the local history," Will said. "Look at those paintings. They're aerial survey maps of vast parts of this district. They're bomb maps. And look here, pictures of the dude climbing into his plane and here, he's standing together with the rest of the wing. It's obvious he must've fought around here. I wonder who he is and if he's still around. He's got to be about fifty-five. Shall we ask?"

"No," Frank said. "Let's save that for later. Maybe we can find out who this guy is some other way. Now, it's time to eat. I'm hungry."

Lu was lost in her thoughts. She could tell it was going to be a long day; the work was not underway yet and it was lunchtime already. She felt the stress building up. How would she explain this to Prim, who was sure to feel let down again when she returned from school and found that her mum was not home? School! Had Prim gone to school or not? She tried not to think about it. Why had she agreed to this?

"Let's take a spot in the middle of the restaurant so we can be seen," Will suggested.

It was not a large place with only five tables and a small counter. There was no spirits served, only bottled beer. It shouldn't have been hard for the staff to notice the new guests. By the time they had been waiting for a quarter of an hour, Will was getting frustrated.

"I'll go and knock at the door to the kitchen," he said.

He did so but nothing happened. He opened the door. Inside, stood two women dressed in jeans and t-shirts with the restaurant's name, 'Crater Bar & Restaurant', printed over their chests. They turned and stared in surprise at the intruder.

"You've got guests in the restaurant," Will told them.

The women were still looking at him as if he were an extra-terrestrial being. After exchanging a few words in Vietnamese, one of them walked up to Will.

"Would you like to order something?" she asked.

"Yes, please. People do eat here, don't they?" he said ironically.

"Yes, sometimes," she replied, honestly, "but not very often."

Will spoke quietly to Lu and Frank when he'd walked back to the table with the waitress in his wake. "Listen," he said, "we should probably do some thinking before we order. The food turnover isn't that great here."

"I'll have a hamburger," Frank announced.

"So will I," Will said. "Lu, what are you having?"

"I'll have the chicken stew and water."

"Us guys will each have a Beerlao," Will added.

The waitress disappeared, looking pleased.

Just inside the door, a couple of German tourists were sitting and following the conversation with great interest. They had both been given their beers forty-five minutes earlier, but they had not heard or seen a thing from the kitchen since then.

After a while, the waitress emerged with two beers and a glass of water. Will and Frank were thirsty and drank their beers quickly. Will resumed his study of the pictures hanging on the walls.

"I'm curious," he said to Frank.

"Don't be," was the reply.

"I'll tell you something else, too. A quarter of an hour has passed since she came in with the beers and since then, we haven't seen anything of the staff. What kind of fucking place is this? And those people over there haven't gotten anything either. We'll go somewhere else. I'll just pay and we can take off."

"No, wait a bit," Lu said. "It might take a while, but it'll be okay. You'll see."

Time passed and eventually, Will got up again and went to the door, knocked and went in. He was met by the same vacant stare as had greeted him earlier.

"What can we do for you?" one of the waitresses asked.

"I want the food we ordered one hour ago!" he said trying to hide his exasperation.

"It will come soon," she told him, smiling.

"Well, if we don't get it, we'll just pay for the beer and leave," he confirmed.

"Just wait a bit; it will come," she assured him.

Will returned to his seat in a foul mood.

"But hey, Will, at least now we've established some local connections," Frank said, grinning.

"Yeah, yeah, you never know, maybe they can even help us to find the skeletal remains of Tom and Nick," Will replied.

"What do you mean? That they might have boiled them or what?" Frank said laughing.

Lu didn't enjoy this humour and kept silent, lost in her thoughts about Prim.

Eventually, the food came to the table, before the German couple got theirs.

"What a weird way of doing things," Will said to Lu. "Is it the same thing everywhere around here?"

"Yes," Lu told him with a resigned expression. "I think you ought to be glad that you got the food at all. As you might have noticed, they're Vietnamese and they reckon they own this area. There's always one conflict or another going on here. And besides, they've already figured out that you guys are Americans."

"But look at the walls," Will said. "Obviously, there's an American living here."

"Yes, but that doesn't mean that everybody here likes Americans. The one living here probably worked hard at being accepted," she explained.

"Now, let's eat and get started," Frank said and dug his teeth into the hamburger. But his bite transformed into a frozen, vacant expression. The hamburger he'd just attempted to start eating would have made a hole in the wall if he'd thrown it. It was hard as rock.

"That was the most hellish thing I've ever had in my mouth!" he said.

"Then you haven't had a lot of things there," Will replied laughing. "Wasn't it any good?"

Will's hamburger looked similar to Frank's: the same meat, the same onion rings and mayonnaise in worryingly large quantities. He took a bite.

"No, this crap is impossible to eat. Now, I understand why you always have a local dish," he said to Lu, who was tucking into her stew with great enthusiasm.

"Yes, it's about time you learned your lesson," she said.

"I'm not paying for this crap," Frank said, his appetite gone.

"Order something else," Lu suggested.

"No thanks. I don't want anything from this place. Besides, we'd be waiting an hour. We'll have to eat later. Lu, tell them we'd like to pay and get out of here."

"Alright, but I'd like to finish my meal first," she said.

"Of course," Will confirmed. "You probably have to be able to handle bombs and dynamite in order to cope with eating here," he continued. "But I'm still curious about the person behind the pictures on the walls. Looking at those aerial survey maps, I can't help being struck by the fact that there are people here who were actually there at that time and there are buildings left, still standing today."

"Yes, sometimes, you do wonder how our people could've survived," Lu said, "but many thousands didn't."

"That's it. I'm out of here," Frank announced. "I can't sit here any longer. Lu, if you're finished, we can try to find a place where we can sit down and start to plan how we are to go about this. I want us to find out the whereabouts of the camps, stores, military bases and hospitals from that time. We've got to meet people who were in the area when Nick and Tom were here, Vietnamese or Lao. I'm getting stressed."

"I just have to ask for the men's room," Will said, "you'll have to wait for me."

*

Will was shown around the corner into the neighbour's house and led through an old, smelly garage. Judging by the odour, not many people had managed to make it all the way to the lavatory. The toilet door consisted of some broken boards bound together with a piece of string and he decided to use his foot to open it: it looked so filthy, he was worried he would end up in hospital if he were to touch it with his hands. Even his foot appeared to dislike the assignment, edging out slowly and cautiously. The door opened and a signal immediately flooded Will's brain: don't go in here, the germs will kill you. Instead, he held his breath, kicked the door shut and walked swiftly back. Not until he came out to the car, where the others stood waiting, did Will inhale again.

"Fucking hell! I swear that toilet hadn't been cleaned since the war," he said in exasperation. "And you know what? It's just next door to the kitchen. I'm gonna puke! I'd thought I'd seen it all but obviously not!"

"We could go to Maly Hotel," Lu suggested. "I was there with my ex-husband a long time ago. They had a little corner with some sofas and tables, where we might be able to sit undisturbed and look at the maps. And we could talk with the family who run the hotel as well. I know they've been living here for generations."

"Okay," Frank said, "Let's do that."

"We've got to drive back a bit," Lu told them. "Then, we will turn left towards Muang Khoun. We go further on for about three kilometres and then left again. After that, it's just a couple of hundred metres to the hotel."

"Fine, let's go," Will said.

"Look!" Will cried out as they proceeded. "There, on the right. That's got to be the largest junkyard of undetonated bombs I've ever seen. Those B-52s didn't realise the gifts they'd bestowed on these entrepreneurs when they dropped their bombs here. I can see why people around here still collect them, remove the powder and then sell the metal to industries in northern Thailand. It's got to be a lucrative business, especially those Daisy Cutters, one of them must weigh almost seven tons, for Christ's sake. Did you know they can spread death and destruction over an area of two kilometres?"

"Yes," Frank said, "it's probably lucky that a fair few of them didn't work. The worst of it were the chemicals. You can still see their after-effects. They killed off everything immediately below and anyone who was nearby received permanent injuries, not to mention the developmental harm on foetuses, which you can hardly miss round here. That stuff became known as 'Agent Orange' and there are probably a hundred thousand children in Vietnam, Laos and Cambodia who have it to thank for their lifelong injuries."

"Yeah, I know all about that. It's fucked up. We used it a lot in both Vietnam and Laos," Will added.

Frank slowed down in front of the hotel. He didn't want to make the entrance of the small house all dusty. It was built in the British country style.

"Come, let's go inside," Lu said briskly, with a smile which Frank understood to be an invitation.

Will struck Frank lightly on his shoulder from behind, so Lu would not see the action.

"Lay off," he said, "you'll just get a guilty conscience."

"What?" Frank replied, pretending not to understand.

Lu was out of the car and already on her way through the hotel door. Will and Frank were so far behind that the door slammed shut in their faces. Lu couldn't hear their dialogue as it took place outside.

"Dammit, drop it, Frank! We've talked about this before, remember!" Will said.

"But you have to admit it, she's attractive," Frank said.

"We're here to work, not to fuck the local chicks," Will replied.

"Okay," Frank said, realising the conversation was going nowhere. "To work, then!"

Inside the lobby, Lu had already talked with the owner. He showed them to a good spot, where they could eat and talk undisturbed.

"I'll be back with some water," he said, vanishing like a spectre through the premises.

"Nice place," Frank remarked.

"I'll go and talk a bit with the owner," Lu said, implying that she would try to find out what he knew about the district and its history.

She followed him and called out, "Excuse me, Sir, may I ask a question?"

"Why, of course," he replied. "I'm Surasak."

Lu greeted him in the manner one often sees in many Asian countries: by placing the palms of her hands together and bringing them up in front of her chin towards her nose. When the greeting, which, since time immemorial, had signified "I approach unarmed," had been performed, the path lay open for dialogue and questions.

"I remember your hotel," Lu told Surasak. "A long time ago, my husband and I stayed here."

"That's nice," Surasak replied.

"But this was some years back. Your family has been living in this district for generations and we talked about this with your wife when my husband and I were guests here. She mentioned that you'd built the hotel on the land where she was born," Lu said.

"Yes, that's right. My wife was born here, but that part of the farm was lost in the bombings during the war. Nowadays, it's just one of the many waterholes where our animals go to drink. I, myself, hail from the mountains up at the Xieng

Khuang-province near Nong Haet after Road 7, that is, further on toward the Vietnamese border. That place wasn't exactly peaceful either, the day I was born in October 1945," he replied.

Surasak was easy to talk to and there was no need for Lu to ask many questions. The hotel did not have a lot of guests, so he was happy to make the most of his time with those he actually came into contact with.

"Then you were in the army during the war, I guess and helped out with the protection of the areas around here? You wouldn't happen to be Hmong, would you?" Lu asked.

"Yes, I am, but not my wife. She's one of the local Khamu." Surasak excused himself, "I'm afraid that I have to go away on an errand, but I'll be back in an hour."

He returned to the table with a jug of water, as promised and then he vanished once more. Lu returned to Will and Frank, who were discussing whether it was possible to approach the alderman of the village for more information. They had come to the conclusion that it was a good idea, but that it might get pricey, given this information might be the only thing the alderman had to sell, with everything else already sold.

"I can find out who the alderman is and the chairman of the local board," Lu told them. "It can't be hard. These things are official, you know."

"Alright then, do it," Frank said.

"Talking to them might not be as easy as you think, though. If I tell them it's two American guys from CILHI asking the questions, their curiosity will quickly turn into suspicion, alongside thoughts of how much they might make out of it and that's no good," she emphasised.

"Do you think we should have a chat with the local police?" Will asked Frank.

"Yes, that might be a good idea," he replied, "not that I think that it'll pay off. They'll be the first to get suspicious about our inquiries and movements up and down the same road.

They'll probably be camped out there watching us. It would make things easier if they just waved at us when they saw us."

"You mean wave us in and ask for our cash," Will said.

"Yeah, that's part of the rules around here," Frank said.

Lu told them what she had discussed with Surasak and that she was sure he'd be familiar with both the people of the area, including what had happened during and after the war."

"We'll put him on our list," Will said, "and you, Lu, ought to go on interviewing him."

"Lu," Frank said, "we'd really like to know who participated in the war here in these districts and where the military camps and any possible prison camps were."

Frank glanced at his watch and exclaimed, "Dammit, it's already half past three in the afternoon and all we've achieved is this. I'm itching to get cracking."

"Cool down a bit," Will said. "First things first. We need to see the alderman. Lu, find out who it is and we'll go there."

Lu went out to the reception. The counter was small, covered in worn paint. There was no computer, just an old telephone, a filthy note pad and an ash tray that didn't appear to have been emptied for several days. Behind the counter stood an old woman, just as worn out, looking idly at Lu as she asked who the alderman was and where he lived. The woman answered the questions and Lu returned to Will and Frank with the information.

"He lives up at the old airfield behind the tourist station. The house is easy to find, apparently, since it looks like an old communist-built administration building," she said.

"Did the old crone say that?" Will asked.

"Yes, those were her very words," Lu confirmed.

"Let's go then," Frank said, "What did you say his name was?"

"It's not his real name," Lu replied, "but they call him Mr Aei."

"Let's just hope he's not Vietnamese," Frank said. "I guess we'll see."

They went swiftly out to the car as all three of them were eager to get going.

"We better hurry up," Lu said. "If he's in the office, he'll be closing up soon."

*

They went back through the small village of Phonsavan towards the airfield. This time, Will was driving and Lu sat in the back seat. He drove fast and efficiently, which meant the people walking by the roadside got particularly dusty.

"Hey," Frank said, "we'll probably double back by the same road, so it might be a good idea not to irritate the people living here. For the time being, I think they'll remember this Toyota."

"Yeah, but it's weird how fast people forget," Will replied.

"No," Lu said, "you're wrong. They don't forget a thing here, especially when it's foreigners behaving badly."

"Okay, I'll ease up in a short while. I just wanted to pass that restaurant where they wasted our time. And we're almost there. It's just to the left at the tourist office over there. I can see the sign."

He parked in front of a house. It looked bare, boring and relatively new. A typical building erected on communist funds, dating from a time when there were bricks left over from the construction sites of the education establishments, usually top secret political prisons which were abundant in this part of Laos.

"Alright," Frank said, "let's go and talk to the old man. Would you like to go first, Lu?"

With Lu taking the lead, they walked up to the door of the building. She rang. Nobody came.

"Try again," Will said.

At last, they heard steps descending a staircase and the door opened. A small woman stood before them in the doorway. She asked what had brought them there so late in the day, as she was about to go home.

"Good afternoon," Lu said, "we would like to speak with Mr Aei."

"What do you want from him?" the woman replied. "He's got no time to see you now; you'll have to come back tomorrow."

"No," Lu said, "we have to speak with him now. Please help us."

"What's it about? Has there been an accident?" the woman asked.

"No, but we wish to speak to Mr Aei now. We're from Luang Prabang and have to go back tonight," Lu confirmed.

"Then, I cannot help you. Come back tomorrow if you still want to speak to Mr Aei," the woman exclaimed.

"Wait a second," Lu said, turning to Frank, who was wondering what was going on.

"She doesn't want us to see Mr Aei today," Lu explained. "We'll have to come back tomorrow."

"That's crazy. Can't you talk some sense into her?" he said.

"No, she refuses," Lu said.

"I get it. She's one of those bloody gatekeepers who like to show off their power," Will chimed in.

"What are we to do?" Lu asked. "We can't stay here overnight. I must get home to my daughter."

Suddenly, it struck her that no matter if they left now or tomorrow, she would barely get a minute with Prim.

"What the heck. Bribe her," Will said. "Ask her how much she wants."

Then, the door shut, calmly but decisively and there they stood, three snubbed people, looking at each other in astonishment at the woman's behaviour.

"Alright," Will said, "what shall we do now? Suddenly that old man has become even more important to us."

"Yeah, what shall we do?" Frank asked. "Go back to Luang Prabang or stay here overnight?"

Lu felt a terrible feeling in her gut but said nothing.

"I've got an idea, even though it might sound weird," Will said. "We'll go back to that shit bar where we stopped for lunch and take another look at those maps hanging on the walls. Then, we'll talk with the staff to see if we can get in touch with the guy who hung them there. Maybe, he knows something about what's happened around here."

"That means we'll have to spend the night here," Frank said. "Should we make a reservation at the hotel we were down at today, or some other place? I think we should stay at the hotel we visited today. It was nice. What do you think, Lu?"

"I think we should go back to Luang Prabang," Lu said morosely.

"Maybe, you could do that by yourself," Frank said. "Why not see if there's a bus going there? Let's go to the bus station to find out. If there's a bus, you can be home tonight."

"Yes, that would be great," Lu said relieved.

"Come on then, let's go down to the village to find out," Will said.

It was to be another fast and dusty trip through Phonsavan. The bus-stop resembled a sandy football pitch with a broken shack in place of a goal at one end. The shack had no doubt been built out of old timber scavenged from some nearby facade bombed by the B-52s.

There was a door on the longer wall and at the side of the door was an opening without a pane. On the door was a sign: 'Be back soon'.

Will stopped in front of the shack and looked with surprise at the sign and then out at the surroundings.

"I think I'd go mad in this society," he exclaimed. "How do they make it work without any structure? Lu, you and Frank stay here and wait. I'll go up to the village and ask if anyone knows when there are buses leaving this place. If a bus comes while I'm away, we'll see each other soon, Lu."

Will drove off toward the village, a little calmer now. It would only be a kilometre or so before he caught sight of an old man by the road.

"Hello there!" Will called through the open window.

The old man gawped at him as if he were from another planet.

"Hello!" Will called again.

The old man started to laugh and look around while he spoke in Lao, which Will could not understand.

Oh, fucking hell! Of course, he doesn't understand English, Will realised and wound up the window to continue to the town centre and the closest restaurant or hotel where he could find someone who did understand him.

*

Lu and Frank walked round the broken shed that was supposed to be the village bus-station. Frank peeked through the hole in the wall.

"There are papers on the table," he said. "That must mean someone's been here, at least."

Lu walked up to the opening, a bit more curious than Frank.

"Yes," she said, "there's an old newspaper as well, from the day before yesterday. I have no idea what to make of this except that probably, two days have passed since anybody was here which does not instil much hope."

"No," Frank said, "but we have to wait anyhow, either for a bus or Will."

Will had arrived at a little hotel where he stood, trying to talk in English and the few words of Lao he knew, accompanied by violent gesticulations, in the hope that this would make the staff understand him more easily. After a couple of minutes of one-way communication, they started to get the idea that he wanted to go by bus to Luang Prabang.

"Tomorrow bus, tomorrow bus," they said in chorus, happy in their belief that they could rent out a room to him for the night.

Will walked out to the car again and drove back to the others at the station.

"Any news?" he asked.

"No," Frank said, "you've been gone ages! What have you been up to?"

"I couldn't find anyone who could understand me," Will replied.

"What happened?" Lu asked.

"There's no bus until tomorrow," Will replied. "That's what they said at a small hotel in the outskirts of the village."

"It seems we're stuck here," Frank said, not sounding too disappointed.

"This was not what I had expected," Lu said, "I told Prim I'd come home. Ah well, there's nothing to be done about it now."

"So, what do we do now?" Frank asked, "Go back to the hotel we were at earlier and book some rooms there, or choose some other place down the road?"

"Let's take the one we were at. I know the place and it's nice and clean." Lu said.

"We'll do that and later we'll go to Crater Bar. But there's no fucking way we're gonna eat at that place again," Will told them.

*

Darkness had begun to fall over the mountains and just an hour later, it was pitch black. The mountains, the jungle and the buildings in the vicinity simply disappeared. But they found their way to the hotel regardless.

"This can't be the same place," Frank said. "What the hell have they done? I've never seen anything like it."

Will just laughed and said, "They've got to be mad about lighting. I've never seen so many light bulbs."

"It's like you're home at Christmas," Frank said.

"Lu, you lot seem to go bananas over lights as soon as you have a chance," added Will, still cackling.

"Just imagine," she said, "most of us have only lived in a hut without electricity and then an opportunity arises to use it. So it's quite natural that there are people like Surasak making the most of it."

"I wonder how we'll sleep with all those lights," Will said.

They walked in line through the door with Lu in front.

"Oh!" cried Surasak when he saw them. "You're back."

"Yes," said Lu and Frank simultaneously.

Politely, Lu asked Surasak whether he had had a nice day and had been able to seize its opportunities, which seemed to brighten him up. Then, she excused herself and went to the ladies room.

Frank walked up to the small reception where Surasak was standing and asked whether he had a single room and a double room overlooking the backyard.

"No, not facing the rear," Will objected. "No way am I going to wake up with a wretched rooster tormenting my ears. I'd rather have a room facing the front."

"Alright," Frank said and asked about a single room facing the front instead.

Lu, who returned at that moment, overheard them.

"But I don't want a room facing the front," she said.

"No, that's Will's room," Frank said.

"What? Is Will having a room all to himself and you and me are to share a double room. Is that your plan?"

"Yes," Frank replied, this time in a questioning tone of voice.

"It might be true that I look cheap, but I'm not so cheap that I'll just jump into bed with you," Lu said, smiling, a look Frank would remember for some time.

Will was standing behind them in silence.

"Oh, I see, Frank. Then it's going to be you and me that do the cuddling," he said.

Lu took the key to her single room and went up the narrow staircase that led to it.

Frank was left standing at the counter as silent as Surasak, who after a while, had got the picture.

"How are you going to get out of this, Frank?" Will asked.

"Jesus Christ! Why do I always have to mess things up? I totally misunderstood. I've got to apologise to her. If I don't, I'll ruin everything," Frank said exasperated.

"Yes, you probably should," Will said.

Frank followed Lu up the staircase to her door. He knocked tentatively.

"Lu, it's me, Frank. I've got to talk to you. Lu, please open the door."

He didn't have to wait long. The door opened and before him stood Lu, her expression far more serious than Frank could have imagined.

"What do you want, Frank?" Lu asked, looking him straight in the eye.

"Forgive me," Frank began. "I was very clumsy and I wasn't thinking. It was stupid of me to have such an idea, but down at the bus-station, I got the feeling that you were interested. I misunderstood you and I hope you can forgive me. It'll never happen again, trust me."

"Well, Frank," she replied, "when I came up here, I was asking myself why you wanted to bring me with you in your search because I might be helpful, or because you thought that I might just be something you could fool around with."

"No, no, no, Lu, that's completely wrong," Frank insisted. "The only reason we want you with us is that you can help us make connections that lead us to what we're looking for."

"I really hope so. If this happens again, I'm out of this thing, no matter if it's in the middle of the night and there are no buses going for a week," Lu confirmed.

"I promise. How much time do you need before we drive up to Crater Bar?" he asked, his tone submissive.

"I'll come down soon. Just give me fifteen minutes and then I'll be all set," she confirmed.

Lu laid her hand on Frank's upper arm. She looked him in the eyes and made him understand that he was forgiven, but that he should never try it on with her like that again.

When Frank came back down the stairs, Will was still at the counter talking with Surasak. Will gestured his apology to Surasak and turned to Frank, "Are you two okay, now?"

"Cut it out," Frank said, "it could just as well have been you. I just happened to get in trouble first, so of course I had to be the one to take the consequences. The worst thing, Will, is that I feel it's just making me more interested but I'll have to back off."

"Yeah, let's focus on something else. We need something to eat, but perhaps not at Crater Bar?" Will said.

"No, I spotted another bar on the opposite side of the street. Let's try that," Frank suggested.

At that moment, Lu came down the stairs. And Frank sensed that all the spotlights and light bulbs that were supposed to be lighting up the house were aimed in his direction.

Although Lu's brown eyes were the only ones that he paid any attention to.

"Now then, let's go back to the village again," she said.

"I'll drive," Frank said.

"That's okay, then Lu and I can sit in the back seat," Will said and laughed teasingly.

"You do that," Frank replied, taking his place behind the wheel. The back doors opened almost simultaneously as Lu and Will got inside.

Lu smiled at Will and said, "Great idea! You drive, Frank, so we get to ride in the back as if we had a chauffeur."

Will laughed and looked at Frank in the rear-view mirror, getting a glare in return.

"Perhaps you'd like me to drive extra slow," Frank said.

"Not at all, that's not necessary. We'll have time for what we plan on doing back here anyway," Lu said, enjoying her cruelty a little.

*

A thunderstorm drew over the north of Laos that night. The dusty roads turned wet and muddy and the trip took longer than it might have done. In Phonsavan, however, it became easier to see in the dark. Their hotel was not the only heavy user of light bulbs: there were plenty of others who thought it impolite not to light up the night and this looked like it had been done with the greatest enthusiasm.

"Let's eat first, at that place opposite Crater Bar. Then we can go back and just for the sake of courtesy and have a beer, if they're serving tonight," Will said with his usual, wry smile.

All three left the car and walked across the muddy street, which was only partly asphalted. Walking on tip toe was no use. The best thing would have been to take off their shoes and walk barefoot.

"It's no good running," Will told Frank, "you'll get just as muddy either way."

"Yeah, but it takes less time," Frank replied, doing everything he could to laugh off what had happened earlier that evening.

Lu could sense something was wrong, but she couldn't make out what it was. She was, however, quite certain that it had something to do with Prim. But she couldn't put her finger on whether this sensation was caused by her guilty conscience, or by her worry about the prospect of Prim taking advantage of her absence. Whichever it was, it killed her appetite and more than anything, she wished she were home. To distract her from her thoughts about Prim, she'd have to get properly engaged in her assignment and that way, she might manage to suppress some of her worries.

When Lu stepped in through the door to the bar where they were planning to eat, she could tell at once that the place was wrong.

"No," she told her companions, "let's get out of here. Anywhere but this place."

"I'll be damned, back in the street again," Will said, a little moodily.

"Well, if you want to stay, that's your business, but I won't," Lu said.

"Oh, cut it out," Will said. "That wasn't what I'm complaining about, but the fact that no matter where we go, we meet the same thing: crappy service or hookers."

"Why, there's not a lot of other ways to make a living up here," Frank pointed out. "And don't forget who started this shit. It was our guys; our soldiers on leave."

"No Frank, you've got it all wrong. Why do you let our guys take the rap? This thing has always been around here in Asia. It's just that the exploitation of it has gotten much worse. And then, if you take a look around, how many people can you have hiding out in a place just like this, up here in the mountains and be into all kinds of shit, even taking small boys to their rooms. And it's not just the men who are twisted, there are old hags too and young ones."

Will could feel his moral indignation spilling over as he spoke. "You do know that these girls are all but slaves, don't you? They're not here for their own sake. I can bet my shirt on that they've been abducted, smuggled and sold to this place from the south of China, Oh, I'm sure they were promised a job at some restaurant in some nice tourist resort and then they were beaten until they joined this shit here. Frank, they have to fuck at least ten guys a day, you know, for their asshole of a madam to be content. And she's a woman too! Just imagine it."

"Yeah, it's weird that so many of those that deal in women are women themselves," Frank agreed.

"And what do the poor chicks get for it? Maybe forty or sixty dollars a month, tops. Really, someone ought to blow all of this shit to kingdom come," Will continued.

"So what do we do now?" Frank asked. "Are we to blow up the place, cross the street and surprise the waitresses there, or go back to the hotel?"

"Let's cross the street," Lu said. "It wasn't that bad after all."

*

Crater Bar was almost empty, just as it had been before. There was a single customer, a man, just skin and bones.

"He's starving to death, by the look of it. He's probably still waiting for his food," Will joked.

They sat down at the same table as before. After five minutes, the kitchen door opened and one of the staff came out and greeted them cheerfully, as if they'd been there a thousand times before.

"I'll be damned," Frank exclaimed. "They recognise us after just one visit! I guess they don't get a lot of customers."

"For the moment, that may be to our advantage, given our assignment," Will said. "I think I'll just go and have a chat with that girl in the kitchen right away, so that they'll get to work while we're waiting for the food."

Lu agreed. "But it should probably be me talking to her, if you don't plan on using body language, that is," she pointed out.

"Alright, Lu. Ask her if she knows who put up the pictures on the walls. Whoever they are, they seem to know this district pretty well," Will said.

Just as they agreed what to do, the kitchen door opened and out came the same waitress from their first visit, holding something in her hand.

"Here's the menu," she said.

"Thanks," Lu said. "I'd like to ask you something. Do you know who put up these pictures? Do you know them?"

"Yes, it's my husband. He was an American pilot during the war," the waitress replied.

"Oh, I see. I'm Lu, by the way. This is Will and Frank," Lu said, introducing the others.

"I'm Aee," said the woman, "and it's my sister and I who run this bar. Well, not bar exactly. We call it a food-bar."

"We would like to meet your husband. Is that possible?" Lu continued.

Aee became suspicious immediately.

"What do you want with him? He's old and sick. He's had heart problems and can't manage much. I don't think he has long to live, either. What would you like to eat? Look at the menu," Aee said, attempting to change the subject.

"Okay," Lu said and turned to Will. "Have you decided what you're having? I am having the chicken casserole with rice."

"Then I'll have the same," Will replied and Frank tagged along.

"All of us want the chicken casserole," Lu told Aee, who disappeared into the kitchen.

"What did you say to her?" Frank asked.

"I asked her if we could meet her husband, since he's the one who put up the pictures. He was a pilot during the war here. But she said that he's old and sick and she wanted to keep him out of it. I think she got scared."

"Lu, go and talk with her! Take our IDs and tell her she can make copies of them if she wants! If her husband was a pilot, he'll know about CILHI. He'll come. I'm sure of it."

Lu went out into the kitchen and the smell of cooking.

"Excuse me. I can talk while you're preparing the meal. It smells delicious, by the way. I'm looking forward to having a proper chicken casserole," Lu exaggerated.

"I can't help you," Aee said, as she whipped intensely the contents in a saucepan. "I told you, my husband is old and sick. He'll be seventy-five soon and he ought to be left alone."

Lu looked at Aee. She reckoned the woman was no older than thirty-five.

"But Aee, please just show these IDs to your husband. I think it might be important to him," Lu lied. "These two guys are serious. They mean you no harm. Just look at the documents. Make copies and show your husband."

Aee took the IDs reluctantly and scrutinised the portraits.

"Yea, it's those guys sitting out there. But what does CILHI mean?"

"Your husband will know," Lu said, not wanting to go into detail. "Make copies and show them to your husband this evening."

"Okay," Aee said. "We'll see. Now leave, so I can get the food ready!"

Slowly, Lu walked back to where the guys were chatting.

"How did it go?" Frank asked. "Did you make contact?"

"Yes, I think so. We'll see. She kept your ID documents, anyway."

"What the fuck!" Frank erupted. "Why did you give them to her! I told you they were to be copied, not handed over!"

"Well," Will said, "I guess we'll be here for a while."

Aee came out from the kitchen with water, glasses and three sets of cutlery but without knives. Also on the tray were Frank and Will's IDs.

"Here you are," Aee told the relieved Americans.

"May we meet him?" Frank asked.

He figured it was likely Aee spoke English, if not, her conversation with her husband would be meagre indeed. When it came to getting a young wife, it wasn't just about sex. You had to be able to communicate too. But this wasn't the sort of thing he'd be telling anyone else.

Just as Aee was about to answer, the service door opened and out came a vigorous, fit and grey-haired man, six feet tall, with clear blue steel eyes, the very image of health and strength. He looked Will straight in the eyes, walked right up him and Frank and raised his hand as if about to salute them. Will sensed immediately that this was the man they wanted to meet and acted swiftly: he got up, straightened his shoulders and stretched out his hand. It felt like a vice. The only time he had experienced a similar handshake was when he'd greeted a New York Rangers hockey star.

"I'm Spencer Smith," the man announced.

"I'm Will, this is Frank and this is Lu, our assistant," Will replied, introducing them all.

Frank shook the man's hand as well and got to experience that handshake. The man didn't look as if he had ever experienced any cardiac issues. His wife probably thought they'd been sent by a very different organisation.

"Spencer," he said, "we happened to notice the pictures on the walls and as I'm sure you know, we're out here looking for the remains of our guys, so we got curious and wanted to meet you."

"I'm familiar with your work," Spencer said. "Just a short while ago, your colleagues found the remains of an old acquaintance of mine who crashed thirty-five years ago outside of Hanoi. A great deal was written about this case. Looks like CILHI did an excellent job."

"Yeah," Will said, "the guys who found those remains were some former colleagues of mine at the 'Prisoner of War/Missing in Action Office'. There were two guys inside the plane that day, the spring of '68, Captain Keith Hall and Captain Earl Hopper. Keith Hall managed to escape the crash using his ejector seat. But unfortunately, he ended up in enemy hands. He remained a prisoner of war up until '73. It was an ugly business. The guy was ruined for life. It might've been better for him if he'd met the same fate as Earl Hopper. Earl didn't manage to bail out."

"But it wasn't until '93 that MIA started searching for remains," added Frank. "And it wasn't until '96 that the results were presented."

Spencer responded, "They knew, of course, that the plane had crashed in the Son La province, but if the team from MIA hadn't come to the right village and met the right people, they would never have found the actual spot. Once they'd sent the little they found to CILHI for DNA analysis, they managed to confirm that the remains belonged to Earl Hopper."

"Yeah," Frank said. "Later on, we read that he'd been buried in consecrated ground in the National Memorial Cemetery in Phoenix, Arizona."

Lu felt a bit left out, but listened carefully with interest. Temporarily at least, Prim vanished from her thoughts.

"That's why we're here," Will said. "We're searching for two sets of remains we believe to be here in the district, two advisers who worked closely with the army the CIA set up, chiefly made up of Hmong people."

"Yeah, I know quite a lot about it. It was established right here, you know," Spencer told them.

"Spencer, how long have you lived in Phonsavan?" Will asked.

"Nearly thirty years," he replied.

"That's a long time," Will observed.

"Yeah, but time flies," Spencer said.

The kitchen door opened again and this time, the food was brought to the table.

"Would you like something to eat?" Aee asked her husband.

"No darling, just some water would do fine," Spencer said, turning to the group, "I'm about to head out, so I can't stay and eat with you."

"Spencer, can we ask you a couple of questions about this district? And we'd love it if you could help us out a bit with our search? Of course, it's all up to you," Frank said.

"Well, alright," Spencer began. "As long as it doesn't involve me in person."

"No, that's okay," Frank said. "But I understand you know this area well, especially Phonsavan."

"Yeah, of course I do," Spencer confirmed.

"Spencer," Will asked, inquisitively, "how come you chose to move to this godforsaken place?"

"After the war, I went back to New York, where I'm from, but I couldn't stand the city or the US anymore. And besides, I felt for the people here, so I decided to come back to the district I'd flown over so many hundreds of times, hoping that I could help to drive the commies out. You're not supposed to speak like that these days, but that's the way it was back then. I longed to return, so I did. Another thing was that I had a sweetheart here in this country, at that time. Yeah," Spencer said and smiled, "and as you can see, I've still got one."

"That's quite clear," Will replied with a glint in his eye, which Spencer, thankfully took the right way. Will continued, "We'd like to get in touch with people who know this district, every detail of it and what happened here when the Vietnamese soldiers were in Phonsavan, all this so we can find out what happened to those two guys, Nick and Tom, who we're looking for."

"I see," Spencer replied.

"We've tried to get in touch with the alderman of this place, Mister Aei," Will said, "but he didn't want to speak with us earlier today."

"Your food will get cold if you don't eat it now," Lu pointed out.

"Yeah," Frank replied and started to poke about with his fork in the rice, so that steam rose up in a thin mist over his dish.

"Mister Aei is a very special man, with many good qualities, but when it comes to meeting people, he's never got the time, so don't count on him," Spencer told them.

"We're going there again tomorrow," Frank cut in. "Would you consider meeting us to go more into detail, before we set off? Maybe, we could meet here, in the morning?"

"Yea, that'll be fine," Spencer confirmed.

They thanked Spencer and he walked out the same way he'd come, just as sprightly as when they'd first seen him.

"Well," Frank said, "I really need to finish my food. But damn, wasn't that a weird meeting?"

Will agreed and commented, "If you have to live like this, despite the fact that you're from the other side of the globe, you've got to have very good reasons. I wonder what they are because I sure wouldn't settle down here, up in the hot mountains, hell no, not when the ocean and the islands are so close."

"I can tell you about a guy that settled down on an inhabited island outside of Australia, north of the Great Barrier Reef," Frank said. "He was a diver during World War II and specialised in mining ships in harbours, one hell of a risky assignment, that. Like Spencer, he went back to the States after the war, but decided to return to one of the islands with his wife, who, just like him, was from Chicago. Anyhow, they settled down on the one island where no one could reach them and they had three children. They almost stayed there for forty years and do you know why?"

"Nope," Will said.

"Well, the guy knew about a couple of Japanese boats that had been wrecked and inside them, there was for them, a significant fortune. That damned rogue began diving non-stop among those wrecks and bringing up all he could and he sold it all through contacts in Europe and the States. This financed the rest of his daughters' lives and they're still living off it. This was his little secret. So, you're probably right, everybody has their reasons."

"It's starting to get late," Lu said. "I think we should head back to the hotel for the night."

"Yeah, I'm looking forward to lying head to tail with you, Frank," Will said and laughed.

There was nothing wrong with the hotel, as it happened. But, as was so often the case, the rooms were dull, the ventilation inefficient and the smell musty and stale. The decor was simple, the rooms unpainted and there was an old TV set which showed just the one propaganda programme, apparently still lingering from the old communist days. Lu was glad she couldn't see herself in the shabby, partly blackened, mirror. The bed looked welcoming though, but it would be. This was to be only the third time in her life she had slept in a proper bed.

At the foot of the bed, on a stool, was a small, enamelled washbasin. By the side of the stool was a hot water bottle, filled with water. It was obvious that this was the washing water and that there was no hot water on tap. Lu washed herself as best she could with a facecloth. The cool water felt good. Her legs were so tired that she could barely feel her feet when she slipped in between the warm, clammy sheets. But it was no good. She pulled off the blanket and rolled up the top sheet to her side.

Her thoughts turned to Prim. Lu hoped that her mother, May, was taking care of her. But Lu's mother was not very helpful these days and to expect any help from Prim's other grandmother, Mak, was out of the question. Mak felt that Lu had driven her son, Fang, away from the home and ruined life for everyone. It was more realistic to hope that Songchai would look after Prim. But he always seemed to have other matters to attend to these days.

Chapter 13

Ten Fateful Minutes

Songchai reached Phonsavan early in the morning. He had a strange feeling about seeing Lu in this district in an unfamiliar car. It had to be those skeleton hunters. But there was no time to dwell on the issue. He had to focus on his own assignment.

Despite the early hour, the villagers appeared to be up and ready for the day's chores. Nat, Songchai's old lover, was back at the workshop.

"Hi, Nat!" Songchai said as he stepped in and spotted her behind the small counter which served as the firm's reception.

"Oh, hi!" Nat exclaimed, surprised. "What are you doing here? You seemed at little uneasy when we bumped into each other yesterday."

"No, not at all. I was just a bit stressed out and needed to get home for the evening," Songchai lied. "Sorry about that, Nat. I didn't mean for you to take it that way."

"Well then, what brings you back? You must've come here before without paying me a visit," she said.

"Well, the truth is, I knew you were still living in the area, but not exactly where. Now I know and I'm glad that we met again," Songchai replied.

"Honestly, I doubt this is the only reason for your showing up like this. So, there's nothing else on your mind?" she said.

"Yes, well, I have this small problem that I'd like some help with. I need to borrow or rent a small truck. Since I don't know anyone else in the area, I thought you might have one," Songchai explained.

"I thought so. You haven't changed, Songchai. But you've struck lucky! We've got a Toyota pick-up, which we use to rent out to our customers. Will that do? It's not too old and probably won't break down on you. I'm glad to be of help. You only need to pay thirty thousand kip per day, not much for a vehicle like that," Nat confirmed.

"I'm very grateful," Songchai replied. "I'll need to hold onto it for a couple of days and I'd like to take it now, immediately."

"I'll write a rental agreement, just as a formality. It's not exactly every day you visit this place, you know," Nat said with a smile. "But it would be nice if you did."

"Maybe, we can find a bit more time to get together when I'm back with the pick-up. Where is it?" Songchai asked.

"Behind the house, in the parking lot. It's a white Toyota with a cargo bed. You can't miss it," she said.

"Thanks," Songchai answered as he signed the agreement form, put some money on the counter and grabbed the keys. "Bye bye, see you soon!"

Songchai walked out into the dusty street. It was lined for the most part with low wooden houses as Phonsavan city centre did not have many buildings in it. He went around the corner of the building and headed for the parking lot. At that moment, he froze. Some twenty or thirty metres in front of him, Lu was standing outside a car talking with the two men who had been in the car with her.

Songchai pivoted and went back into the alley, hoping that Lu had not spotted him. He waited for them to leave before he walked back to the pick-up and took off. There weren't many cars going through Phonsavan in the morning, maybe just five or six and some twenty or thirty trucks. It was easy to keep an eye on who was coming or going.

One problem remained to be solved: Supot's pick-up was still in Phonsavan and had to be driven up to the cave. But now, they had two pick-ups for transportation. Naturally, it would have been better with one big lorry, but this would do. They had all night.

*

Up by the cave, everything was ready to be loaded and transported to Ban-Pak Ou. Songchai parked the Toyota and found the others, who were in excellent spirits.

"Supot, your pick-up had to be left in Phonsavan. You've gotta fetch it. Take Surachai's car and take one of the guys with you. We'll load this one, in the meantime and drive it down to Ban Pak-Ou. That should only take a couple of hours, so if we get going now we ought to be finished before nightfall."

"But wouldn't it be better if you were to go back and I took care of the loading and transportation?" Supot replied.

"I can't," Songchai replied. "There are some people I know in Phonsavan and it wouldn't look good if they saw me. Before I took off, I got a glimpse of my daughter-in-law."

"I see. I'll go then. It's safest to have someone along that she doesn't recognise. It'll have to be you, Voratep. We'll take Surachai's car."

"It would have been much easier if someone had joined Songchai this morning," Supot said in irritation, once they were on the road. "Everything's messed up, dammit!"

Voratep sat in silence, but after a short while, he spoke.

"It's the strangest thing. On the one side of the road, there's a memorial site and a graveyard for the fallen from Vietnam while on the other, directly opposite, there's one for the fallen from our country. It's weird how quickly we forget."

Back at the caves, Songchai took command and ordered that everything be taken down to the parking area. Since it was impossible for anyone passing by to see what was going on in the jungle, he thought it safe to get going.

Surachai was becoming irritated by Songchai constantly changing their plans. First, there were carriers coming, then there were trucks and now, they were supposed to take care of it all by themselves. On top of that, there was a new timetable to manage.

"This is looking more and more like sheer drudgery," he said to Pooi.

"My mind's on the dough," Pooi replied.

"But you do see, don't you, that suddenly we've got to do the whole fucking job ourselves," Surachai pointed out.

"Yeah but don't you know your own folks? Pooi said. "This has probably been Songchai's plan the whole time. Did you really think he'd be willing to share the loot if it wasn't absolutely necessary? Quit whining and start carrying! That'll make life a lot easier." He hoisted a grenade box on his shoulder like he'd been doing it all his life.

In the forty degree heat, they carried down hundreds of boxes to the parking lot. They were sweating buckets and gulping down water. The sun was in its most unforgiving position, set right in the middle of a clear blue sky; not even the shade of the palm leaves offered sanctuary.

*

Suteluck was carrying a box of machine guns on his back. He had just passed the spot in which they had seen the landmines for the first time, when he caught sight of a big brown snake with bright stripes slithering across his path, a king cobra, five metres long. He stopped, stiff as a pole, in front of the snake. The others were far behind, too far to see what was going on. Suteluck held his box tight and backed away carefully. Now he was a metre and a half from the snake. Suddenly, it reared, almost as high as Suteluck himself and stared at him. Not thinking, Suteluck adjusted his grip on the box. The snake took this as a threat and moving too fast for him to react, bit his inner thigh beneath the testicles. Suteluck had no chance. The cobra had sunk its teeth eight millimetres into his flesh.

Contently, as if in slow motion, the snake slithered away and vanished into the bushes.

Suteluck did not notice the animal's retreat. He was staring at his groin. It was one of the worst places to be bitten. He dropped his machine gun box and cried out in pain and anxiety. He called for help and shook with fear as he tore off his trousers to look at the wound. At that moment, Pooi, Surachai and the others reached him. When they saw Suteluck's twisted facial expression, they dropped to the ground where he was lying and discovered the bite on his inner thigh, unmistakeably, the marks of snake fangs, the traces of a poisonous bite capable of killing an elephant in three hours.

"It was a cobra," Suteluck managed to stutter, "it was a cobra."

Pooi was sitting with Suteluck's upper body in his lap, squeezing him tight, stroking him over his sweaty forehead.

"There, there, my friend, hush now. Try to relax," Pooi said.

Thirty years had passed since they had first met, not far from this very place. Then, they were happy at having survived the war. They promised each other friendship for life and had kept to that promise, religiously.

"I'll run and get some water," Surachai said.

"Let me have a look! Can we cut out the poison?" Songchai asked, inspecting the wound thoroughly.

Carefully spreading Suteluck's legs and holding his testicles to the side, he was able to get a clear view of the bite. It had already begun to swell up considerably. He turned his head to the others and whispered that it was looking bad, really bad. He had a long experience of gunshot wounds, bites and other wounds.

Then, he turned back to Suteluck, "We'll pull your trousers up and carry you down to the car and don't you move. This will work out just fine. You just need to keep still and save your strength. Pooi and Surachai, you'll have to grab each other's hands and make a chair, so Suteluck can sit on your forearms and hold himself around your necks. I'll be walking behind and holding him up to make sure he doesn't fall backwards. You others, put away the boxes. Stay and stand guard! This could take a while. We need to get Suteluck down to Phonsavan and Lao-Mongolian Hospital as quickly as we can."

They carried Suteluck down to the vehicle, the pick-up Songchai had rented that morning.

"Please, put me down," Suteluck said.

His face was ashen, his limbs shaking from the shock and from the spasms caused by the poison. His whole body was aching with muscular pain beyond description. But before long, the paralysis had set in and the only thing still working was his head. Soon, he realised that he could no longer talk. He went into a coma as they pulled his body into the back seat and they had barely backed the car out of its spot when he choked to death. It had taken less than ten minutes. It had been a painful end.

"Suteluck is dead," said Pooi, on the verge of tears, "and for what, for greed? Fucking unnecessary! Stop the car! I've got to get out!"

They were all equally bewildered. No one knew how to deal with the situation.

"Pooi and I will take Suteluck to his family," Songchai said. "You others need to continue. And you, Surachai, will make sure that everything's going according to plan. All of it is to be down in Ban Pak-Ou before nightfall. I'll be there to meet you and help reload the goods onto the boats."

"Yeah," Surachai said, "we'll in for one hell of a job, but we'll make it."

*

Suteluck's family did not live in Ban Aen, in the outskirts of Luang Prabang where Suteluck had lived, but in Muang Sing, about ten kilometres from the borders with China and Burma, one of those places where they traffic everything from women to counterfeit branded goods. Songchai and Pooi had only been sitting in the car for a few minutes when Songchai realised what they had got themselves into.

"Hey, Pooi," he asked. "Do you know where Suteluck's family lives?"

"Yeah, up in Muang Sing," Pooi replied.

"Have you got any idea how long it'll take us to get there? He'll start stinking up the car long before we arrive. The question is, how important is this, actually? We could just bid farewell to our friend here and make sure he gets to his family by some other means. We can pay for the transportation."

"No way!" Pooi said. "We've been friends a long time and it's my duty to take him home to his family so he gets a dignified journey to the other side."

"Okay," Songchai replied. "But you'll have to drive him there by yourself. It'll take you twenty-four hours there and back, you know, so you'd better get cracking. But first, you have to turn around and drive me back."

"It just has to take the time it takes," Pooi said. "I'll join you somewhere along the route."

They drove back to the parking place. The others were still there and had not yet got over the shock. All of them had seen death by poison before at close range as a result of nerve gas or pesticide. But those recollections were of the remote past and the fact that they'd seen similar things before didn't mean they were any less shaken by what had happened to Suteluck. All their work had ground to a halt when the pick-up showed up unexpectedly.

"I changed my mind," Songchai explained, stepping out of the car. "Pooi will have to arrange for the funeral on his own.

The rest of us have to do what we've agreed to do and more, since we're two men short, for now."

"You get the feeling that we're going to snuff it one by one on this job," Surachai said. "Firstly, Tatchacon, of natural causes, then Suteluck. Who's next?"

"Bullshit! We have to forget about this. We need to get working," snapped Songchai.

"Yeah, what kind of weapons are we lugging around, really?" asked Kitepong, one of the hands Supot had recruited. "Those Russian bastard Simonovs or RPDs, machine guns constructed long before the Second World War. RPG7 and RPG2 bazookas. I understand why someone would want those and even those American rifles, the MI Garand, M14 and M16, but the rest of it, well, I think we just ought to leave it."

"No," Songchai replied. "We're leaving nothing. We've promised to deliver it all and that's what we'll do. For now, it's just us here, so roll up your sleeves and let's get to it!"

They worked in silence, carrying the goods that would make each of them a small fortune, but would also result in long prison sentences if the wrong people within the police learned about them. It was true that most of the police were already bought or involved in some other way - everything could be bought, even protection - but you could never be absolutely sure.

Clouds of dust were rising, announcing the approach of cars; soon Voratep and Supot would be with them. From now on, there would be four men doing the job.

*

After a couple of hours, it was time to drive the first load down to Ban Pak-Ou, on the banks of the Mekong River, where they would have to reload swiftly. Songchai had made sure that the boats that were intended to transport the load further on along the Mekong were already in place, so the boxes could be packed beneath the floors while they were unloading. He was pleased. Nobody in the area appeared to suspect a thing and if they did, they were smart enough to keep their mouths shut about it. Nobody wanted to get their tongue cut off, or their throat cut, for that matter.

They shuttled to and from until late in the night, when everything was loaded and ready.

"That's that, then," said Songchai to the exhausted bunch, all of them long-experienced smugglers. "Now we'll eat and park the cars and then we'll take off right away. We've got four boats, filled and ready to go and for the moment, we're four guys. Pooi will join us later, so for now, we'll take one boat each. Tonight, we'll go down to Ban Pak Man. We'll rest tomorrow before we continue."

Once out on the river, everybody felt relieved. Songchai in particular had been worrying about Phonsavan. Too many people there suspected that he and Surachai were up to something. Songchai and Surachai were hardly unique, of course. For many people, there was no other way to make ends meet than by trafficking weapons, opium and counterfeit goods from China, or even worse, by abducting and buying girls and young women from poor districts and selling them to brothels elsewhere in Asia.

Chapter 14

Recruiting New Models

Up in Phonsavan, darkness had fallen. Frank was sleeping, but Will lay awake thinking about the day's events, especially about Spencer who he had found to be the archetypical, fit old soldier, but a very difficult character to make out.

Lu lay tossing and turning in an adjacent room, not used to sleeping in a bed. It would have been better if the floor had consisted of trodden earth and the bedding merely of bast carpet and blanket. But it was not just the room and the bed that caused her sleeplessness. The uncertainty of what Prim was up to and whether or not she had been to school, was playing on her mind.

That day, Prim had seized the opportunity to do some more exploring of the world outside the village. She had not gone to school and she had no intention of going there the next day either, unless Lu came home. She had met her friend Lek during the morning. They had hung out in the outskirts of Luang Prabang to avoid being seen by their teachers, or any fellow pupils who might have given them away. She planned to tell her teacher that she had fallen ill and had to stay at home. Everyone had always trusted Prim; she was never up to mischief. But those days were gone and it would take a while for those close to her to understand that from now on, she was going to be a very different person from the one they had known before.

*

Lek and Prim were the prettiest girls in their class. The boys always swarmed around them like bees around honey. There were a few of the older boys that the two girls liked to hang around with, boys who were into exciting things who were not as childish as the others. These were the same boys that the girls had had a little too much fun with in the hotel a couple of days earlier, when they had got themselves thrown out.

Prim had never had sex. But Lek had been with a boy a couple of years her senior who was from her neighbourhood in Luang Prabang. She was fourteen but looked older. Most people thought she was around seventeen. Prim was soon to be fourteen and was very curious. She had begun to explore her body and was enjoying doing so.

In the park, north of central Luang Prabang - lying where the Nam Khan River meets the Mekong and the riverbanks were at their finest - Prim and Lek sat on a shabby wooden bench in the morning sun. They were chatting away about guys, school, family, their grandparents and their parents, who never seemed to understand anything they talked about or wanted. As Prim was looking down at a group of Buddhist monks harvesting their salad in one of the many plots of vegetables that lay along both riverbanks, she glanced at the boats passing by, carried slowly by the current.

"Lek," said Prim, "tell me what it was like to sleep with Ian. Also, why him? It makes no sense, really. You two aren't even together."

"No, we're not," Lek responded. "But we had met a couple of times and he's kind. He's not like other guys, just groping everywhere. And he's not childish. He likes to hug. He's nice. Sometimes, we go out for a cup of coffee although I have a Coke. His dad is American and doesn't live here, but he sends money to Ian's mother so she doesn't have to work; she does though, anyway. I don't know what she does. I think she works at one of the hotels. We usually go to his place since he's always alone there in the afternoons and the early evenings. My mother doesn't suspect a thing."

Prim sat listening in silence. Now and then, she asked a question, but she didn't want to interrupt Lek.

"What about the first time?" she asked.

"We were at his place and he put on some music, a CD his dad had sent him from the US. We were sitting and listening to it; we went through the whole thing a couple of times. We both liked it. It was an American band but I can't remember their name. When we'd been kissing for a while, he started to undress me. Then, he took off his clothes. Next, we were lying naked on the floor in front of the speakers, kissing and hugging. It felt great when he caressed my breasts and I loved how stiff or hard he got; I don't know how you say it," Lek replied, describing everything as well as she could.

"No, don't stop," Prim said, giggling. "Tell me more!"

"Careful, it could be harmful!" Lek said, laughing.

"You must!" Prim insisted.

"Alright," Lek said, giving in. "Anyhow, we were lying there stroking each other when I suddenly felt him groping between my legs and touching me. I was tingling all over and could feel my whole body yearning for him. I've heard that it can be really painful the first time, but I just had to do it and eventually, he was inside me. It didn't hurt as much as I'd feared, but it was all over pretty quickly. He came almost right away. He said it was just because he was so incredibly horny. It was a bit of a letdown to be honest and it meant that I didn't feel so good afterwards. He didn't want to hug anymore; he just wanted me to leave. He said his mother might be home any moment, but I knew he was lying. He wanted me to get dressed quickly, so I did. And as I was walking away, I felt all wet between my legs. It felt so gross!"

"But you slept with him once more, didn't you?" Prim said.

"Yeah, but I've realised that I've had enough," Lek replied. "I don't want to see him again and I regret going with him. I got horny, okay! But it wasn't a nice debut. I think it's better if you find a guy that really wants you, instead of somebody who only wants your body when they just feel like it."

"I'd kind of like to try it. Sometimes, I wake up in the night feeling horny, but I don't know what to do about it. I remember when dad lived with us; sometimes I woke up in the night because mum and dad were doing it, whispering to each other about how great it was," Prim recalled.

"Well, that's the way we make children," Lek said. "I want to have lots when I've found 'Mr Right' and we're married."

"Anyway, what time is it? I'm starting to get a bit hungry," Prim said.

"It'll be two o'clock soon," Lek replied.

"Why don't we go to your place? You'll be alone at home, won't you? Maybe, you've got something we can eat, just some rice or something?" Prim asked.

"Yes, let's go. Nobody comes home until evening anyway," Lek confirmed.

*

The girls went over to Lek's home. She lived on the opposite side of the Nam Khan, so they had to walk south along the Phommatha Road and across a bridge that allowed only pedestrians and two-wheelers. When it had been built, the bridge was intended for the few cars that had existed in Luang Prabang at the time. Although it had only been constructed in the mid-seventies, it looked as if it had been standing there for centuries. Parts of the ironwork, especially the railings, were so corroded that they threatened to break in several places. To lean against them was to risk your life. The boards were so rotten in places that large holes gaped along the walkway, revealing the sharp heads of the nails that were supposed to hold the rest of the wooden structure together.

"It's dangerous here when it's dark. You can't see a thing. Many people have fallen and hurt themselves badly, usually old men drunk on beer," Lek said, laughing. "Dad says it's an outrage, that those men in the council responsible for the repairs have been given government money many times, but the money just ends up in their own pockets. They don't give a damn about fixing this bridge. It doesn't matter who's in power because they all go about it the same way."

It took the girls almost an hour to get home. During their walk, Prim told Lek about her dad and how he had moved to live in Chiang Mai in Thailand where he now worked as an estate agent, selling plots and houses.

"I don't know what that actually means, but it sounds nice. He's been living there for some time now," she said.

"Haven't you seen him since?" Lek asked.

"Well, once," Prim replied before Lek interrupted.

"This is my place and this is our yard," Lek said. "We rent this house from the family next door. They're Chinese and we don't like them, but they're letting it cheaply, dad says. They own several houses and make their living by letting them out. Dad drives tourists around the river in our boat, but now, he's told us he'll be away for a couple of days. Mum will be coming home at sunset. Come on! Let's go inside and see if there's anything to eat."

The house Lek lived in stood on poles two metres high. Beneath the house, the family's motorbikes were parked, together with some of the lumber Lek's dad used to bring home. He collected unexploded landmines, of which there were still tens of thousands out in the fields. Eventually, they ended up maiming or killing almost everyone that dug for them. Landmines contained copper, for which you could get a good price. Her dad saved the explosive powder, for what reason, was anybody's guess. And he actually kept these things under the house where his family lived.

Leks' dad had been incarcerated in Samana Camp, a re-education camp for anti-communists. He was supposed to stay there for three weeks, but it was five years before they released him. During his imprisonment, he acquired the knowledge of how to handle various bombs, not from the prison staff or the school staff, as they were technically titled, but from others who, in some cases, never made it out at all.

Lek and Prim climbed up the ladder leading to the first floor and the entrance of the house. Immediately inside the door was yet another ladder, which led up to an attic where the family slept. Lek went directly to the part of the house used as a kitchen. The whole house was quite small, so the dining area was not large. Lek undid the lids of some jars and found a bit of this and that for them to eat.

"Wow! Would you like some fish?" asked Lek.

"Yeah, that sounds good," Prim said.

"There's rice as well," Lek added.

"I'd like some of that too," Prim said expectantly. She had not eaten properly for two days.

"It feels so weird, as if I were all alone," she said. "Mum is always away and the others at the yard don't care about me. Nobody would notice if I didn't come home at all, except maybe the cat."

"For me it's the same," Lek agreed. "I think I'll get out of this place as soon as possible. I'd like to get a job in some shop or restaurant. I've heard they pay well."

"Not me," said Prim. "When I'm old enough, I'll find myself a rich guy, who can take me to all the places in the world and buy me everything I point at."

"Only princes do that," Lek told her, laughing.

"Then a prince it must be!" Prim confirmed. "At least, you have the luxury of living in a house made up of boards. Mum and I live in a house of bamboo branches, bast and leaves."

"I would probably like to live in the centre of Luang Prabang, or some other city," Lek said.

They kept on talking as they ate.

"When do you have to be home?" asked Lek, when they had almost finished their fish and rice.

"Nobody cares," Prim said, looking sad.

"After we've finished up, how about we take mum's motorbike back to town and hang out with some friends?" Lek suggested.

"Okay," Prim agreed.

"I think I know where we can find Ian and his mates. We can tag along," Lek said.

"But you said you didn't want to meet Ian again," Prim remarked.

"Yeah, I know but he's got some nice friends, so I don't have to be with him. It might be fun," Lek added.

"Let's go!" Prim said enthusiastically. "Where's the key to the motorbike?"

"I've got to change first," Lek said. "I can't go dressed like this and neither can you. We look like we've just come from school and we'll end up being mocked by the guys. Come here! I've got some other things we can wear."

Lek opened a box that contained trousers. She said they were hers, but when she put them on it was obvious to Prim that they belonged to her mother. Prim mentioned this to Lek, but she didn't seem to mind. "It doesn't matter. We can borrow them. Nobody will be able to tell whether they're mine, yours or anyone else's. We've gotta look a bit cool too, you know. Just check out the other girls sitting in the bars."

"Yes, but they're older than us," said Prim.

"Perhaps, but we look older than our age. Get dressed now! Then we're outta here," Lek responded.

They went out and down the ladder. Being naive, they left their clothes lying in a pile inside, assuming nobody would notice them.

*

Lek went under the house to drag out the motorbike. She put the key into the ignition, pushed the start button and the engine started with a roar. This was not the first time Lek had used her mother's motorbike; she had been doing it for a couple of years now. Prim sat behind Lek and slowly, they drove along the riverside, down to the bridge. Twilight was setting in. As ever, it went from dusk to dark in an instant.

"Stop, Lek!" Prim cried out as they approached the bridge. "I want to get off. I'll walk it! You'll have to drive over on your own."

"I'm going to walk as well and lead the motorbike. This bridge is just too scary," Lek agreed.

On the other side, they immediately mounted once again.

"Let's go down to Martin's Pub!" said Lek.

But just as Lek was about to accelerate, they heard someone calling, "Lek, Lek! Hi, it's me!"

It was Moa, a friend of Lek's with whom she had hung out in the past, but who had lately gone her own way.

"Hi, Moa! What are you doing here?" Lek asked her.

"Well, I could ask you the same thing and who's this?" Moa asked, scrutinizing Lek's passenger.

"This is my friend, Prim. We go to the same school and we thought we'd have some fun tonight. Are you coming?" Lek asked her.

"Sure! Where are you headed?" Moa replied.

"We thought about going to Martin's Pub," Lek confirmed. "I think some guys I know might be there, well, you know, Ian and his mates."

"But I don't think they'll let us in at that place," Moa said.

" Let's try! I can ask Ian to come out and get us in if there's a problem," Lek said enthusiastically.

"Prim, have you hung out with Lek and her friends before?" asked Moa.

"Yes, a few times," replied Prim.

"It usually gets quite wild," said Moa, who was only slightly older than Prim, although it would be hard for anyone to figure out the girls' ages in the dark anyway.

"Climb on and we'll head straight there!" said Lek.

To have three or even four people riding on the same motorbike was not considered strange in Laos. Often, you saw a whole family riding along on just one motorbike. The police would never stop you for a thing like that.

Quite soon, the three adventurous girls arrived at Martin's Pub. As expected, Ian was standing outside the bar talking with some friends inside. Bars in these districts were seldom, if ever, surrounded by high walls or anything else that might block the view of their interiors. That customers had this clear view from outside is actually part of the pitch to them to come inside. Above all, male customers had to be able to see into the bars to find out whether there were any young girls for sale.

Ian, who was well known by the owners of the bar, was talking to a man with fair hair who stood to his right, either a European or an American. To Ian's left were his old buddies, Nong and Lim.

"Hi, Ian," said Lek.

He replied with an arrogant "Hi!" and didn't even bother to look at her, but he did look at Moa and Prim. Lek felt hurt; she could never have imagined that he would ignore her like that. It seemed as if he didn't even want to pretend to know her.

Lek kept a stiff upper lip while confirming to herself what a bastard he was. The blonde guy understood the situation, turned to Lek and introduced himself.

"I'm Stephen, from England," he said confidently, as he looked into Lek's inquisitive eyes.

She had had lessons in English in school, as well as a little practice in various situations, but she had never spoken with an Englishman before.

Moa and Prim grasped the opportunity to greet Ian and then Ian's other mates approached the girls.

"I'm Nong; this is Lim."

The girls were trying to appear urbane, but not very successfully. Neither of them had had much experience of the night life of central Luang Prabang. Nong became interested in Prim right away.

"Do you live here in the village?" he asked.

"Village? This is the town! I live up in the mountains," said Prim, revealing neither her village's name nor its location.

She did not want to bring her village into the discussion and hoped it was a place she would soon forget. As she spoke, she could hear the conversation beginning between Lim and Moa. Lim should have been called 'Slimy', really. He was a smarmy customer, buttering the young girl up right from the start.

Nong kept on talking with Prim, even as he noticed her attention was drawn elsewhere.

"Are you listening to me at all?" he asked her. "Maybe you don't like me standing here chatting with you?"

"Not at all, I was just thinking that I'd better be off home soon." she said.

"But why? It's just seven o'clock," he said.

Getting home would probably take two hours but Prim decided that she would stay a little longer.

"May I buy you a drink?" Nong asked Prim and turning to Moa, he asked her as well, "Would you like a drink too?"

"Yes please," she said.

The guys would have no problems ordering the drinks as they were all over eighteen.

"What would you like?" Nong continued.

"I'd like to taste one of those margaritas," said Moa.

"I'll have one too," added Prim.

"Are you having drinks?" asked Lek, in awkward English.

"Yeah," replied Moa and Stephen.

Stephen – who did not know Lim and Nong – closed in on them now, with the help of the girls.

"Are these your friends, Lek?" he asked.

"Yeah that's right. This is Prim and this is Moa," said Lek trying to be suave.

Ian had now been shuffled to the back of the pack and quickly became aware of it.

They went into the bar and sat down at a table. Nong ordered Margaritas for everyone. "Large ones," he told the bartender. "We don't want any ice in the glasses. Just shaking them with ice will do. Ice takes away some of the flavour." Nong sounded as if he wanted to teach the bartender his job.

"My treat!" said Ian.

"No, I've already paid for it," Nong pointed out.

"Okay, I'll buy the next round," Ian replied.

Ian tried to establish contact with Moa, but she knew what he and Lek had been up to and wanted to have nothing to do with him. The drinks were carried to the table.

"Bottoms up!" Ian cried out.

"No, easy does it!" said Stephen, who was older than Ian.

"Easy? I'm going to down mine in one go," Ian replied.

While the others sipped carefully away, he knocked his drink back and ordered another straight away.

Lek was receiving more and more attention from Stephen, who was stroking her cheek lightly while drinking to her health. The Englishman was much older than her. Old enough, in fact, to be her father.

"What do you do? What is your line of work?" he asked, although he was quite aware that she would probably lie about both her occupation and her age.

"I've just finished school. I know I shouldn't be here, drinking but I'll be sixteen soon, you see," Lek replied, blushing.

"I see," Stephen said. Her honesty had not been unanticipated.

"Where are you from?" asked Lek. "And how old are you?"

"I'm from a city in England called Bath and I'm twenty-seven," he replied.

For some time, they said nothing. Both of them were sipping their drinks, waiting for the other to break the silence.

"Damn, it's quiet here!" exclaimed Ian, who had had two large margaritas while the others were still halfway through their first.

"Yes, we think before we speak," said Stephen.

Ian turned and addressed Lek. "Come! Let's go to my place!"

"No thanks," she replied, rejecting Ian in the same cold manner with which he had treated her earlier.

"What the hell! Why don't all of us go to my place?" said Ian, turning to the others, "Lim, bring Moa and let's get out of here."

"Yeah," Lim said and turned to Nong who objected. The rest of them wanted to finish their drinks first.

"Okay," said Ian. "I'll just have to wait."

"I don't want to go back to his place," Lek said quietly to Stephen.

He imagined the two of them doing just that. He reckoned he could teach her a thing or two.

"Have you drunk up?" asked Lim. "Let's have another one that'll be tastier and go down quicker."

"Which one's that?" asked Moa.

Ian sighed in resignation.

"The B-52. It's great and it'll suit us fine," replied Lim. He called out to the bartender, "We'd like seven B-52s, all at once."

The guys all knew exactly what a B-52 was. In contrast, none of the girls had drunk them before and in Prim's case, the margarita was the first alcoholic drink she had finished. She thought it was rather good and would gladly have had another, if someone had offered her one. It was half past eight now and Prim's worries about the trip home had vanished. She was having a great time with the guys.

The B-52s were brought to the table and all disappeared quickly down the throats of the seven drinkers. Nong and Lim mentioned that they lived in Vientiane, the capital and that they worked at an advertising agency. Moa and Prim were all ears.

"What is it that you do, exactly?" asked Moa.

"We take photos and make adverts for cars, books, motorcycles, food, amongst other things," Nong replied.

"Okay, so if you took a photo of me on a bike and put me in an ad, you could make me famous overnight, could you?" Moa asked.

"Yes of course! Come to Vientiane and I'll get you a job as a model," Nong confirmed.

"Did you hear that?" Moa said to Lek and Prim. "They can get me a job as a model!"

"Okay," said Lek. "If Moa is to become a model, then so shall I."

"No problem," said Lim. "I'm sure that can be arranged."

"Well, are we leaving, or what?" said Ian, "Let's go! Are you coming, girls?"

"Yes," all three said, "we're coming." Prim's objections to going back to Ian's place had vanished entirely with the second drink.

"You can come too, Stephen," added Ian. "Despite your arrogance."

"Ian," Stephen said, pulling him to the side, "I'm not being arrogant. It's just that if you go on like this, you'll mess everything up for the rest of us and we'd really like to pull these little cuties. Ease up a little, will you? That's all."

"Alright," said Ian. "But Lek's mine; I've fucked her before."

"Oh yeah!" said Stephen. "But it's time you found someone else. I understand why she's turning away from you. You're downright rude to the girl. I think it's too late."

"I don't give a fuck about her!" said Ian, "And if she's a dead-end, I'm sure Moa's willing."

"Lim seems to be hell-bent on buttering her up, so let her be for now, you hear!" Stephen insisted.

*

All seven of them were quite drunk when they finally left Martin's Pub. Ian lived on Kitsarat Road at the corner of Witsunarat, so it wasn't a long walk. Along the way, Ian and Stephen were rather quiet. Lim and Nong, on the other hand, were chatting away with Moa, Prim and Lek, who managed to lead the motorbike all the way to Ian's place despite her being very tipsy indeed.

"Would you really like to become models?" asked Lim.

"What type of models?" asked Moa.

"The kind we talked about in the bar," said Nong. "Photographers' models, of course. We can get you jobs pretty quickly."

All three of them were delighted and said they were interested.

"How cool is that!" Lek said to Moa. "My classmates would never believe me if I told them."

"Neither would mine," replied Moa. "And what would my brother say? He would be so jealous!"

As usual, there was no one home at Ian's place this time of the evening. His mother was working late and didn't care whether there would be people in the house when she came back anyway. She would just be pleased that Ian was home. It was a corner house, sparsely lit outside. Ian led the way inside, showing everybody into the rather dark accommodation: two rooms and a small kitchen. The kitchen was located at the rear of the building, outdoors naturally; only the well-to-do and westerners did their cooking indoors. Ian went to fetch beer and a bottle of Mekong whiskey, which he took from his mother's collection.

"Here's, some beer and whiskey. Who wants beer?" Ian called out.

"We all want whiskey," replied Stephen, without any objection from the others.

Ian poured seven whiskies, gave everybody a glass and shouted "Cheers!" as they all drank.

Prim did not feel well at all. It was getting too late after all. She asked Lek whether she could borrow the motorbike to get home. If not, she wouldn't be able to make it tonight.

"Of course you can, but you could wait a while, couldn't you?" Lek said.

"No," said Prim, "I want to get home now." She was firm. The feeling that she was about to lose control had scared her.

"Here's the key! Go whenever you like, sourpuss," Lek replied.

"I'm not sour," Prim responded. "It's just that I feel I have to."

"That's okay," Stephen cut in. "We'll meet some other evening. Can I get in touch with you in some way? Do you have a number I could call?"

"No, I haven't," Prim told him, playing hard to get.

What she actually longed to say was that she lived up in the mountains, among the Hmong and that they had neither telephones nor electricity, sometimes not even food on the table and that they couldn't really afford the clothes she was wearing, which were borrowed. Everybody up there was poor and would do anything for money, including risking their lives. But she kept all of this to herself.

"We could meet. Where do you live?" she asked him.

"I'm staying in Satri House, at the northern part of the sports field, but I'm probably leaving next week. I can accompany you outside and make sure that the motorbike starts up alright," he suggested. His manners and apparent decency made Prim feel secure.

"Bye, bye then!" she called out and went off with Stephen.

Inside the house, Nong was leaning toward Lim. They were looking at each other cunningly, leering and whispering.

"Shall we give it a try?" said Nong, nodding in the direction of Moa's breasts.

"Hell, yeah!" said Lim.

"Hey girls, about that modelling job. I think we should find time to talk about it a bit before we take off," Nong said.

"Yes," replied Moa and Lek at the same time. "We'd love to."

"Would you like something more to drink?" Ian asked with a smile.

"Of course," said Lim.

Ian topped up everybody's glasses once more.

"Put on some music," suggested Lim.

Ian put on a record by Rod Stewart which his father had given him a long time ago. It was almost worn out. But good old

Rod could apparently still make young girls move and move they did, more and more.

"Turn it down a bit!" said Lim. "We've gotta talk about this now."

"Moa, take off your top so we can see if you have the right figure for modelling!" said Nong. "And you too, Lek!"

"I don't know," said Lek. "I don't think I want to."

"Come on! It's important. All the models do it," Lim told them.

"One part of the job is to model bikinis, so you have to have nice breasts," Ian pointed out. "Lim and Nong just have to make sure you have what it takes."

"Come on now," said Lim again, "or we can just forget about it."

"Okay," said Moa and removed her tank top and blouse.

Suddenly, she was standing half nude before the guys, who scrutinised her in silence.

"You too!" Lim said to Lek.

"Okay, I guess I have to do it then," she said and pulled off her tank top.

"Hey, we gotta celebrate this with another drink," shouted Ian.

Ian poured once more and everybody drank. Before long, Moa and Lek felt it was actually okay to stand around half undressed.

In the meantime, Prim and Stephen were still standing, talking outside. Stephen was trying to keep her from leaving by talking about things she liked. But suddenly, it was as if she had woken from his spell. She said she had to leave and there was nothing he could do about it. She said goodbye and drove away while he went back inside. To his surprise, he encountered two half-naked girls.

"Oh, super!" he said. "What's going on here?"

"They'd like to be models at our firm," Lim explained. "So we have to take a look and mull it over."

Stephen cried out in delight, "I want to become a model too!"

He tore off his shirt and placed himself between Moa and Lek, holding the laughing girls against his naked torso.

"If you have a camera, Ian, take our picture!" he cried out.

"Me too," said Lim and jumped in.

"I want to be a part of this too," Nong said and pulled his shirt off too.

Ian was snapping away as they posed. Suddenly, he jumped to attention.

"Oh hell! My mother will be home soon. You gotta put on your clothes and leave! Hurry up! It'll be eleven soon. You've got to get out of here."

"Okay, we're off," said the guys.

"What's happening?" asked Lek.

"I don't know," said Moa, "But I know that if Ian's mother saw us all here half-naked, she'd go bananas. Mine certainly would."

Everybody put their clothes back on and ran out.

"We'll get in touch," said Lim. "Trust us. It'll take a couple of weeks, though."

"That's okay," replied Moa. "I'll be expecting to hear from you."

They parted outside the house. Moa and Lek headed home, part of the way together.

The guys took a different road. One that led them back to Martin's Pub, not with a view to having more drinks, but hoping to fulfil their objective of finding new girls for the 'model' jobs. This was what they were paid to do, to recruit girls on commission. The boys were young and smart and could easily make contact with young girls and lure them with pipe dreams.

This was all the more true when it came to girls from the poorer districts.

Prim was riding the borrowed motorbike on her way home, without the faintest inkling of what was about to befall her friends.

Chapter 15

Mekong Secrets

It was probably fortunate that the five men had navigated the river before, many times in fact. The remains of a number of boats along the stretch testified to the power of the Mekong. When the river was in its worst mood, it was best to stay on dry land. If, on the other hand, it was fairly sensible, which could be seen clearly enough from the behaviour of the water on the surface, it was not so dangerous, provided you had some experience of riverboats and knew how to avoid the rapids.

Songchai knew his Mekong and so did the others, for that matter. He knew exactly where there were good hideouts along the riverbank, practically all the way down to Vietnam. A long time ago, they had carried weapons along this same route and just as they were doing now, had risked their lives in the process. Back then, it was for war, however, rather than profit. At the moment, they were on their way to Ban Pak Man, a river trip of about one hundred and sixty kilometres, which would take the rest of the night and the lion's share of the next day.

Along the way, there were no more than five hamlets. Plenty of glances were cast at the boats from within the huts that they passed by. The risk involved was low because the Mekong was used for transport and smuggling of all sorts of things and few people along the route cared. But Songchai knew, all the same, that if they ended up being caught by soldiers who weren't willing to take bribes, the odds were they'd be shot on the spot. Of course, the soldiers might choose to arrest them and torture them to death instead, not because they were smugglers but because they were Hmong and therefore, legitimate prey.

For the time being, they were each sitting in their respective boats. Songchai was in the first; in his wake came

Surachai, then Supot, Kitepong and lastly Voratep. They could barely see one another, just the paraffin lamps on their aft decks. The only things in existence seemed to be the night sky and its stars with the moon rising over the trees bathing the river in a silvery glimmering light. As they were gliding down the Mekong, they were also gliding down memory lane.

*

Kitepong found himself transported back to Sala Phukhoun in 1975. He was on Road 13 between Vientiane and Luang Prabang. He had a crucial decision to make. Was he to desert, thereby putting his life at stake?

Just as the Americans were withdrawing their aid from the Hmong leader, Vang Pao and the Secret Army, the communist movement Pathet Lao, was driving the Hmong forces away. Kitepong had heard rumours that Vang Pao had surrendered, after the loss of more than a thousand men. Vang Pao had managed to escape to the US, thanks to the American help, taking with him his six wives along with his twenty-five children. These flights took the supposedly important figures first of all. Only then, was there room for others. Kitepong believed Vang Pao had betrayed his people.

It was in the village of Ban Sen, further south on Road 13, that he had met her, the woman who had told him what had happened, the woman whose name he had forgotten, perhaps she had never found the time to say it. He had become fond of her. They had ended up in the same hiding place along the road, just the two of them. There was heavy fighting in this area, the so called Plain of Jars, all the way down to the border with Vietnam. To move about was to dice with death. Kitepong was not the only one hiding; thousands were doing the same. They lay hidden for three days without any food with only rainwater to quench their thirst.

The final day and night, they held each other tightly, two bodies united in one. Was it the horror, the fear of death and the overwhelming craving for security that made it happen? They did not even know one another and she was no prostitute. She simply had the same yearning to be loved in the midst of this horror. Was this why he was thinking about her now, out here on the river? She, who happened to be there then, only to disappear from his life.

*

In the boat behind Kitepong's sat his friend, Voratep, lost in his own thoughts. Now and then, he found that he was speaking to himself, though not loud enough for anyone else to hear, although it was difficult to hear anything above the six-cylinder engine of a Lao riverboat with straight exhaust pipes. It was a miracle that they managed to install these engines in such slender vessels and to make them stay put. This type of boat was only a little more than one metre wide and just half a metre high where the planking was at its lowest. Usually, it was made up of both old and new timber, painted with surplus paint and equipped with a pair of seats and a steering wheel from some old Isuzu pick-up. With their raised floors, designed to hide weapons and mines and curtains of plastic and canvas, it was a wonder that these boats managed to stay afloat at all. Boats like these were used for transporting everything, including people, staking their lives on the journey.

Voratep was mulling over what he would do with the money he would earn from delivering his portion of the cargo down in Khemmarat, if they managed to make it there. During the war, he had swum, hidden and killed in the Mekong. On this river, he had sat crying many times in the stillness of the night. "River of memories," Voratep said to himself as he sat beneath the moon. The very same moon that once had been his enemy, when during the war, its light had revealed both him and his enemies. All these years later, he was still on his guard, constantly suspicious of people.

He had lost his whole family under the most horrific of circumstances. But they were always with him, even now. In his solitude out on the Mekong, his wife and his two daughters were with him. They had not survived to see the end of the war. The sorrow ground his heart and his loved ones were in the river, in the trees, on the ground on which he trod, among the stars he was looking at, yes, in everything. The worst times were when he felt like he actually recognised one of them in a crowd and walked up to grab hold of them before realising this was a complete stranger.

His daughters and his wife had been arrested by Vietnamese soldiers at the border. They were not killed, but handed over to army brothels, which had always existed, especially during times of war. Hundreds of thousands of women and young girls were abducted by military forces and transported to these brothels. Many of them did not survive for long. There might be up to sixty soldiers, young as well as old, waiting outside a room with only one bed and inside, just one girl or young woman who, in many cases, never left it.

The moment Voratep realised that this was how his daughters had met their deaths, he was overwhelmed by a hatred that would never fade for as long as he remained among the living. There, sliding down the river, he spoke with them and told them what he planned to do when the journey was over.

He knew that there were a great number of brothels along the borders between Burma, Thailand and Laos and that some of them were located around Mea Sai in Thailand. The most terrible of them were in Tachilek on the Burmese side, just at the border and not more than sixty kilometres from Chiang Rai in northern Thailand. A steady stream of so-called VIPs visited the great Golden Triangle Casino there, guests from as far away as China and Japan. The reason for the casino's popularity was that it offered virgins, who could fetch a price of up to five thousand dollars.

The brothels of these districts were known as 'breaking-in stations'. This meant that those who were sent there were forced to endure six months of violent adjustment to brothel life and to get used to spending the rest of their lives as prostitutes, wherever in the world they might be sold. At the brothels, there were girls not older than thirteen. What age they would reach was another matter.

Voratep was keen on the idea of putting this practice to an end. The casino was located close to the Mekong, so it was possible to get there by water. At his disposal, he had both a boat and weapons.

He had objectives of his own which no one else knew about. He would have been glad to know how many organisations there were in the world on his side, but using very different methods from those Voratep had on his mind, his plan was both drastic and ruthless.

*

Supot steered his boat skilfully between the small dangers that poked up through the surface of the water. Now and then, he looked up at the stars to which he owed his life. He was one of the forty thousand Hmong who had escaped into Thailand during the final days of the war, over and via the Mekong. He had been positioned close to the banks of the river, just south of Sanakham and now, he felt a pang of anxiety over returning there. All of those who had tried to flee to Thailand had been gassed with 'Yellow rain', a poisonous gas the Lao regime used against the Hmong.

From his place aft, he found himself unconsciously listening out for slowly flying biplanes, planes that would drop a type of bomb that exploded just over the treetops, spreading a cloud of red, yellow and white. After such an explosion, the people who came into contact with the poison would lie on the beach vomiting blood, bleeding from their nose and their eyes. Later, they would experience blood in their faeces. Supot himself had endured terrible pains in his chest and been unconscious for two days and nights before he woke to continue his escape. He ended up in the village of Phu Nio, only about ten kilometres north of Sanakham, where he recovered after a day or two. Then, he took himself on to Sanakham in order to try once more to get into a refugee camp in Thailand.

A great number of people came under fire from border guards, or were tricked by guides into walking straight into the jaws of the Lao army. If they were men, they were shot. If they were women, they were raped and taken to military brothels, re-education camps or made to vanish in some other way.

Supot reckoned that the damned river ought to be red, from the immense number of people who had lost their lives in it and along its banks. But it was just as brown as ever. All those thousands upon thousands of restless spirits, desperate to rise to the surface and into freedom. What a waste of human life. Supot longed for his scrapyard back home.

*

Surachai kept a constant eye on Songchai and his boat. He was aware how well the old man knew the river and it was easiest to follow him. But if Songchai happened to founder on a rock and capsize, he would most definitely not interfere. He would be happy to see Songchai vanish, just not too soon.

Although younger, Surachai was a more experienced smuggler than the others. He earned his keep chiefly from the transport of counterfeit goods from China including clothes, watches and jewellery. It was a profitable market for those who sold within the larger tourist cities of Thailand, where his travels had taken him a number of times.

He had been considering certain business proposals he had been offered, which might turn out well when he returned. A couple of times, he had managed to sell opium to visitors up in Luang Prabang, transactions that had gone very smoothly. Together with a mate, he would ride about in Luang Prabang on a motorcycle. They had cruised slowly past the bars, turned to the guests as they came out and asked them quietly if they were interested in buying opium. Often, they struck lucky and made some cash. But Charlie, his partner, got into trouble. He had become reckless and was caught by the drug squad in Nong Kai on the Thai side. He had wanted a larger slice of the cake and had taken the drugs to a buyer in Bangkok all by himself. The affair ended with him sitting in Klong Prem prison – popularly known as the Bangkok Hilton – in the company of ten to twelve thousand other prisoners, of whom around five hundred were usually foreigners. Charlie was given a life sentence and that was the end of the drug business for Surachai.

He thought about his lover, who had planted a seed in his mind, a seed that had grown into a business concept. Naturally, it involved smuggling, but it also involved buying and selling, a sort of agency. In the end, it would help the poor and those in distress. It's really an honest job, he decided, to provide work for poor girls.

*

Bam! The noise came from underneath, in the bows. The current had grown stronger and his attention to Songchai had waned during the last few minutes. The boat swayed roughly. Then, there was another bang, this time, in the aft.

"Bloody hell! What's happening?" Surachai said out loud.

Supot had seen the boat ahead of him sway and had heard that last bang. Voratep and Kitepong had also grasped the situation and darted towards Surachai. Songchai, however, just kept on going.

Surachai noticed that the engine was out of balance and the boat was shaking, causing him to lose control. He had to turn off the engine and drift on the current. Supot accelerated and was the first to reach Surachai, but Voratep and Kitepong were not far behind.

"What happened?" Supot shouted.

"I think the propeller's bust," Surachai replied. "I had to turn off the engine, since the whole boat was about to shake to bits!"

"Okay, hand me some lines when I pull up beside your boat!" Supot shouted.

Supot positioned his boat along Surachai's port side, with Voratep along Surachai's starboard and Kitepong at the bow. They knew exactly what to do. With deft fingers, they tied the boats together and when everything was rigged, they floated skilfully on the current like one boat without any serious loss of speed. Surachai was impressed by their skill and determination.

"All you have to do," Supot told him, "is to stay at the helm and hold it like you did before, otherwise you'll just be getting in the way."

It was then that Songchai became aware of what had happened and that the others had come to Surachai's rescue. He simply slowed down a little to check everything was under control and then on he went, down the river.

Songchai lost himself once more in thoughts and memories: Mak, Fang, Pom's death, the yard. Why had they stayed in Laos after the war? They had only become poorer and poorer. They should have left the country when they saw that all the civil servants were being replaced and all the official buildings were being ransacked. The commies had taken everything and grown rich. And then, there was that prime minister, Souvanna Phouma, who said he felt sorry for the Hmong people and made the comment, "since the peace will exterminate them." What an idiot!

*

Before long, they were down at Ban Pak Man, which was to be their first stop and their camp for the night. Despite Surachai's incident, the journey had gone more swiftly than Songchai had anticipated. He waited for the others, who were not far behind.

"I suggest that we put in at the small harbour coming up soon on our right," he shouted.

"Got it," said Supot smiling at the others.

"Let's rest until daybreak. Then, we'll fill up with fuel and figure out the easiest way to fix the damage on Surachai's boat."

"Sounds fine," Supot said and nodded to the others. "Everything's under control."

Ban Pak was a fairly small village at the edge of the Mekong. The population, a few hundred families, lived off river freight, animal husbandry and the cultivation of rice. Songchai reckoned that it would be easy enough to find a propeller for Surachai's boat here. There was always some wreck lying around with the propeller intact with the rest of the vessel so rotten that you didn't even need tools to remove both the engine and the propeller shaft.

Soon, they saw the piers and the buoys stretching out in the water. Songchai switched off his engine and turned towards the sandbank in front of the jetty, letting his boat glide up onto land. A pole, two metres long, rose up by the stern and Songchai lashed his boat to it, safely anchoring his vessel to the land.

For the others, things did not go quite so smoothly. They had to go about it the same way as Songchai, but they were heavier and had problems manoeuvring towards land.

"Crank up the gas!" Supot ordered. "We've got to push ourselves up onto the beach by force. When the prow of the first boat is on land, I'll throw a line to Songchai and then you can all turn off your engines. Then, you need to jump into the water and untie the boats from each other. Pull up the boats by hand, one at a time and lash them down for the night."

Supot led everything like a general. It was a relief for Songchai, who followed all of Supot's orders, that there was someone else who could assume responsibility.

In thirty minutes, everything was done. Meanwhile, Songchai had managed to work himself up over Surachai's negligence.

"Bloody hell!" he erupted. "From now on, you'd better pull your socks up, kiddo! You gotta be on the alert! Were you sitting and dozing off in the boat, or what? Don't you understand what we're trying to do here! I don't give a damn whether you get wrecked or not, but if you risk our cargo one more time, or our lives, I promise I'll fucking kill you! Let's get some damn sleep."

When they had cast a final glance at the moorings, each man returned to his respective boat. Swiftly, they fell into much needed sleep, except Surachai. He lay awake thinking about Songchai's reaction. There was always something that displeased that man. It was quite obvious that the old fart had a grudge against him. What could it be about, though? Surachai couldn't figure it out. Songchai had had yet another go at him, in front of the others. The old man made jibes at him. Songchai, who would do well to look out from now on as a lot of things could happen on the river.

Chapter 16

The Woman with One Tooth

Lu did not get much sleep. There was more than one reason for that. Obviously there was the bed. There were the events of the day. There were her worries over Prim. But there was also a racket going on all over the hotel: people talking, cars coming and going and other strange noises she could not identify. The morning came, with light filtering through the plain cotton curtains. Lu got up and opened the window to let the air into the small room. The thin curtain was swinging back and forth in the morning wind, which came down from the mountains like a caress of silk. Then she did what was forbidden, once dawn had broken, she laid herself down on the bed again since it was not yet time for breakfast. And this time, she fell asleep deeply, very deeply. She dreamed herself back to times past, all the way back to when Pom was alive. He was out in the yard playing, hunting the cat in the heat of the sun. He was so alive and real that Lu could touch him. She saw his smile, heard his laughter and his shouts, saw how he was teasing Prim and then suddenly, a bang. Lu woke up, cold sweat all over. The bang had been a hard knock on the door. Then, she heard Will calling.

"Lu, open up! Are you there?" he said.

"Yes, I'm here," Lu replied, still half asleep and more than a little jittery.

"Why didn't you answer?" Will asked from the other side of the door.

"I fell asleep," she called out.

"Have you any idea what time it is?" Will asked without thinking. Lu had no watch and followed the sun. "Lu, it's nearly half past nine. And if you'd like some breakfast, you'd better hurry to the dining-room. Frank and I have been there a while already."

Lu freshened up quickly and ran, shamefaced, down to breakfast and the table where they had planned to meet a couple of hours earlier.

"I'm so sorry. I got up as I'd intended. But once I'd dressed, I lay down again. I shouldn't have, of course, but I slept badly last night and was still tired."

Will had some sympathy for her.

"What was going on here last night, in this godforsaken hotel? It was like the whole village spent the night here. It was all a bit weird, I reckon," he said. " I have my suspicions, but let's not talk about it here," Will continued, wearily.

"Let's hurry over to Crater Bar to see if we can get hold of Spencer," Frank suggested after nodding in agreement.

"He's probably not there yet," Will said.

"Well, I don't want to wait," Frank said. "We need to talk to him as soon as possible. Otherwise, today will go to waste as well and I can't accept that."

"Let's pay and take off. We won't be coming back here for the night, anyway," Will said.

"You go out and pay the check. I'll just finish my tea before I fetch our stuff from our room. Have you got your things ready, Lu?" Frank asked.

"Yes," she replied.

Frank finished his tea, got up and went off with Lu following. When they passed the plain reception counter, Surasak was smiling at them, a knowing smile with clear sexual implications. However, he had got all of that wrong. Those were not Frank's motivations.

After Frank had returned to the room, they went to the parking area where their car stood waiting, thoroughly warmed by the sun. In fact, it was hot as hell.

Frank opened the door to the driver's seat and was immediately hit not only by the high temperature, but by an odour as well, the odour of sweaty human bodies, not just theirs but of everyone who had ever rented the car before them. After a couple of minutes, they managed to get seated in the car like before with Frank at the wheel, Lu by his side and Will in the back.

"I'll drive. You drive like a bat out of hell and we don't want the people here getting hostile just because you're covering everyone you pass on the road with dust," Frank remarked to Will.

He drove slowly and greeted the few people they saw along the route as if he had known them for years. At Crater Bar, they piled out of the car and went inside where Spencer's wives, or whatever they were, were standing in line, as if they had known that the trio would be coming in through the door at that very moment.

"Hello," they greeted the new arrivals cheerfully, "what would you like for breakfast?"

"Nothing thanks," Will said, "we've already eaten something you might call breakfast."

"It's probably better here," Frank pointed out and looked at Lu.

"I'm quite sure of it," she replied.

"No, no breakfast, but we would very much like to meet Spencer again. We hope that would be okay. He's not ill, is he?" Frank asked with a glint in his eye, which the women understood.

"No, I don't think so," they replied, almost simultaneously. "Mr Spencer is just out on his regular walk stretching his stiff joints."

"Yeah," Will answered, smiling. "I remember back when my body was supple and soft, except for one thing and now, it's the opposite – everything else has stiffened up – except for one thing."

"That can be taken care of, really quickly," Frank observed, "with some Viagra." Everyone laughed.

It was a relief to be able to joke a bit with these ladies.

Although it had taken Lu a few days, she was now used to the Americans' jargon and their sense of humour.

"We'll get you some coffee while you wait. Just be seated," one of the women said.

The coffee arrived at the table much more quickly than it had done on their previous visit. It was hot and to their great astonishment, tasted really good. Will and Frank slurped their drinks with delight while they walked around the room, looking at all the aerial photos. Suddenly, the door opened and in came Spencer.

"Good morning," he said and shook hands, just like on the previous day. There could be no mistaking his background.

"Guys, if you don't mind me calling you that, except you of course," Spencer said and looked at Lu.

"It's okay," she replied and smiled at him.

"I've done some research," he continued. "As you may know, you don't sleep as much when you get old, so I've spent a couple of hours on our lost boys, Nick and Tom. If you guys hadn't turned up, this would never have come to light. It all happened such a long time ago, you know and everybody here in this country, as well as in Vietnam, most likely believe that everything that can be found already has been. But I've come to the conclusion that this isn't the case and that there are probably more guys left out there in addition to Nick and Tom."

"We need to know everything about this area, both its past and present," Will said.

"And meet other people that know something about it," Frank added.

Lu sat silent, feeling like the odd one out, but she knew her time would come.

"You have to bear one thing in mind," Spencer told them. "You are in an area populated mainly by Vietnamese, that is, people who might have killed the men you're looking for. I hope you understand that you'll have to tread carefully around here and things might get dangerous. And you, Lu, do you know the background of all this?"

"Yes, some of it," she said. "The idea is that I am to translate when needed and try to find people who can help us out."

"Yeah," Will cut in. "We got in contact with Lu in Luang Prabang and found her easy to get on with and she is Hmong to boot."

"That might pose a problem for you," Spencer warned. "Be wary of speaking about it. You do know that Lao and Vietnamese forces cooperated to do everything in their power to drive the Hmong out of the country? And now, thirty years later, it's still dangerous for the Hmong to stay around their former enemies. But enough of that. Like I said, I've done some research among the people I know around here and I've discovered that down by the lake, Nong Nam Nyam, there was a military camp where they used to take prisoners of war, Hmong folk, usually. A bit further south down at the village of Lat Kai, there used to be another camp. I'm talking about the place right before the tanks that now stand there, on the opposite side of the road. Those are Russian tanks, by the way, used by the commies. Of course, these days, they're just standing there, corroding away. The camp down at Lat Kai was more of a barracks, in contrast to the one up in Nong Nam Nyam. That one was a camp where military advisors, usually Russians and Chinese, stayed, together with officers from the Vietnamese army. I can tell you this now, since I know who you guys are. But I don't want to advertise my background. I've left the war behind me now and

I'd rather not be reminded about it. But this kind of thing is important and what I'm doing right now, I do willingly, for my country and my people."

"Okay," Frank said. "We understand, Spencer. There's no reason for us to let other people bother you. We will be as discreet as we can be regarding your involvement."

"We'll investigate the places you've mentioned. What do you reckon our chances are of finding people who were at these camps during the period we're talking about?" asked Will.

"Well, I guess there still are a couple of them living in the valley. But it might get quite pricey," Spencer replied.

"How much are we talking about here?" Frank asked. "A thousand dollars?"

"Wow," Spencer said. "That's what most people here make in half a year of labour. It'll be enough to get most of them talking. But if you throw that kind of money around without being careful, you'll end up hearing too many stories, half of them untrue, so you'd better take it easy until you find the right informant."

The day had hardly even got started, but already it felt like they were on the right track.

"Okay," Frank said. "Let's head down to the camps and check them out. For now, we'll just take a look. And we'll come back to you later on, Spencer. We would appreciate it very much if you could help us to get further when we do."

"Of course," Spencer replied.

"We'll get going, then," Will said as he got up.

"What a fluke we didn't get stuck in the bar on the other side of the street," Will observed when they got into the car to drive off.

"Yeah, you probably ought to steer clear of that shithole," Frank said, making a U-turn across the street.

"Let's go down to Lat Kai first," Will suggested. "I'd very much like to check out those old Russian tanks."

"Alright, but remember, that's not the main reason we're going there," Frank reminded him. "Now, we're beginning a new phase of this job."

*

On the way to Lat Khai, they passed the small lake on their left. They also passed the camp they planned to visit later on, if they did not find anything interesting first. As they passed the small village of Lat San, Will spoke up, "Damn! I've never seen so much scrap from a war. They even make tractors out of old army lorries."

The narrow road got them swiftly to Lat Kai. It was obvious that the place had been a military camp, some of the barracks were still there. Nowadays, however, they served as accommodation for homeless people, among other uses.

"Well, it's clear we're in an extremely poor area," Frank said.

"Yes, there are plenty of those in Laos," Lu told him, thinking of her own village.

"Do you think it would be alright if we were to do a bit of door knocking, to see if we can find anyone who experienced the war and has been living here ever since?" Will asked.

"We could give it a try," Frank said. "We've got an interpreter with us. Let's stay on the outskirts of the camp, not go in, just the closest houses here."

"Why is that?" Lu asked.

"Well, I don't think people who were living in a military camp during the war would want to feel like they still live in such a place in peacetime. I'd imagine our questions will stir up some painful memories," Frank replied.

The car stopped and they all got out. Frank saw a little black pig running across the road, screaming as if someone had stuck it with a knife. On the other side of the road, there was a gravel track in serious need of repair, as usual, despite the fact that the authorities had most certainly received funds for its maintenance. Beyond the ditch, an old lady was standing, looking at them in wide-eyed wonder. Her old, pyjama-looking clothes were worn-out to the extent that they no longer clung to her body. Will had seen poverty before, many times, but this was something different.

"How old do you think she is?" he asked.

"I don't know," Frank replied, "but I'm curious enough to find out. Lu, could you talk with her and tell her that we just intend to take a look around? She looks scared."

"Sure," Lu answered and took a stride across the ditch to the old lady. "I'm Lu," she told the woman, who just stood silent and listened. "These people are friendly and are from another country," she continued, trying to sound as pleasant as possible.

"I see," the woman replied and when she started to speak, Lu saw that she had only one tooth, at the very front of her mouth.

The old woman was just over four feet tall, but the stick she was holding was a good six feet long. Suddenly, she laughed.

"I'm Noi. I just find them a bit odd looking," she said and laughed again. It was amusing to observe westerners.

"Have you been living here for a long time?" Lu asked.

"Almost all my life but before that, I lived up in Lat San," Noi replied.

"When did you move to this place?" Lu asked the next question.

"Well ..." Noi began to answer.

Meanwhile, Frank and Will had also crossed the road and were now standing just a few metres from her.

"I didn't move here. I was brought here by my superior officer," Noi said. "Since then, I've remained here about thirty-five years now."

Noi came across as very friendly and seemed to be enjoying the experience of someone wanting to talk with her.

"Where are you from?" Lu went on.

"I'm from the village of Ban Na Ka in North Vietnam, about a hundred kilometres the other side of the border," Noi began. "Like so many others, I fought against you during the war. I was a communist, you know. After the war, I wasn't allowed to go back to my village. Instead, I was ordered to help by living in this part of Laos. This would give me great advantages, they said, but look how it turned out. I have nothing and I'm getting no help. I have to get my food the best way I can. All I have is my little hut back here and these clothes I'm wearing. If we had known how things would turn out, a lot of people, me included, would have stayed home and not fought. Now, they bury us side by side."

Will and Frank stood in silence. They understood nothing of what Lu and Noi were saying. They just looked at the old woman, the way her cheeks turned hollow as she spoke and at her only tooth which looked like it was hopping about in her mouth.

Lu interrupted Noi to tell Will and Frank what she was saying. They listened with great interest.

"This is exciting," Will said.

Noi followed a Vietnamese pot-bellied pig with her eyes as it ran across the road into the yard. It was hers and made Lu think about Prim. For some reason, she was reminded of her own hut when she saw how Noi lived. Lu was adamant that she had to get home later in the day; she just had to.

"Lu, ask her if it would be okay for us to talk some more, in her yard," Frank said.

Lu did as he requested, but wondered why. What she said to Noi was that they wanted to talk about her time in this place and that they were journalists from a famous magazine in

Thailand on an assignment to make a tourist report. Noi brightened up.

"How interesting! Are they going to take my picture?" she asked.

"Sure," Lu said and smiled.

Noi invited them all into the yard asked them to sit down by a fire that had probably been kept alive for decades in the very same spot.

"This is nice," Will said. "There aren't many houses around here. Lu, you'll have to translate what I'm saying."

The yard itself was quite tidy, but around the edge of the plot were piles of lumber and plastics, highly dangerous, even for a pig.

"Do you live here all by yourself?" Lu asked tentatively.

"No," Noi replied. "I have a husband. He's out working for the day. You don't get many opportunities in this district."

"What's your husband's name?" Lu asked again.

"His name is Decha. I met him after the war. Or more precisely, I took care of him because he was so badly injured that if I hadn't nursed him, he would have died. He was so damaged that nobody else wanted him!" she added, laughing so hard her tooth almost fell out. "He's not Vietnamese; he belongs to the ethnic group called Khamu."

Lu understood now why Noi was so talkative. She lived here with a man who was not Vietnamese and she had probably been expelled from the social network of her village, not that she'd told them that, however. Noi would probably bring it up later on herself.

"Anyhow, things turned out that way. I took care of him and patched him up," Noi said, laughing again. "Later on, he recovered, but by then, I was already pregnant. It was too late. I liked him and that was enough to seal my fate. Back in the old days, when we were young, we said that we should leave Laos and go to Thailand to find work somewhere along the coast. But time flew and things just got worse."

"How old are you?" Lu asked.

"Well, I think I'm about fifty five," Noi replied and Lu was astonished.

"Wait a bit. I've got to translate what we're saying to the guys here."

"Of course," Noi said.

Lu told them what Noi had just said.

"Great, Lu," Frank replied. "Keep it up. We'll just sit around here for a while. Something useful might come up."

"Frank," Lu said seriously, "I must get home today. I'll take the bus leaving Phonsavan this afternoon. If I miss it, I'll hitchhike back."

"No, not at all," Frank told her. "We'll spend the day here and then we'll go back together. Will and I can return to this place if you need to be free. It's completely okay."

"Fine," Lu said, feeling a little more at ease.

"But Lu, go on. Keep asking the same sort of questions. Try to find out as much as you possibly can. Tell her we're willing to pay for certain information that might draw tourists. You know, we need to find out things about the camp on the other side of the road. But take it easy, so you don't frighten her," he said, cautioned her.

"I could never have imagined there being people this poor here," Will said.

"Well, come to my home district and you'll see," Lu told him. "You might not believe it, but at certain times of year, the only type of meat sold there is rat, especially during the rice harvest. Then, the rats get big enough to be attractive as food, so attractive that around that time of year, they're even sold at markets."

"Wow," Frank said. "I had no idea."

"I really hope that we don't have to eat rats," Will said.

"You can never tell, because people here are very clever at cooking them." Lu pointed out.

"Don't lose the thread now, Lu," Frank said.

Again, Lu turned to Noi, "When is your husband coming home?"

"When the sun sets," Noi replied.

"What a shame. We won't get to meet him today. But we can come again some other time," Lu confirmed. "So, you've been living here since the war?" she continued.

"No, not here precisely," Noi said. "I lived in an out-of-the-way spot, outside the village for a year before I moved to Lat San. After that, I joined in to help out clearing up this place when the camp had been evacuated. We were a couple of women who stayed. I've been here ever since."

"Have you got children here as well?" Lu asked.

"I had two daughters, but they are long gone," Noi replied.

"What do you mean gone?" Lu asked again.

"I'd rather not talk about it. I sold them," Noi said looking sad.

"What did you say? You sold them?" Lu said.

"Yes. They promised us that the girls would receive an education and good jobs," Noi explained.

"Do they send you money?" Lu asked.

"No. I got money when they left," Noi confirmed.

"How much did you get?" Lu asked, shocked.

"I got two hundred dollars," Noi said.

"Two hundred dollars for two girls! How old were they?" Lu asked.

"They were twelve and fourteen," Noi confirmed again.

Lu felt the hair rising on the back of her neck.

"What is it?" Will asked, staring at Lu.

Lu related the conversation to Frank and Will and concluded, "There are not many alternatives, but this is, by far, the worst one."

"Now that we have her warmed up, you could ask her what sort of establishment was on the other side of the road. But circle around the subject a bit first, so she doesn't realise we're ferreting about," Frank suggested.

They had been sitting for an hour around the fire, which now was merely smoking. If they did not get any further in this conversation soon, they would have to end it and try to talk with someone else.

"Noi, those Russian tanks over there by the roadside must have been a playground for the kids round here over the years. Is that right?" Lu continued.

"Yes, but they also meant a small income for us. Sometimes, an occasional tourist comes here. The tourists are attracted by the tanks and later, they want to see more of the valley and hear about what happened here," Noi replied.

"So, you're a kind of guide as well, then?" Lu asked.

"Yes, but not that often these days," Noi said.

"Could you tell us a bit about this place and what you've experienced here?" Lu said, a smile on her lips.

"Then I'd like to get paid," Noi said and looked pointedly at Frank and Will. Immediately, they understood what the old lady was after.

"How much?" Lu asked.

"One hundred thousand kip," Noi said, smiling.

"Okay," Lu replied and turned to Frank to inform him of the rate.

"It's just ten dollars," Frank said. "Go for it."

"We've got a hundred thousand kip for you, if you tell us what we would like to know," Lu told the woman.

"Don't beat about the bush," Will said. "Get straight to the point and ask her about the establishment on the other side of the road."

"Noi, during the war, this valley was full of Vietnamese soldiers, everybody knows that. It's even in the schoolbooks and the papers. But what type of camp was that one on the opposite side of the road?" Lu asked.

"It was barracks, accommodation for soldiers," Noi replied.

"Soldiers only?" Lu asked.

"Yes, that's what it was," Noi responded.

"So prisoners were never taken there?" Lu asked again.

"No, this place was just a training camp and accommodation, not a prison camp," Noi confirmed.

"Was there a prison close around here?" Lu inquired.

"No, there wasn't," Noi said.

"Was there any prison camp in the valley?" Lu tried again.

"None that I know of. There was a camp some ten kilometres from here, but that was no prison camp either. It was a camp for officers and advisors," Noi stated.

"Where was it situated?" Lu asked again.

"Down by the lake, towards Phonsavan," Noi confirmed.

Lu reported what Noi had told her to Will and Frank. Frank wanted them to round off the interview and leave.

"This has been most interesting," Lu said, "but now, I think we'd better be going. It's getting late and we have to move on."

"What a shame," Noi said, who was anxious not to lose the opportunity to make more money than she and her husband could make in a week of hard manual labour.

Everybody had just got up from their uncomfortable semi-recumbent positions on the ground when Noi suddenly spoke again.

"A long time ago, I heard that there were some prisoners of war being held at the camp by the lake, Americans, I think they were," she said.

Lu stiffened and then she looked at Frank and Will. Both stopped short.

"What did she say?" Frank asked.

"She said that many years ago, she heard a rumour that there were some Americans being held prisoner in the camp by the lake."

"Ask her what she knows about it!" Frank insisted.

Lu asked a couple of questions, but did not get the answers she was hoping for.

"She says that there was some talk about it at the end of the war. She just heard about it. She knows nothing more."

"Ask her if she knows of any people that might know more about this and where we could find them," Will said.

Lu asked her, but Noi fell silent.

"Please Noi, think hard," Lu encouraged her.

"It'll cost you a hundred thousand kip more," the old woman replied.

"A hundred thousand kip more? No, you can't have that. You get fifty thousand kip, not one kip more," Lu said.

"Yeah, we won't pay more than that," Frank said. "And it better be something concrete, otherwise we can do without it."

You couldn't mistake Frank's curiosity. Noi had noticed this as well. Frank's voice was like music to her ears and meant more money.

"We didn't get to know everything," Noi began, "but like I said earlier, we had to clear up the place when peace was declared. There was still money to be made by killing Hmong. They were chiefly against our programme, just like the Americans. A group of our battalion got the order to make sure nothing was to be left for history. It was then that a couple of us learned that the camp by the lake had not only been a military camp and that they had also held prisoners there, together with the Americans. Two of them, there were. Those prisoners who were still here after the end of the war were taken to North Vietnam and the prison camps there. There were several around Hanoi."

"Ask her how many prisoners were being held in that camp." Will said.

Lu continued her interview of Noi, who by now, was really showing off her gift of the gab. While they had been talking, the group had moved. Now, they were standing at the edge of the ditch, close to the car.

"Go on, Noi," Lu said.

"Well, we didn't get to learn very much," Noi said. "Only that there had been Americans in the camp and that it was very important that there were no traces left of them having been there."

Lu told Frank and Will what Noi had just told her.

"Lu," Will said, "I'd like to know what kind of camp it actually was. Was it a liaison camp, an education camp, an officers' camp, or what?"

Lu translated and now she began to feel stressed. "Noi, what kind of camp was it, down by the lake?"

"It was an education camp, where there were Chinese and Russian advisors among our officers. The privates there belonged to a special force. I can't tell you anymore. I just can't remember," Noi replied.

"She's lying," Frank said. "She knows plenty more. But I think we should end this conversation now. Let's go back to Crater Bar, have a chat with Spencer and then take off for Luang Prabang, so we can get you home, Lu. Tomorrow, we'll drive up here again and continue our investigations. I think we've come quite far today."

They thanked Noi and got into the car. In the rear-view mirror, Frank saw the old woman still standing by the road, watching as they drove away, probably pondering on what had made all this come about and why anyone would be interested in such old information and be willing to pay for it.

Lu felt happy that the work was done for the day and that she could turn her focus to getting home.

Chapter 17

Drinks with Something Extra

Prim's journey home went almost too quickly. She was not used to riding mopeds and she had been drinking alcohol. When a dog jumped out from a ditch, she wobbled and was on the verge of losing her balance until she managed to slow down and resume control over the vehicle. But when she put out her feet to keep from falling over, she found that her shins hit the pegs. First, she considered stopping, but quickly changed her mind and proceeded at the same speed as earlier. It would not do if someone saw her and it was not completely safe for young girls to be out alone at night.

When Prim got home after her adventure, she hid the moped in the jungle a short distance from the edge of the road so that no one would see it. It was not hers and she had not received the owner's permission to drive it, so she thought it best to walk the last part of the journey up to the hut. She stopped in front of it and listened. There was no sound from within. Carefully, she stole into the hut and tried to look around in the dark. Everything was silent and empty.

"Dammit!" Prim exclaimed. Mum wasn't even home. Prim had done everything she could to get home and the place was deserted! Should she go back? No, it was probably too late. She'd stay where she was, or should she? It had only been a few hours since she'd left Lek. She eyed the exit. It was a long drive, she reasoned with herself.

Eventually, she decided to speak with Lek the following day to hear how things had turned out. Her last thought before she went to sleep was that her mum would probably be home soon.

*

Prim woke up just as lonely as she'd been when she went to bed. Her only company appeared to be the rooster making the usual racket outside. She got up, rubbed her eyes and looked out over the beautiful mountains while sunbeams played over the yard and through the palm leaves that wafted gently in the light morning breeze. With the cloth she used as a towel, she went down to the brook beyond the end of the yard to wash herself properly.

On her way down between the huts, she spotted a car approaching and slowing down. It was a police car. As it went on by, Prim reckoned that it was probably from Luang Prabang. Good. She felt safe. It was a police car with three constables inside. It was a rare thing, though, the police going all the way up in the mountains just to check that everything was alright. Usually, the villagers had to take care of things themselves. Calling the police wasn't really an option and neither could they read smoke signals. The police only did what they were bribed to do anyway, that was the prevailing opinion up in the mountain villages. The police belonged to the regime and the mountain-dwellers were considered to be little more than a commodity, to be used for anything, including sex.

Prim arrived at the brook where she and Lu would get undressed and bathe naked to wash from top to toe. That was what Prim wanted most of all; to wash away yesterday's groping and regret. She looked around and there was no one in sight. They were always alone at their washing spot. Other than themselves, the place was only known to their family and their neighbours. The others, however, didn't use the brook the way Lu and Prim did.

Prim took off her blouse and her slip and let the borrowed trousers fall to the ground. They were slightly too large and came off easily. Finally, she took off her underwear and dropped them in the water. They would have to be washed anyway, she told herself. She stood, her feet in the cooling water. She sat down and let the water enclose her hips, belly and legs, pleasantly tickling between her thighs and down to her feet. After a while, when her skin had become used to it, the water did not feel so cold and she laid herself down on her back, only her face remaining above its surface.

Prim was looking up at the palm trees and the fish trees swaying in the sun, hearing nothing but the water in her ears. She was just lying there, enjoying herself, unaware of what was to happen in the future, which was of no interest, not to Prim or to any other youngster of that age. They lived in the present. She lifted her upper body and remained sitting for a while before she rose from the water, grabbed the towel and wrapped it around herself. She picked up her clothes and walked back up to the hut.

Just as she was about to enter, she noticed the police car coming back. She wondered why they were driving back and forth. There could not possibly be anything of interest there for them. She shrugged it off and began to focus on getting something to eat. Neither her paternal grandmother nor maternal grandmother and grandfather seemed to care whether Prim was home or not. She went out to the chicken run, to fetch herself some eggs, but nobody had been there for a long time and it was impossible to make out which eggs were old and which were new. She thought it safest to throw them all away. Next, she went looking in the hiding places of her maternal grandmother, May. She found some dried fish, which she took with her back to her hut. She ate it, lay down on her bedding and fell asleep again.

It was already afternoon when Prim was woken by the rumble of an engine. Since the hut was located quite close to the road, one could easily be woken by the bus stopping outside. Around these parts, the buses were rarely equipped with effective bafflers, if they had any at all. In most cases, they just made do with a pipe leading straight out from the engine.

A minute or so later, Lu entered the hut. There they were, Prim still half-asleep, Lu wide awake, but their smiles were equally broad when they saw each other.

"Hello, my darling Prim," Lu said.

"Mum, it's great that you're home! I've been so worried about you," Prim said.

"Have you really?" Lu asked.

"Yes, of course. When I got home yesterday, you weren't here," Prim replied, although she was lying a little. It was actually rather fortunate that Lu had not been home when she had returned during the night.

"My poor little girl," Lu said.

It was a good thing there was no telephone and no way for Lu to check what Prim had been up to during the last twelve hours. As things were, Prim could take advantage of the situation.

"Yes Mum. It's terrible to be alone," she replied.

"I don't like it either. Have you talked with your grandmothers?" Lu asked her.

"No," Prim said, hoping that they would not have noticed how late it had been when she'd come home. "I was in the chicken run this morning and had to throw away all the eggs. They were too many and it was obvious no one had fetched any of them for a while." Prim was hoping to divert Lu away from talk of yesterday or the previous night.

"You did the right thing, throwing away those eggs," Lu agreed.

"But where have you been, Mum?" Prim asked.

"Up at Phonsavan, together with the two Americans who are paying my salary. I help them out with translations and contacts," Lu explained.

"I know. But do you really have to be away so much and for such a long time?" Prim said.

It was her intention to aggravate Lu's bad conscience enough to improve her own situation in the event her activities were discovered.

"Prim, I have to ask you something," Lu said, startling her. "You haven't been to school today. This is obvious, since I can see you've been sleeping here until I arrived. Please, tell me why you're not going to school!"

"It's childish, they tease me and the teachers are mean. I've got no friends and I'm tired of it all," Prim said, building up her energy for the shouting match she expected to come soon.

"Calm down, now!" Lu insisted.

"What do you mean 'Calm down?' You're away whole days and nights with a pair of bloody Yanks and then you have the nerve to grumble about me not going to school. You've got to be out of your mind!" Prim yelled, so loud her words reverberated through the village.

"Calm down, Prim," Lu repeated. "You've got to understand that I worry when you're not at school. I'm not stupid, I know you and your older girlfriends come up with things to do and I don't like it. And if you keep going on like this, I'll have to find other ways."

"What ways? What do you mean? Start to make some sense!" Prim shouted, grabbing her clothes and preparing to run out.

"Oh no you don't, young lady! You're not going anywhere and where did you get those trousers?" Lu said grabbing hold of them, trying to tear them out of Prim's hands.

"That's none of your business, you old hag!" Prim grabbed the trousers back and at last, managed to get out of the hut.

Out in the yard, Mak was standing completely transfixed. She had heard every word and was staring admonishingly at Lu.

"Well, Lu, you reap what you sow and your harvest appears to be failing," Mak said, turned and walked away.

Lu was so furious that she had to fight the urge to run after the old scarecrow and hit her with something hard over the head.

Behind the hut, where no one could see what she was doing, Prim pulled on the trousers and ran off to the spot where she had hidden the moped. She dragged it out, got on and turned the key which still was in the ignition, pushed the start button and turned the throttle. The automatic transmission brought the moped smoothly up to a decent speed and Prim found herself feeling cooler after the heat inside the hut. Prim pondered on how crazy her mum was. She'd show her that she could make it on her own. She was of no use to Prim anyway. Her mother was too self-absorbed to give a shit about anyone else. Angry, bitter and downcast, she decided to find Lek and return the moped. It would take slightly more than an hour. Fortunately, there was enough petrol.

While Prim was cruising past the holes in the road, she was thinking about Stephen, the man she had met the previous evening and about Moa and about her mother and how she would have to lie her way through the evening when she got back home to the hut. She decided to get home late enough to be confident her mother would be asleep. Prim did not want to hear Lu's incessant moaning. The woman could go on all night sometimes and Prim wouldn't get a wink of sleep.

*

Lu felt totally powerless as she watched Prim running away. She went back into the hut and closed the door, for fear of May or Mak coming in. She gave a lot of thought as to what she would do about Frank and Will the following day. Should she go up to Phonsavan again, or stay home and try to find Prim? Lu wasn't sure but at the same time, she knew that what they would get from Spencer, together with what they already knew, would probably lead them to Tom and Nick's remains.

She decided to go to bed early. She had slept badly the previous night and was exhausted after everything that had happened. But first, she would make sure to kindle a fire at their old spot by the road, sit there in solitude and drink clear soup until darkness had fallen and all had become quiet. She would just sit there, drifting off in her thoughts and be by herself for a while. Perhaps, she had become a little self-absorbed after Pom had died and Fang had gone away.

While Lu was sitting reflecting at the fire, the police drove slowly past the village. She noticed that there were three of them inside the car and that they were looking at her. She was surprised. During her lifetime, she had only seen police in the area on three occasions and it was late, too. It would have been better if Prim had been with her, there at the fire. Lu wondered if she had been as badly behaved as Prim was when she was fourteen, but she could not recall. She had probably repressed it years ago. Sure, she had heard about girls of that age being difficult, their hormones spurting about inside them and that all they wanted to do was to break free from everything and everyone, especially their parents. But Prim had never shown such tendencies before.

Lu let her thoughts wander freely. They came to rest at the old lady up in Lat Kai, who had sold her daughters. Nothing could be more horrible than being a virgin from a poor family, sold to a filthy brothel. Every day, thousands of girls and young women were forced into sexual activities by physical or psychological violence. And every day, there were men willing to pay. The customers didn't want to have sex with an experienced prostitute as for some reason, they found it repellent and would rather buy sex from a young girl who they could dominate. And of course, the girl would have to be a virgin. Probably the girls had been sold down to Mae Sai in northern Thailand, one of the worst places. That poor family, what had they got for it and what had the girls got? Nothing, really. Just their daily food and somewhere to live.

One third of all the girls in the mountain districts became caught up in this slave trade one way or the other.

It seemed strange to Lu that it was all so hard to stop. There was probably just too much money in the business. Suddenly, she remembered Tim, her girl friend who worked at Gulu's bar in Luang Prabang who had come so close to dying when that Swedish guy had rented the bar for the night.

Lu had certainly experienced many things, but she had never heard anyone tell her to her face that they had sold their children. She knew it was not an uncommon practice, but nobody spoke about it. If the subject was ever brought up, everybody looked the very picture of bewilderment: No, it's not true! But now, it was time to go to bed. Lu gathered her things and went into the hut. She went to sleep without giving Prim another thought.

*

When Prim reached Luang Prabang, she took the shortest route to Lek's house. She drove in via the southern bus stop, past the Chinese market and further on along Naviengkham, which took her all the way down to the bridge. It struck her that there were no streetlamps on the bridge, so she decided to lead the moped over it. On the other side, she took off to the left and just a few hundred metres further on, she arrived at Lek's place.

It was fortunate for Prim that Lek's mother had left for work, since she was furious that Lek had lent out her moped without asking. As it was, she was unaware that Lek had let Prim use her clothes, too, but her anger over having to walk to work at the post office was more than enough. Lek had argued that it was not very far and that it was much worse for Prim, who had such a long journey home. The way she told it, Prim had only missed the bus because she had been keeping Lek company at home.

Prim turned off the motor and walked into the yard. When she reached the steps, she called out, "Lek, are you home?"

Hearing no response, she walked up a couple of steps and called again. There was still no response. Prim decided to put the moped under the house. That was probably where it should be parked. Or should she take it to Luang Prabang? She remained standing, weighing the alternatives. Finally, she decided to take the moped to the bus station and take the bus back home if it was not too late.

Prim rode back to the bridge and again, felt fear grip her as she passed over it. She held her breath until there were just a couple of metres left. Back on firm ground, she decided to drive up to Martin's Bar to see if Lek was there. But she was nowhere to be seen and there was no one else Prim knew, either. She drove on to get onto Kingkitsarat and when she came down to the end at Wat Khili, close to Tum Tum Cheng's Bar, she spotted Lek, Moa and a handful of others sitting outside. Lek noticed her immediately and came towards her from across the street.

"Dammit, Prim! You can't still be using Mum's moped. She'll go nuts!" she said.

"What was I to do? I went to your place to return it, but no one was home. I thought about putting it under the house and then walking here, but I would've missed the bus," Prim replied.

"But you're here now and isn't that 'using' it?" Lek said.

"Yes, but I decided to go looking for you. What are you doing?" Prim asked, attempting to change the subject.

"Let's drive to mum's work with the moped," Lek said. "She'll be happy that she will be able to ride it home. She got so bloody mad that I let you borrow it that she almost burst."

Lek turned to the gang.

"Moa, will you stay here for a while? We'll just go to the post office and we'll be back soon."

"That's okay, we'll wait," Moa replied.

"Take Sakarin to the right and then it's just straight on up to the post office," Lek instructed Prim, climbing onto the back of the moped.

"What happened yesterday after I left?" Prim asked when they had covered some ground.

"First, I want to know what you did with that guy Stephen!" Lek demanded.

"I did nothing. We just talked a bit," Prim said.

"I thought he was talking your pants off," Lek said laughing. "Moa and I went home after they had taken pictures of us half-naked."

"Took your picture half-naked!?" Prim cried out, veering to one side and only steadying herself, seconds before she'd have crashed into a cart full of vegetables.

"I know, I know but let's not talk about it now. I'll tell you while we walk back," Lek assured her.

There was a lot of activity at the post office as soon, it would be closing time: there were parcels that had to be sent, tourists that needed to send postcards to their loved ones back home, stamps being sold and documents copied for customers.

Lek's mother saw the two girls entering, innocent expressions on their faces. They walked up to her and Prim looked her straight in the eyes as she said, "I'm sorry, I had to get home somehow and the only way was to borrow your moped. I've parked it outside so you can use it to get home. I hope you're not too angry."

Lek's mother almost choked.

"Angry? I am, I guess," she said. "I had to walk to work. But it probably did me some good. I need to walk more than I do. I'm glad it turned out well." she turned to her daughter, "Lek, you're to be home in time! I'll be home later on."

"Yes, Mum," Lek replied.

"And you can take the moped home, I won't need it tonight," she said.

"I don't think there's very much petrol left in it," Prim said.

"Lek," her mother said, "here, take some money and fill it up on your way home."

*

The two girls walked back outside, looked at one another and burst out laughing. They covered their mouths so Lek's mother would not hear them.

"Come on," Lek said, "let's go back to the others! I'll drive."

"Yes, but you promised to tell me what happened yesterday. Tell me now! I'm as curious as hell," Prim said.

They sat on the moped and drove off towards Tum Tum Cheng's Bar.

"We drank a little bit, as you know," Lek told her, "and after a while, Lim and Nong wanted us to take our tops off, so they could see what we looked like."

"You have to be out of your mind," Prim said.

"Don't interrupt me now," Lek continued. "Well, anyway, we needed to have our pictures taken, they said. So they could see if we were suitable as photographers' models. We let them do it and then we went home."

"You're crazy," Prim said.

"It was nothing!" Lek replied.

"Nothing?" Prim exclaimed. "They took pictures of you in the nude!"

"Yes, but just our top halves. I didn't have time to take my trousers off," Lek replied, laughing.

"Did you intend to?" Prim asked.

"Yes, if I had to and if it got me some money, it would be worth it. Just a few nude pictures! That's nothing," Lek said.

They did not have time to speak any more on the subject before it was time to get off the moped and join the others.

"That was quick," Moa said.

"Well, we can't keep on sitting here," Ing, another of Lek's friends pointed out. "What about heading somewhere else?"

"Where to?" Lek asked.

"Well, if we're looking for some extra fun, we shouldn't go to places where there's only the kind of guy who barely buys us a Coke," Ing replied.

"Alright," Moa said, "You know, we're game."

"We're not going to Martin's Bar, that's for sure. I suggest we go to Night Stalls. We can get anything there," Ing said.

"That's not a good idea," Prim told Lek. "I can't go with you to that place. That's where my mother used to work!"

"But surely there won't be anyone there that would recognise you?" Lek suggested. "Come on now, it'll be fun. We'll take the moped and leave it at the ferry terminal's motorcycle park and then we can walk up to the bar."

"We'll walk," Ing said to the rest of them, "We'll be there in no time."

Prim and Lek jumped up on the moped and went on ahead. After five minutes, they reached the parking spaces for the ferry terminal. The place was crammed with mopeds. Oddly enough, nobody ever took the wrong one when leaving.

"I'm a bit nervous," Prim said when they had dismounted. "I've heard a bit about that place. It's one of those places tourists go to buy sex."

"I know. If someone wants to buy me it'll be pricey and he's got to be a prince," Lek confirmed. "But seriously, we're just going there to have a look. And if someone wants to treat us to a drink, we can say thanks but no alcohol."

"Well, I find it scary anyway. And Lek, how am I to get home?" Prim asked.

"We'll deal with that later," Lek said. "It'll sort itself out. Come on now!"

They reached the bar and waited for Moa and Ing to catch up.

"Alright girls let's head on in," Ing said, apparently street-wise and confident.

The place was already packed with guests, an advantage for the girls who could disappear into the crowd.

"Bring the other two," Ing told Moa, "We'll go up and hang out at the bar. Then they'll buy us something for sure."

Prim, Lek and Moa placed themselves at the left end of the bar. A large mirror behind the counter reflected all the bottles standing on the shelves and in it, the guests could see themselves as well as everyone else. Prim spent a moment scrutinising her own reflection pleased that she looked quite adult. And then, she noticed a man staring at her reflection. Immediately, she turned to Moa and said, "Look at the way he's staring, that old man!"

Moa turned to the mirror. "Yeah, well, he just wants to make contact. You see that, don't you?"

"Good grief. He could be my dad!" Prim said.

"Yeah, of course. Do you think guys our age can afford to come here? Even our parents can't, you know. These men spend the more money in one night on food and drink than my dad makes in a month," Moa said.

The man in the mirror knew what was going on and had told his mate they should move closer to the young girls. It was obvious that this group of girls was naïve, but still wanted to have a good time.

"Hi, I'm Stewart," he said, "and this is Mel."

"Hi," said Mel and stuck out his hand for a handshake, a greeting typical of a Westerner.

"May I buy you something?" Stewart asked, looking at Lek and Moa, who replied carefully, "Yes, we'd like a Beerlao."

"And how about you?" Mel asked Prim.

"No thanks, I don't want anything. I'll be going home soon," Prim said. She gazed imploringly at Lek and went on. "Do you think I can take the moped? Would it be okay? I'll be back with it tomorrow. I promise."

"Alright, take it then. But you know that tomorrow it has to be back in time," Lek replied.

"I promise," Prim said.

Prim lingered, talking with Lek while Stewart and Mel spoke to Moa. Mel fetched the beer from the bar, paid and handed the bottles over to the girls.

One of the men was from England and the other from Austria. Mel said that they had met on the flight from Vienna and were here on holiday. At that instant, a man pushed his way forward to the group.

"I'm Gulu," he said, "and I own this bar. Do you know these girls? Do you know how old they are?"

Moa and Lek were on the ball and immediately said they were eighteen.

"She's just sixteen though," Moa said, turning to Prim, "but she's not drinking anything and she's just about to leave."

"Is there a problem?" Mel asked Gulu.

"No, I just don't want any problem with the police," he said.

"We understand," Mel said, "But you heard the girls, Moa and Lek here are eighteen and Prim, the little lady here, is leaving."

"Can you show me your ID cards?" Gulu asked.

"No, I don't have mine with me," Moa said.

"Neither do I," added Lek.

"Then I must ask you to leave the bar," he said.

"Hold your horses," Stewart said, "There must be some misunderstanding here."

He put his hand in his pocket, brought out a bundle of banknotes and counted out fifty dollars. As he pressed the notes into Gulu's hand, he took the opportunity to shake it and thank him for his brief introduction of the bar.

"If this works out, we'll come here often," he confirmed.

Gulu got his meaning, nodded casually and disappeared into the crowd.

"Bye, then," said Prim to her friends and returned to the ferry terminal to get the moped and drive home. But even as she turned the key, a very different plan occurred to her: it wasn't that late, not really and Lu was surely sleeping, so why not drive by to see if Stephen was at his hotel?

Prim drove away towards the northern end of the sports field and up to the small hotel, Satri House.

In the meantime, the conversation in Gulu's bar continued.

"Alright," Mel said, laughing, "so you're eighteen and you live here in Luang Prabang I guess, or you go to school here and maybe have another year left before you're eighteen."

"Not at all," said Moa, who was the cockiest of the three. "You've got it all wrong. We've finished school and we're looking for work."

"Great," Mel said.

"How old are you, then?" Lek asked.

"I'm twenty-nine," Mel said, "and Stewart here is a little older."

"How old?" Moa asked.

"Thirty-two," Stewart replied.

"It doesn't show," she observed.

Moa had learnt this line from her maternal aunt who was twenty-five and constantly trying to pick up wealthy men. She didn't sleep with them, just fooled them into paying and then took off. Moa had begun to understand that men were daft enough to fall for this sort of trick, especially tourists.

"Well, you seem to know what you're talking about," Stewart said, smiling.

"Have you guys eaten?" Mel cut in, "I need something to eat. I'm a bit hungry, actually."

"Me too," Stewart said. "Would you ladies like to come along, or should we eat here?"

"No," Mel said, "let's go to Baguette Stalls. It's practically next door and they've got some nice fancy dishes. You'll come along, won't you?"

"Gladly," Lek said.

"From what I can see, you probably need something to eat, as well," Stewart said, grabbing Moa around her waist and lifting her from the floor. "Wow, I could just put a handle on you and carry you away," he said.

They all laughed and went on to the next bar.

*

At the sports field, Prim was increasingly uncertain about whether she should go up to the hotel. It was really more of a guesthouse and was run by a family known for being meticulous about which guests were allowed in. Their yard was enclosed by a plain wooden fence, one metre high, with a gate that opened onto a gravelled path leading to a terrace. From the terrace, one entered the small lobby that was always manned by a member of staff, handing out and receiving the guests' keys. Prim drove slowly up to the gate and parked the moped. She walked in. Her legs were a bit shaky.

"What do you want?" said the woman at the reception desk, glaring at her.

"I'm looking for Stephen," Prim replied.

"That's all very well, but he's probably sleeping at this late hour. You'd better come back tomorrow."

"Alright, I'll be back tomorrow," Prim said. "But could you please tell him that Prim was here."

"I will," the woman said.

Prim returned to the moped and headed for home. She was glad she'd taken the initiative to go to Stephen's hotel, as well as relieved that he was sleeping. This sentiment made her journey home much easier, as she rode along the dark road up into the mountains, towards Lu, who would hopefully be asleep too.

Lek and Moa allowed themselves to be lured with food, drink and pleasant company. Inside the bar, there were many unoccupied tables. Most of the guests had already eaten and were now standing at the bar. Mel and Stewart found a spot where they could be alone with Lek and Moa. The table was not big, so the group formed a cosy bundle of arms and legs. They had barely seated themselves before the waitress showed up, asking them whether they wanted to eat or drink.

"Both," Stewart said.

"Then, you'll have to hurry, because we're closing the kitchen soon," the waitress replied, a little sulkily. She had been working since the early morning.

"We'll decide very quickly," Mel told her. "I'll have a hamburger and some red wine. We could all have that, couldn't we? That'll be simple enough but hurry up with the wine!" He turned to the others, "That's okay for you guys, right?"

"Sure," Stewart said. But Lek and Moa looked sceptical.

"It's our treat," Mel told them.

"Then, it's alright," Moa said.

Red wine was brought to the table along with four glasses, white paper napkins and cutlery. The wine was poured.

"Let's toast success and a nice evening," Stewart said.

Moa and Lek were struggling to follow the men's English. They had been practising for a long time and understood most of it, but their pronunciation was not quite that of a native. Sometimes, it was difficult for Mel to understand what Moa said. Most of the time, Moa and Lek talked with each other just as Mel and Stewart did, except for when their arms and legs came in contact with each other's, which happened frequently.

"Cheers," Mel said, lifting his glass to his lips, drank and took a peek to check whether the girls were doing likewise.

He looked at Moa. "You are very pretty," he told her.

Moa blushed.

Meanwhile, Stewart was stroking Lek's arm lightly. "You too," he said.

"Bloody hell," Mel said quietly to Stewart. "Damn, they're nice."

"Do you mean those small tits?" Stewart replied. "I'd like to lick them."

"I'm sure that can be arranged," Mel said. "Cheers again, Moa and Lek! Dammit, we're out of wine! You can't get many glasses out of a bottle like that."

"It can fill just as many as all the other bottles of the same size," Stewart said and roared with laughter.

Moa and Lek did not get the joke, but smiled anyway.

The hamburgers were brought to the table.

"This looks bloody delicious," Stewart said, "Another bottle! We want that as well!"

The waitress returned to the bar, fetched another bottle of wine and asked if Moa and Lek wanted some water with their wine.

"What was that about?" Mel wondered, "What did you say?"

"Oh, I just ordered some water as well," Moa told him.

"Alright," Mel said.

"*Sábqai-dii baw*," Moa said to Stewart, whose face had creased into a big question mark.

"What did she say?" Stewart asked.

"She asked you if it wasn't yet time for you two to go to your hotel room," Mel said and tittered.

"Sure, yes, that sounds like a great idea!" Stewart said.

"I'm just pulling your leg, man. I don't understand what they're saying either," Mel added.

"But it really is a great idea," Stewart said. "We'll have our dessert at the hotel. Were your hamburgers okay?"

"Yes," everybody said.

"Fine, let's have another toast!" he suggested.

Moa was starting to feel affected by the wine and turned to Lek, "We'd better drink more water so we won't get too drunk."

"Yes, that's probably a good idea," Lek said.

Under the table, the leg-contact had now become more intense and Stewart had his arm around Moa.

"Cheers, Moa. This wine sure is delicious. Let's take the last of it along with the last bite and then it'll be time for 'dessert'," he said and smiled.

"Are you serious?" Mel asked.

"I've never been more serious. Let's order a couple of shots and knock them back before we take off," Stewart said.

Mel ordered two shots for each of them, along with the bill. Stewart began trying to bargain with Moa, assuming that she was a professional prostitute. But Moa had not got to that place in her life and had no plans on getting there at all. Stewart became a little more careful. When the shots came to the table, Mel placed two glasses in front of each person.

"Here you are, Moa and here you are, Lek. Now! Let's have some fun!" he said.

Everybody grabbed their first glass at the same time and knocked them back. They did the same with the second one.

"Let's go," Mel said. He got up from the table while holding Lek, who was now unusually giggly and was having some trouble keeping her balance.

Once out in the street, Mel pointed at Hotel Ancient Luang Prabang. "That's our hotel," he said.

Moa and Lek both thought this was a good idea. Neither of them was keen on going home. Given their condition, it would probably have been inappropriate.

Ancient Luang Prabang was a three-star hotel with a generous entrance that was enough on its own to lure any poor girl. Neither Moa nor Lek had ever been beyond that massive entrance.

"Do you know that one room here, for just one night, costs almost as much as my dad makes in a month," Moa said.

"Yeah," Lek replied, "I wonder if they've got silk sheets in the beds here."

"Lek, we've got to stick together," Moa reminded her.

"Yes, of course," she agreed.

Mel walked up to the reception and gave the man there a bundle of banknotes so he would look the other way as they went up to their rooms. Room 103 faced the rear and was silent and rather large, which suited Mel just fine. Room 105, also facing the rear and shut off from anyone's view, had been Stewart's choice.

"Let's go into your room," Stewart said, "it's a bit bigger than mine."

Inside the door was a small hall. To the right was a large bathroom, clad in marble and adorned with all the trappings. The room itself was spacious. It had a giant TV, a desk, a bar and an enormous bed, the kind of bed which could easily fit four people.

"Wow, I would never have thought it could look anything like this," Moa said, laughing now, a little drunk, while she looked at Lek.

"May we offer you something to drink and some snacks?" Mel asked and opening the door to the bar, took out four glasses, a bottle of gin, lemon and tonic.

Mel poured out four drinks, but in two of them, he added something extra. Stewart took out nuts and sweets from the fridge and put on some music. They all ate nuts and drank. Stewart, who was now keen for his 'dessert', sat down beside Moa on the bed, stroking her lightly on her chin while asking if everything was alright.

"Yes, yes it's okay," Moa said and drank some more.

"Cheers," Mel said to Lek.

She felt exhilarated and laughed. Mel took her in his arms, lifted her up and kissed her lightly on her chin and her mouth. He had the impression that she was into it. He gave a yell of delight. He decided he wanted to drink again, so they drank some more. Moa and Lek felt as if they were starting to get drunk and lose control. Little did they know that this was not the effects of the alcohol alone, but also the drug Mel had mixed into their drinks.

"No," said Moa quietly, still chuckling. "No, not like that."

Stewart was slowly pulling up Moa's shirt to caress her breasts.

"No, no," she insisted.

But Moa was not strong enough to remove Stewart's hands.

"Come, Lek," Mel said, "and I'll show you the other room just next door."

Lek barely heard what Mel was saying. She just did her best to walk alongside him, reeling with his arm around her waist in order for her to at least remain on her feet. Mel flicked at Stewart's leg and pointed to his room.

"Great," Stewart said, "See you later."

Finally, he was alone with Moa. She was in a world of her own, barely aware that Stewart had removed her shirt. The bed was comfortable and more than anything, she wanted to sleep. She lay there in a sort of torpor and just smiled.

Stewart got up from the bed and took his clothes off. Then he locked the door, pulled the curtains and dimmed the light. He lay down beside Moa again. First, he stroked her breasts and then, he started to pull off her trousers. Once more, Moa held on to them and repeated, "No, that won't do. You can't."

Stewart pulled harder and Moa could no longer hold on to them, could only say "no, no, I don't want to" with a pronunciation that barely held together and which Stewart had no desire whatsoever to understand or listen to. He was the stronger of the two of them, of course. Moa was powerless and by now, she had closed her eyes and begun to feel the bed rolling and the room spinning around her. She was naked now, not frightened, however, since she could not really grasp what was about to happen. Stewart's hands were everywhere on Moa, around her and between her legs.

"No, no, no!" she said.

Stewart was finally where he wanted to be and Moa had no chance of defending herself.

Moa and Lek spent the next five hours being raped and abused at the Hotel Ancient Luang Prabang, in the two rooms facing the rear.

*

Early the next day, they were thrown out by the hotel staff who had been paid to allow the night before to take place. Their side of the story was that the two girls had been extremely drunk, vomited all over the place and behaved inappropriately.

Moa and Lek stood out in the street. Lek had fifty dollars in her hand but no idea where the notes had come from.

"What are we to do?" Lek asked in despair.

"We have to get away from here. Let's go down to the river and sit there for a while. I feel very ill and need to sleep," Moa said slowly.

"Let's go home," Lek said.

"No, we can't do that! I can't go home now. Let's go down to the riverbank and sit on the sand. Lek! What have we done?" Moa asked.

Lek burst into a flood of tears.

"Not now, people are watching us. Come! Hurry up!" Moa said.

They walked to the river bank. There were already many people there, taking their morning plunges and washing themselves. Lek did not stop. She just walked straight into the water, still wearing all her clothes.

"What are you doing?" Moa shouted.

"I've got to wash myself. I'm feeling so filthy all over. Come in too!" Lek said.

Moa did the same and they sat silently up to their waists in water, fully clothed. Lek swam out between two empty boats resting with their bows up on the beach. She undressed and washed herself in the pale brown water. Nobody saw anything except Moa.

"Lek, what are we going to do?" Moa asked.

"Nothing. We've done enough already," Lek replied.

"That's not what I mean. You do understand that don't you? We can't just sit around here all day!" Moa said.

"Well, that's exactly what I'm going to do, until I'm dry at least. And then, I'm going home," Lek confirmed.

"I'm going now," Moa said.

"I don't give a damn about what you do! You just leave me here! What was it we said yesterday? Have you forgotten it?" Lek said angrily.

"What?" Moa said.

"We were not to leave each other, no matter what," Lek said.

"But it was you who left with that bloody Mel when you went to his room. You were the one that left. Not me!" Moa reminded her.

"Dammit! Are you trying to say that everything that's happened is my fault?" Lek asked starting to cry again.

"No, but I'm starting to have the feeling that we're in an awful mess now, whether we like it or not. We both know no one's going to want to marry us if we're not virgins. My family will demand that I get a job. They'll want me to pay back the debt they think I owe them. You know, I am to be grateful to them for giving me life and that's why I've got to pay them what they've earned. What am I to do? No, Lek, I'm not going back home. I'm getting away from here. You got fifty dollars from them. Half of that is mine. If I borrow your twenty-five, I can get to Thailand and away from all this. The idea of doing that has crossed my mind enough times before now," Moa said.

"Then I'll come with you. We'll be two and that's better," Lek said.

"Yes, but then we need to get more money. How are we to manage that? Sell the things we own? They won't bring us much. Sell your mum's old moped?" Moa suggested.

"No, Prim's got it. And if I did sell it, I could never go home again," Lek replied.

"You could send the money home," Moa said.

"That would make me into a thief and I don't want to do that. Couldn't we borrow money from someone?" Lek asked

"Well, for the moment I need to borrow some clean clothes. These feel like shit." Moa said.

"If we just hang around here for a while, the sun will dry us."

"Let's go and sit on that stone wall over there. That way, we'll avoid the sand and get dry quicker," Moa said. "Then we could go to my place and then yours to fetch some clean clothes. Once that's done, I don't plan on going home again, ever. I know how it'll turn out if my mother gets hold of me. She'll demand that I travel and take a job that my aunt in Udo Thani in Thailand will arrange for me. That's what they did to my sister and we haven't heard from her since she went away. The only sign of life is some money we get every month via my aunt. Mum thinks she takes half of it."

"What does your sister do?" Lek asked.

"Everybody says she's working in a bar waiting on tourists. That may be true, you know. But I think I know and it's that sort of thing you don't talk about. It's the weirdest thing, thousands of girls work in bars to serve men in every possible way, yet no one talks about it," Moa said.

"But apparently they're making good money, since they can all afford to send money home," Lek said.

"You know what my mother does with the money she gets from my sister, don't you? She buys clothes, invites her friends to dinners and buys my brother a new moped. I'm not subjecting myself to that. I'd better look after myself from now on," Moa said.

"Prim should be back with the moped this afternoon," Lek said. "Maybe, we can take it down to Vientiane?"

"You've got to be out of your mind! That's over two hundred kilometres away. It's way too far to go by moped. For now, I think, I'll just lie down in the sun for a while," Moa said.

"Me too," Lek agreed.

Both girls fell asleep in the sun.

*

Lu was asleep when Prim got home, so no-one could tell when the girl had crawled into bed inside the hut. She had hidden the moped in the same spot as last time.

Morning came and along with it, numerous questions. Prim was prepared, however. And so was Lu. She had decided not to attack her daughter, but to go easy on her.

"Prim, did you have a good time yesterday?" she asked.

"Yes," Prim replied.

"Do you want me to make you some breakfast?" Lu asked.

"Yes please," Prim replied hesitantly as usually, Lu never asked if she wanted breakfast.

"Those trousers, where have you got those? They look smart," Lu said.

"I've borrowed them from Lek," Prim replied, not expecting any follow-up questions.

"Lek is a nice girl, from the sound of it," Lu said, keeping to her strategy.

"Yes," Prim agreed.

"Do you see a lot of each other, just the two of you?" Lu asked.

"Yes. You sure are inquisitive this morning, Mum!" Prim responded.

"Well, I'd just like to know. I'm probably a bit worried I regret leaving you alone so often," Lu said.

"It's alright," Prim said, smiling at Lu. "I have plenty of friends. And sometimes, it's just nice to be on my own a bit."

"Yes, you're probably right" Lu agreed. "I'll be going down to Luang Prabang during the day and I might have to go on up to Phonsavan. I take it you've got no plans to go to school today?"

"No, I haven't," Prim confirmed.

"Prim, that's a bad idea. It's important to finish everything at school," Lu observed.

"I know, but why does it matter? I finish this year anyway and I'll never get the opportunity to study further. We haven't got the money for it. So how can it possibly matter if I finish now or in a month?" Prim stated.

Lu was at a loss for a reply.

"Please, take care of yourself," she said.

"Sure, everybody takes care of themselves, don't they?" Prim said.

Prim was worried. Under no circumstances did she want to bump into her mother in Luang Prabang.

"Well, then," Lu said, "let's go down to the brook to wash ourselves and make sure we make the most of the day."

Out in the yard, they met Mak, Prim's paternal grandmother, who was standing outside her hut.

"Good morning, Grandma," Prim said.

"Good morning, Prim," Mak replied, refusing even to give Lu a glance.

"I wonder where grandpa is," Prim asked Lu.

"I don't," Lu replied. "He's probably busy with one of his shady businesses."

"Like what?" Prim asked again.

"It's for the best that you know nothing about it," Lu replied as they made their way down to the brook.

Chapter 18

A Lesson in Trafficking

Morning dawned over the Mekong River. Surachai's night had been fitful, but the others had slept deeply.

"How are you?" asked Voratep, rubbing his eyes as he folded the tarpaulin that had been his quilt for the night.

"Oh, just fine," lied Surachai. "I lay and watched the river glimmer like silver at dawn. It was very beautiful."

In reality, the night had been torture. No matter how hard he tried, he could not refrain from thinking about Songchai.

"It was probably the silver we'll be getting when we arrive," said Voratep.

"Oh yeah? I thought we were supposed to get gold," Surachai said.

"What are you two prattling about?" Songchai said scanning around. "Kitepong, you'll get us a new propeller. Supot will get petrol with me and you others can get us all water and something to eat."

All these things could be found nearby and the village market was already a hive of activity. Getting petrol and food were simple enough tasks, but finding a propeller proved to be harder.

Kitepong had walked to the closest boat workshop to buy one that didn't cost too much.

"If you'd like a cheap one, you've got to remove it from this shaft here yourself and buff it so you can use it," the owner had told him.

The propeller shaft had been terribly corroded and if Kitepong had realised what the task would entail, he would have declined. But he hadn't and now, he was finally standing by Surachai's boat with a propeller in his hand. When he returned, the others had already begun eating their breakfast. They had sticky rice with fish, rinsed down with fresh water.

"If we take off as soon as we've eaten and replaced the propeller, we should be able to make it all the way down to Phon Pisai," said Songchai.

"Wow," replied Voratep, "that's some stretch! All the way past Vientiane!"

"Yes, but if everything goes smoothly, there should still be some daylight left when we're passing Vientiane," Songchai confirmed.

"Yeah, let's give it a try," said Surachai, "We'll see how far we get."

"I'll take the lead as usual," Songchai told them.

*

As he turned around to head for his boat, Songchai heard someone calling behind him. Down at the beach, just some twenty metres from the boats, a woman was standing in front of a rather big car. No one had noticed it stopping there. Songchai eyed the woman, intrigued. She appeared to be about forty, but it was hard to tell since she wore heavy make-up.

"Hello there," she said again and walked towards Songchai, who wondered what she could possibly want with him. "Is this your boat?"

"Yeah," replied Songchai. "Why do you ask? It's not for sale," he continued as he walked.

"That was not what I was asking you. I asked if it's your boat. I'm Jinn, by the way," she continued.

"Yes, it's mine. What can I do for you?" he asked, suddenly softening up a little.

"Well, I've got a problem," Jinn said. "I've got some girls in my car who are bound for Sanakham, but the car's broken down. So I'd like to ask you if it would be possible for us to go with you down to the village. We'd pay, of course."

"Alright. And how many of you are there?" he asked.

"There are just six of us," she confirmed.

"How much would you pay to ride along?" Songchai asked.

"You're going in the same direction, so what about me buying you and the others something to eat when we get there?" Jinn suggested.

"No thanks. We've got no time for that. Tell me what you're willing to pay, or forget about it," Songchai said, not wanting to waste any time.

"Alright, I can give you fifty thousand kip per head," said Jinn seriously, her eyes fixed on Songchai's.

Songchai told Jinn to wait by the boat while he went to discuss it with the others.

Standing by his own boat, Surachai looked thoughtfully at Songchai and the woman. She was a hooker, that much was obvious. There was both the glow and the smell, fish or perfume. Only the devil knew what.

"Has the old man gone out of his mind? Is he about to buy himself a hooker this time of the morning?" he asked Voratep, laughing out loud.

"Hardly," replied Voratep, "I think this is about something completely different."

Songchai walked up to the others. They were standing on Surachai's boat, which was all set to go. Wide-eyed, they were all following what was going on.

"What are you up to?" asked Kitepong.

"Well, what does it look like?" replied Songchai.

"If you ask me, it looks like a cheap tart is trying to scrape up enough for her breakfast," Kitepong continued.

"Yeah, that could've been what this is about, but it's not. It's about something else. She'd like to hitch-hike with us down to Sanakham, but there are six more of them in the car and it's broken down. She says she's willing to pay three hundred thousand kip for the ride. What do you think? Should I take them there?" he asked everyone.

"It's your call," said Voratep. "You're the one who's gotta take them in your boat. But you should probably make sure none of them can see what you've got on board."

"You needn't worry as everything's properly packed," Songchai replied.

"Do as you wish, as long as I'm not disturbed in my solitude," said Kitepong. "It's nice not having to speak to people, especially ones you don't know."

Songchai walked back to Jinn, who was waiting by his boat.

"Well, what did your friends say? Can you take us along?" she asked, giving him a buttery smile.

"Hurry up!" said Songchai, "Get your things on board so we can shove off."

"It's not much and the things will get themselves on board," said Jinn, smiling again.

She turned around to fetch the rest of the passengers. A woman of about Jinn's age got out of the car, followed by five girls. The girls looked bewildered, afraid and lost, but followed the two older women. None of them had much luggage, just a small case each, probably containing only their absolute necessities.

"Who are these young ladies?" asked Songchai as they got on board and got seated.

Instantly, Surachai called out, "Come over here! We've got a problem."

"There must be the same number of girls on each side of the boat," Songchai told Jinn.

Then, he walked swiftly over to Surachai's boat.

"Don't you understand what's climbing into your boat?" asked Surachai , who was getting worked up. "I bet my ass these girls have been sold to some whorehouse on the other side of the border."

"Is that what you think?" asked Songchai.

"I'm dead sure! Check out where they're from but do it casually. These women know what they're doing," Surachai added.

"Sure, I will. But it's time to get out of here," said Songchai, returning to his boat. As he drew closer and heard them speak, it was obvious to him that the girls were Burmese, but they fell silent as he approached.

"Alright! Let's cast off and push out the boats!" shouted Songchai. With that done, they climbed on board and started their engines.

Jinn sat immediately behind Songchai, so they could talk as they proceeded along the river. The motor was twelve metres further towards the aft. Despite its straight pipes from the cylinders, it did not disturb them much. Songchai found Jinn pleasant and easy to talk to after just a short while. Her friend or colleague, however, sat silent behind the girls the whole time. Songchai thought that Surachai was probably right and he suspected that she was guarding her investment, or her commission, from one of the thousand brothels along the border. Had he got himself involved in human trafficking, all of a sudden?

"Where are you from?" he asked Jinn.

"I'm from Wan Lemfai, on this side of the border with Burma. But I work and live in Pattaya down on the Thai coast."

"Yes, I know where it is. What about the others?" he asked again.

"They're from various places in northeast Burma, mostly from the Shan State," she replied.

"And where are you heading?" he asked.

"Well, I'm going to help some of the girls get jobs in Khon Kaen and I'll take a couple of them down to Pattaya," Jinn replied.

"What will they be doing there?" Songchai wanted to know next.

"They'll wait on tourists and work in a couple of bars. Well, not just tourists, really. And if you guys would like to have a good time before we part, as payment instead of money, all you have to do is ask," said Jinn smiling.

Songchai was surprised and a little angry. It occurred to him that he had asked too little for this transport. And screwing little girls wasn't exactly his cup of tea, either. He couldn't refrain from asking more questions, however. He had heard that there was a lot of money to be made in this business.

"How come you're mixed up in this type of thing?" was his next question.

"Why, maybe I can tell you. You seem to be a decent guy," said Jinn. "Like I said before, I'm from a village pretty close to the border up in Burma. Our family wasn't rich, but not exactly poor either. I had two sisters and a brother. My mother was a sex worker in Bangkok during the Vietnam War and as you probably know, there was a need for a great many girls to entertain all those soldiers. When I went to school, I made up my mind to start working in an office."

"Why an office, exactly?" Songchai cut in. "That's gotta be boring."

"Well, I had good grades in maths and languages. I've always been interested in languages. But when I turned fourteen, I started to work with what I've been working with ever since. My mother told me and my sisters that we could make much more money by entertaining men. So I did the same thing as my mother. I went to Bangkok to work in a massage parlour. That is, what you see all over Asia, along all the streets and pavements, in all the villages and cities. But the job was no fun. The customers weren't at all nice and they didn't want to pay properly. I worked there for three years, until I'd paid my debt to those who had fixed me up with the job. While working there, I had got to know some of the customers a bit. And during my last year, I started to follow them home, offering them extra services and they paid well because they liked me. A short while later, I managed to get a job at a bar in central Bangkok on Sukhumvit Road, you know, 'The City of Angels', as Bangkok is called. I guess it's us who are the angels," said Jinn, laughing again.

She continued, "The only ones visiting that bar were the foreigners, so it was quite easy to make money. Most of them had no chance of getting a girl on her back in their own countries, but with us, it was easy. All they had to do was to pay. They were easy to fool, too. Often, they stayed in Thailand for a couple of weeks and for all that time, my friends and I pretended to be in love with them. Most of them had fallen for us after the first night. Before they left Thailand, they'd given me their telephone number and address. A few days after they had got home, it was time for me to call and tell them how much I missed them and how I longed for them to return. After that, I would ask them if they could help me with two thousand baht for my mother's birthday which they often did. If I called them all during the course of a week, I could easily get seventy to a hundred thousand baht."

"Not bad at all. Why wasn't I born a woman?" said Songchai and laughed for once. "But seriously, it's got to be tough, especially since people look down on you all the time."

"You're wrong," Jinn told him. "Nobody looks down on me. On the contrary, all the customers are happy and we're making money with what we're doing. That's a great benefit. The only ones looking down on us are those who know us from our native villages. No one there talks about what we're doing, though. And I've got no reason to go home. I'd rather go to other places. In fact, once I went to Japan, just for a couple of months. I made a lot of money. It's a good job and I can send plenty of money to my family. I've bought my brother a motorcycle and soon, I'll be able to give him a car. My family have already renovated and extended their house thanks to the money I've sent them. My parents are proud of me for making more money than any of the other girls from my village."

"Yeah, I can see that," Songchai said, "but what are you doing here, now, with those girls? Where do they come from really?"

"Poor families," Jinn replied.

"Yeah, there's a lot of those around. Families selling their daughters to ward off poverty has been a last resort around here for ages," Songchai pointed out.

"When my mother got started, in her youth, only a small proportion of the girls came from Burma. Ten years ago, it was half of them and now, almost all the girls in the brothels come from Burma, particularly in northern Thailand, Chiang Mai, most of all," Jinn explained.

"There are probably lots of people making money from this in various ways, aren't there?" Songchai said.

"Yes," said Jinn, "just like any other commodity. But everyone isn't sold by their families. Many of them get in touch with me directly, all by themselves. They're looking for work and they want to get out and make money. Then there are others, who are tricked into it and get abducted, but I won't touch those. That business is far too dangerous. Those girls who are sold by their families or relatives and believe they are bound for the big city to get a job in a restaurant as a waitress, get the shock of their lives, at first, although it passes quickly. Most of the girls that I help get jobs come to me just because they get food on the table and they're tired of getting raped by soldiers who are faithful to the junta. They'd rather get themselves to the brothels in Thailand where at least they get paid for their services."

"But, what about those who are abducted and tricked into the job?" asked Songchai.

"The worst thing is that the customers can't tell the one from the other," Jinn said. "All they want to do is to pay and get some sex. These girls are often at brothels that are fenced-in and locked up. I don't think we have so many of them in Thailand, but in Manila, there are lots of them. Those girls aren't allowed to leave the brothels and the buildings often have blacked-out windows. The only people allowed to enter are a certain kind of sex buyer. They are disgusting; even I find them revolting."

"It's tragic. That line of work is not for me," Songchai confirmed.

"A lot of men pay well for cute young girls. You should see those that come from the Yai-Thai district, who have slightly fairer skin. If you get hold of a virgin, you might get up to fifty thousand baht from the right buyer, just for her virginity. I'll give you some facts I've got from a mama-san, an older brothel-keeper who'd been in the business for many years," Jinn said.

"Gladly," said Songchai, slowing the engine, since the river had become rather fast and they were moving quickly enough anyway.

"Well, this mama-san had a lot of information," Jinn began. "In Yunnan, which is an inaccessible mountain district in southern China at the border with Burma, the standard of living is extremely low and literacy is almost non-existent. It's worse than anywhere else in that region. This makes Yunnan a great place to find girls for the sex trade in Thailand. There is an enormous market for young girls there, preferably virgins. Since 1990, thousands of girls have been abducted and taken to Thailand. The mama-san said official sources had it that during just one year, two and a half thousand girls were sold from

Yunnan to brothels in Thailand and still, I think this number is far too low."

"I think you're telling me this to silence your conscience," said Songchai.

Jinn sat silent for a while before she spoke again. "You're probably right," she said. "Lately, I've started to see things from another perspective. But I'm attached to a couple of brothels and have to perform these tasks. If I don't, I might get into a lot of trouble and so might my family."

"Alright, I see," said Songchai. "They have a hold on you."

"They have a hold on everyone that is, or has been, involved," Jinn said.

"But why don't you go to the police, to help you get out of it?" Songchai asked.

"The police," replied Jinn, smiling, "own brothels too."

"How much are you getting, then? You've got to be experienced and up to your ears in it," Songchai said.

"Three hundred dollars per girl," Jinn confirmed.

"That means," said Songchai, performing a mental calculation, "that you've got fifteen hundred dollars coming when you arrive tonight and after that, you go back up again and get some new girls."

"Well, at least I don't have to lie on my back," Jinn replied.

"Hell only knows what's best," Songchai remarked.

They fell silent. Songchai could not hear whether the girls were talking at the back of his boat. The only thing he could hear was the monotonous sound of the motor. It was not long before Jinn fell asleep.

Songchai reflected on how he was trafficking weapons and she was trafficking girls. The police owned brothels and allowed themselves to be corrupted on all levels. Songchai had friends who both grew and sold opium, as well as relatives who smuggled goods over the borders. It was rumoured that people got kidnapped in order to provide other people with body parts and there were also those who made a living out of killing. It didn't seem like we had come very far in our civilisation, even though it was the twenty-first century. No, this human trafficking was not a business for him to get involved with. Actually, he should probably let the girls go, but he knew he'd probably get himself murdered if he did.

*

They had arrived at the ferry port where the girls were supposed to go ashore. Jinn woke up as the boat slowed down.

"Are we there?" she asked.

"Yes," said Songchai.

"Up you get everybody. Sit up properly!" shouted Jinn. And then, she spoke quietly, "Songchai, could you be kind and let us go ashore on the Thai side before we reach the jetty?"

"No. We discussed your destination and agreed it would be Laos. I refuse to be involved in any sort of human trafficking. You have to take care of that yourself. I am letting you off here, nowhere else and I want to be paid now," he said firmly.

Surachai glided up alongside Songchai and told him that he and the others would continue and that Songchai should hurry and catch up.

"I'll come soon. As soon as I've received our money and they've left the boat," he confirmed.

"Take out the money and jump ashore," Songchai told Jinn.

"All this time, I've had the impression that you would let us go ashore on the Thai side," said Jinn. "I'll only pay you half."

"Hell no, you'll pay me now what we've agreed on. If you don't, the girls aren't leaving the boat and you'll never see a brothel again. You can be sure of that."

"Okay," said Jinn, "then I'll just have to bribe the border guards. It always works out since they're usually keen to try out a new girl."

She paid the agreed sum and jumped ashore. Two of the girls came after her, accompanied by Jinn's woman-friend who had been sitting silent the whole trip. Songchai felt disgust as he saw her pushing the girls in front of her. He could have reversed the boat and taken the other girls with him, but it would have been too risky. It would not be hard for the human traffickers to intercept them from any of the roads running along the river.

The others had slowed down to await Songchai and soon, they were together again on the river.

"That took a while. How did it turn out?" Surachai shouted when Songchai came up alongside in order to take the lead.

"Well, there was a bit of fuss, but I put an end to that. We'll go on to Ban Pak Ton now to rest, fuel up and eat and then we should continue as far as we can manage.

They reached Ban Pak Ton towards the late afternoon. Songchai was feeling tired, not through lack of sleep or from the arduous journey, but mainly because the episode with Jinn and the hapless girls had taken its toll. He shouldn't have given them the ride. All that misery had come too close. He was all too aware that this sort of thing went on in the neighbourhood and around the mountain villages from where the girls were sold. But this was different. Songchai had had the opportunity to save these girls and yet, he had not. Sure, it would have meant risking his life, but all the same, he could have saved them.

"It's nice that we've come this far," said Voratep when they drove their boats to the water's edge near the ferry port in Ban Pak Ton.

"I need to sleep for a while before we continue," said Songchai. "You've got to get water, food and petrol. A half-hour nap will do the trick."

*

Songchai lay down on the floor of his boat, or rather the magazine and fell asleep immediately. He was sleeping deeply on the arms boxes until he was woken by what sounded like the war starting all over again. There was a lot of commotion and someone was standing above his head with a big steel object.

"What the hell is going on here?" he cried out, looking around drowsily even though he had only been sleeping for half an hour.

"Stop shouting, Gramps. Are you out of your mind?" he heard someone say.

"What is going on here?" he repeated himself.

"Calm down! It's just me filling your boat with petrol," said Surachai, who was straddling over him with a jerry can in his hands.

It was not easy to fill up the boat in a space that was no more than one cubic metre. He had to contend with the old man in there, too, practically lying on top of the fuel cap.

"Do you need anything else before we leave?" asked Surachai.

"No, just water and then I'm fine. Does everybody know where we are, by the way? Maybe, we ought to have a little meeting before we take off. Everybody to my boat and we'll have a quick chat," he called out.

The others jumped on board and placed themselves at the fore, which was the flattest area. Songchai took out the map. This was unnecessary, since everyone had travelled this part of the Mekong before on several occasions, by boat or by raft.

"As you can see, we are up here now," said Songchai, "and we've got Sang Khom on the Thai side. It will take us about two hours to get down to Vientiane and then maybe half an hour to Friendship Bridge. It would be nice to pass it in the evening darkness."

“I’d like us to stay in Phon Phisai for the night,” said Voratep, “instead of pushing on towards Muang during the night. Doing that might cost us our lives.”

“Not at all,” argued Supot. “You don’t have to worry about fireballs rising from the bottom of the river and sinking your ship. Unless you actually believe in ghosts?”

“I don’t give a fuck what you think; I won’t go down that stretch of river at night,” Voratep insisted.

“Alright, alright,” said Songchai. “We’ll have to see. Let’s get past the bridge first and then we can have another meeting. Are you alright with that?”

They all agreed.

*

It was not long before Songchai’s thoughts returned home to the village. The hours just went on and on. Ahead, lay a long, uneventful journey down to Phon Phisai and the night’s camp.

Phon Phisai was on the west side of the Mekong and therefore, belonged to Thailand. It was typical of villages close to rivers, whose people lived off fishing, agriculture, the cultivation of rice and the tourists who visited to see the famous ghosts rise up out of the river a little to the north. All of the north-eastern part of Thailand was very poor. Many farmers could not even gather more than thirty kilos of rice per year.

On arrival, as usual, Songchai assumed the role of guide and was the first to get his boat up onto the beach. The others arrived shortly afterward and the boats were laid close to each other, at a slight angle, firmly lashed together as well as to the poles which were always set up along those beaches.

“We’ll be staying here for the night, eh?” asked Voratep.

“Yeah, you’re afraid of the dark, so it’s probably for the best,” said Surachai, smiling to the others. “Oh, I’m just pulling your leg. We’ll do that, right?”

"Well, it's probably for the best," replied Songchai. "This was a tiring stage."

When everything was ready for the night, all five of them sat down in Voratep's boat and ate their sticky rice and fish.

"Where is Pooi?" asked Kitepong, "I expected him to have joined us somewhere along the route by now, as soon as Suteluck's funeral was over."

"So did I," said Supot.

"Maybe, Suteluck's journey to the 'other side' took longer than expected. Perhaps, the rooster-spirit had to work hard, given Suteluck was rather heavy," said Songchai laughing.

"I've got some Mekong whiskey here," Voratep said. "I'll get you guys a glass."

"Thanks, it might be nice to have a nightcap before bed," replied Surachai and held out a mug.

"Songchai," said Supot, "I didn't really understand what happened back up in Ban Pak Man. Fill me in on it."

"If you start doing something, you've got to finish it," said Songchai, knocking back his whiskey. "That was nice. I'll have another one. Well, I've got some money which we can share, or use for food, when all of this is over. I got three hundred thousand kip for the transport, but it probably could have brought us much more."

Voratep poured another drink. Mekong whiskey was cheap, so this time, he filled the mug closer to the brim.

"What do you mean? Could you have taken more passengers, or what?" asked Kitepong.

"No, not that. I could have received much more money if I'd agreed to let them go ashore on the Thai side. The girls had been sold and were to be smuggled down to some brothels in northern Thailand. The two older women were supposed to deliver two of them to brothels in Khon Kaen and then, take the other two with them to Pattaya to work. Jinn, that's the name of the one I was speaking too, is tied to a couple of brothels herself, which are probably owned by the same people. One of her assignments is to supply her employers with new girls," Songchai explained.

"It's big business this buying and selling girls to brothels," said Surachai, who had been keeping an eye on the business a little, without getting involved.

"And filthy," said Voratep, who knew what it was all about from what had happened to his family.

"Sure, but we all know that it's all around us," said Songchai.

"And nobody does a thing to stop it. It's a slave trade, pure and simple!" spat Voratep.

"Who is there to stop it? A business with a turnover of billions of dollars and controlled by politicians and the police?" asked Kitepong.

"What do you mean?" asked Supot, lying back over the wheel in the slim boat's fore. The others were hardly more comfortable, sitting on boxes and pallets. The whiskey had done its job, however and softened up their joints a little.

"It's simple: the politicians don't want to intervene because the sex trade brings a huge number of tourists in, mainly men from other parts of the world, who gladly spend their money in our countries, just because there are, as they believe, lots of willing women here. They don't realise that those women are only doing what they do under duress and have to make a certain amount of dollars every day. In some places, that means that they have to take up to thirty guys every day. The police own some of these brothels and therefore, it's a matter of course that they turn a blind eye. Also, those policemen who aren't owners, also get paid by the brothels to look the other way."

"Yeah, you're probably right," said Supot.

"Have you got some more?" asked Surachai and held out his mug yet again.

"Yes," said Voratep, "I bought a couple of bottles up in Ban Pak Man."

"Well done. Why didn't I think of that?" Surachai asked out loud.

"I know that up in Mea Sai, at the border," continued Kitepong, "there are many brothels, staffed with generally very young girls. During the first six months, they are kept locked up to get acclimatised to the system, as they put it. They're only about fifteen, these girls, but have to attend to at least ten men each day. After that, they are sold on to various brothels, mostly in Thailand."

"Bloody hell," said Voratep. "I could happily kill the men who are responsible for that, without so much as blinking!"

"I'll tell you a story about what happened to a family in my native village," said Kitepong. "And bear in mind, this is nothing out of the ordinary. The husband was a furniture dealer and his shop did rather well. His wife was home attending to the children. They had a daughter, who was thirteen and quite beautiful. The man of the house had started an affair with the woman who ran the shop next door, a very attractive woman and his furniture shop started to go downhill. Eventually, he had to borrow money to maintain his family. He borrowed about four thousand dollars - a year's income for him - and promised to pay back his loan shark a month later. But he couldn't. The moneylender decided that the rate of interest should be twenty dollars per day until every cent had been repaid. As usual, no one else in the family knew what was going on as all of this was done behind their backs. When the lender paid them a visit, he got wind of the fact that there was a beautiful daughter in the house. His demand turned out to be painful and quite simple. 'Your daughter is mine, from this day forth. I demand that you sell her to me and in this way, you can pay back a part of your debt.'"

Everybody sat riveted in silence as Kitepong went on. "The man and his wife, who had known nothing of any of this, were forced to sell their daughter, who was taken away as soon as she came home. She was taken to a brothel up in Mea Sai. She's probably still there, working off the debt that she'll never escape from."

"Disgusting," said Voratep.

"The worst thing is when buyers come and buy children that haven't even been born yet, or mere babies, to have in readiness," Kitepong continued. "The parents might get a few hundred dollars for the baby and they're taken away at a young age."

"Why isn't anyone doing anything?" asked Voratep once more.

"Too much money," said Kitepong.

"Well," said Songchai. "I'm prepared to do almost anything when it comes to making money—"

"This we know," interrupted Surachai.

"Smuggling arms is okay and clothes, watches but to sell children and young women. No. Even I won't stoop to that," Songchai said.

"Just think about it," said Kitepong. "If Thailand banned the brothel business, banned all prostitution and criminalised the buyers, a great number of the tourists would disappear and the country's economy would collapse. How many young women from our villages and from villages in our neighbouring countries, are working at Thai brothels? I don't think a single one of them is out there spreading their legs of their own free will. One way or another, they're forced to do their job."

"You seem to know quite a lot about this," Surachai observed.

"You just need to keep your eyes and ears opened," Kitepong replied.

"Well, I think I'll go to my boat while my legs can still carry me," said Supot. "It's starting to get late and we've got to be up early in the morning."

They thanked Voratep for the whiskey and walked over to their respective boats.

Songchai, who had taken a nap earlier on, had trouble falling asleep. He returned to his thoughts about his own village up in the mountains and the toll poverty often took. For some villagers, the only way to get food on the table was to sell their daughters, or to fool them into travelling to a relative in another part of the country who, in turn, would make sure that the girls ended up in a brothel somewhere. Certainly, there was prostitution up in the villages too, but on a very different level, cheaper and filthier.

Even in villages as small as these, there were brothels for the men of the area. They were called songs and in places like that, it didn't cost more than a few dollars to buy a young girl.

Chapter 19

Leaving Home

Lu and Prim walked slowly down to the brook. The day had started well and they had both decided it should continue that way. The water was, as ever, refreshing and cool, since it came streaming down from the mountains. Prim had often thought about going upstream to find out where it originated, but it had come to nothing.

They were standing before each other naked, in several senses of the word. They looked alike. Prim looked almost as if she were an identical younger version of her mother. They were sitting with their feet in the current and washing themselves.

"Don't forget to keep yourself clean down there, particularly when you get your period," Lu said.

"Mum, you're a bit late with this. You know I can take care of myself, right? And I know what might happen if you get bacteria from bad water. You don't have to remind me about those things," Prim reassured her.

"Sorry," said Lu, "but sometimes I forget that you're about to become an adult."

"Mum, I am an adult," replied Prim in a huff.

"I didn't mean to step on your toes," Lu continued. "But you're my child and it will take a long time before I can look upon you as an adult."

Lu tried to smooth things over so they wouldn't get off on the wrong foot again, which would have been a shame given how well they had started the day. Besides, she had a pang of conscience, knowing she would have to leave again soon, without being able to tell Prim if or when she would be home.

"Come, let's go back up again," said Lu. "I have to try to leave as soon as possible for Luang Prabang."

Prim remembered the moped that lay in the bushes on the other side of the road. It could easily take both of them down to the city. But no, no, mum could not find out that she was using a moped. They put on their pyjama-like clothes and walked slowly back again while chuckling over the mischief the little pigs were up to.

"Mum, look over there! What are the police doing here in the village?" Prim asked. "They've been here several times. I saw them the other day, when they drove by and just looked around. Has something happened?"

"Nothing that I know of. But you're right. I saw them yesterday too. That aside, I haven't seen them here for several years. It's weird. Well, they've probably got some reason for driving around up here. But now I've got to get dressed and take off right away. And Prim, go to school today!" Lu said firmly.

"No, never. We've been through that," Prim replied.

They walked up to the hut, where Lu changed quickly and then went off. Prim remained inside the hut. She did not want to leave at the same time as her mother, so she took the opportunity to arrange the bedding, clothes, books and the things they had used for breakfast. With this done, she sat down outside the hut in the morning sun and enjoyed the warmth.

She looked away towards the road, which veered slightly left outside the village and noticed that the police car was motionless. It was all a bit strange. Prim squinted in the sunlight and followed the police car as it started and slowly drove away. No, this won't do; better to get ready and head down to meet Lek. Besides, the moped had to be returned, after all.

*

Lu had managed to get a lift and had already left the village, so Prim would not run the risk of bumping into her mother along the way. Prim hurried, dressing herself in the borrowed trousers which by now had become a little dirty. Then, she ran to the moped and drove out on the road to town. Prim had got used to driving the moped by now and had developed a thirst for speed. The moped's top speed was seventy kilometres an hour. At first, Prim had only been driving at forty, tops, but now, it was to be full throttle almost all the way to Luang Prabang.

When she reached the bus terminal, she decided to pass by Stephen's hotel first, to see if he was in, before continuing on to Lek.

After about a minute, she was at the hotel.

"Well, young lady, you're back again," the woman behind the reception desk said.

"Yes," replied Prim.

It felt easier today; she was not nervous at all.

"I'm looking for Stephen," she continued, as if she had done this numerous times before.

"He just left with his jogging shoes on, so I'm pretty sure he's out running at the sports field," the woman said. "He usually exercises for a couple of hours in the morning. Would you like to wait, or should I give him a message when he comes back?"

"Tell him, Prim was here and that I'll be coming back later," she said.

Prim left the hotel, planning to drive to Lek's place. But even before she came to the unpleasant bridge, she could feel the knot of anxiety in her stomach.

In the meantime, Moa and Lek were walking on Setthathirat Road along the Mekong, which was on the same side of the river and parallel to the street Prim was riding. When Moa and Lek were about to turn off down by the river, they spotted Prim just as she was about to drive onto the bridge.

"It's Prim!" Lek cried out. "Prim! Prim!" She called out so loudly that everybody around them turned to see what was happening.

Prim heard Lek calling out her name. Surprised, she managed to turn the vehicle just as she was about to drive up on the bridge. She stopped the moped in front of her two friends and looked at them.

"Where have you been?" asked Prim. "You both look terrible. What's happened? And you, Moa, you're all wet."

"Me too," said Lek.

"What have you been doing?" Prim asked as she turned off the engine.

"You tell her!" said Lek turning to Moa.

Lek started crying again.

"What is it?" asked Prim, more emphatically.

"We've been through hell," Moa began, but struggled to say any more.

"Come," sobbed Lek. "Let's sit down by the river and talk."

This time, they sat down by Nam Khan, the river that passed by both Lek and Moa's homes.

"I don't know how to say this," said Moa. "But we stayed with those two guys and went with them to a place close by. Then, they took us to their hotel where they drugged us, undressed us in separate rooms and then raped us for several hours. And on top of that, when the guys had thrown us out of their rooms, the staff threw us out into the street. They didn't listen to a word we said and just assumed we were the reason for the whole problem and all the commotion at the hotel. If we hadn't left straight away, they would have called the police."

"It might have been a good thing if they had done," said Prim.

"Are you out of your mind? Don't you know that if the police had come for us, we'd have just been raped all over again? By the police themselves!" Lek exclaimed.

"Raped, without getting paid at that," Moa filled in.

"What, you got paid?" Prim said aghast.

"Yes, we got fifty American dollars to go with the filthy feeling," Moa admitted.

"Actually, I'd like to buy a gun for the money and go back and shoot them," said Lek.

"But what are you going to do now?" Prim asked.

"We're going to clear off," said Moa.

"Clear off? Where to?" asked Prim.

"Anywhere," said Moa, "just as long as we get out of here. Right now, we're just going home to change, take some things with us and then we're going. We'll probably try to take a bus this evening down to Vientiane and then head further on to some tourist resort. It's easier to get a job there at a hotel or a bar. Prim, by the way, have you got some money to lend us? We need quite a lot."

"No," said Prim. "I've got nothing. Why don't you get in touch with Nong and Lim? They live in Vientiane, you know."

"Oh yeah. Why didn't we think about that?" said Lek and turned to Moa, "It's a great idea!"

"I could drive to Stephen's hotel and ask him whether they've set off or are still around," said Prim.

"In the meantime, we'll go to Moa's place to get our clothes. But Prim, don't tell anyone about what happened. You must promise us that! And you can't tell anyone we're leaving. That'll come to light sooner or later anyway."

"But won't you tell your families about it?" Prim asked.

"No, they'll understand," Lek said. Besides, they'll be happy since there will be one less mouth to feed."

This was true.

"Okay," said Prim, "I promise."

"Come along, Lek!" said Moa. "Off we go!"

Prim drove back to Stephen's hotel. The woman at the reception desk looked surprised.

"That was quick. He hasn't come in yet. But if you go out in the sports field, you'll probably see him," she said.

"Thanks," said Prim. "I'll do that."

Out in the sports field, there was a variety of training equipment along with a track with logs, ropes leading up to beams, climbing nets and an eight metre high climbing wall. A man was busy climbing the wall alone, with no other help than a thick rope. He leaned backwards while holding the rope firmly. While moving his hands swiftly, his feet ran up the wall until he heaved himself over the edge and then jumped down into a heap of sand. Then, he moved onwards to the next assignment: a loosely hanging net attached to a beam five metres up. It was when Stephen was partway through his ascent that he noticed someone walking towards him whom he recognised. His eyes were smarting from perspiration and he had to use the sleeve of his sweatshirt to wipe his forehead and eyes. His vision cleared and he jumped down.

"Prim, is it you? Why are you here?"

"I was just passing by. I've been at the bus stop close by," Prim lied.

"What do you mean again?" he said and smiled. "Have you been up at the hotel before?"

"Yes, I came by yesterday for the same reason," Prim lied again.

Stephen saw through Prim's little lie, of course.

"Alright, what is it you wanted to see me about? Would you like to start training or something?" he asked.

"No not me. Why should I start training? Only guys are into that sort of thing," Prim replied tentatively, in her halting English, which usually sounded better when she had drunk a beer or two. "No, I wanted to ask you if you know where Lim and Nong are staying and if they're still here in Luang Prabang."

"No, I don't know where they live. They never told me, but I don't think they're still here. Why are you asking about them?" Stephen said.

"Moa and Lek would like to get in touch with them, so I promised to ask you since I would be passing your hotel anyway," Prim replied.

"Oh I see, that's why. And there was me thinking you were after me. But I'm a bit too old for you I guess," said Stephen, smiling, as he laid his hand on Prim's upper arm and stroked it lightly.

"Oh, I don't know about that," Prim said, smiling at him.

"What, is that an invitation or how am I to take it?" he asked her.

"Why, take it as you like," said Prim smiling evasively, beginning to blush a bit.

"Oh, I do," replied Stephen. "No actually, I don't know much about them. I just happened to tag along. I didn't know them. I had met Ian a couple of times and he knew the other guys, so if you'd like to know where they are, you should get in touch with Ian."

"No, I don't want to do that," she said.

"What are you doing today?" Stephen asked.

"I have to run some errands and then head for home," said Prim trying to come up with an explanation for why she would be occupied.

"Could we see each other tonight? You could come here or we could meet at Martin's Bar at eight o'clock. What will be best?"

"Yes, that sounds okay," replied Prim quickly without thinking about the time. "But now I've got to get moving. See you later!"

"Okay!" Stephen replied as he returned to his ropes and obstacles which he now undertook with renewed vigour.

*

Prim drove to Moa's house. Moa had started to pack the things she would need for her journey, all of it fitting into a small rucksack: a pair of sandals, underwear, a blouse, a sweater, a pair of trousers, toiletries. Moa had washed and changed all the clothes she had been wearing. Lek and Prim waited out in the yard.

"How did it turn out?" asked Lek. "Did you find out where Nong and Lim are?"

"No, Stephen thought they had gone home and he didn't know where they live, either. He suggested that we should get in touch with Ian. I didn't want to, but you can if you want to," Prim replied.

"No, I don't want him to know that we're leaving," Lek replied and called out to Moa, "Hurry up!"

"Is Moa all by herself in the house too?" asked Prim.

"Yes, her mother is always working and her father is never home; he has moved in with another woman," Lek explained.

Moa came out, the colour in her face fresher than it had been a couple of hours earlier.

"All of us will ride the moped," said Moa. "That way, it'll take less time."

"Did you have a look to see if there was any money lying around the house?" asked Lek.

"Thanks for reminding me. I forgot to do that! I think I know where Mum hides her money."

Moa ran back into the small house and looked among her mother's things. This wasn't the first time she had stolen money from home. Moa felt under the mattress, under clothes and private things and there, she found what she was looking for, a bundle of kips and dollars. There were eighty dollars in addition to the fifty they already had. It was a lot of money.

"We're going to take it," said Moa to herself and went out again.

"I found some money," she said to the others. "I took eighty dollars."

"Are you out of your mind?" said Lek. "You took eighty dollars from your mother!"

"Yes. My sister worked for this money and sent it to us. I don't think she'd mind my taking it. Anyway, mum will get more money one way or another."

"Get on the moped now and let's go to my place," said Lek.

Off they went, all three of them. Moa would never see her home again.

"Let's hope it falls down soon. Then, they'll have to give us a new one," said Prim when they reached the bridge. "It's scary to walk across it, if you're more than three years old. I'm always frightened."

"Yes, this is what everybody's always talking about when they're crossing this bridge," said Lek. "It's weird."

"Not at all," argued Moa. "They are all scared, that's why they're talking about it."

"Moa, you're always so logical," said Lek. "Why didn't you make use of that brain of yours yesterday?"

"You fool! Back then, I had none," said Moa and laughed. "Let's cross it now."

When they came to the other side of the bridge, they all jumped up on the moped again for the last stretch. They drove into Lek's yard and stopped in front of the house, which was standing there with all that lumber beneath it, as had always been the case whenever Prim had visited the place.

"I'll go in," said Lek. "You wait here."

Moa looked at Prim and asked, "How did it turn out with Stephen? Did you find out anything about the other guys?"

"No," said Prim. "He knew nothing."

"What is that junk lying under the house?" asked Moa.

"Lek's dad goes out looking for land mines up in the fields towards the long valleys around Muang Khoun," Prim replied, "He brings them home and takes them apart. He sells the precious metals but he saves the powder. It's a bit nuts and extremely dangerous. I also know that Lek's mother, in addition to her job at the post office, also sells counterfeit ferry tickets to tourists. That's quite dangerous too, but no one ever reports her."

"I think my brother is the one doing the best business around here," said Moa. "He helps tourists with their luggage when they get off the ferry from Huay Xai down on the Mekong. He picks only the fair skinned ones, takes their bags and offers to carry them up to the road, you know that narrow, steep path and almost all of them say 'yes please'. He puts down their bags in the street and the tourists walk up to him thinking they will get their luggage and that's when he says he wants three dollars. When the tourists say no, he calls for the police, who are always waiting in the wings and when the tourists see them approaching, they always pay without a fuss. And afterwards, my brother gives half of it to the police."

"Well, my uncle sold fake lottery tickets to tourists as well as counterfeit bus tickets," Prim admitted.

"Enough of that," said Moa impatiently and shouted, "Lek, come on!" Since the walls were made of plain timber frames, clad in reeds and large leaves, there was nothing to stop the sound of voices travelling through them.

"I'm coming!" Lek shouted back.

She was writing a note to her mother, explaining that she had left home but would get in touch. In it, she explained that she was going together with Moa, meaning that she would not be alone. She also mentioned that she had taken some of her mother's money. Admitting this made it feel a little less like she was stealing from her own family. Half a minute later, Lek was out in the yard again with a shoulder bag filled with what she needed most.

"Did you find any money?" asked Moa when she emerged.

"I took what I could: forty dollars," Lek said.

"Wow!" shouted Moa. "That means we've got one hundred and seventy American dollars, about one and a half million kip!"

"Okay," said Moa. "Let's head to the bus terminal. It would be good if we could catch the bus to Vientiane at noon. The journey takes about eleven hours and costs about nine dollars, but we'll be in the lap of luxury since the bus is air-conditioned."

"Why don't we buy something to eat to take with us on the journey?" suggested Lek.

Prim was completely silent, almost shocked over how fast all this was happening.

"But Lek, what are we to do with the trousers I've borrowed?"

"What about them? Keep them!" she said.

"What about the moped?"

"Park it up at the post office when you're finished with it. But don't show yourself to my mother because she'd go crazy. And whatever you do, make sure that you don't get caught in any roadblock. You've got no papers for the moped, so the police will take it to the station. Once they've got their hands on it, my mother will have a hard time proving it's hers."

"Alright," said Prim. "But are you telling me I've been riding around on a moped your mother has taken from somebody else?"

"Well, yeah, almost. It's actually my sister's," Lek said.

"Let's go now," said Moa and got up on the moped. "I'll drive this time, otherwise we'll never get there."

*

They drove out of the yard and up on the dusty gravel road. The potholes were nearly big enough for the whole moped: it dipped half a metre and up again with each hole. The road was so uneven that it felt like they were travelling on water. The suspension seemed soft because there were the three of them on the vehicle – three laughing girls – all possessed by the spirit of adventure.

When they got to the bridge, Prim got off. Lek and Moa continued out on the bridge without flinching. Moa drove on the walkway, which was the best strategy when it came to staying alive.

"Look out!" cried Lek, as the front wheel got stuck between two boards and the moped stopped abruptly. Moa almost flew off. The moped fell on its side and Lek had to jump off so as not to land upon Moa.

"Oh, bloody hell! That was close," said Moa.

The moped was lying on one side, its front wheel jammed by a broken board.

"This could've turned out very badly," said Prim when she got there.

"Well, it didn't," replied Moa, a little sulkily. She felt that it was enough that she had been scared and did not want to be reminded about it. "Don't just stand there! Help me get this thing free," she added. "Lek, lift up the front wheel while I crank up the gas! That should do the trick."

Once the moped was free, Moa mounted it again, but the others continued on foot.

"When you've left, I won't have to cross that bridge ever again," Prim told Lek, "and that'll be marvellous."

Moa was waiting impatiently at the corroded and torn bridge stanchion. She looked at the frayed cables that held the bridge. The rivets, supposed to hold the iron construction together at the stanchion, were heavily corroded. The beams that led into the concrete foundation were also partly broken. The very foundation itself was displaced and its collapse into the river appeared to be imminent.

All three of them got up on the moped again to continue to the bus station. Moa was driving fast, but Prim felt as if the two kilometres were taking an eternity. Her new friends were about to leave town.

"This feels sad," said Prim as she sat at the very back of the saddle behind Lek. She held her friend tightly, although mostly to avoid falling off.

"But we'll be back soon, when we've found jobs and saved some money," Lek said.

"Yes," added Moa, "but it'll probably be a while, since I'm not so sure my mother will be happy about me taking all that money."

They drew nearer to the bus terminal and Moa slowed down.

"Stop a little way before," said Lek. "I have to see if there's anyone there that knows me or mum. If mum finds out I'm getting aboard a bus, she'll come here and stop me."

The bus terminal looked like a large, asphalted football field, with buildings along each long side. At the short northern side, there was an entrance and an exit at the southern end. The buildings were worn out, just like every other old structure and their facades were stained by damp. Their window panes were protected by bars, but those were unnecessary as there was nothing worth taking inside. At the spot where the busses stopped, there was a small, raised ramp which made it easier for the passengers to get on and off. By the stop was a sign which stated where the bus was heading. Three buses were in, but none of them was bound for Vientiane.

"Have we missed the bus?" asked Lek.

"No," said Moa. "It's probably not come in just yet. Let's wait here outside until we see it coming."

The three girls got off the moped. They placed their bags between themselves and the moped, so no one would see that they were about to leave.

"This is going to feel really strange, all of it," said Prim. "What am I to do?"

"You could get together with Ing and her friends," said Lek.

"No, I wouldn't like that; they're not my type," Prim replied.

"But Stephen probably is," Moa said and laughed. "It's time you got a boyfriend."

"No," said Prim, "he's too old."

"Too old! You can't be serious. Have a look around. Would you like to run about with young guys who can't afford to take you out and who only want to show you off for their friends and be childish? Never!" said Moa, answering her own question.

"I suppose you're probably right. But it doesn't have to be an old man," replied Prim.

"I think Stephen will be perfect for you," said Lek, turning towards the buses. "Here it comes. Come on Moa, let's go and line up so we can get nice seats."

And then, they said goodbye to Prim, hugging her tightly.

"Bye then, Prim! See you!" Lek said. "Moa, we forgot to buy something to eat for the journey."

"We'll have to get it while we're on the road. The bus will stop a couple of times," Moa responded.

*

Prim stood leaning over the moped and watched her friends as they walked towards the bus. She remained standing for a short time but after a while, she waved goodbye, got back on the moped and began driving away. After a while, she caught herself feeling totally void, her whole body screaming out for something unknown. She drove down to where the rivers met, where she and Lek had sat by the river bank on a half-broken bench just a couple of days ago, looking at the monks growing vegetables, talking about guys.

She wondered what on earth she was going to do now. The monks were still there, watering the same vegetables as before. Nothing ever happened. No, she decided. She'd go home. She wondered whether Lu could be coming home that night, or if she would be staying up in Phonsavan together with those men who were looking for corpses.

Prim drove homewards, very slowly.

Chapter 20

Surprising Discoveries

Lu was a little late. By the time she arrived at Luang Prabang, Frank had already gone up to Phonsavan to try to meet with Spencer. Will remained at the hotel. He had been suffering severely from a stomach illness during the night. Frank said it must have been the heat. But Will thought it was the chicken he had eaten at that street kitchen. Perhaps it had been lying about too long. He was sitting on the terrace when Lu arrived.

"Hi, are you sitting here all alone?" asked Lu.

"Yes," said Will.

"You could easily get into trouble if you're not used to kitchens of that sort," she said. "The best thing to do is to stay clear of them. I always do, even though I'm a local."

"Every cloud has a silver lining; I think I've lost about ten kilos during the night," Will said trying to joke about the situation.

"I guess it can be a way to lose some weight but it's hardly the best one. Make sure you drink properly," Lu advised him.

"Frank went up on his own to meet with Spencer," Will continued. "He didn't want to wait for either of us, but if you want, you and I could go up there in a car of our own or take a bus, if there is one."

"But what if Frank returns during the day? We would have gone up there for nothing," Lu said.

"You could be right. But we can't hang around here all day either. I'm feeling much better now and if we're not going up to join Frank, there might be something else, something fun, we could take the chance to do," Will said.

"Well, have you been to the Tham Ting Buddha caves at the village of Pak Ou?" Lu asked.

"No, I haven't," replied Will. "Where's that?"

"It's an old cave system located a few hours up along the Mekong. For a long time, it was a secret place known only by the monks and the locals. It's definitely worth seeing. What do you think about us taking a riverboat up there? There are departures all the time and it's not more than eight dollars. I think you can afford that," said Lu and smiled the sort of smile a guy wants to see when he's got his mind set on getting lucky; the smile women use when they want to make guys agree to do something.

"But, what about Frank? He might come back early," wondered Will.

"If he does, he'll notice that we're gone and by the way, he doesn't know that I'm here. He might believe you're out and about on your own. But when we meet him, we'll tell him where we've been so he won't start sulking," Lu suggested.

Along the Mekong, just before the meeting of the rivers, there were a couple of boats that didn't seem to be very busy. When one of the boatmen caught sight of Lu and Will approaching, he shouted eagerly, "Come here! Over here!"

Lu guided them to the man's boat. It was a typical Mekong riverboat, with a cabin on top which looked like an old derelict hovel painted with surplus paint from some earlier hotel construction. Lu and Will told him where they wanted to go and were shown to their seats which were made of wood, had crude backrests and were attached directly onto the floor.

"Damn," said Will, "we're in for a rough ride. Are we really going to sit here for several hours?"

"Yes," said Lu, "But the time will fly by quickly, you'll see. There's a lot of things worth seeing along the way. And besides, this is somewhat of an adventure and you're into that sort of thing aren't you?"

"Couldn't you ask the man if he's got a cushion I could put behind my back?" Will asked.

"Sure," Lu said.

Will had not slept at all during the night, so shortly after the motor got started and the cushion was in place, he fell asleep, dead to the world almost all the way to the caves.

*

Frank arrived in Phonsavan during the morning and drove straight to Crater Bar to get in touch with Spencer as soon as possible. When he stepped into the bar, the women were fully occupied in the kitchen. As usual, they appeared to be totally unaware of the fact that there were customers in their restaurant, or perhaps they simply didn't care. If it hadn't been for Spencer, they probably would have worked their shirts off to make sure everybody got the best service possible. He walked up to the kitchen door and knocked hard. There was a hive of activity on the other side but nobody came, so he opened the door himself and stepped in.

"Hello!" shouted Frank. "Hello!"

He poked his head behind a screen at the corner of the kitchen and one of Spencer's wives was standing there holding in her hand the day's special, a struggling hen. She stretched out the other arm to keep her balance, as she held the hen by the neck and swung it around as if stirring a pot until its head separated from its body. Frank swore to himself and hurried out of the kitchen, probably without her even noticing him. He wondered why she couldn't have used a knife instead. After a moment of consideration out in the restaurant, when it had become quiet, it dawned on Frank that this was probably the easiest way to slaughter a chicken if you didn't have a knife and that perhaps, she had been raised without one. There were enough of them in the kitchen, though. Spencer's wife came out into the dining area as if nothing had happened.

"Hi Frank," she said, smiling. "What would you like today? Lunch?"

"No thanks, I would like to meet Spencer," he replied.

"That can be arranged," she said.

"Great, I'll go out, sit down and wait," Frank responded.

"I'll get you some coffee," she said and went back through the door again.

Frank went out and got seated. After what he'd just seen, he couldn't possibly eat there again. How disgusting! Maybe, he did eat a lot of meat and chicken, no question about that, but when you got to see what happened before it wound up in the casserole, you weren't so keen to have anything to do with it anymore. He looked across the street and noticed that there was activity inside the strip bar even at this early hour. He thought that the bars wouldn't open until after lunch but he saw men coming and going during the forty-five minutes he sat waiting for Spencer. Suddenly, he heard a voice beside him.

"Good morning, Frank! Nice to see you here again."

Frank almost jumped, jerked back to reality by Spencer's words.

"Good morning, Spencer," said Frank. "Yeah, duty calls, but Will's suffering from a tummy bug, so I've decided to go on with our assignment on my own today."

"Way to go," said Spencer. "How far have you guys got?"

"We've been down at Lat San, where the Russian tanks are and further on along Lat Khai up to the old barracks. But we haven't had time to see the camp down at Nong Nam Nyam yet. This was actually supposed to be today's destination, but I'll have to wait until Will can come along. What are your thoughts on that?"

"That you're on the right track," Spencer confirmed. "I'll talk with a couple of older Vietnamese guys I know, but they aren't in the area for the moment. I've found out they were here during the war and I believe one of them served at the camp during its later years. If we want to make the guy talk, it'll cost you. But let's go for it. I'll find out when he might be available today."

"Great, thanks!" Frank said. "When we were at the camp at Lat Khai, we met an old lady, well maybe not that old, but she was so haggard, she looked about two hundred. She was called Noi. She's Vietnamese but lives in poor conditions compared to the other Vietnamese people in this valley. Is that just because she chose a man from a different ethnic group? I've given it some thought since we left that place yesterday."

"Yeah, that's the way the cookie crumbles around here," said Spencer. "They get frozen out and regarded with great suspicion. If they get poor, they get extremely poor and live on almost anything. No denying that it's terrible."

"Yeah, it's weird that. Your woman is Vietnamese as well and she's living with you, but from what I can see, you seem to have a certain economic standing," Frank observed.

"That's correct, but there is a difference," Spencer began. "I could, so to speak, buy myself into this society and even help others. In addition, I'm an American, which in itself, could pose a problem, but we do have a high status here and most of the anger about the war has waned. Recently, I have not really noticed any of it and there are a lot of Americans around here, in this valley. There are also some mixed couples, like we are. Those from groups with high economic standing are allowed to join the fun, just look at the Chinese in this area, people are careful not to freeze them out. So you see, there's a lot of hypocrisy even here, Frank. But I agree with you that those who do get frozen out haven't got a chance."

"Yeah, Noi told us, among other things, that she had sold her daughters and I'm pretty sure I know what kind of life she sold them into," Frank said.

"Well, I'm afraid that's more common than people realise in many other parts of the world. But you must understand that these individuals are unbelievably poor. They try to live on a few kilos of rice and a pig per year. Everywhere, there are brothels that buy up girls. If there are about one hundred and thirty thousand families in this valley, I guarantee you that one percent of them have sold one or two daughters to middlemen who take them to brothels. That makes one thousand three hundred families, from this area alone," Spencer said.

"Why is this a subject that only crops up when one's sitting and talking like this?" Frank asked.

"Oh, it's quite simple," said Spencer. "This all happens so close to us that we don't really think about it until we get some distance from it. Just look at the opposite side of the street here. It's a brothel bar and it popped up over there a couple of years ago. And who owns it? No one knows, or likes to talk about it."

"Would you like some more coffee?" a voice called from inside.

"Yes please and make us a sandwich with cheese and ham! That might go well with the coffee," said Spencer, who turned back to Frank. "I always have some coffee around eleven in the morning. It's the best time of day and the coffee always tastes best then. After that, no more coffee. But back to what we were talking about. Men stream in to that place all day. It's really filthy. It's one of those cheaper brothels and a screw doesn't cost you more than five dollars, tops. I've never seen the girls go out. I think they're kept on a very short leash in there. Little more than slaves," said Spencer, with a glare of outrage. "But no one does a single thing about it. That would mean putting your life on the line."

"I'll be damned!" said Frank. "We actually went in there a couple of days ago, when we were looking for some alternative place to eat. But once we got inside, we realised it was a bit of a go-go bar, so we went back out again."

"Yeah, yeah, go-go it is," Spencer said, fixing Frank's gaze.

"Well, gentlemen," said a female voice from behind Frank, "here's some fresh coffee and some bread with cheese and ham. I can't understand why you eat so much bread!"

"No," replied Spencer. "You're missing out on the fruits of life."

"And I've realised that I won't be getting a lot done today," said Frank. "But I really welcome this opportunity to get to know you better."

The conversation waned while they drank their coffee and each took bites of their sandwiches. Frank thought about Spencer, who had been so reticent at the start, but was now chatting away. It was nice.

"Have you ever thought about going back to the US?" Frank asked.

"Nope," Spencer replied. "I'll never return. I don't have as many years left as you have, probably, but I'd like to live those years well and living well is what I'm doing here. Besides, I've lived in this part of Asia for a longer part of my life than I lived in the States. Alright, I was born American, but that doesn't mean that I have to live and die there."

"Yeah, you're right about that," said Frank.

"Besides, I'm making a great living here on my pension from the air force. There's no way that I could keep the standard of living I have here, if I had to move to the States or to Europe," Spencer confirmed.

"Is that a fact?" Frank said.

"Oh, yeah, it is. I'm living really cheaply. I can't even manage to spend my monthly pension here," Spencer revealed.

"Do you like it here?" Frank asked while Spencer chewed away.

"Yes I do and above all, moments like this one, with a nice cup of coffee," said Spencer.

"It is nice. I get your drift," Frank said.

"I like it here, here in Asia I should say, since I mostly keep myself in Laos, Thailand and Cambodia," Spencer continued. "I go to Thailand when I feel the need for a vacation by the sea and to Phnom Penh when I need to see my son, Peter, who's been running a large restaurant and a bar there for a couple of years. When he moved from the States, he settled down in Thailand, where initially, he worked at a restaurant. Nowadays, he runs a bar called Riverside Bistro, probably the most popular bar in Cambodia."

Frank sat listening in total silence, dumbfounded. For a moment, he thought he must have misheard.

"It's not possible!" he said, finally. "It's true that I've experienced many strange things in my life, but to be sitting here up in Laos and hear this, takes the biscuit."

"What do you mean?" asked Spencer.

"I know your son!" Frank exclaimed. "I lived at his place when he started decorating for his bar. I lived in that extra apartment in his house that he rents out. My God, it's a small world! But as far as I can remember, he said that his father lived in Thailand, not in Laos."

"Well, that was probably just because he didn't want to go into detail about me," said Spencer, who was as surprised as Frank. "How did you meet?"

"As you're probably aware, Peter campaigns against child pornography and the sexual abuse of children," Frank said.

"Yeah, I know," said Spencer.

"I met him when he'd just finished helping the police in Cambodia catch that famous rocker and infamous paedophile Larry Glister. Peter was at the station with information, at the same time as I was there on an errand. As you know, we have to cooperate with the local authorities and it resulted in us getting to know each other. From then on, we got on well."

Frank shook his head, rose up, took a step towards Spencer. Moved, he stuck out his hand, "Spencer, I must shake your hand once more."

Spencer rose up, put his hands on Frank shoulders and embraced him. Then they both said, almost simultaneously, "I have to call Peter."

*

The Mekong offered a beautiful boat trip up to the Buddha Caves. But Will saw none of it. When he opened his eyes, they were almost there.

"What the hell? I must have fallen asleep," he said.

With his hand, he scooped up some water from the river to wash his eyes.

"Yes, so I noticed," said Lu. "It didn't take long for you to fall asleep and to crown it all, you were snoring so loudly that you almost drowned the engine."

"No, that's not true," said Will laughing. "Pull the other one!"

"Good morning, sir," the boatman said and smiled at Will.

Ten minutes later, they reached the caves, or rather the steps leading up to them.

"Are we supposed to go ashore here?" asked Will.

"Yes," said Lu. "We're in for a bit of climbing."

"Up those steps?" Will said.

"Don't be silly, come on now!" said Lu, laughing.

The steps leading up the mountainside were precipitous. The first stage was narrow, with small steps. There were a lot of them stretching upwards and they were in poor condition. After the next terrace, it got a little easier, but before long, Will had started to feel the effort in his calf muscles and thighs.

"Ouch! What have you got me into? I'm starting to feel my unused muscles," he said. "I really must rest for a while. How much is left?"

"Okay, let's take a break," said Lu. "After that, it's maybe just another two hundred metres."

"Don't you feel anything in your legs at all?" Will asked.

"No," Lu admitted.

"This is worse than a Stairmaster at a gym," Will observed. "I never run into problems on those things, but this, bloody hell!"

"Come on now," Lu said trying to encourage him, "we can't remain standing here. Let's walk slowly and I'm sure you'll be able to handle it," Lu said.

After a "God-awful amount of steps" as Will put it, they finally arrived at their destination.

"Oh!" exclaimed Will, amazed. "What a cave entrance! Absolutely fantastic! So it was Buddhist monks who found this cave a few hundred years ago? It's remarkable. And see how it's placed with the entrance towards the Mekong. What an eagle's nest!"

"Go in and have a look," Lu said.

"I've never seen the like - so many Buddha statues - thousands upon thousands of them and each one unique," he remarked.

Will grew lyrical; the pain in his legs had vanished.

*

Road 7 wound its beautiful way up to an altitude of fifteen hundred metres between Nong Tang and Nam Chat. Frank was starting to feel tired of driving and it didn't help when he pinched himself on his legs or slapped his cheeks. "Fucking hell!" he said loudly to himself. "If I can just make it to the crossroads down at Phou Khon and Road 13."

But by the time he'd reached the main road out of the village of Phou Vien, Frank's energy was sapped and he had to give up. He stopped the car, got out into the cool mountain air and drew a few deep breaths. He was lucky that the mountain people had not begun to burn the fields, or those deep breaths would have been an extremely unpleasant experience. The mountain people burnt everything during certain parts of the year; as a result, the smoke lay thick over the mountains. During these periods, it was best to avoid travelling up here, or down in Luang Prabang.

Before his departure, he had eaten a slap-up dinner with Spencer. He was slightly concerned that had become so full up and lethargic. This wouldn't do. Time to get home.

Frank took a stroll along the road, but was reluctant to stray too far from the car. He was afraid that it might get stolen, or perhaps get vandalised. He hopped and skipped as he went, alone. If anyone had seen him, they might have called the police and the police would have taken away his licence. He was acting strangely, but only so as to prepare his body for the drive ahead.

He was on his way back to the car when two men on a motorcycle drove up towards him.

"Wanna buy opium?" one of them asked him.

"No," said Frank. "I don't. Get lost!"

But the men did not get lost. Their minds were set on something else.

"Money! Money!" they shouted to Frank, who suddenly grew afraid as he backed slowly towards the driver's door.

"Wait, I've got some in the car!" he said trying to buy some time.

Frank got the door open and jumped into the driver's seat, turned the ignition key, which was already in place and slipped into gear. He heaved his car up onto the road, causing the men to lose control over their motorcycle. Frank didn't look back, just drove on, hell for leather. He had never before driven this fast on this type of road. He didn't slow down until he reached the exit to Road 13 and turned onto it. Then, he realised that there was no one behind him, trying to catch him up. Frank pondered how creepy the experience had been. Those drug dealers could be a real pain-in-the-ass. They weren't to be played around with. If they didn't snuff you out, the police would.

After the exit, the driving got easier and Frank decided to make a stop in Nam King for a cup of coffee. While drinking, Frank wondered what could have happened to the drug dealers. Had they pursued him, or had he run them over? Fuck! And how was Will doing?

*

Will was surrounded by Buddha statues of all shapes and sizes.

"Wouldn't you like to go a bit further up?" asked Lu. "A hundred steps higher up, there's more to see."

"Yes, since we've come all the way up here, it would be a shame not to see everything," said Will.

"Come on then, let's go. We could take it a bit easier so you won't get so tired," she told him and gave him a motherly smile.

"Look here, quit doing that! There's much more power left inside this guy, believe you me!" he said.

"Will, you don't have to prove anything to me. What's important is that we'll get there in one piece, since it's just as hard to get back down again as it will be to get up there. You've got to stay focused: if you put your foot in the wrong place, it can get ugly and I've seen strong young men make that mistake, so take it easy," Lu emphasised.

"Alright," said Will and they proceeded up to the last ridge and the last cave.

"Just think of it!" he cried, when he reached it. "Nature has created all this and then the monks have lived and worshiped here. It's a pity we don't have a flashlight," he said.

"That's not the way it's intended. You're supposed to contemplate this holy mountain cavern with your own imagination. All of us see different things and this is what you are to bring with you on your journey back."

They left the large mountain room and began to descend slowly.

"Hell! I didn't believe you when you said it would be just as strenuous going downwards as upwards. I guess now I know better," he announced.

Once they made it down to the boat, Will recovered his breath.

"Lu, thank you so much for bringing me here. I would never have thought of it by myself. For the moment, there's only one thing missing," he said.

"What?" Lu asked.

"I'm incredibly thirsty and hungry," Will said.

"As far as your thirst goes, I can be of assistance," Lu said. "There are usually bottled drinks for sale on board these boats but they are often pricey."

"It doesn't matter," Will said. "He can ask whatever price he likes. Ask him what he's got and I'll buy you one as well."

"He's got Beerlao and water," Lu told him.

"Then I know what I'd like: a Beerlao," Will confirmed.

"I'll have water," said Lu.

"Would you like to go back right away?" the boatman asked Lu.

"Yes, I guess so," she replied. "But I'll ask him, just to make sure."

"Will, would you like us to go home the direct route or would you like to make a stop along the way?" She asked him. "Passengers usually stop at a whiskey factory close to the river."

"No thanks," Will said. "I'm no whiskey lover, so let's skip that. And, by the way, I think we have to be back early, preferably before Frank gets back."

"Why? Are you afraid of him?" Lu asked.

"No, not at all, but it would be nice if all three of us could eat together, don't you think?" replied Will, gulping down his beer.

"Then, we have to leave at once and not stop anywhere on the way. And Will, don't fall asleep this time! You'll miss out on a spectacular sunset over the Mekong," Lu said.

"Don't worry, I'll stay awake. Do you really think I'd be willing to miss a romantic sunset together with you, Lu?" he said.

Lu was grateful that the boat was narrow and that she had to sit behind him. She wasn't interested in a romantic trip; she just wanted to make sure she gave something of value for the money she was getting. And that could be anything but sex and romance, since that wasn't what she was selling.

This time, Will saw how beautiful it could be along the Mekong, the villages, the yards, the animals and the many boats.

"Such lives they live by the river," he said.

"Yes, you missed out on a lot on the trip upriver," Lu remarked.

"But I'm making up for it now," Will said. "It's the weirdest thing," he continued, after a short while. "It always feels like the journey back goes quicker. I thought you said that it would take a couple of hours for us to reach Luang Prabang, but I can already see the beach, the ferry port and the other boats."

"Time goes quicker when you're experiencing nice things. Even if I've been a thousand times or more on this river, I see new things every time and I often experience the trip as if it were for the very first time. Things are changing all the time," Lu said.

"How far can you get on the river?" Will asked.

"All the way down to Cambodia," Lu replied.

"Have you been down that far?" Will asked again.

"No, I haven't. But I've travelled down to Vientiane on a few occasions. It's very beautiful. Go there if you ever have the time. There are boats that leave from here," Lu said.

"Yeah, I'll suggest to Frank that we do that when we've finished our assignment. It's a great idea to do that trip instead and skip the flight when we go back," Will commented.

The boat reached the beach they had departed from several hours earlier. This time, they were greeted by a stunning sunset over the river behind them.

"I'll go ashore from the side," said Will. "I can hardly get up. I'm as stiff as a board."

"Be careful, it could be deep. I'll go ashore from the bows," said Lu.

Will made sure the little bag he had brought with him stayed on the inside of the gunwale as he slithered off the boat. And that was lucky: Will, all five foot six of him, disappeared completely into the water. Luckily, he was holding on to the gunwale with one hand.

"Oh hell!" he said, astonished. "It sure is deep right here. I can't touch the bottom!"

"Well, I warned you didn't I?" said Lu with a laugh.

Will pulled himself towards land with help of the gunwale. And there he stood, soaked to the skin.

"My first time in the Mekong. That's something to brag about! Lucky it's not far to the hotel. I just hope everybody won't laugh when they see me," he said.

"Oh, I don't think they will. People around here have seen most things, both with and without clothes. You needn't worry. Come on!" Lu replied.

They walked towards the ferry port to the steps which led from the beach to the street. These steps, which covered a distance of fifty metres, had been there since the war. Originally, there had been two hundred and fifty steps. Nowadays, however, every other step was broken, askew, in pieces, cracked, filled with concrete or mended with wood pieces inserted into its wounds.

"I think I'm about to get a stitch," said Will. "What bloody strenuous steps! They're a metre high, dammit and broken too. It would probably have been easier to walk beside them."

"Come on now!" said Lu. "It's true that they're broken and high, but we'll soon be up there." It crossed her mind how so many men seemed to whine.

*

In the meantime, Frank was driving into Luang Prabang. Lingering still was that unpleasant feeling following the incident with the men on the motorcycle. It was a shame that it should happen on such a nice day. For now, he wasn't far from the hotel and on a whim, he put on the radio. It had been off during the whole trip, but he felt that a murmuring radio could ease his stress and make for some relaxation. Frank turned into the hotel street and was met with a sight he had not expected.

Will and Lu stopped short and stared at the approaching car.

"This can't be true," said Will. "Why should he pop up out of nowhere right now? Why wasn't I allowed just one minute's advantage?"

Then, he began to laugh, almost struggling for breath as Frank got out of his car with an astonished expression.

The guests and the staff at Merry Lao Swiss open-air café looked on inquisitively at the accidental theatrics, as Frank spoke.

"What are you doing here? And just look at you! Has someone thrown you into the river, or what?" Frank had a hard time trying not to laugh as well. "Lu, what have you both been up to?"

"Don't drag me into his sudden bath. For now, I leave you to each other. I guess you guys have a whole day to talk about," Lu said.

"But tell me, Lu, what's been going on?" Frank asked.

"No, Will has to tell you. I'm going home and don't want to miss the bus. You can talk to each other. I'm taking a motorcycle taxi to the bus terminal. Bye then! I'll be back early in the morning," she confirmed.

"Sounds fine," Frank said. "We have quite a lot to do."

Lu quickly found a motorcycle taxi, relieved that she had not had to answer any questions. The driver took the same way back towards the bus terminal as Will and she had just walked, past the ferry port, the steps, the wall and the memories. They sprang quickly to mind: the memories of all those times she had come here to take the boat to her friend across the river and of all those times Fang had been sitting waiting just to catch a glimpse of her. It was inevitable that she would come to think about Fang. No matter whether Lu liked it or not, he was there in her mind, in so many places and so many mental images. Lu had come to understand that Fang was a butterfly nowadays, fluttering from bed to bed. This was no surprise really as Fang's father Songchai was a butterfly too, but this was never spoken of. In that sense, Songchai had been no different from many other Asian men, other than the fact that he avoided brothels. Those cost money, after all; it was better to have a lover here and there, away from his own village.

Chapter 21

River Threats

Songchai had arranged a comfortable seat, furthest out in the aft of his boat. He had made up his mind to remain sitting there all night, to gaze out over the river and enjoy his solitude, to just 'be'. The night could offer much more than the sounds from the village. Large and round, the moon cast its light over the river valley and the calls of the animals, alongside the endless rippling of water against the boat's hull, had a soothing effect.

Songchai realised that they still had a long stretch ahead of them. Perhaps it was foolish to choose the river. Should they change strategy and go hauling by road earlier than planned? On the other hand, that might prove to be dangerous, since there were so many road blocks by the police and the army along the way. To be discovered smuggling weapons to a foreign country through Thailand would lead to incarceration. Safer then to stick with the existing plan, but they'd have to try to get down to Khemmarat a bit quicker. He'd speak with the others tomorrow, early in the morning.

Songchai decided to try to sleep for a couple of hours, nevertheless. But not in the moonlight, since he believed that doing so could cause you to wake up angry and he did not want to be like that the following day. He altered his seat to make it more comfortable, pulled a tarpaulin over himself and tried to fall asleep.

*

Morning came with all that it involves in a small village by the Mekong: dogs barking, roosters crowing and boats without silencers coming and going. Voratep was the first to wake, so he made breakfast for everyone, the usual: tea, rice, vegetables, fish and eggs, everything the body needed. One after the other, his companions came for their breakfasts, all except one.

"Where is Songchai?" asked Voratep. "Surachai, go and have a look and make sure that nothing has happened to him."

"Sure," he said and jumped over to Songchai's boat.

Suddenly, the tarpaulin in the aft came alive.

"Oh my!" said Songchai. "I must have sat up for so long last night that I lost track of time."

"Good morning," said Surachai. "Come on over to Voratep; he's made us some breakfast."

"Great, I'll get over at the double," Songchai replied enthusiastically.

He joined the others.

"Today, we have to make sure that we speed things up and take fewer stops; only to fuel up. This journey is beginning to take too much time," he said to them all.

"I thought we had agreed that we should hurry, so I've got no problem with that at all," said Kitepong.

Neither had the others. As long as they kept to a reasonably rapid pace, they would be able to avoid the balls of gas. Along the stretch down to Muang, a gas was formed in the river bed, which ignited and sent up fireballs in various bright colours. These fireballs lit up everything on the river during the night and could rise up to a hundred metres above the surface of the Mekong. This phenomenon had been going on for thousands of years and there was much speculation as to whether this could be Buddha's way of expressing his discontent.

"I hope that there are no fireballs during the day," said Voratep. "I don't want to get on bad terms with my Buddha."

"Alright, here's an idea: we just push on and whoever arrives first simply waits for the others?" Songchai suggested.

"No, that might prove risky. What would happen if one of us were to get machine problems or nod off?" objected Voratep.

"You've got a point there! Let's stick together," said Surachai.

"You'd all better stay on the alert, for you own safety. We don't want any more accidents. Well then, are we all set?" Voratep continued. "I just need to clear up after you guys. It'll only take a couple of minutes and then, we can be off."

*

Each went to their separate boats to continue down the Mekong, against the background of the monotonous sound of all the engines. For someone standing on the beach, it was impossible to single out one boat from the other. They all looked the same. That was also the idea; they should be hard to identify. No serviceman or policeman would be able to catch a boat on the Mekong, filled up with weapons, on the basis of a generalised description. Pointing out that the target vessel was a typical twelve metre riverboat, painted in blue and with a bit of white, maybe also some red and green, just wouldn't suffice; there were about a hundred of these almost identical boats every kilometre.

When they had passed Muang Paksane, the river seemed to flow faster. Everything went according to plan and by noon, they were approaching Ban Paksa. Songchai signalled to the others that it was time to fuel up and to have something to eat. They stopped after the port camp in Paksa where they could get petrol.

"I'll fill my jerry cans as well," said Songchai. "You lot do that too, so we're equipped to get through the night. Let's have something to eat before we continue, but we have to move first. If we stay here, we're in the way of others. Let's anchor a hundred metres further down."

Songchai had heated some water for tea and laid out some food as the others moored side by side.

"Why do we have to take the cargo all the way to Khemmarat?" asked Voratep. "I gave it some thought as we were approaching Paksa but I can't figure it out."

"Why? I thought I'd explained all this," said Songchai. "I guess I'll have to go over it once more. As you all know, I'm familiar with certain parts of Thailand and above all the areas around here. Just like our districts in Laos, there are poor areas here as well and Khemmarat is situated in the region of Isan, the poorest region of Thailand, one that is in a class of its own. It's the worst region I've ever come across. This means that it's easy to get help for almost no money at all and they don't give a crap about what kind of job it is."

"Yes, yes, you're right," said Voratep. "I had forgotten about that. That's a good enough reason for me."

"They'll do anything for money there: load and unload arms boxes, transport pigs to the slaughter houses in Bangkok – pigs that might contain other things than meat – get little girls for the brothels. Yes, they'll do anything, since they have no other way to support themselves," Songchai said.

"I understand now," said Voratep. "I just need to get it clear inside my head to be able to build up some motivation."

"It seems as if the river flows faster here," said Kitepong. "It sure feels that way, at least. Maybe, we can save some time."

"Alright guys! Let's take off again," said Songchai, before they had time to chew down their meagre meal. "If we keep up this current pace, I think we can reach Khemmarat in twenty-four hours and it'll be enough if we just fuel up in Muang Khammouan."

Surachai reckoned that Songchai was the worst slave-driver in Asia. "If we push on too hard without sleep," he said, "there's a risk that someone will doze off and then we're all in trouble. Not having breaks and rests along the way is idiotic."

The others agreed with Surachai.

"Alright, I suppose that's the way it has to be then," murmured Songchai. "But let's get a move on, for now!"

They cleared up quickly, boarded their boats and cast off. Before long, they were on their way, like a line of colours strung along the river. Songchai and his men were already a good distance from Luang Prabang and they would have to cover another five hundred kilometres before they reached their intermediate goal at Khemmarat.

*

Just as Kitepong had observed, the river flowed more intensely now, which meant that the section down to Muang Khammouan would go faster than the previous ones. Songchai cranked his engine and took the lead, but after a short period of time, he slowed down and waved to the others to come up to him. They placed their boats side by side and allowed them to drift with the current.

"One thing sprang to my mind. Down in Muang, there is a ferry port quite similar to the one in Luang Prabang. It's about the same size. But it's also a frontier station which means that there are lots of police and servicemen in town," he said.

"Oh yeah," said Voratep. "And you tell us this now! Then it's probably for the best that we stop either before or after Muang."

"Yeah, no bloody way we'll step right into that hornets' nest," said Kitepong. "Do you think that we could get down to Ban Kengkaboa? I was there on a few occasions during the war and have some friends in the village. They might be still living there."

"Sounds fine," said Songchai. "But it's even better that you know the village and the way it's situated in relation to the sea.

If we manage to get there on the fuel we have, it's a better place to stock up."

"Fine by me. Let's do that," said Surachai. "But we still have to tread carefully through Muang. Let's keep proper distances from one another and if something happens, we'll just act as if we're all strangers."

*

After another couple of hours, they had Muang Khammouan to their left and Nakhon Phanom to their right. Out on the river, there were a number of ferries travelling between the two cities, as well as a patrol boat.

Songchai decided that he should go towards Muang; there seemed to be a greater distance between the patrol boat and the shore on that side. He slowed down, so as not to draw attention and crossed the river towards Muang at low speed. After Kitepong had done the same, he noticed that one of the men on the patrol boat was pointing at them and that they had started their engines. The patrol boat began a wide turn in order to intercept them further on. Kitepong felt his adrenaline rising and drove up towards a couple of boats, joining them so as to be less conspicuous. Surachai and Voratep just drove on as if nothing had happened, albeit with their hearts in their mouths.

Songchai had also noticed the patrol boat's manoeuvre, but he was no longer looking back, since he wanted neither to see nor to know if something went wrong. If any one of them were to get caught, he'd be looking forward to life imprisonment, something they all knew. Suddenly, Supot regretted his participation. What would happen if he was discovered? Would they sink his boat, drown him, take the cargo, find out where he lived and then take the rest of the family and claim that they had all been involved? No, not initially. First, the local chief of police would contact the press, place himself behind Supot and the others and make sure that the photographers took pictures of the capable policeman with his catch. And when they had received all the attention they desired, every means available would be used to reveal the truth; among other details the fact that Supot was Hmong. An 'accidental drowning' seemed quite possible.

The patrol boat slowed down, closing in on them at low speed and squeezing itself between them with just a few metres on either side, determined and without concern for the smaller boats. They knew exactly what they wanted. The waves they formed forced all the boats around them to heel hard and they almost collided.

Supot had a gun ready to hand, not to fire at the crew of the patrol boat, but to liberate himself from suffering and misery. One hand was on the wheel; the other held the pistol below a covering. No one saw him turning the muzzle towards his face. But just as the patrol boat was at its closest, it accelerated again, shooting past Supot and up towards the shore on the opposite side. Slowly, Supot lifted his finger from the trigger.

Suddenly, he saw that he was about to ram into a boat in front of him. At the last moment, he managed to yaw away and steered towards a group of boats in the middle of the river. He put his gun away, grateful he had not been forced to use it.

The others sat on edge in their boats, keeping a good distance from one another as they passed Muang. Each of them understood that if any one of them were to get caught, he would have no friends and no helpers. Voratep was sure that Supot would talk. Maybe, he'd hold out for one or two days, so they might have time to get away. When he had come far enough down the river to feel safe again, Songchai slowed and waited for the others to catch up.

"Did you have time to see what happened?" he asked Surachai when he came up alongside.

"I'm not sure. The only thing I saw was Supot steering in among the boats that go between the ferry ports and then there was this patrol boat going up towards him. We'll have to ask the others."

Voratep drove up alongside Surachai. He slowed too late and glided into Surachai's boat, hitting the gunwale on the port side.

"Oh, sorry, but I'm a bit shaken. I just wanted to tell you that nothing happened back there. It turned out well."

"We'll wait for Supot," said Songchai. "He'll have to tell us himself when he gets here."

Supot chose to take it easy. He needed to catch his breath after the stress of the near miss. He decided to put the gun out of reach so he wouldn't be tempted to use it again. As he approached the others, their boats were now idling while they waited for him.

"What happened?" asked Surachai.

"Nothing, but it was a close call," Supot said. "A great deal of things could have happened, but I don't want to talk about it now. Let's go on! I'll tell you tonight when we take a break."

"I couldn't agree more. Let's get the fuck out of here, at the double!" said Voratep, driving out to the middle of the river to see if Songchai would take the lead again.

As expected, he did. The engines roared, fully cranked up. Nobody looked back. There was no reason for that now. Foam whirled about. The bow waves were whipping the river banks behind them and it would not be long before they arrived at Ban Kenkaboa. Kitepong signalled that he wanted to be the first to arrive at the village. He drove past Songchai. This time, Songchai was not the one who knew best. Kitepong signalled with his arms that everybody was to follow him.

They passed the village's anchorage and continued for about a kilometre until a natural bay opened up on the river's west side. Inside it, a couple of jetties appeared, stretching out some twenty metres into the water, a perfect place to bunker up and rest.

Chapter 22

Three against One

In Luang Prabang, Lu was on her way to the bus station, hoping to get home after having spent the day with Will. At the same time, Prim was riding the moped out of the same city, dazed by the day's events. She wondered why she had decided to go home. She asked herself why she wasn't staying and meeting Stephen. Something inside her said yes and no to this idea both at the same time. She was curious and yet hesitant. She could meet him some other day. She couldn't think straight. Everything was so confusing. Prim jammed on the brakes, drove to one side and sat herself down, a short distance from the roadside. She held her arms around her legs, her chin on her knees and then she began to cry, the tears she had wanted to shed when Moa and Lek climbed onto that bus. It was this grief that had kept her from thinking clearly. It had blocked the way and now it all heaved out in streams of tears by the roadside. A car went by and then a bus. No one who saw her knew what had happened to make the girl cry.

The air began to get cooler, almost a bit chilly, which was often the case up in the mountains when the sun was about to set. Prim's conscience was troubled, since she had not returned the moped. Of course, the vehicle was a very practical asset. But this was a problem that would have to wait until the next day.

Prim felt better after having a good cry. She got up, returned to the moped and took off. When she was almost home, she decided to ride all the way into the yard. If anyone saw her, she would just tell them how it was - well, almost how it was - she would say that she had borrowed the moped from Lek and was going to return it tomorrow, which was, she told herself, not so very far from the truth.

Prim rode all the way up to the entrance of the hut. Lu was already at home. She had arrived with the bus that had passed Prim as she sat by the roadside.

Lu heard the engine sound outside the hut and went out.

"Prim, it's you who's turned up here on a moped!" Lu exclaimed. "How did that come about? You've certainly changed quickly! What are you up to? Besides, are you even allowed to drive one of those?"

Showered with questions, Prim struggled to get a word in.

"Answer me! Where did you get that moped?" Lu repeated herself

"Chill out, Mum! I've borrowed it from Lek, otherwise I wouldn't have come home in time. Everything's okay. I'll return it tomorrow. Don't make a big thing out of it," Prim said, trying to smooth things over.

"Oh yeah, 'No big thing!'" Lu responded. "You come home in other people's clothes; you skip school - in fact, you don't give a crap about it - you don't come home at night, now you show up on a moped you've borrowed and you're asking me to chill out?"

"But what about you? How often are you not home at night?" Prim proclaimed.

"That's me, Prim, not you," Lu replied. "I'm your mother and you're my daughter whom I want to guide through life and now it feels like I'm about to fail."

"Yeah, yeah, Mum. But you don't need to feel that way. I can take care of myself," Prim assured her.

"Not on your own, you can't. Not for a while yet," Lu stated.

"Mum, I promise, tomorrow I'll go down to Luang Prabang to return the moped and I'll take the bus home. So, when you return in the evening, I'll be home, okay?" Prim said trying to reassure her mother.

"Yes, that's okay, but I hope you fully understand me," Lu continued.

"Yes, but no more now, or else we might fall out," Prim said.

"Alright, which one of us will do the cooking?" Lu asked.

"I'll fetch some eggs if you boil the rice," suggested Prim. "I'll go to grandma and ask her if she's got some chicken."

"Yeah, you do that. If I'd go, we're guaranteed not to get any," Lu replied.

"Mum, why can't grandma stop being so unfriendly towards you?" Prim asked.

"She feels that I've ruined her and grandpa's chances of getting a better life since your father moved away. They're holding me responsible. And there's something else. They feel that I should support them which is something that I refuse to do. I think they're perfectly capable of getting their food on the table themselves, just like they've always done," Lu said.

"So, that's why it's better if I go over there and ask her," said Prim.

"Yeah, you could try. I guess you'll get what you're asking for. Go on and I'll take care of the rest here," Lu agreed.

Prim went to the chicken run, which now was in a much better shape than it had been the last time she was there. She took a couple of eggs and left the rest alone. Then, she went to her grandmother and asked if they had some boiled chicken. Fortunately, grandma had just done some cooking and Prim got what she wanted.

"What have we got here?" said Lu, grinning at Prim with a slight grimace. "Are we to sit outdoors or indoors?"

"Indoors, it's a bit cold tonight and I think it takes too long to kindle the fire. Couldn't we just wrap some blankets around us and eat indoors and then hit the sack?" asked Prim, imploringly.

"Sounds fine. Let's do that," Lu confirmed.

Before long, they were sitting wrapped in blankets with the food in their hands. Prim had so many things on her mind that she felt she might burst. How would she hold back from speaking about what had happened over the last few days? To prevent herself revealing her secrets, she decided to asked her mother some questions instead.

"How's your day been, together with those guys? What have you done?" she asked.

Lu told her about Will and their outing to the Buddha caves, about Will's stiffness after the climb, the trip back, his dip and how they had bumped into Frank. But before Lu had finished her story, Prim had almost fallen asleep, her food still in her hand.

"Mum, I'm so incredibly tired," she said. "I think I have to go to bed now."

Prim put away her food bowl, lay down with the warm blanket wrapped around her and fell asleep instantly. Lu remained sitting for a while, looking at her. Where had the years gone? They'd flown by without her even noticing. Silence fell in the hut as the night enclosed both mother and daughter.

*

Prim woke to the sound of Lu ferreting about in the hut before she left. It was still early morning.

"Prim," called Lu. "Could we go together on the moped down to town? That way, you'll have returned it in the morning and I'll get there well in time to go up to Phonsavan with Will and Frank. And you can come home by bus later in the morning."

"Of course," said Prim, who was happy to be able to help Lu.

"Then, let's get a move on. Shall we go down to the brook to wash ourselves?" Lu asked.

"No, I'll wash out in the yard, it's quicker," Prim replied.

"So will I," said Lu and left the hut before Prim.

They both heard a car approaching and soon, they could see it too.

"Funny," said Lu. "That police car again. I can't figure out why they're skulking about in the mountain villages like this. What are they looking for, really? At first, I thought it was nice that they were cruising around making sure that everything was alright, but now I smell a rat. Sooner or later, their purpose will become clear, I suppose."

Prim and Lu washed in the tub and made themselves ready.

"Do you mind if I drive?" asked Lu.

"No, not at all, please do. But drive carefully," said Prim, as if Lu had never driven a moped.

Prim soon find out that Lu knew what she was doing; Prim had never travelled this quickly to Luang Prabang before. When they got there, she laughed.

"Mum, you're crazy," she said. "I would never have thought this of you."

"There are a lot of things you don't know and some things you'll never know," Lu replied, grabbing Prim about the chin and kissing her on the cheek. "Drive the moped to Lek's now and return it. Drive carefully!"

Prim took the handlebars and drove slowly towards the bridge and Lek's house, but at the bridge, she changed her mind. She would park the moped by the post office instead. That way, Lek's mother would see it when she got there. Prim parked it by the steps, so it would be impossible to miss and then walked away.

It was still morning and there were a couple of hours before the bus was due to depart. Prim took the sunny southward road along the Mekong and it occurred to her that Stephen's hotel was not very far away. Should she go there? No, it was probably too early. He was probably eating breakfast, or already gone out to exercise. Her instincts told her not to go there, but all the while her legs were carrying her to the hotel. It wasn't right. She didn't know him at all and he was a lot older than her. What was it Moa had said? That Prim needed a real guy? But she couldn't stop her curiosity getting the better of her.

Excited by her thoughts, but a little frightened too, she stopped at the hotel gate and peeked inside, but didn't open it. Then, she looked towards the sports field. There was no one there. What a relief! She pivoted quickly and walked at a rapid pace with her back to the hotel, hoping that no one had seen her.

Prim was curious about what it would be like to really sleep with a guy, not just kissing and fondling, but with someone who didn't just touch her breasts, but touched her properly, felt all over her body, someone she could caress just as she pleased, someone to enjoy and who enjoyed her. She had never felt this way before and the hormones were bubbling inside her. But was Stephen the right man? He was certainly the most interesting one, Prim reflected, growing frightened by where her thoughts were taking her.

*

Lu arrived at the hotel and went into the lobby where the staff said hello. Everybody knew who she was now and their friendliness was sincere.

"Do you know if Frank and Will have come down for breakfast?" she asked.

"Yes," the receptionist replied. "They're in the restaurant at their usual table."

"Then, I'll join them," Lu said.

She saw them at a distance as they sat talking. Will and Frank caught sight of her at the same time. Frank got up and pulled out a chair.

"Hi Lu, please have a seat. Have you had any breakfast?"

Lu greeted both of them and took her seat.

"No, not the kind of breakfast you're eating, but I'd like to taste it. We don't eat bread here, but I'd love some tea and some of that ham and egg. It's okay, though. I'll get it myself," she said.

"Yeah, you do that and come and sit down. We have some plans that might interest you," Frank said.

Lu went away to get what she fancied and then she returned.

"Lu," said Frank. "I've heard all about your adventure yesterday, about the gentleman here and how he slept through the lion's share of your journey and that I've missed out on something worth seeing."

"Yes, that's about right," said Lu. "But I hope he didn't forget to mention his bath."

"Not at all," Will cut in. "I couldn't possibly leave that part out."

"Lu," started Frank. "We won't be going up to Phonsavan today. I don't feel I can manage to get up there. I hope you're not disappointed but I don't think it matters if our assignment takes one extra day."

"It's okay," said Lu. "In the meantime, I can do other things."

"But since you've come here, we'll pay for a cab, so you can get home easily," Will said.

"That's out of the question. You don't need to do that at all," Lu insisted.

"But we want to," said Frank.

"Okay then, but it has to be a motorcycle-cab," Lu said.

"Just as long as you'll be getting home easily," said Frank, happy with the compromise. "But while you're eating, you'll get to hear what happened up at Spencer's place yesterday. Sit tight, because you'll be surprised."

Frank told them about the activities on the other side of the street opposite Crater Bar, as related to him by Spencer, as well as the peculiar coincidence regarding Spencer's son and about his own journey home including his escape from the opium dealers.

"Unbelievable," said Lu. "It really is a small world, isn't it? And those opium dealers can be really unpleasant. There have been incidents where they've scared tourists into buying their stuff and the tourists have ended up in an even worse situation, in prison. But I'll be getting along, for now. So then, shall we start here early tomorrow morning instead?"

"Yeah, that's a good idea," said Will.

"At the same time as today?" Lu asked.

"Yes," confirmed Will.

*

Lu left the hotel, aware of eyes following her. There was always some new guest, one of those people who had ridiculous preconceptions about Asian women, people who didn't know who she was but felt they had a clear picture.

Lu decided to walk for a little way before she hailed one of the many motorcycle-cabs that operated in the city. She passed Martin's Bar, which was situated fifty metres from Merry Lao Swiss on Phommatha Road and looked into the empty room, which displayed obvious traces of the previous night's events. She was utterly unaware of the fact that this was one of the places Prim and her friends had visited. Lu carried on another hundred metres, turned right across the street, passed the petrol station and walked up to the stone wall of the temple situated at the corner of Phommatha and Wisunarat. She stopped and looked into the yard on the opposite side of the temple. Before her, was Lane Xang Guest House, a small plain hotel owned by the parents of an old friend of Lu's, a schoolmate who no longer lived in Luang Prabang. The hotel had few guests and it was easy to see why: it was built out of surplus timber and other material the owners had come across cheaply. And the walls were very thin. On one occasion, Lu and Fang had borrowed a room, but since you could hear every sound outside, which meant that people outside could hear every sound within, the room did not serve its purpose. Instead, they had spent an hour or so listening to all the neighbours who had rented rooms and who probably left after a single night as well.

Lu strolled on. Up at the bank, only a couple of hundred metres further on, were some motorcycle-cabs waiting for customers. Sometimes, they had to wait for days. About twenty drivers jostled for Lu's attention when they understood that she wanted to rent a cab. It was important for Lu to make the right choice: not a young man keen to impress or an old man who would never get going and would drive so slowly that she would become nervous. She identified a suitable driver, walked up to him and suggested a rate. He accepted and led his motorcycle up to Lu, got up and offered her the place behind him on the saddle.

"Sitting comfortably?" he asked.

"Yes, thank you," she replied.

"Off we go," he said.

The trip took the usual time: one and a half hours. Lu asked the driver to stop a short distance before the yard, out on the road; she paid him and walked past her neighbours, who ignored her as usual. Lu passed the spot where Pom had been found and although she had walked by it a thousand times before, it was not until today that she stopped and looked down into the ditch. Why precisely now? Was there something Pom wanted to tell her?

The yard was deserted as usual or was it that everybody hid as soon as she arrived? She went into her hut and up to her bedding, which still was untidy. She folded the blankets, swept out all the straw and wood shavings, looked through the leftovers from that morning and the previous day and sat down to eat. All was peaceful and quite. She thought about Prim and her little adventure with the moped. Without Lu noticing, her daughter had become an adult and she had already missed out on some of it.

Lu collected the food bowls and saved some leftovers for Prim, who would be home later. Lu decided to go down to the brook to bathe and wash properly; the quick splash with Prim that morning hadn't been enough to make her comfortable. She placed her toiletries in a cloth which she rolled up and made a knot on either side of the contents. Then, she tied those ends together so it turned into a small cloth bag. With this bundle over her shoulder, a rice hat on her head, wearing a plain blouse and a skirt of cloth around her waist, all in various colours, Lu went off.

The brook, well-hidden below the yard and surrounded by vegetation, ran endlessly from the surrounding mountains, spreading its freshness, giving the trees and the bushes all they desired. The place had become a private oasis for Lu and Prim. Here, they could bathe in seclusion, with no one there to see what was going on at the spot she had arranged for their needs a long time ago. All of the stones were placed with the smoothest side up. She had made a depression as well, so the water could wash over their bodies when they lay down. She had also made a seat of a bigger, half-buried rock, to be used as a stool when bathing their feet. The deepest place at their spot was convenient for standing in while washing their hair.

As she always did, Lu put her things down on a flat, larger stone she used as a table. Then, she undressed in the warmth of the sun. Not even the wind could reach her. The only things noticeable were the sounds of the brook and some birds in the surrounding valley. Lu let her clothes fall onto the grass and the stones. She leant forward and dipped her head while she twisted her body to get wet, trying to get used to the cold water as she rinsed her hair, took shampoo in her hand and rubbed it in thoroughly from the scalp all the way out to the ends of each strand. Her black hair, which she usually wore tied up in a knot or in a ponytail, fell all the way to the small of her back. She stood with her head down in the water up to her ears until the shampoo was completely rinsed out. Then, she sat down slowly, to wash her upper body with water from her cupped hands. The water felt warmer now and Lu grew more adventurous. She half rose and with her arms stretched out backwards, took a couple of small, light steps out to where the water was a little deeper so she could sit down and allow the water to enclose her upper body completely. She leaned backwards to lower her shoulders down into the water, as she bent her head backwards so the water could reach her forehead, until she was looking at the opposite shore upside down.

While Lu was bathing in the brook, a familiar car had slowed and stopped on the road. The three men had observed Lu as she walked down into the valley, unaware that she went there to bathe. They went down too, from a different direction. As they approached Lu, their plans were taking shape.

The water's edge, the stones, the grass, the babbling water, were all as they should have been. But suddenly, there was something else, something that was not supposed to be there: voices, uniforms, boots and legs. Horrified, Lu flew up to a sitting position and crossed her arms over her breasts while she instinctively pressed her knees together.

"What do you want?" asked Lu, frightened.

The men did not answer, just stared at her doggedly.

Lu rose carefully and moved over to her clothes as she asked them to leave. It was a stretch of only one metre and took just a second, but to Lu it felt like minutes. She got hold of the piece of cloth she had used for a skirt and wrapped it around herself. Then, one of the men strode quickly through the brook, grabbed her arm and dragged her out into the deeper part of the stream. Lu was so frightened she couldn't even scream.

"Please, let me go, let me go, it hurts," she sobbed and whispered.

At that moment, the second man got up, took a firm grip of Lu's hair and held her down while dragging her up from the brook. Lu just cried and whispered weakly, "Don't, don't, please." But the men didn't listen.

She felt herself being pressed down toward his legs; to keep her in place, the man jammed her head between his thighs and knees as he sat down. Lu's face was pushed into the ground, which forced her down on her knees and her arms stuck out to her sides.

She had no chance at all of fending off the rape. She could not hear anything, since the man who held her down was blocking her ears completely with his thighs. She tried to kick backwards but received a punch in her side which caused her to lose her breath. It hurt so dreadfully that she began to vomit. The man she could feel inside her did not stop; instead, he became rougher, grabbing her hips and pushing deeply. Lu whimpered, on the verge of losing consciousness. She could not breathe. Suddenly, she felt him easing off, releasing her hips and leaving her. No, no, it's happening again. Not the same hands this time, these pushed her knees outwards before the man forced his way into her. This time, it finished quicker.

The man who had been holding her in an iron grip let go of her and allowed her head to come loose. She was bleeding from her forehead and her nose. The three men were still holding her when the man who had jammed her between his legs announced, "I'll be taking her from the front." Lu tried desperately to resist when they dragged her down in the water and pushed her head beneath the surface. They held her there until she was nearly dead and she coughed and vomited when they pulled her up again. Then, they pushed her down onto the hard rocks and with their jagged edges against her back, the third man completed his turn.

Lu felt them taking her again and again in various ways, but she had no strength to fend them off. Everything went black and she lost consciousness. She collapsed like a rag doll.

At the edge of the water, in this deceptively peaceful valley, Lu was left to her fate. The three rapists vanished the same way they came, driving quietly away as if they were just out on another patrol.

*

Prim was still down in the city. She had made up her mind to take the later bus home. This was not so she could make time to meet Stephen, however, even if it had taken a lot of mulling over. Prim's decision had been to postpone the efforts to see him. Instead, she had bumped into some friends and they had gone to a café, where they were currently sitting talking about Moa and Lek. Rumours were circulating about what had happened at the hotel where they had been taken by those men.

"They only have themselves to blame if they were crazy enough to follow them to their rooms," said Ing.

Mo, one of the older girls, agreed.

"That's the only thing guys want and Moa is well aware of this," she said. "I know her. This wasn't the first time she's had sex with a guy."

Prim listened curiously, but it was time to leave her friends and go home. She walked to the bus terminal to take the same old rickety bus that had plied this route for an eternity, probably all the way back to when the route was established, but before that, it had first been employed in southern China. After that, it probably had served in Hanoi for a couple of years until the Communist Party there gave it to the poor and needy of Luang Prabang. Its worn out red paint was sun-bleached, almost pink, the sash windows were broken and the doors, which you were supposed to shut with the help of a button, stood permanently open. This bus really needed a loyal and devoted driver.

The driver, always the same man, recognised Prim.

"Hi Prim, I see you're heading home," he said and smiled as she climbed into the bus.

"Yes," replied Prim, showing him her best smile.

"Come on in! You haven't got a ticket, have you?" he asked.

"No, I haven't and I haven't any money either," she said.

Bus drivers had children too and they knew how it was for them. Where would a child get money? The bus drivers that drove in the area around Luang Prabang gladly took the children home free of charge, since they were heading in that direction anyway.

Prim found a seat in the middle of the bus, where the bumps were least felt. Quickly, she fell asleep. When they reached her village, the driver called for her; if he hadn't, she might have tagged along all the way back to the city after the turning point, further away in the next village.

"Oh, I fell asleep!" said Prim, darting up from her seat drowsily.

She crossed the road through the dust cloud left by the bus, walked into the yard and up to the hut. She decided to start a fire for the evening and make sure that they had a pleasant time. Although the fire had not been used for two days, you only had to turn the ashes over and you could find live coal beneath it. Sometimes, it could take days before it died out completely.

*

When Prim reached the hut, she saw that Lu had been there. "Alright," she said to herself, "Mum's home, since she's taken care of this morning's leftovers. But where is she?"

Prim looked around and saw that Lu's clothes from the morning were lying on the stool by the mirror. She walked out onto the yard and looked around. She went to grandma's hut. It was unlikely that Lu would have gone there, but she had to ask.

"Grandma, have you seen mum? Is she here?"

"No," grandma replied sulkily, "she's not. You should probably look in the city."

Prim walked back to their hut, where she sat down and resumed picking dry wood for the fire. Before long, the flames were rising again in the old fireplace. When she got into the hut again and looked around once more, she noticed that Lu had taken their toiletries which were usually kept on a plain shelf by the mirror. Prim realised that mum had gone down to the brook to wash herself. Prim prepared some blankets and some of the food that was left and brought it out to the fireplace, to make everything ready for a comfortable evening by the fire.

Soon, she returned to the hut to change clothes, a skirt instead of the trousers she had been wearing for several days now. Lu used to say, "It's nice to liberate your body," after she had taken off some uncomfortable piece of clothing. Once you'd done that, all you needed was some sort of covering, which was why Lu's clothes from the morning were on the stool. Prim felt also liberated after shedding her used clothes. She folded them and went out.

How long had mum been down there now? Maybe, she wanted to be by herself for a while. Prim made sure that the fire caught properly, so that they would have something to warm themselves with later on. She organised things around the fireplace a bit. The area was rather untidy and the others around the yard didn't seem to care. Grandma never came here and grandpa was away, although as to where he had gone, no one wanted to say.

Time passed, dusk drew closer and the sun began to spread streaks between the palmtops. She'd had enough. Prim decided to go down to the brook. She called out ahead as she walked down the path.

"Mum! Mum! Are you there?" she called out.

Down by the brook, she spotted Lu's toiletries immediately, as well as her clothes, which were spread about.

"Mum, what are you doing?" Prim scanned around and there Lu lay, seemingly lifeless and bloody, vomit all around her battered body.

"Mum, Mum!" Prim screamed and rushed over to Lu, who showed no signs of life. "Mum, what's happened?"

Prim dropped to her knees and took Lu's head in her hands.

"Mummy, Mummy! Please answer me! What has happened?" said Prim, crying.

Lu gave no reply, but Prim could see that at least she was breathing, albeit with difficulty. Prim looked at her mother through eyes so full of tears that she could hardly see what had obviously happened to her. She got up and fetched the remains of Lu's clothes, then tucked them under her mother's head. Crying and slipping about, she ran up the path to the yard to get help.

Nobody reacted until Prim was outside her paternal grandmother's hut. "Grandma, come quickly! Mum's had an accident! You must help me!" she said.

"What's happened, child!" her grandmother asked.

"I don't know! You must come quickly!" Prim said.

Grandma came out of the hut and Prim ran ahead.

"Down by the brook," said Prim. "She's lying down there."

"Is she lying down?" grandma asked, increasing her pace, now understanding that something had to be terribly wrong.

Prim reached the brook first, with grandma hot on her heels.

"Oh, what has happened here?" exclaimed grandma when she got there.

"I don't know, but we must help her up!" sobbed Prim.

"Prim, hurry up and get some blankets that we can wrap around her. Then, we must get help from the village, some strong people. Hurry!" she said.

Grandmother had seen many wounded bodies before and had no difficulty in recognising a rape, although not one this rough. She laid Lu on her side and felt inside her mouth to make sure she could breathe properly.

"Lu, Lu, can you hear me? Can you hear me? Can you speak to me?" she shouted.

There was not a sound except now, Lu was shivering. She was just staring blankly ahead, breathing heavily.

"Lu, can you help me? Can you get up?" she asked.

There was no visible reaction. Lu stayed on her side where grandmother had placed her. Prim returned with the blankets and then she ran to the village washing place, where she knew there were always people. She arrived there crying, short of breath, sobbing out her words.

"Help! Please! Come and help us quickly. Come quickly, mum is hurt. Come down by the brook!" she pleaded.

"Why? What has happened down by the brook?" asked one of the women who were doing their laundry.

"Mum's hurt, lying, bleeding," Prim managed to say. "Come quickly, please! Grandma and I need help!"

"We understand," another woman said. "We're coming."

Prim ran ahead, not as fast as before, since she had to make sure everybody was following. Usually, the village was peaceful, so when something unusual happened, it received a lot of attention. Everyone she had found in the washing place – seventeen people, three of them men – made up a train that followed Prim, half-running, down to the brook.

There they stood, leaning over Lu with sad eyes while grandma told them about what must have happened. Lu was lying still with one blanket around her and another beneath her head, which was still bleeding from a nasty wound on her forehead. Five people placed themselves on either side of Lu, stuck their arms beneath her and took a firm hold of one another. This way, their hands and arms constituted a stretcher, onto which they lifted her. No one said a word; everybody knew what had to be done. Grandma took Prim and went ahead. Everyone was silent except for Prim, who could not stop crying.

"You have to go ahead," said grandma, "so you can get mum's bedding ready. I'll fetch Lu's mother. She and I will have to work together to wash Lu's wounds."

Prim rushed into the hut to prepare Lu's bedding. The bearers, with Lu on their arms, arrived shortly after.

"Here," said Prim, holding the doorway covering out of the way. "Mum is to lie here."

Prim dried her tears as she moved items around so they could lay Lu down on the bed. Almost everyone in the village of Tat Kuang was standing in the yard. They were wondering what was going on as Prim's grandmothers Mak and May walked to the hut together, discussing what might have happened. There was little doubt that it involved a rape. This was the first time for a long while that Mak and May had cooperated. They stepped into the hut as the helpers came back out. They looked at the two older women and shook their heads.

"She's in a bad way," one woman said.

"Some people from the village?" another asked.

"No, I don't think so," replied a third.

"Has anyone seen anything unusual?" an older woman wondered.

"No, not really," said the others, thoughtfully.

"Strange," the old woman concluded.

Inside the hut, May stood looking at her daughter.

"Oh my, my, my girl! What have they done to you?"

There was no response from Lu, nothing at all.

"Prim," said May. "I want you to go to my hut and fetch the hot water which is standing over the fire. Then, you're to take some of my rags that are hanging close by. Bring them here, so Mak and I can wash your mum. Then, I want you to fetch something to eat from my place. I want you to stay outside when we're washing mum. We want to be alone with her."

Prim went quickly to carry out May's instructions. She took a bit of her grandmother's food and sat down outside, not by the fire, the place she had arranged for Lu and herself, but in the opening to their hut, close, in order to hear if her mum wanted her to come in.

By this time, more villagers had gathered at the fireplace, to be ready if May or Mak came out and asked for help. They did not, but the talk and the speculation grew. When May came out to check on Prim, the girl had fallen asleep. May put a blanket over her and let her be. Mak and May had now washed Lu's body all over, bandaged her wounds and wrapped her up in blankets. They had not succeeded in getting any words out of her, however. The movement of her eyes suggested she was awake, but she was not present. She did not communicate with anyone and didn't move.

"Mak," said May. "I'll stay here tonight and watch by her; I need to get some fluid into her. Besides, it's not good for Prim to be alone with her right now."

"You do that," replied Mak. "I'll go out to the others and then, I'll go home."

Mak went out to the others, who still sat in the warmth of the fire. One of the women observed that for a little while now, there had been some policemen driving slowly through the village, looking curiously at everyone and everything.

"Yes, that's correct," another added. "We've seen them as well and have been wondering what they wanted."

"Was it those policemen that did this? If that's the case, we'll never get to know the truth. If we go to the police and tell them about what has happened – that we think it's policemen that are responsible – then we'll just get into trouble ourselves," one woman said.

"The police back each other up, we know this. And we know that they rape, just like the soldiers. The worst thing is that this has always been going on and always will. We'll never be able to do anything about it except being more careful and making sure never to be alone," said another.

"If it is them who are behind this, I wonder why they don't go to their own brothels and rape the girls there. Why do they come here?" the first woman wondered.

"It's quite obvious why they don't go to their own brothels to rape. For men like that, it's not exciting enough. Besides, then they would hurt their own income, wouldn't they?" another of the women said. "We're a minority who will always suffer for our role during the war years, even though we fought for what we believed was right. We should have left this country, like so many others did."

"But for what kind of life?" asked Mak, who had now joined the conversation. "Very few of us are better off somewhere else. We are and remain who we are."

"Yes," the woman said. "But here we are without legal rights."

"Well, now I'm off to my place," Mak said. "I think that you ought to do the same. I'm deeply grateful to all of you for your help."

The people around the campfire returned Mak's thanks and then they dispersed. With gloomy eyes, they all went to the respective places.

Prim woke up freezing. She went into the hut where Lu and grandma had fallen asleep and she lay down behind her grandma. The woman's warmth felt good. Lu's mother, May, felt Prim close to her, took her hand and held it, stroking the back of her hand.

"Go to sleep, now, Prim," she said.

Prim looked up at Lu and could see she was sleeping. Before long, Prim too, slept for the rest of the night. Mak sat down outside her hut and pondered about what had happened and where Songchai could be. How long would he be away?

Chapter 23

Lots of Muscle

Kitepong was in a hurry. He wanted to say hello to his old friends and get some help stocking up with food and drink.

"I know the people who live here," he said to the others. "Let me be the one to go in and dock first. We'll be moored fine just here, no currents."

This was a good strategic spot, he reflected when he got up onto the jetty. He climbed onto the river bank and up the hillside to the houses and huts situated along the crest, crossed an enclosed salad garden and on through a small pig pen and past a hen-house with terrified chickens.

"Hello! Anybody home?" he shouted when he got there.

An old woman came out into the yard.

"Who are you?" she asked.

"I'm Kitepong. I'm one of Aroon's old friends," he announced.

"Aroon doesn't live here anymore. I think he's dead. I live here now, but Aroon's son lives just a couple of houses away," she replied.

"I'm sad to hear about Aroon. Can you show me how to find his son?" he asked her.

"It's just a stone's throw away, up the hill, over there," she replied.

"Thanks," said Kitepong. "Are the nearest jetties yours?"

"Yes," she said, "but we share them with the neighbours. And Aroon's son owns one of them."

"Would it be okay for us to berth there as we're doing now, while we fuel up and eat? We'll leave again in an hour or so," Kitepong asked.

"Yes. I don't mind at all if you berth there," the woman responded.

Kitepong thanked her and walked towards Aroon's son's house, a good leg stretch after his many hours on board the boat.

*

Up at the house, there was a Toyota pick-up which looked rather new. Obviously, this man was not a poor fisherman like his father. He went on into the passage, which was laid with stone and concrete and up to a proper door, where he knocked. The situation made him feel awkward. This was a rich guy, not someone on his own level.

"Come in!" someone shouted from inside.

Kitepong remained where he was standing. He barely knew how to turn a door handle.

"Come in!" he heard again together with the sound of someone approaching the door.

It opened with a jerk and revealed a tall man with muscular arms and tattoos which described a life journey. Despite the fact that this was a young man, he seemed to have had the time to experience many things. He had to be well over six feet tall! Kitepong wouldn't have liked to meet a man like that on a dark night but he could probably help them stock up the boats. Kitepong was not daft.

"Hello, my name is Kitepong and I'm an old friend of your father," he said. "I wonder where I can find him. Does he live around here? When we berthed at your jetties, I was convinced that they belonged to your father."

This bundle of muscles stared at Kitepong, his brown forehead wrinkled in concern. He stroked his almost bald head with his hand, beside a tattoo depicting a samurai sword which stretched from his right temple up to the top of his head. Kitepong had never seen the likes of it. Up in his district, you might bump into one or two tourists wearing tattoos, but nothing approaching the art on this man's body.

"Alright, your name is Kitepong," he said, finally. "So then, where are you from?"

"I'm from the Luang Prabang district and I had a lot of contact with your father after the war. Aroon is your father, isn't he?" Kitepong explained.

"That's right, my name is Khanawat and I'm Aroon's son," the man confirmed.

They remained in the doorway. Khanawat did not let Kitepong in. He still wasn't sure about Kitepong's identity and he was a thorough man who had come far in his line of work thanks, in part, to his constant wariness.

"Tell me more! How come you know my father?" he asked.

"After the war, we were in the same re-education camp and your father was released just a few days before me," Kitepong began to explain. "We were supposed to have stayed there for two weeks, but as you probably know, it ended up being over a year for us. After that, he stayed around our district for a month or so. He lived with some mutual friends who we later helped escape to Thailand. And during the escape, which was via the Mekong, we stayed here, in a house down by the jetties, where you were living at the time. I remember you as a small boy, but wouldn't have recognised you now. I remember that it was your grandmother who took care of you during our short stay here, before your mother passed away."

"Yes, you're right," said Khanawat. "That's the way it was."

"There were other people here who were involved in the escape as well, but we were the ones most involved, especially your father. How is he? And where is he?" Kitepong asked.

"A couple years ago, he was out on an assignment, one quite similar to the one you did with your friends. He had become skilled at that sort of thing. But he has been missing ever since that job and we don't know what happened, just that he's disappeared. Anything could have happened and I do mean anything. In the meantime, what do you want and what can I do for you?" Khanawat asked.

"I'm one of a group of guys with boats heading further down the river. We need fuel, water and some rest so I thought that I'd take the opportunity to pay my old friend a visit," Kitepong said.

"I'm so sorry. I'd very much like him to be standing here with us right now. But let me help you. How many boats did you say?" Khanawat asked.

"Five," said Kitepong.

"Five? Is it a charter trip, or what? Or is it that you've stayed in the same business too, just like my father?" said Khanawat grinning. "If you have, I have to tell you one thing and be clear about it: be damned careful. Nowadays, it's not just the police and the military out there, but also gangsters who steal cargo from defenceless old men like you."

Kitepong was a little annoyed at this comment, but he was a careful man. He had been mistaken; this bundle of muscles was clever.

"Okay," continued Khanawat. "I'll help you. Let's take my car. It's no problem to drive down to the jetties and thinking about it, I probably owe you a favour. Come!"

They went to the pick-up and jumped in.

"It's been a long time since I've sat in a car as fancy as this," said Kitepong, although the truth was that he had never actually sat in such a vehicle. "May I ask you what you do?"

"Sure, but I won't answer you. Not even the police get any answers from me, so I hope you'll understand. But let's just say that I'm into business and I'm good at what I do. Sometimes, I'm a bodyguard as well and I'm good at that, too," said Khanawat, glancing at Kitepong as he drove down to the jetties. Then, he counted five boats, wondering what could be done with such a number.

*

Songchai, Surachai, Supot and Voratep waited in their boats. Surprised and on their guard, they watched as the Toyota pick-up came down to the jetties.

"What the fuck is this?" said Surachai, turning to Songchai.

"I haven't got a clue!" Songchai replied.

That very instant, a man who looked more gorilla than human hopped out of the driver's seat just as Kitepong emerged from the passenger seat. From their seats in their boats, they could watch the two men closely as they forced their way through the tall grass towards the jetty where the boats were tethered.

Songchai had difficulty restraining his anger.

"What is he up to? We don't want any guests!" he said.

"Wait here a while," said Kitepong to Khanawat. "I just have to explain who you are."

He had anticipated Songchai's rage and thought it would be for the best if he bore the brunt of it himself.

"This is Khanawat, the son of my friend, Aroon," said Kitepong, as he walked up to Songchai's boat. "He's promised to help us stock all that we need. He'll take our jerry cans in his pick-up and drive to the fuel depot. It's nothing to worry about."

"Listen, you," said Songchai, "just the look of him makes me worried. You'd better be right about this."

Khanawat understood that they had become suspicious when he showed up, so he walked up to Songchai. He looked into the older man's eyes as he greeted him with his palms together, demonstrating that he was both unarmed and friendly by bringing his thumps up to his nose. Songchai returned the greeting and after him, the procedure was repeated by Surachai, Voratep and Supot.

"Alright," said Khanawat. "I've heard that you're out on a little river trip and going all the way down to Khemmarat."

"That's more than I've heard," said Surachai, glancing at Songchai, who had joined him up on the jetty.

"I've never said that!" said Kitepong.

"No, you haven't. But isn't that where everyone who's into trade goes?" asked Khanawat, smiling confidently. "I can help you guys. It's no picnic downstream: smugglers are abundant and the goods vary. And it's not just the authorities who are out to get you, but those who live by stealing goods as well. They're always about, but with my help, you'll get past them without any problems. I know the guys and the police downstream. Kitepong, shouldn't we get going and stock up now? Take out all your cans for fuel and water. We've got no time to loiter around here."

Surachai did not feel comfortable around Khanawat, perhaps because they were about the same age and because he had several friends who also used anabolic steroids. He grabbed some of the cans which the others had passed up and walked with Kitepong and Khanawat to the vehicle to load them onto its flat bed.

"This is what we're going to do," Khanawat told Kitepong. "I'll go and fill up with water and petrol and you can walk back the way we came to the crossroads. At the corner, there's a shop with all the groceries you'll need to make it all the way down to Khemmarat. Take your friend; he looks strong."

Khanawat gave a broad and friendly smile and got into his pick-up. Kitepong and Surachai walked back to the boats to discuss the situation. Things were suddenly happening awfully quickly.

"What the bloody hell are you doing?" asked Surachai. "How the hell could he know that we're going down to Khemmarat? Have you told him about our cargo as well?"

"I swear," said Kitepong. "I haven't said a word; neither about our cargo nor our destination. I just went up there to contact my old friend, Aroon. But nobody knows where he is. He went missing a couple of years ago. Khanawat would like to help us on our way, in return for the help I gave his father in the past. If I'm not mistaken, he knows all this and he has the contacts we need."

"I think he's got some secret motive," said Songchai. "Whatever it is, it'll come to light. You'll see."

"He's an unpleasant customer," said Voratep. "I think we ought to get out of here and forget about him."

"Great idea," said Surachai. "It's just that he's got our water and fuel cans, so we'd better play along for a while and see how things go. We are actually five men, with guns at that, so we're not totally helpless, are we?"

"Alright, get cracking now!" said Songchai. "If I'm not mistaken, you both received an assignment."

Meanwhile, the others took the opportunity to rest. Songchai lay down to sleep for a while stretched out on the jetty. It was not very wide, so when the delivery eventually turned up, he would be woken by the sound of the engine and the swinging of the jetty boards. And, sure enough, the jetty swung like a hammock when Khanawat came walking down carrying four jerry cans, two in either hand. Songchai looked up and saw him holding them as if they were a couple of plastic bags with bread. The load he was carrying must have come to about a hundred kilos, fifty in each hand.

Songchai wondered what they could use him for.

But Khanawat's thoughts ran in the same vein. He knew what he wanted from his father's old pal. That was why he'd wanted to go and fuel up by himself, without a chaperone.

"Have Kitepong and his mate returned yet?" he asked.

"No," said Songchai. "Not yet."

"If you help me out with the cans, things will go much quicker and then we can talk a bit so you'll know how to go about this."

"How to go about what? I don't understand," said Songchai.

"Well, I know you don't, but you will soon. Come on and unload this stuff now," Khanawat instructed him.

Everybody went to the pick-up and grabbed the goods from the bed.

"What's in that wooden box? Are we to take that as well?" asked Voratep.

"Yes," said Khanawat.

"No," said Songchai. "It's not one of ours."

"It is from now on. It contains extra water and food and it is to go with you as well, so take it!" Khanawat insisted.

"Okay," said Voratep.

Everything was carried to the boats and loaded onto them. Khanawat was last out onto the jetty and when everything was in its place, he spoke again.

"Let's sit down for a while so I can tell you how things are. I wasn't born yesterday; I know exactly what you're up to, but I don't know what you're transporting and I don't give a damn. But if you don't agree to cooperate, you won't get far. That I can guarantee. The fact of the matter is that a great deal of what takes place here and on the stretch down to Khemmarat is controlled by, let's just say, some guys I know. And if you don't pay to travel that way, it might just happen that your goods sink or are simply taken from you by guys who think they've got a better use for them than you do."

"We're armed," objected Supot.

"Wait a moment," interrupted Songchai. "Obviously you've got some reason to tell us this."

"Yes, old man and we should probably deal with this in an adult way. This is what you have to do, straight away: You have to bind your boats together so they're working like one. Bind two together alongside each other and the next two to the sterns of the first two and the fifth boat you take in tow. This way, my guys will have no trouble identifying you and you'll be granted safe conduct," Khanawat explained.

"It seems awkward," said Voratep.

"Indeed, you'll see for yourselves. It'll be your ticket down to Khemmarat. But there are these other matters," Khanawat confirmed.

"Oh yeah, here it comes," said Songchai.

"I want you to travel in darkness. And I want you to take some passengers with you, my goods, you could say," Khanawat said.

"Passengers?" said Songchai. "What sort of passengers?"

"It doesn't matter," Khanawat replied.

"No!" protested Songchai. "We won't do it!"

"Then, you'll be going nowhere!" Khanawat responded and got up from his half sitting position, turned around and began to walk towards his car with steady strides. When he reached the middle of the jetty, Kitepong and Surachai were heading back and with them, two more men stuffed with anabolic steroids, obviously friends of Khanawat.

"What is this?" Songchai said aloud to himself and looked at Supot. "I don't like the look of it."

Khanawat said hello to his mates, went back to the boats and resumed the conversation.

"I guarantee you that everything will turn out well, as long as you just do as I say. One of my guys will come along just to make sure you won't do anything stupid. You scratch my back and I'll scratch yours," he said.

"Let us discuss this on our own a bit," said Songchai. "And then we'll come back up to the car."

Khanawat went up to the Toyota and stayed there with his friends while Kitepong and Surachai continued to the boats with the groceries.

"What's happening?" asked Kitepong, looking at Songchai.

"What's happening?" Songchai responded. "I'll tell you what's happening. That gorilla of yours is demanding that we take a number of passengers with us, people he won't tell us anything about and he wants us to bind our boats together so his river robbers can see that it's us. I understand why. It's so we can take more cargo. Plus, we have to go in the dark. I can understand why too. And I really don't like him threatening that if we don't do as he says, we won't get out of here. Also, I don't like the suggestion that they control all the contraband on the river."

"I see," said Kitepong. "But I think we can trust him. He knows what I've gone through to keep his father alive, so I don't think he'll be up to any tricks. Let me speak to him."

Kitepong went up to the car.

"Khanawat," he said. "I have to ask you if I can trust you that nothing is going to happen to us or our cargo?"

"One hundred percent! All I ask is that you do as I tell you and take some passengers," Khanawat replied.

"What sort of passengers?" Kitepong asked.

"My merchandise. Nice girls who are going down to Khemmarat and don't like to travel by road, especially not through the frontier stations. That's all. They've got a guide with them, you could say and you're out on a trip anyway, aren't you?" said Khanawat, glaring at Kitepong. "Go down there now and tell your friends to start working. I can guarantee you that you'll meet some new people along the way, but you will have my blessing."

Kitepong begun to understand why Khanawat had such a large house and a new car. He was one of the gangster bosses in the area, a dangerous man to be meddling with.

"We'll be transporting girls," said Kitepong when he came back down to the boats. "They have both food and guides with them and we're guaranteed to get there without any problems."

"Oh yeah," said Surachai. "It's those bruisers who'll be the guides and I suppose they'll be our guides, too. It seems like we're their hostages."

"I've got a bad feeling about this," said Songchai. "I'm sure there will be problems."

"No, not at all. Come on now, let's get cracking so we can get out of here," said Kitepong. "I know how you all feel about this but we have to bite the bullet."

"I really hope that this doesn't go down the drain, because if it does, you'll end up likewise," said Songchai. "Take out the lines and let's bind the boats together side by side."

The work began and before nightfall, the boats were lashed together and fuelled up. Everything was ready for the final stretch.

*

A large motorcycle rumbled down towards Khanawat's car. It drowned out all ambient sound. It was followed by a white minivan with 'Tropical Trips' painted on the side. It looked just like any regular charter minibus. The motorcycle stopped in front of the jetty. On it was yet another brute; now there were four of them. He remained on his bike and waved with one hand to Khanawat, a wave signalling that everything was okay. The van stopped behind Khanawat's car and out jumped a woman, who got in position to wait for the next signal. Khanawat looked at Songchai.

"Are you ready?" he asked.

"Yes!" shouted Songchai.

"Let's load!" Khanawat said, signalling to the woman by the van to bring out the passengers.

They got out one by one and Voratep, who had not participated in the last discussion, became almost paralysed with fury.

"But bloody hell! Are we bringing young girls with us again? In that case, I'm out of here!" he hissed at Songchai.

"Cool down, it'll be just fine," said Songchai, but took Voratep to the side so that everyone else couldn't hear him.

"No, Songchai, I'm bailing out now. You have to arrange for my boxes to be reloaded to the other boats. Then, I'll undo the lines and make my way back."

"No! We can't do that. We would reveal what we have in our boats," Songchai pointed out.

"I don't give a shit, I want out and you've just got to live with it," Voratep insisted.

"You'll cause a lot of problems. We might all get into trouble if we start to mess with this gang. You must realise that," Songchai said.

"You don't need me now and I refuse to take part in transporting young girls who've been abducted, fooled, sold, bought or whatever the fuck you want to call it. I just won't do it. We can go about it this way: I get out of here and you tell them that this was our deal from the start. Then, I can stay here in the village until you come back. You won't be more than a couple of days. This way, I won't be involved and you don't have to pay me more than half of what was agreed at the start. Is that okay? Answer me! Is that okay, Songchai?"

"Wait a little, so I can speak to Kitepong and ask him to bring it up with that pal of his."

Kitepong was standing on the jetty. He was pre-occupied by what was happening ashore so he had missed the conversation between Songchai and Voratep.

"Kitepong!" called Songchai. "I have to talk to you. Come here!"

"What?" asked Kitepong, going over to Songchai.

"Voratep wants out, here and now. He refuses to transport young girls," Songchai said.

"Well, at least one of us has got some morals. If it was possible, I'd do the same, but that would lead to even more problems. What do you want me to do about it?" Voratep asked.

"Speak to Khanawat and tell him it was agreed all along that Voratep should leave us here," Songchai advised him.

"Okay, I'll do that," said Kitepong.

He walked over to Khanawat and relayed the news.

"Sure, no problem," said Khanawat. "But you have to make one thing clear. If this man should speak to anyone about what's happened here today, or about us, he's not the only one who'll die, but you others will as well. I guarantee you it will be an excruciating death. And that's not all. We'll also seek out your families and what we'd do to them, well, I don't think you'd like to know. I just wanted you guys to know what the deal is."

"I'd never have expected that you'd resort to such threats," Kitepong said, shocked.

"Well, I can see that. And I don't intend to hurt either him or you. But if he comes up with the idea of speaking to the police or any other authority, well, you have to understand that we have to protect ourselves and our people," Khanawat emphasised.

"I understand," Kitepong replied.

"Yes, I believe you do," said Khanawat.

Kitepong went back to the jetty. He did not tell Songchai everything that Khanawat had said; he didn't want Songchai to lose his wits in a fury.

"He said it was okay. Voratep can stay here, but he should remember that ..." And Kitepong reported the essentials.

"Alright, then," said Songchai to Voratep. "Take your things and go ashore. We'll pick you up on the way back, as you suggested."

While Voratep's participation during the remaining journey was being discussed, twelve young girls had been escorted onboard to take their seats on various places within the tied-up vessels. The girls looked frightened and Voratep turned away when he picked up his things. He hurried to get away.

"Surachai!" he called out. "Just a word before I leave."

They exchanged a few words on the beach before Surachai said goodbye and walked back again.

"What was that all about?" asked Songchai, slightly anxious, since Voratep had not asked him to come and say goodbye before they parted.

"Nothing special," said Surachai. "Just that he wished me good luck and that we'd see each other in a couple of days and that he'll be waiting for us in the village here. I promised to get him on our way back."

"Alright," said Songchai. "Nothing else?"

"No," Surachai confirmed.

One of the thugs and the woman up at the car were also coming with them and when he climbed on board, the whole raft wobbled.

"Take a seat further back," said Songchai. "That'll be best. We have to remember that we're pretty heavily loaded now. The water is just some a short distance below the gunwale."

Surachai realised how heavy they were with guns, girls and a big bundle of muscles with tattoos on his head. Surachai didn't think the man was from that part of earth. Maybe, he'd risen up from hell.

"You girls over there," said Songchai. "You have to disperse yourselves."

Four of the girls had sat down together in the middle.

"You two must sit here!" he said.

"No," one of the girls said. "I want to sit with my friend."

"Yes, Moa has to sit here," said her friend, who already had tears in her eyes.

"Okay, then you two are to sit here," said Songchai, pointing at the others.

When this was done, the engines were started and everything began to move. Khanawat was standing on the jetty and told the two guides that he would come down to their meeting place to take the delivery further.

"Off we go," said Songchai, casting off from the jetty into the darkness of the night.

*

Within the bay, the water had no current, but when they got out on the middle of the river, everything shifted and so did their strange vessel. Everyone who was sitting in the boats, except those with river experience – Songchai, Surachai, Kitepong and Supot – felt unpleasant and a little sick as the tied up boats rubbed hard against each other and began to lurch.

"I hope this holds together all the way down to Khemmarat," said Surachai. "And the possibility of the police not noticing us now is as likely as Buddha being my father. We might as well be signalling 'here we come'."

"Well, that's precisely the idea," said the goon. "They're supposed to notice us and let us pass without any fuss. They're on our pay roll and won't touch us."

The boats heeled over and twisted, water flushing up between the gunwales as the whole contraption carried on, slightly askew.

"Can't you make her go straight and follow the current?"

Songchai and Kitepong, who were handling their respective motors, shook their heads.

"Not a chance, it's the river that's in charge now. All we can do is to tag on the best we can," said Songchai. "It's possible that things would go easier with just one motor. If Kitepong turns off his engine, we'll find out."

"My guess is this will only result in you having to strain your engine and that'll be harder on you. But sure, let's try it," said Kitepong.

Then, he choked his throttle. The whole raft careered even more in the currents and manoeuvrability became even worse. As a result, they began drifting back towards land.

"Watch out! Dammit! We're getting too close to those rocks at the river bank!" screamed the bruiser. And at that very instant, the craft's port side hit something hard, which made it heel considerably.

"What are you doing?" screamed the thug.

"Nothing," said Songchai, enjoying himself, even though he felt a bit worried too.

"Why did we choose to travel with these people?" said Lek to Moa. "I'm scared. I've been on water before, but never like this."

The tattooed guard was holding onto the gunwale and his face had begun to change colour.

"For fuck's sake! Get that other motor running as well before everything goes to hell!" he shouted to Songchai.

"No, it won't. Things will just be a bit uncomfortable. It sounds much worse than it actually is," Songchai said.

None of the new passengers had any idea what Songchai was up to. Songchai wished more than anything that the two guides would get seasick. He laughed up his sleeve when he saw the woman furthest back holding both her hands over her face, looking terrified. And he certainly didn't mind when the boat heeled so hard that their guard almost flew out of his seat as water cascaded all over him.

"My, my, my," said Songchai. "This is no good. This won't do. I guess we'll have to get to the shore."

"No!" yelled the guard. "We won't!"

"But we can't see anything and we might break up!" shouted Kitepong.

"We're not going towards land. You must go on!" the tattooed man yelled back.

"But surely you can see where this is heading, can't you?" Songchai said. "We'll end up on the bottom of the river if we go on."

"Can't you hear what I'm saying? You're not to go towards land!" the thug shouted. By then, his face had turned deathly pale.

"It won't just be my merchandise that'll go down the drain if we don't, but yours too," said Songchai as he drove the boat on.

"We can always get new ones. The supply is unlimited, so I'm willing to take that risk. But as for the money we get on delivery, well, I do care about that," the bruiser said.

"As do I," said Songchai.

"What did he say?" asked Moa looking at Lek with a frozen stare. "I don't understand a thing."

When they reached calmer water, the brute leaned over the gunwale and threw up. Surachai looked at Kitepong and smiled.

"If you get worse, we can put you ashore," said Songchai.

Not a sound came from the steroid-stuffed hoodlum. Slowly, he lifted himself up to a sitting position and laid his head in his hand.

"Can it get much worse? I feel like shit!" he confessed.

"It's called seasickness and it won't be passing any time soon," Songchai told him.

"Just keep going and shut up," the brute said, in an attempt to show that he was tough despite the fact that it wasn't working.

Since they had one oil lamp at the front of the raft and another aft, they attracted attention all the way along the river, both from other boats and from people on the shores who lingered outdoors in the night. In silence, they saw a typical long-tail boat coming towards them. It was about one metre wide, six metres long and was moving so fast that it clearly had an extremely powerful engine, excellent for smuggling. The boats used by the police could never catch up with this speed boat. Quickly, it approached Songchai's craft, which now was slightly the worse for wear. Songchai could see that there were two men in the boat. They were sitting in a sort of tandem manner with the man behind driving. They kept themselves some ten metres from the raft and circled around the tied up boats before they swiftly moved up and boarded them.

"Who are you?" asked Songchai.

"We're just here to check everything is okay," said one of them.

It was obvious where they had come from.

"Has everything run smoothly?" asked the other one, turning to the tattooed thug.

"Yeah, but I don't feel very well, probably a bit seasick," replied the guard, whose face had now regained some of its colour. "I think we ought to change positions. You take over here and I'll go to the shore. I have to get off this bloody ferry."

Songchai could not hear exactly what was being said and grew nervous when the bruiser changed places with one of the two men from the other boat.

"What are you doing?" he asked.

"We're just making some arrangements so you can get there safely without anything happening to you," said the driver of the long-tail boat grinning at him. "We've got our orders. You've met Khanawat, so you know the deal."

"We probably ought to be both careful and a little grateful," whispered Surachai to Songchai. "I think these guys know what they're doing."

"Get going! You've got no time to lose and we'd like to see you in Khemmarat tomorrow."

The substitute for the seasick thug took the same seat as his predecessor had, lay down a filled white plastic bag in front of his feet and got settled in. After a while, he happened to give the plastic bag a kick and a gun barrel poked out. He bent down and adjusted the bag so the barrel was covered again, without the slightest concern as to whether anyone had seen it.

Chapter 24

Making their Way

Lek shook her friend lightly. "Moa," she said, waking her up. "Listen to what they're saying. They're talking about Khemmarat but we're not supposed to be going there. We're supposed to get off at Mukdahan!"

"Yes," said Moa. "That's what they promised us."

Earlier, when Moa and Lek had got on the bus in Luang Prabang, neither of them had given much thought as to where they should go, except to Vientiane and then onwards. The bus trip had been an adventure and had taken almost nine hours due to bad weather. It was fortunate that the bus had been forced to stop a couple of times along the way so they could get off, buy something to eat and visit the lavatory. On the whole, the trip had been giggly and fun and they had become acquainted with several of the other passengers.

When they had arrived in Vientiane towards evening, they had walked, bewildered, away from the bus terminal in the city, trying to remember the places Lim, the guy at Martin's Bar in Luang Prabang, had mentioned, the bars he and his friends frequented in the evenings. They recalled that Lim had talked about the Chicago Bar, so they asked around and found out that it was on Nokeo Khumman in the centre, no more than twenty minutes' walk. Once there, they positioned themselves outside so they could peek in through the windows, but the place was so crowded it was impossible to try to recognise any one.

It was growing late, so the girls decided to go in. But just as they were about to pay the entrance fee, they were stopped by the guard, who told them they were too young. By this time though, Moa had already taken out her money and when the guard saw she had dollars, he gave a grin and welcomed them to the bar. They found it odd. In the past, they had never had to pay entrance to a bar with a discotheque attached.

After an hour, they had connected with a guy who knew Lim. He told the girls that Lim was away and would not be back for a week. But he knew about Lim's work and offered to help the girls. They told him they had left Luang Prabang for good and that Lim had said that he could fix them up with jobs, modelling jobs.

"Yes, I know. That's no problem, but you have to go to Thailand since there are no jobs here for the moment, unless you want to work at filthy bars and you girls don't want that, do you?" he said.

"No," the girls replied.

"I'll fix you up with a good contact. I just need to make some phone calls and it's done," he confirmed.

He went away to make the calls and when he came back to Moa and Lek, he was smiling.

"Everything is set," he told them, "but you have to leave tonight. A guy we know is going to help some other girls to go to Thailand and you can tag along. It'll be cheaper for you that way. They're going to pick you up in a minivan shortly and you'll ride along to Mukdahan. From there, it's easy to get into Thailand without papers. You're going to meet some people that Lim and I know. They'll help you."

Moa and Lek felt safe as their adventure continued.

After an hour, a woman entered the bar and greeted the girls. She was polite and friendly. She asked them if they had eaten and made sure they had some drinks and a good time. She gained the girls' confidence. She spoke fondly of Lim and the work his firm had done for many girls who wanted to advance and make money. In turn, the girls told the woman how they had met Lim at Martin's Bar in Luang Prabang and she laughed heartily, "That's Lim for you!"

Then suddenly, Nong, Lim's mate from Martin's Bar, was standing by the woman's side.

"I heard you were here. Great!" he said. "And you've already got some help with the journey as well. Once you're there, the jobs are sure to come too! But hurry up now! Not many girls get this lucky, to tag along and ride for free."

"Yes, girls," said the woman. "Come on, let's hit the road!"

Moa and Lek had walked towards the door, happy they had the chance to go directly to Thailand, the jobs and the money. Outside Chicago Bar, a minivan stood by the kerb side, a small tourist bus for twelve people. There was a man at the wheel who greeted them in a friendly manner and in the back, there were two other girls, who said hello, cheerfully.

"Where's your luggage?" the driver asked them. "Is this rucksack and shoulder bag all you've got? Alright then, it's easier if you travel lightly. If you've got your money and IDs in them as well, I think you should hold on to them until we get there."

"We've got some stretch ahead of us," said the woman, who had not told them her name.

She told the girls not to speak with the others sitting in the bus or to those who joined it along the way. It could create a disturbance, she said and that might cause problems at the border crossing and nobody wanted to run into problems there. She sat down so that her back was towards the driver's seat and she could observe what every passenger did or said.

"We'll be picking up another four people and after that, I suggest you sleep until we get there," she advised.

They had stopped just east of Vientiane in a small village called Dongkalum, where another four girls climbed into the minivan. They came with a big, dark, tattooed guy who had no hair on his head. As he climbed into the bus and settled himself, he grinned broadly at everyone. When they were all in their seats inside the warm bus, they drove on, at high speed. They stopped in Hongtong to change drivers. The pleasant driver handed the wheel to one who looked more like the guy with the tattoos. Moa had trouble sleeping and whispered to Lek, "Why do we have to be silent? That's strange, isn't it?"

The minivan proceeded at a fair pace and during the trip, they were only granted one break.

"No talking," repeated the woman, who seemed to have altered her attitude. "We have water, so we don't need to stop for anything except pee breaks."

They went on all night in that crowded minivan, which at first, had seemed comfortable but after a couple of hours, felt more like an old hovel which was getting more and more stuffy. The tattooed guy reeked so badly of sweat that Lek was developing a headache. By morning, they had reached Ban Kengkaboa, but they were still not allowed to speak to each other, or to leave the bus, except for a brief moment. Lek asked for the windows and doors to be opened to let the air in and this was permitted, albeit reluctantly.

"We have to wait here today so the rest of the journey will be as safe as possible. We have to take care of some paperwork," the woman told them. "So, you have to give us all your IDs."

Everyone did as they were told.

"You'll get them back later on," said the sweaty guy, smiling at them.

*

Khanawat, who had intended to take the girls onwards to the border in the bus, had changed his plans when earlier, Kitepong had showed up unexpectedly. Kitepong's visit provided an excellent opportunity to transport the girls by river instead and to get them into Thailand where it was most convenient. Now, the girls heard the surprising news that they would be continuing by boat and that this would make it easier for them to get into Thailand.

When the bus came down to the boats, which were tied up together and moored to the jetty, the girls remained inside the bus wondering what was going on and why there was such a hullabaloo all around with guys who looked like gangsters, both with or without motorcycles. Moa felt that things did not feel right. As they walked between the bus and the boat, she spoke to Lek.

"We're not doing this! We're not going with them!" she said firmly.

"You can't do that!" the woman interrupted, aggressively.

"But we don't want to come with you," said Moa clearly to the woman and to the guy in the bus. "Come on, Lek, get your things! We're getting out of here!"

"You can't! We've got your IDs and they are at customs now," the woman lied.

The tattooed guy grabbed Lek hard by the arm and led her to the boat. She was beginning to become afraid. The boat was going to be gliding down the river towards a destination that had never been included in their plans.

"I have to ask," said Moa to Lek. "I'll ask that old man over there." Moa turned to Songchai. "Where are we heading?" she asked.

"We're heading for Khemmarat," replied Songchai. "And all of you are supposed to disembark there."

"Why Khemmarat?" she asked again.

"You are to be silent," said the guy who had replaced the tattooed thug. "No talking!"

Songchai ignored him.

"It's easier to get into Thailand through there," he said.

"Alright, I see. But we thought it would be easier to go via Mukdahan," Moa said.

"No," said Songchai. "That station is too closely controlled."

Moa realised that things were adding up. Perhaps the woman and the tattooed guy weren't lying after all.

"We should probably calm down," she told Lek. "Everything seems to be alright."

Lek sat thinking about how things must be back home, what everybody would be doing, whether they were worried, or just happy to have one less mouth to feed? It was the weirdest feeling.

"Moa, what do you think the others back home are thinking and doing at this moment?" she asked her friend.

"Well," said Moa quietly. "I think the bores are getting bored. The others are jealous of us getting away and probably wish they were here with us now."

"I hope you're right," Lek said.

"Shut up!" said the guy again.

"But we're just talking to each other, you fool! What could possibly be wrong with that?" Moa said.

"You'll see. You'd better pack it in!" he threatened them.

"I can't understand why you go on like this," said Surachai to the guy. "A bit of conversation doesn't harm anyone, does it?"

"Anyhow, I think things are probably okay back home," said Moa, wrapping up the conversation so as not to annoy the guy too much.

Chapter 25

Lu's Nightmare

Up in Tat Kuang, Prim had been lying behind her grandmother all night feeling the reassuring warmth of her body, a sensation Prim had missed for quite some time. Morning came with the roosters incessantly crowing at the as the sun spread its pleasant morning warmth over the village. But this was not a day like any other. It was a day that would change the lives of many people, above all, Prim. She felt grandma waking up and moved her arm, which had been holding the older woman tight during the night. Grandma rose carefully, so as not to wake those she thought were still sleeping.

"How's mum, Grandma,?" Prim asked quietly.

"I think she's sleeping," replied May in a soft voice. "Come, let's go out," she said. "You can eat at my place so mum can sleep. She needs to rest as much as possible."

May went out of the hut and Prim came after her, ever so quietly, all the way across the yard up to May's hut.

"Are you going to wash at all?" asked May on their way to her hut.

"Yes," said Prim. "But I'm going to use the tub. I don't want to go down to the brook."

May could easily understand that thought.

"Alright Prim, do your morning wash and tell me when you'd like some food. I'll go and speak with grandpa about what's happened. I'm not sure he'll understand, or want to understand. He's not very well, you know."

"Yes, I know," Prim confirmed.

When Prim was done, she sat down outside grandma's hut to eat her breakfast.

"When you've eaten, you should go down to the town and try to get hold of some bandages and maybe some medicine for Lu," grandma told Prim.

"Yes," said Prim. "I will."

Before she left, she wanted to speak to Lu, since she would probably be away all day. She went into the hut. Lu lay in the same position as she had done the previous night, but now she was awake, staring at the wall.

"Mum," said Prim, but she got no answer.

"Mum!" she repeated, a little louder this time. Lu still didn't answer and showed no sign of having heard or seen her daughter.

Prim felt with every fibre of her being that something was very seriously wrong.

"Grandma, come quickly!" shouted Prim at the top of her voice from inside the small room. "Grandma! Come quickly!"

Some neighbours, who had heard Prim calling, came to her aid.

"Look at mum!" sobbed Prim, shaking all over.

Grandma came and joined with the neighbours in getting Prim, who was now crying uncontrollably, out of the hut.

"There's something terribly wrong with mum! I can feel it. Please, help her!"

Prim didn't stop crying for a long while. Grandma sat and hugged her as if Prim was a small girl, which indeed she was and now, one burdened by sorrow and tears.

"I'm in pain," said Prim as she lay in her grandmother's lap, her arms around her grandmother's waist. "I feel pain all over. What am I to do? What are we to do about mum? We must call for a doctor!"

"Prim, my dear, we have no money for that and anyway, I don't think we could get any doctor to come all the way here."

Prim had started to calm down and it was easier now for grandma to speak to her.

"Prim, it's important that you go to Luang Prabang and get the things I need," grandma told her.

"Yes, I can see that. I will," Prim said.

Prim rose from her grandma's lap, went to wash her face and got herself ready to go to town. While she got dressed, she spoke to Lu; this was important to her, even though she knew she would get no answer.

"Mum, I'm going to town to get you bandages and some medicine. I'll also try to get a doctor to come here, even though grandma says we have no money for it. I really think you need one."

Prim walked with quick steps out onto the road to hitch-hike with the first car or motorcycle going in the right direction. Before long, an old wreck of a car came by and stopped. There were new cars in Laos as well, but those that drove around up in these districts were usually much older and often had missing lights, suspension and body parts.

The driver was a kind old man from the neighbouring village who was on his way to sell a pig which was in a box tied to the roof. The pig squealed and grunted so loudly that it occasionally drowned out the engine, even though the car had no silencer. Since the car had almost no suspension, the trip to town took longer than usual and Prim had time to tell the old man everything that had taken place. He grew more and more upset as Prim told him what had happened to her mother.

"Prim, if I can drive you back later on today, I will. We had better decide where I should pick you up in advance, but if you're not there in time, I'll have to drive off anyway," he said.

"That'll be fine," said Prim. "Thank you."

The old man, who was heading for the airport, wanted to help Prim and took a small detour to the ferry port where he let her out. Prim went directly to the post office where Lek's mother worked.

"Hi," said Prim when she spotted Lek's mother behind the counter-window, just as she was about to help some customers. "I'd like to speak with you when you've finished."

"And I'd like to speak with you!" replied Lek's mother.

When she had served the last customer in her line, she closed the counter-window and asked Prim to come in behind.

"Prim, do you know where Lek is?" she asked.

"No, I don't, but I do know that she and Moa took the bus to Vientiane and that they were planning to try to get a job there or go on further. They didn't intend to come home until they'd earned enough money to afford it," Prim told her.

"Well, I gather that, since she took my money before she went away," Lek's mother confirmed.

Prim looked as if she knew nothing about that.

"Why have you come to me right now?" asked Lek's mother. "Have you got something else to tell me that I don't know?" She was visibly upset. "If you have nothing else to say, I want you to leave and pay me for the time you've been riding around on my moped."

Prim was uncomfortable about asking for money but felt that she needed to give it a try.

"I need to borrow money. I need medicine and a doctor for my mother." Prim failed to hold back the tears as she tried to explain what had happened. Lek's mother listened in silence.

"I'm sorry," she said, "but I can't contribute much. Possibly just a few thousand kip."

"Thank you!" replied Prim. "That will help us get part of the way. I'll ask some more people. I know my mother has a friend called Tim, who works at a bar nearby."

"Yes, I know who you mean. I know who Tim is, everybody does. She's the hooker all our men go to," said Lek's mum, not even trying to hide her resentment. She had caught her husband with Tim a couple of times herself. "But don't you mind what I think about her. You go and talk with her and maybe she can help you. I think she's still working at Night Stalls. You do know where it is, don't you?"

"Yes," said Prim.

"Here, take this money and come back with it whenever you can," she told Prim.

"Thank you," Prim said. "I'll try to pay you back as soon as possible."

*

Out in the street, she braced herself again, both mentally and physically and then she went onwards to Night Stalls.

The place was already crammed with customers, who were sitting at the tables or standing at the bar with drinks in their hands. Before Prim had made her way to the kitchen, she had received half a dozen proposals from the men at the bar, filthy old men as far as she was concerned. She stopped just short of the door to the kitchen, before knocking and entering.

"What do you want?" asked a voice from behind a sink unit, where a shelf packed with kitchen utensils covered the speaker's face.

"I'm looking for Tim," said Prim as she tried to look up from under the shelf.

"I'm not absolutely sure about Tim's whereabouts. Can I take a message?" the voice said.

"Yes, my name is Prim and my mother and Tim are friends. I would like to talk to her."

"I see," said the voice and now a face appeared along with it. "What's your mother's name?"

"Her name is Lu."

"Oh, I see. I know who Lu is. No problem. If you'd just wait for a while, I'll make some phone calls. I expect Tim will come right away."

Prim did not want to relate what had happened again and decided to wait until Tim arrived. "Could I wait here in the kitchen, so I don't have to stand out there?" she asked.

"I know what you mean. Sure, that's fine. Stay here, I'll go and make my calls," the woman said.

Prim sat down to wait on a bench by the back door to the kitchen. While she waited, she listened to the sounds of the restaurant and the bar. After a while, the woman came back into the kitchen.

"I'm Som, by the way and I know Lu as well, but it was probably with Tim that your mother had the most contact," she said.

"Will she come soon?" asked Prim, who felt pressed for time.

"Yes, she will," said Som. And at that moment, Tim came into the kitchen.

"Som, who's asking for me?" she asked.

"I am," said Prim.

"Who are you?" Tim asked.

"I'm Lu's daughter and I need your help," Prim explained.

"With what?" asked Tim, surprised.

"I know that you and mum are acquainted," Prim began and went on to relate the story from the beginning. "I've already borrowed two thousand kip from a friend's mother, but that won't even be enough to buy painkillers."

"No, my dear girl, it won't," said Tim.

"Such bloody bastards," said Som. "I could shoot them! Do you think it was the police?"

"I wouldn't be the least surprised," said Tim. "We all know what they're capable of and they won't stop at anything, those pigs. Prim, I can help you with some of the money and I'm sure Som can too, so that you can go down to the hospital and ask for help. Maybe, they'll give you something there."

"Thank you," said Prim. "I will. I have to hurry so I can get a lift back with the same old man who drove me here."

Prim left the bar. She decided to go to the hospital first, before she visited a chemist.

The hospital was not very far from Night Stalls. It was on the same street, Kitsarat, at the corner of Chao Sisophon Road, so it did not take Prim long to get there. The building, situated on a large corner site, was undergoing restoration and was covered in bamboo scaffolding on which people stood scraping the façade in order to re-plaster the surface and then paint it. It wasn't a big investment for the city as the building was only two stories high and about twenty metres long. Prim had never been to the hospital, but had heard what the locals said about the place, "If you enter here, you'll never get out alive. It's a laboratory, an institution for tests, a place you should avoid at all costs."

But for the moment, she had no other choice.

Prim went into the yard and up to the entrance. The door was stiff, but using both hands, she managed to force it open. Concrete dust in the lobby, from the scraping of the façade, rendered everything slightly grey. She entered a long corridor lined with doors; she could hear voices coming from behind them. When she found a door with the sign 'Doctor', she knocked. After a short while, the door opened and a nurse stood looking at her.

"What do you want? We have closed the reception and the day staff will be going home soon."

"I need help," said Prim. "I need help with bandages and medicine for my mother. She's been taken ill."

"I see and that's a shame, but you'll have to bring her here."

"I can't. She ..." Prim continued.

"What is this all about?" interrupted a voice.

"There's a girl here who says she needs bandages and medicine for her mother who is ill somewhere," the nurse explained.

"We can't give her those things without her mother coming here," the voice confirmed.

"It's impossible! You must help me! I live all the way up in Tat Kuang," Prim insisted.

"Tat Kuang?" said the voice. "Isn't that up among the Hmong villages?"

"It is," replied Prim.

She looked at the nurse while she waited for some response from the person behind the wall.

"We can't help you at the moment and the hospital is full. You have to leave and if your mother needs help, she'll have to come here herself," the voice stated.

Prim walked away from the hospital in despair and continued to the chemist's next to the Luang Prabang Hotel, thankful that there were tourists whose demands meant that the hospital stayed open. Inside the pharmacy, she tried to find what she needed. What she couldn't buy, she would have to steal. Prim had never stolen before, but now, she had no choice. She looked around and saw that the only assistant in the shop was busy attending a customer; meanwhile, the other customers paid no attention to her. She located the shelves stocked with bandages, plaster, surgical spirits and the vital Betadine to counteract infections, which could take hold quickly when it was hot and humid. Prim decided on a small bottle of Betadine and slipped it into her pocket. Then she picked a gauze bandage which was easy to squeeze into a small space. She walked half a lap around the display case and observed that the assistant was now occupied with a customer who was suffering with stomach pains.

Prim finished her circuit and returned to the same spot. How would she manage to take the surgical spirit? The plastic bottle was too big to shove into her pocket, so instead, she slipped it inside her blouse. If she kept it in place with her elbow, maybe nobody would notice. She walked straight past the assistant, who seemed to have made little progress with her customer.

"I'll be back soon," she said.

"Please do," replied the assistant and Prim went out.

Just opposite the hotel's chemist was the park Phu Si, which was enclosed by a stone wall. Prim squatted down with her back against the wall. Here, no one could see what she was doing. She allowed the items to slide down into the high grass, kicked some leaves over them and made sure her loot could not be seen. Then she went back to the chemist's to buy the rest: painkillers and penicillin.

The assistant was now occupied with other customers who also wanted penicillin. Their complaint was gonorrhoea. They received help quickly and when it was Prim's turn, she told the assistant exactly what she needed and why.

"My mother is seriously ill," she said. "She's been raped and beaten. I know I don't have enough money, but I must have painkillers and penicillin."

The assistant looked at Prim and from what she saw in Prim's eyes, there was no doubt the girl was telling the truth.

"I can't really sell half packages. How much money have you got?" the assistant asked.

Prim took out what she had, about thirty thousand kip, in the neighbourhood of five US dollars.

"Well, I'll take the money you have there, but in reality, that would only just be enough for four boxes of aspirins. I'll give you this, though. It's enough penicillin to last six days. They are powerful pills, so I hope your mother's got a strong stomach. They are effective, though," she said.

"Oh," said Prim. "How will I ever be able to thank you?"

"Pay me when you can. I know what it's like up there in the villages," said the assistant, smiling. "They don't give you much help."

"Thank you!" said Prim again. "I must hurry. Do you have a bag?"

"Here you are," the assistant said, handing one to her.

Prim left the pharmacy with a sense of shame. It felt wrong to retrieve her stolen goods, but she had no alternative. She looked around as she rounded the stone wall and aimed for the hiding place. No one had seen her and quickly, she picked up her stolen items and dropped them into the plastic bag. Then, she dashed to the meeting place. Her allotted time had already passed and it was time to get home. It would be fortunate if the old man could give her a lift back, if only she could get there in time.

Prim walked at a frantic pace and prayed she would not be too late. When she arrived at the meeting place, the old man was not there. Half an hour passed, but finally, she saw the old man and his tattered wreck of a car approaching. Only one of the headlights seemed to be working.

"Hi there, my little companion," said the old man. "How have things worked out for you today?"

"Fine," said Prim doggedly. "I got some help from the mother of a friend of mine, from mum's friends and from the woman working at the pharmacy. But not at the hospital. They had no time for me and they told me I should take mum to them. But the place was full in any case, they said."

"Weird, that," replied the old man. "I thought hospitals were supposed to give people help when they needed it."

"Yes, but not to those that live up in the mountains," Prim said.

*

She fell asleep on the main road out of Luang Prabang and did not wake up until the old man nudged her as they approached her village. She had not noticed a single bump or hole along the road. The old man stopped outside Prim's yard and as she got out of the car, he wished her good luck.

"Hope to see you soon!" called the kind old man.

When Prim entered the hut, May, Lu's mother, was sitting on the dry earthen floor with Lu's head in her lap.

"How's mum?" asked Prim.

"Not well," said her grandmother. "I haven't managed to make her eat anything all day and it's been difficult to get any fluid into her. It's like she has shut down. I just don't know, Prim."

"Has Mak been here?" asked Prim. "Maybe she can help."

"Yes, Mak's been here and those in the village who know some medicine. Nobody has managed to come up with a solution, though. They all say we just have to make sure she drinks enough not to dehydrate. That would be very dangerous indeed; you could dry out and die within three days," May confirmed.

"We won't let that happen, Grandma," said Prim.

Then she showed May what she had managed to bring home.

"I've got hold of bandages, surgical spirit, Betadine and penicillin," said Prim.

But Prim did not tell her how she had acquired everything, only that she had received help from Tim and Som, her mother's friends in town.

"Great," said her grandmother. "Then we'll try to make her swallow some of the pills and re-bandage her wounds again. You have to help me clean up mum's bedding. I think she's wet herself." Grandma's eyes were filled with sorrow as they met Prim's.

"Okay, I'll help you so you can change the blanket," Prim said.

When Prim rolled her mother over, she realised Lu was totally limp and had no way of helping herself. Once more, Prim had the feeling that things would never improve. But although it was unexplainable, a new strength was growing inside her.

"I'll help you, Mum," she said.

"Yes, we all will," said grandma.

They both meant two separate things, but Prim didn't bother to explain.

"Grandma, will you stay here with me tonight? I don't think I want to be alone with mum," Prim said.

"Yes, I'll just go home to my place and get some food and you need to eat something, too," grandma said.

"I haven't eaten all day, Grandma. If you go to your place and prepare the food, I'll try to get mum to drink some water and then I'll take care of the fire outside so we can sit there," Prim said.

"That sounds fine," said her grandmother before leaving.

Prim organised everything in the hut in the way Lu had always done it. She spoke to Lu as she worked, as if she could hear her and she answered her own questions, "I know, Mother." Then, she went out to the fireplace, put on some dry sticks and blew life into the fire and before long, it caught. She fetched two blankets and went to her grandmother to help her to carry out the food. This done, they sat down by the fire.

"Grandma, isn't it just typical that everybody is away when you need them most?" Prim stated.

"What do you mean? I'm here aren't I?" she replied, misunderstanding Prim's point.

"Yes, you are! But grandpa and dad are gone and I think dad ought to be here now to help us, Grandma. If mum doesn't get any better tomorrow we have to take her to the doctor or a hospital," Prim said.

"Yes, but how are we to pay for it?" grandma asked. "That kind of treatment will cost a fortune and we just don't have the money for it."

"I must try to find help. I wonder what kind of people Will and Frank are. Mum's working for them, you see. Why didn't I think of tracking them down when I was in Luang Prabang today? I must do that tomorrow. I have to go down into town early tomorrow morning and contact them before they go up to Phonsavan, that's where they work. Mum's mentioned it several times," she confirmed.

"Yes, that sounds like an excellent idea," said grandma.

The evening passed and it grew late. Prim was tired now and wanted to go in to Lu and sleep.

"Come, Grandma, I've had enough of the fire for tonight. And we have to get up early in the morning."

Chapter 26

French Connection

After breakfast, Will and Frank had been sat waiting for Lu for over two hours. Then, Frank spoke. "I've had enough of this! Will, if we don't leave now, we'll get nothing done today."

As had become their custom, they took the car up to Phonsavan and the nearby plain with all its two metre high jars. These jars were still standing, despite the deluge of bombs they were subjected to during the war. They were the main attraction of the valley and the principal reason for its fame. These gigantic rock jugs had the same shape as a one litre wine jug, but were big enough to hold up to two or three thousand litres of wine. They were believed to have been made about two and a half thousand years ago. Frank had told Will everything Spencer had said and what they could hope to accomplish.

"Here," said Frank. "This is the place where I stopped to get some air and those guys on the bike came and threatened me. I would never have thought that anyone would try that kind of business proposal in broad daylight."

"You have to be careful. I think you've become a bit soft and lost your edge. Are you getting past it?" asked Will, laughing.

"I'll get you for that when we come back," promised Frank, "no matter how late."

"Well, let's hope it will be late. If Spencer's managed to get hold of these Vietnamese guys, we might have some more leads to follow up today. Did you bring all our gear and equipment?"

"Yeah, I never took them out of the trunk."

"Uh-oh," said Will. "Do you have any idea what it'll cost to replace those things if they get stolen?"

"Who would have any use for those tools? If it was a bunch of screwdrivers, I'd understand your concern, but not for that lot," Frank said.

*

Arriving at Phonsavan, they went straight to Crater Bar. Spencer's wife stood wiping tables in the restaurant.

"So you're here today! We thought you'd come yesterday, so I made a tasty casserole which stood waiting for you. Lucky I didn't give it to the neighbour's pigs!" she said and laughed. "I'm just having you on. It's still in the kitchen and you'll get it even though you're a day late. I suppose you're here to meet Spencer as well?" she said.

"Yes, but we'd very much like to try the casserole," Frank assured her.

"Why, of course, it's still lunch hour! If you just take a seat, I'll heat it up. And then I'll see to it that Spencer comes as soon as he can," she said.

While they were waiting, they looked out towards the other side of the street.

"Look at that bar where we went in and back out again. See how the guys are constantly coming and going," Frank said.

"Yeah, I see it," said Will. "They sure open early over there."

"Spencer told me that this is one of the village's brothels. Apparently, it's one of the worst. They won't even let the girls leave the house," Frank replied.

"Oh hell, one of those places. Why don't the authorities shut it down? Isn't prostitution forbidden in Laos?" Will asked.

"Well yeah, but nobody would ever admit that it exists and if you make a fuss about it, they won't let you out of the country. The best way to draw attention to it is to write about it, debate about it and work with human rights organisations. The important thing is that people understand what it is, which is sex slavery. And it's not just here but in many other places around the world," Frank commented.

The kitchen door opened and Spencer's wife emerged carrying a tray laden with two steaming plates and a bowl of rice. She served Will and Frank.

"That smell's great. What is it?" asked Frank.

"Buffalo casserole: diced meat, first browned in an iron casserole then boiled in wine for a couple of hours with various spices. After that, I've added carrots, onion, mushrooms, fresh herbs, Yellow Star-of-Bethlehem, fresh coriander, lemon grass and lime," she said, outlining the recipe.

"Who taught you to cook this dish?" asked Will.

"Nobody, it's a common thing around here. Most likely, there's some French touch in it. As you probably know, France has had a major influence on Vietnamese cuisine," she said.

They ate with great relish and the only words Frank spoke before Spencer came in through the front door were to say, "We can't gorge ourselves on this. We have to work after lunch, remember and not doze off!"

"I see you've had some of the casserole my wife cooked for you yesterday," said Spencer as he approached the table. "She was a bit disappointed you guys didn't show up and I guess I was, too."

Frank looked at Will and kicked him lightly in the shin.

"Well," said Frank. "Yesterday, we had a little accident. Will fell into the river and dropped his wallet by the ferry and we had to search in the water for hours. When we found it, with help from some little boys, the passport was ruined. We thought it best to go to the police and arrange for a new set of papers at once."

"Oh, I see," said Spencer. "Meanwhile, I've got hold of the man I told you about, the one who knows something about the camp that used to be down at Nong Nam Nyam during the war.

He lives a little east of here in a small village called Khek. He can tell you a thing or two about the camp. He doesn't want to say what military rank he had during the war, but I have my suspicions. The guy holds quite a position in the local hierarchy and in one way or another, he's managed to become fairly well-off. He's somewhat of a pompous ass, but he likes to be the centre of attention, so he might be the right man for you."

"Let's go see him then. Would you like to come along?" asked Frank.

"No," said Spencer. "There's no need for me to tag along. He knows you're coming. But he expected you yesterday, though. Spin him the same yarn you spun me and we'll find out if he buys it. If he does, tell me so I don't appear to be the only gullible one, since I can say that he believed it too.

Spencer smiled at Frank, who kept a straight face and smiled back. Then, he said to Will, "Let's get going so we can be back before nightfall."

"You'll spot his house to your right before you get in to Khek, since it's the only house that seems to have been built by an Austrian master builder," explained Spencer. "The house has a typical Central European look and I know that he got the idea from a place called Da Lat in Vietnam, where there are lot of houses of that type. They call Da Lat 'Little Paris' and if you ever go there, you'll find that the whole village is still standing. Da Lat was one of the few villages both the US and Vietnam avoided bombing. Superior officers used to meet there. And our man was a big shot, of course and got his idea for his house while he stayed there. You won't miss it. Give him my greetings when you get there!"

Frank and Will hurried out to their sun-baked car.

"Well, we just have to drive eastwards," said Will.

"Yeah and there's even a sign with the village's name on it," said Frank. "All we've got to do is to drive until a new sign shows up."

"There won't be one, given it's just straight ahead," Will said.

"There will be another sign," Frank said.

"No, there won't!" Will disagreed.

"It's guaranteed," said Frank, mocking Will. "There will be a sign."

"Damn, what a nuisance you are!" Will said.

Frank laughed. "Oh yeah!" he said. "When you get to a village there's always a sign and that's the one I'm talking about."

"Yeah, of course, that one, but that's cheating," Will said.

*

They sat in silence, both of them, until they reached the house Spencer had told them about.

"Bloody hell!" said Frank. "It looks just like a place in Austria, where I stayed once. Just look at all the flowers hanging from the balconies and those ones by the parking spaces. It's unbelievable!"

"Frank?" said Will and grinned. "Did you notice one thing when we got into the village?"

"No, what?" Frank asked.

"There wasn't any sign with the village's name on it," Will said smugly.

"Okay, okay, you were right!" Frank said, accepting defeat.

They drove into a wide parking area outside the house and walked up to a fancy door of oiled oak.

"Wow! This door has to be the most impressive one I've seen in this part of Asia. Ornate, panelled, the whole works!"

He leaned forward and pushed a small button to the left of the doorframe.

"I think this must be the first time I've pushed a button to a doorbell of the same type as those we have back in the US," Will said.

A loud signal reverberated through the whole building and after a short while, the door opened. A young woman dressed in a light blue working suit with an apron tied around her waist stood in front of them. She looked at them for a couple of seconds and then she asked, in French, if there was something she could do for them. Frank replied in awkward French, but when she heard Will speaking to Frank in English, she switched to impeccable English instead.

"I'll go and ask my master if he's available. Please wait here a moment," she said and walked away.

"Will," said Frank. "she's hardly Vietnamese, is she?"

"No, I think she's a Filipina," Will replied. "As you know, it's not uncommon for people who can afford it to import cheap labour and I believe it's cheaper to have someone from the Philippines taking care of your house than someone from Vietnam or Laos."

"I guess you're right," said Frank.

They heard voices and footsteps from the room the maid had walked through to find her master and now the man himself approached. He looked like many other Vietnamese men around sixty: a little corpulent and about five foot eight.

"Hi," he said heartily. "I thought you'd come yesterday. That's what my friend Spencer said, at least. I'm Djoe, but my friends call me Jo."

"I'm Frank and this is my colleague and friend Will."

"Come in," said Jo. "We can't just stand in the doorway. There are far too many nosy people around. Let's go out back and sit down in the shade. What may I offer you? I know you've come from Luang Prabang, that's quite some trip just for this, isn't it?"

"We stopped awhile at Spencer's place. His wife had made a casserole, so even if we had to go straight back, the journey would have been worth it," Frank replied.

"Well, you must have some coffee or tea, at least," Jo insisted.

"Thank you! That would be nice. Coffee for me, please," replied Will.

"And Frank?" asked Jo.

"Tea, please," replied Frank.

Jo instructed the maid to go to the kitchen and get some water, tea and coffee.

"My wife isn't home yet. She's gone to a salon to have her hair done," said Jo and smiled.

Suddenly, he grew serious. "I know why you're here and I know all about your organisation. As you're probably aware, we have an equivalent organisation of our own, so I welcome you with respect. If it hadn't been for Spencer asking me, though, I would absolutely have refused this meeting with you as I just have no time for it."

"I see," said Frank. As usual, he was the one to lead the conversation, since he outranked Will.

"I don't know if you're aware, but Spencer's wife and I are relatives and as long as she makes those casseroles, she'll remain my relative." He smiled again. Then he asked, "How long have you been looking for these remains?"

"Well, they've been on our lists ever since the end of the war," replied Frank. "Time passes quickly."

"Yes indeed," said Jo and at that moment, the maid returned with a tray.

"You've got a nice house," said Will, trying to lead the conversation elsewhere while the young woman put everything down. "May I ask you what you do for a living?"

"You may. We work in rubber and my company is one of the largest in the regions where we're active," Jo replied.

"Rubber?" said Will, interested.

"Yes, but not here, since there's not much of it locally. This is my main home but my companies are in Thailand and Vietnam, where I also live occasionally," Jo explained.

"Oh, I see," said Will.

Frank guided the conversation back to their errand.

"Jo, what did you do during the war? And where were you stationed?"

"I don't want to answer any of those questions," Jo replied. "But I can tell you this much: there were two of your guys in the camp at Nong Nam. This I know, but I won't tell you how it is that I know it or anything else about it, only this, that I know that these two were there in the camp along with the other captives."

"I understand," said Frank and drank some of his tea.

"Do you know for how long they were there, or if they were transported to some other place?" asked Will.

"I couldn't say how long they were there and I don't think they were taken somewhere else. This was towards the end of the war and they were captives of particular interest. I guess the Russian advisors wanted to get as much as possible out of people who worked for the CIA and to the best of my knowledge, your guys were agents who trained the so called Secret Army." Jo drank some of his tea.

"Well, out of respect for their memory, we shouldn't go into any details," Will said. "As far as you know, then, should we focus our attention exclusively on Phonsavan and Nong Nam?"

"I believe so, yes," Jo confirmed.

Frank and Will sat pondering in silence for a while. Will could tell from Frank's expression that they were both thinking the same thing: had Spencer known this all along, but pretended not to?

Frank broke the silence. "May I ask you something? Does Spencer know about this?"

"No, he doesn't," replied Jo looking Frank straight in the eye. "The question happened to pop up a couple of days ago, but even then, I didn't tell him what I'm telling you now. I swear it."

"You can probably understand why we're asking you," said Will. "We've met Spencer a good few times now and we would've found it rather odd if he hadn't told us about this."

"Well, Spencer came to me two nights ago and told me about you, Frank and the meeting you two had had at the restaurant. He told me it had been pleasant and reassuring and that you obviously knew his son. You must understand that Spencer and I have left the war behind us and come to terms with the fact that it's history now. When Spencer contacted me, I'd only been home for a couple of hours; I'd been away in Thailand. I was a little surprised by his questions about whether I knew anything or not. Spencer told me it was nothing to worry about and that there would be no consequences. He guaranteed me that. Then, I said, 'Let Frank come to me and I'll help them out.' So, it's true, Spencer knows nothing about it," Jo responded.

"We're truly grateful for the information you've given us," Frank said. "We'll keep you updated about how our work progresses."

"There's no need for that, at all. Let's just hope you find the remains of the guys you're looking for and that they get taken back home to American soil, where they belong," Jo concluded.

"Yeah, many thanks. I hope we'll meet again under more pleasant circumstances," said Will rising from his chair.

"I couldn't agree more," said Frank, also getting up. "Will, I guess we won't have time to accomplish much more today, so we might as well go back and start to check up on the details tomorrow."

Jo stretched out his right hand, something people only did outside Asia. "If there's anything I can do for you, just let me know. I've got contacts within the police and various other authorities."

"Thank you," said Frank. "If something crops up, I'll be in touch."

The young woman returned to show them out. She said goodbye politely in French.

"It's a pity we didn't have time to meet his wife," said Will as they walked towards their car.

"Yeah, or fortunate. For now, at least we have a clear objective to aim for, so tomorrow will be exciting," Frank confirmed.

"Wow!" said Will, as they backed out of the parking place. "Could that be her?"

A woman in her thirties had just emerged from a taxi outside the house.

"Bet she's high maintenance," he added.

"Yeah," said Frank. "Money buys you everything."

*

They drove towards Luang Prabang at high speed, so as not to arrive too late.

"Let's go there directly, without stopping," said Frank. "If I get tired you'll have to take over, so we'll be home in time to get a good night's rest. I think we'll have to get up early tomorrow."

"Yeah, alright, that's probably for the best. I think we should go to our old hotel. I find it hard to sleep in new places. And Frank, don't you stop now or we might get harassed by a gang of opium dealers on a motorcycle," Will said.

"Well, I'll try. But Will, I wonder where Lu's at," Frank mused.

"She'll probably show up tomorrow. How did it work, Frank? You employed her for three months, didn't you? This won't take more than one, tops! That's not very economical. We'd better not say that we hired her for three months. We'll take her cost on the bribe account," Will said thinking of their budget.

"Yeah, that's probably for the best. But we could discuss it with her: she probably won't mind getting two months' pay without having to work for it. That way, she'll cost us three months' pay but only have to work one," Frank said.

"Let's sort that out tomorrow. I think I'll try to take a little nap. Wake me up when you want me to take the wheel," Will advised his colleague.

"Okay," said Frank.

Frank did not feel the least bit tired, not yet at least. He had been exhilarated by the meeting with Jo. The old man knew exactly what had happened, but for various reasons, he didn't want to go into details. But that didn't matter. He'd given them a clear objective.

Will slept, his snoring drowning out the car radio. Frank drove non-stop to Luang Prabang all by himself and Will did not wake until they got there.

"Damn, are we already there?" he asked.

"Yes, travelling goes quickly when you're sleeping," said Frank, pulling up in the parking lot behind the hotel. He got out of the car and stretched. "Now, it sure will be nice to go to bed. I'm going to sleep like a log."

"I'll have a beer in the bar before I go up to my room," said Will.

"Alright, you do that, since you've been sleeping all this time. But remember, we have to be up early tomorrow morning. We won't get many hours sleep," said Frank.

"Don't worry. I'll just have the one," Will assured him.

Frank went up to his room and Will went to the bar, where it soon dawned on him that he was quite alone. It wasn't long before he went to bed, too.

*

Will was first to get up, refreshed and wide awake, at six o'clock in the morning.

He went down to the restaurant. It was completely empty except for the staff milling around preparing breakfast. He took a seat. Frank would probably be down soon. He went to their regular table, which the staff had reserved for them each morning. He waited half an hour. After another ten minutes, he began to wonder where Frank was. He decided to check out what was going on. But just as he was about to walk up the stairs, Frank came down.

"Hell, I got worried. You've never been late or overslept before," said Will.

"I woke up early and then I went back to sleep again. You know what happens: you sleep twice as deep. Besides, I dreamt that type of strange dream, the one where you're flying. Have you ever dreamt about that? You just put your back into it, flap your arms and then you take to the sky. It's crazy. It's lucky I landed, otherwise I would still be flying. It was that real."

"Yeah, yeah, Frank, that's most interesting," said Will. "Let's have a quick breakfast and get going."

Chapter 27

Paid in Full

The morning chores started early for Prim. She had decided to go down to town to try to get hold of Frank and Will. She stole out into the yard and washed herself in the tub, tiptoed back into the hut and got dressed silently, so as not to wake anyone up. The bus would not be due for several hours and she was concerned she might not be able to get a lift at such an early hour. But she did not have to wait long; after a short while, a truck came by with goods bound for the city market.

While Will and Frank were on their way down to breakfast, Prim was half-running towards their hotel. As she passed the parking lot, she had a recollection of her mum telling her they had a Toyota? But there were an awful lot of Toyotas there. She got to the entrance and when she stuck out her hand to grab the door handle, the door opened automatically. She walked up to the reception desk and asked for Will and Frank.

"Wait a moment," said the woman behind the desk and went away to have a look for the guests. When she returned, she said, "They're in the restaurant having breakfast. I'm imagine they won't want to be disturbed."

"Could you please tell them that Prim, Lu's daughter, is here and has to speak with them urgently?" Prim said.

"Oh, I see, you're Lu's daughter," the woman said cheerfully. "In that case, I guess it'll be alright if you go in to them."

Prim strode into the restaurant and up to the two men, who were staring wide-eyed at the girl approaching them. There was something very familiar about her. Prim greeted them by bowing and holding her hands together, her fingertips under her nose. Will and Frank did likewise, without thinking, since they did not yet know who the person before them was or what her errand might be.

"Who are you?" asked Will.

"My name is Prim. I'm Lu's daughter. I'm here because I need your help, or more accurately, my mother needs your help."

"What kind of help?" asked Frank.

"It's serious," she told them. "Mum has been severely beaten." She began to cry. "She's been raped too and we can't seem to get through to her. She hasn't said a word for twenty-four hours now."

"Oh my, oh my," said Frank. "I was afraid that something might have happened, but I would never have believed it could be this bad. Sit down, little girl. Have you eaten?"

"No, I had no time," Prim said. "I know you usually get away early in the mornings, so I came here as quickly as I could. I was here in town yesterday, but I didn't think of looking for you until I got back home yesterday evening."

"Please, Will," said Frank, turning to his colleague, "could you go and get whatever Prim wants, so she can eat while we can have a chat. Tell us what happened, Prim."

"What would you like?" Will cut in. "You don't eat sandwiches like we do, do you?"

"No, we don't," said Prim smiling behind her tears. "I can go and get it myself, but first I'd like to tell you what happened to mum."

"I'll get you some orange juice anyway," said Will. He left, but returned quickly from the buffet table.

Prim begun to tell them about all the horrific things that had befallen her mother and how she had looked when Prim found her down by the brook. Will was back in time to hear almost everything.

"Prim," Will said. "Are there many villagers who have seen that police car over recent weeks?"

"Yes," replied Prim.

"Frank, what are we going to do? We can't just leave Prim here. She's come to seek our help."

"Of course not," said Frank. "Those old corpses that we've been looking for the last few months aren't going anywhere. I think we'll take a different route today, to Prim and Lu's place."

Prim felt happy for the first time in what felt like days. She asked them if it was okay if she got herself some breakfast before they left.

"Absolutely, have as much as you like and we'll have another cup of coffee before we leave," said Frank. He turned to his colleague. "Will, it looks like today will be very different from the one we had planned."

"Yeah, but how often do our days turn out like that? I truly hope we can do something for her," Will said.

Prim returned to the table with a large plate of chicken casserole and rice.

"Wow," said Will. "Are you going to eat all of that?"

Will was not used to the voracious appetites of youngsters, but for Prim, this amount of food wasn't a problem. It took her no time at all to wolf it down and by the time Frank and Will took their last sip of coffee, her plate was clean.

"Something's occurred to me," said Will. "Would it help if we could take a doctor with us to Lu, now, right away?"

"Like I said, we've got no money for a doctor," said Prim.

"But we have," said Frank. "And besides, we owe your mother money which she's got coming anyway, so that issue will sort itself out."

"Frank, let's ask the staff here at the hotel for a good doctor," said Will.

"Good idea, Will. You take care of it while I go up and get my things," Frank said.

"Okay," said Will as he got up. "You can come with me," he said to Prim and started walking towards the reception.

*

Will asked the woman behind the desk where he could find a good doctor and if the hotel could make sure that he came immediately.

"I could ask for one that we usually contact, who lives in this block."

"Great," said Will. "Tell him that it concerns a serious injury in Tat Kuang. We're heading up there today and we'd like a doctor with us."

The receptionist made a couple of phone calls from the office behind the desk. Will understood nothing of the conversation, but Prim did.

"We won't be getting any help," she said and looked at Will.

"What do you mean? Why shouldn't we get any?" he asked her.

"I overheard what she said in there," said Prim. "I think it's because she asked the doctor to go to Tat Kuang. Everybody knows it's a Hmong village and nobody's willing to help us."

"How are things going?" asked Frank when he returned from his room.

"Well, she's in there calling for a doctor," replied Will. "Here she comes."

"I'm sorry," she said, "but there's no one available to go with you."

"Okay, I understand," said Frank. "Give me a telephone directory for the town and a map. We're going to do as we usually do: Will, you go straight to the practice and explain that we need help and that we'll pay whatever the doctor asks. Get the man in the car, tell him that we'll be travelling a fair way outside the city, but not where we're going until we're well on the way, got it?"

"Yes, but that's basically kidnapping, isn't it?" Will said.

"Not if we pay the man for his services," said Frank smiling.

Prim stood silent, listening.

"But Frank, what about going down to the hospital and talking to the people there?" suggested Will.

The receptionist was still standing behind the desk and cut in now.

"It might be a good idea to go to the Chinese hospital and try there instead," she said.

"Yes," said Prim. "I was at our hospital yesterday and they wouldn't help me."

Will looked at Frank.

"Then, the Chinese hospital it must be. Let's get cracking. Time is of the essence. Prim, if you navigate, we'll get there sooner," Will said.

They dashed out to the car.

"Take the front seat, Prim. I'll take the back," said Will. "It'll be easier for Frank if he has his guide beside him. It's where your mother usually sits."

*

During their trip to the hospital, Prim told them about yesterday's meeting with the nurse.

"It's strange that people can be so bloody unforgiving. Or is it just that they have to assume a certain attitude so they don't get in trouble with the authorities?" asked Will.

"You know it is," said Frank. "If you don't have the party card and if you've done something party members don't approve of, you're in trouble."

"It's over there on the left hand side," said Prim. "And there, to the right, is the hospital I went to yesterday."

"Alright, let's park here in the street," said Frank. "Prim, you wait here."

As Will and Frank approached the entrance, a short, plump woman emerged from the door. It was clear that she was one of the staff.

"Excuse me, do you speak English?" asked Will.

"Yes, I do," replied the woman, with a squeaky voice. She had an unmistakable Chinese accent.

"We need some help," Will continued.

"With what?" asked the woman, cautiously.

"Well, the situation is this. A friend of ours is seriously ill several miles from here and we can't move her, so we need a doctor to come with us to where she is."

"There are no doctors here. At best, there might be someone who never finished his studies and who stayed on as an intern," she confirmed.

"But maybe you know someone who's willing to come along and can give better care than we can give ourselves. We'll pay well," Will continued, noticing that the mention of payment caught her attention.

"What is it all about, then?" she asked, grabbing the street door. "Let's go inside. I've got a small office in here. We can talk in detail there."

"A friend of ours, a woman," said Will, entering her office, "has been severely beaten and raped. She works for us and we've been working together for some time now. We have to do something for her."

"I see," replied the woman.

She seemed to understand the situation.

"How much would you need to come along this us? We'll drive you back, of course. We're staying here at the Merry Lao Swiss Hotel," Will continued.

"Oh, I see," she said, as she tried to come up with an appropriate sum. "This will take the rest of my day, of course. If you were to pay me two hundred thousand kip, I'd come."

Although that was one month's pay for her, Frank agreed.

"It's a deal," he said, looking over at Will, who nodded in agreement.

"It's important that you realise I'm not a doctor," she said.

"We appreciate that, but we've set our hopes on you," said Will. "Our car is outside in the street. Should we wait for you there?"

"I'll just gather up the things I'll need. It won't take long and then we can leave together," she said.

Frank watched as she loaded her bag with instruments, bags containing fluids and injection needles, her hands moving swiftly and unerringly from item to item. He reckoned that based on her age, she was probably quite experienced.

"Alright, I'm done. Let's go!" she said and walked towards the door to the office. Will opened it for her, quickly.

"Oh, a gentleman! There's not many of those around these days," she said smiling.

Will winked at Frank, who planned to be first to the main door to hold it open, but Will got the better of him again. The nurse smiled again.

Prim saw them coming and was just about to get out of the car when Frank spoke, "No Prim, you stay in the front seat, you have to guide us to your house."

A house was not how Prim would have described her home. She sat back feeling a little embarrassed.

"Hello," she greeted the new passenger, who was surprised to see a girl in the front seat.

"Who are you?" asked the nurse.

"I'm Prim," she replied quickly and somewhat shyly.

"It's her mother who's hurt," said Frank. "Her name's Lu. It was Prim here who found her."

"Oh, poor girl," said the nurse. "Well, I hope I can help you. It's a major problem for us, that we lack educated staff. Neither of the two hospitals can do much more than clean minor wounds. If the wound is large or has to be stitched, the poor reputations of both hospitals are probably justified: if you get in, you never get out."

"That sounds terrible," said Will, who was sitting next to the nurse in the back seat.

"If there's been an accident, you usually have to take the patient to Vientiane or to Thailand, usually to Chiang Mai or Bangkok," she continued.

"I really hope we don't have to resort to a solution as complicated as that," said Frank.

Prim said nothing and grew more and more anxious as they drew closer to the village.

"We don't live in a house," she said, finally. "Up in the mountains, we live in huts and lie on the floor at night with blankets wrapped around us to keep warm. I just wanted to tell you, so you won't be surprised."

"Dear child," said the nurse. "I know how you live. You need not worry. I promise not to abandon you."

Prim reckoned that it felt good that there was a woman with them, even if she was Chinese.

"Frank, don't go so quickly through the next bend, or we might end up in our neighbour's house. We're almost there now," Prim advised him.

"Okay," said Frank, slowing the car right down to five miles per hour for the last fifty metres before the yard.

"Here it is," said Prim. "You can turn in between those huts and then you'll enter our yard. But watch out for the animals!"

"Wow, there sure are a lot of pigs here," said Will, "and chickens, too."

"I see them every day, so I never think about how many there are. They're just another part of everyday life," Prim said.

Frank stopped the car on a spot he assumed to be a parking space.

"Is it okay for me to park here?" he asked.

"Yes, grandpa always parks here when he's home. But for the moment, he's away and we don't know when he'll be back. If he happens to come back today, we'll know about it. You'd hear it alright," Prim replied.

They all got out of the car.

"Now I see what you mean about living in huts. But that's the way it is everywhere, Prim. What's wrong with that? I've seen all of Laos and almost everybody lives like this."

"Yes," said Prim. "But I thought that—"

"Okay then. Now we have to get started with what we're here for," said the nurse interrupting her. "Where is your mother?"

"Over there," said Prim, pointing towards the hut by the road. "I can go ahead to see if grandma is there. I think she is."

"Let's go," said the nurse, following Prim into the hut. Behind her came Frank and Will.

Grandma sat holding up Lu's head. When Prim saw her, she filled her in quickly on who the people were who had come into the hut with her. Grandma hissed something to Prim that only she could understand and moved aside. It was obvious that she didn't like what was happening. The way she saw it, the fact that a Chinese woman had entered the hut was an ominous portent from the gods. But the nurse took command immediately. She could see what the old lady thought of her presence, but she also knew there was a woman on the floor who needed urgent help and that was more important than making a fuss.

"How much has she been drinking?" she asked May.

"I guess I've managed to get half a litre into her today," May said.

"Oh my!" said the nurse turning to look at Will and Frank who were standing there twisting and turning. "Everybody has to get out of here immediately. You stay," she told May. "You can help me out."

"No, I can't," said May.

"If you want to save your daughter's life, you must!" She turned to Prim. "You have to leave as well! Go and boil water. It must really boil. A couple of litres will be enough and it'll be quicker if the pot isn't full. Those two can give you a hand," she said, referring to Will and Frank.

"Okay," said Prim. "I'll take care of it."

"What do you want me to do?" May asked.

"Make her lie on her back and make sure she has something under her head. She'll also need a rolled-up blanket under the small of her back, so I can examine her. And while you're doing that, I'll wash the back of her hand and put in a needle to give her fluid and penicillin. Once that's been done, hopefully, she'll feel better."

Then the nurse turned to Lu.

"Oh my! Just look at the state you're in! What have they done to you?" she asked, but there was no reply. "Has she been like this the whole time? Have you not been able to talk to her?"

"No," said May. "We found her this way a couple of days ago and she's been like this ever since."

"That's not good at all. Here, wash her wounds with this alcohol! Use clean rags! I can see from what you're doing that you've done this before," the nurse said.

May felt more confidence about the nurse now. "I'll lift the blanket over her chest on the right side," she said. "Can you see that?"

"Oh yes! That's a nasty blow!" The nurse felt carefully around Lu's chest with her fingers. "A couple of ribs are broken and that must hurt terribly. Raping her wasn't enough for these monsters, then. They had to beat her up as well," she said angrily.

The nurse carried on speaking as she examined Lu. "During the war years, I was stationed in Hanoi. I saw a lot of things there and I took care of a lot of things too. It was as if, as soon as the uniform went on, all atrocities became legal."

*

While the nurse had been examining Lu and giving her fluids, Will and Frank sat outside listening to Prim's stories about her grandfathers, their life at the yard and briefly, about her decision to leave school.

"Prim!" she heard, from inside the hut. "Prim, come with water. We need it now!"

Prim ran to her grandma's hut and fetched the water that was boiling over the fireplace. She poured the water into a small bucket and placed a small piece of wood over it and then, she ran across the yard.

"Why did she do that?" Will asked Frank.

"To stop the water splashing out as she ran. It's an ancient technique you don't see much of these days," Frank replied. "But I remember that my grandmother used to do the same thing when she carried water from the well to our house when I was a kid. Try it and you'll see that it works."

"I will. Do you know what, Frank? I think it would be fun to live with people in a place like this for a couple of months, witness their everyday life and get to know them. We're almost here like tourists," Will said.

"I doubt they'd let us into their private lives easily. But for the moment, we have an opportunity to bond, haven't we?" Frank observed.

Prim came out again, with tears in her eyes.

"What's up, Prim?" asked Frank. "Sit down here and tell us more about life at the yard," he suggested, mainly to divert her thoughts.

"Mum's in there with a big needle in her hand with a plastic pipe leading to a bottle they've got hanging from the ceiling. It looks horrible," she said.

"It's called a drip and it's given so that your mother can take in fluids when she can't drink enough," Frank explained. "That's very important, because it's dangerous if you dehydrate, something that can happen in just three or four days."

Inside the hut, the work continued. The nurse noticed May's skills. "How did you learn that?" she asked.

"Probably the same way you did, by patching together and helping men and women in battle. These things stick," May replied.

"So why didn't you do what I did and stay on at a hospital afterwards?" the nurse asked.

"I'd had more than enough of wounds and death," May said.

"Yes, just like the rest of us, except for some politicians," the nurse added.

Grandma was of the same opinion. She had begun to think well of this nurse.

"You have to help me keep her legs apart. I have to examine her and I'd like to take the opportunity to clean her thoroughly at the same time," the nurse instructed.

"This doesn't look good," she continued. "She's already got a genital infection. Could you hand me that spoon over there among my gynaecological tools and that small spatula along with the flashlight, too! Oh my! Poor woman, what have they done to you? If you could only speak. I believe they have ruined her for life, poor girl."

Grandma assisted in silence, realising that Lu's condition was serious, more serious than she had realised earlier.

"She can't stay here," said the nurse. "We have to take her to a hospital as soon as possible. It's lucky we have those guys outside, because I think we have to take her to our hospital in

Luang Prabang. But that will only be for a short period. If she doesn't get better we'll have to move her again, probably to Vientiane."

"Yes," May said. "I think I understand."

The nurse looked at grandma with empathy in her eyes. May met her gaze and shook her head.

"These last few years, everything has gone downhill for all of us. I can't understand what sin we have committed," said May, her eyes welling with tears for the first time.

May had been as resilient as she could, but her strength had deserted her when she realised that her daughter's condition was even worse than she had feared. She kept her eyes on the nurse and expressed her gratitude that the woman had come.

"Will there be time for us to eat before you have to go?" May asked her.

"Yes, sure, let's do that. Lu should stay here for a little while anyway, so she can take in the drip," the nurse replied.

The two women went out into the yard where Prim, Will and Frank were sitting in the shade talking about everyday life in the village.

"Prim," said May. "Come and help me prepare the food. They are taking your mum to the hospital, but I'd like everybody to eat first."

Prim translated for Will and Frank.

"Sounds fine," said Will. "I'm actually starting to get hungry."

"Yeah, that'll be great. Can we help?" Frank asked, attempting to help.

"Yes, you can. You could grill the red meat and the chicken. Prim, show them where the fireplace is so they can get the embers glowing. You know how, don't you?" May said to the Americans through Prim, who was kept busy translating.

"We'll take care of it," Will said.

"This will be interesting," said Frank. "Now we'll get close to the villagers."

"What do you think we're having?" Will asked.

"I think we're having barbecued food, since that's what they usually eat, barbecued meat with vegetables from their own garden and no rice," Frank replied.

"No rice?" asked Will, surprised.

"No. Up in the mountains, people don't tend to eat rice. In Laos only the valley people do that and those living in the Mekong Delta," Frank explained.

"Yes, but when we've eaten at restaurants, Lu has eaten rice," Will pointed out.

"That may be, but that's not what's on their own menu. There's no land suitable for growing rice up in the mountains," Frank explained.

While Prim and grandma walked away to fetch water, the nurse seized the opportunity to take a walk around the yard. Her voice was heard now and then, as she spoke to the animals. The small outdoor kitchen was soon filled with vegetables and meat. Grandma had gathered all the ingredients. She gutted the freshwater fish meticulously and then she salted it and filled it with lemon grass. Eventually, it would end up on the barbecue alongside the meat and vegetables. The prepared food smelled delicious.

"Prim," asked Frank. "Do you always make such tasty food?"

"No, we usually eat simpler dishes, but we do barbeque a lot. Usually, it's chicken with vegetables, herbs and spices. Sometimes, we use dried buffalo hide," said Prim and smiled at Will.

"I don't believe you," he reacted.

"But it's true! It's a common spice when one cooks for many people," she assured him.

"Well I hope I'll be spared that spice!" Will said.

"If you've bought food from the carts in the street, then you've probably tasted that seasoning already," she told him.

"Now I understand why I got so sick the other night," said Will.

"No, it doesn't make you sick," replied Prim.

*

The nurse was done with her round. She had been away to check on Lu once more, before joining the others again.

"I overheard you saying you got sick from eating food from the street stalls," she said. "That has nothing to do with the ingredients, but comes from them having no way to clean their utensils and pans properly. It could be devastating for a tourist to eat from a market stall. And if it turns out to be a severe stomach illness, there is no way to care for it in Luang Prabang. So you were probably lucky, but you'd better confine yourself to more established kitchens with proper hygiene from now on."

"Yes, I've gathered that," said Will. "But what line are we to take as to what we're about to eat now?"

"You need not worry. You're doing the grilling yourself and as long as it's hotter than eighty degrees, all the bacteria die on the grill," the nurse replied. "And it'll be hotter than that, for sure."

Frank had got the barbecue going and Prim and May carried out the food that was to go on the grill.

"Get on with the grilling now," said May.

Frank felt comfortable in his role as head barbecue chef.

"The only thing missing right now is a big cold beer, isn't that right Frank?" said Will.

"Yeah, that would be nice. But something that would be even nicer is to forget for a minute that we're eating now so we're ready to take Lu down to the hospital."

"That won't take long," said Will and looked at Prim, who seemed worried.

"Will," said Frank, quietly. "Let's give Prim the full pay for all of Lu's three months. I haven't the heart to haggle over the price now, especially when I see what they need."

"Prim," said Will. "We owe your mother her salary and even if we now know that she won't be able to come back to work for a while, we'll be paying for the entire period she was supposed to have worked for us. This means that we'll be giving you her three months' pay."

"Oh, thank you!" said Prim. "That's great. That means I can pay this nurse for mum's treatment."

"No, we've taken care of that already, forget about it," said Frank.

May called out. "Prim, go and get some water for the food!"

Prim ran off to the earth cellar where the water was and when she returned, everybody had taken their seats around the barbeque, with a place left vacant for her. May laid the barbecued meat on various wooden plates and soon, the newcomers realised that they would to eat with their hands, once they'd washed them, that is. The food was eaten quickly.

"Incredibly tasty fish," said Will. "Is it the lemon grass that does the trick?"

"It probably is," said Prim. "Apart from that, it's only salted."

"And I don't think I've ever eaten such a tasty, marinated chicken. But if we're to manage to achieve anything else today, we need to get back soon. Prim, tell your grandmother that we need to hit the road."

Will turned to the nurse, who they now regarded as more of a doctor than anything else; indeed, from that point on, she was considered as the 'Doc'.

"Hey, Doc, could we prepare to head back to Luang Prabang? Frank and I have things to do later," Will asked her.

"Yes, that's probably for the best. I guess we're done here now. You could drive up to the entrance of the hut and then we will all help to get Lu into the car," she replied.

"I'll take care of it," said Frank.

As he stood up, he asked Prim to express their thanks for the delicious meal. The car was driven up to the hut and everybody helped to lift Lu into the back. She had remained silent and seemed entirely unaware of what was going on around her. The Doc did not remove the drip as there was still some fluid left in the bottle and she held it up so gravity could do its job. Prim stood watching as they lifted Lu into the car, holding onto May the whole time. When Frank closed the back door and sat down behind the wheel, Will wound down the window.

"See you soon, Prim!" he said.

At that moment, Prim's strength ran out again and she could no longer hold back from weeping. She watched the car drive away through a fog of tears. May stood with her until the car had vanished beyond the bend.

"Everything will be fine now," said May. "Mum is on her way to the hospital and soon, we'll be able to go and pay her a visit."

"I don't believe you, Grandma," said Prim, between sobs. "I have this feeling inside of me that everything's over. I just don't believe you."

"Come, Prim, come in with me. Come to my place," she encouraged her.

"No Grandma, I want to be by myself. You go! I'll tidy up after mum and then, I'd like to be left alone for a while," said Prim, wiping away her tears.

*

The Doc, Lu, Will and Frank soon reached the Chinese hospital in Luang Prabang. During this hour-long trip, Lu had not made a single sound, despite Frank's efforts to get her to respond.

"I think she can hear," said the Doc. "But for some reason, she doesn't answer. I hope she'll recover enough to tell us who hurt her this badly."

"Yeah, so do we," said Frank.

"When we get her admitted to the hospital, we'll have to make sure to lie about who she is. Would you object if I were to use your surname, Frank and put you down as the contact? Otherwise, it might be difficult to get her into our small hospital," the Doc explained.

"That's fine," said Frank. "We'll use my name and address and tell them that she's a relative of mine."

"The reason is that if I were to say she's from Tat Kuang and that she's Hmong, I'd have to put her on a couch in the corridor and pretend she's only here on a visit," the Doc continued. "And then, to be honest, she'd probably die."

"No, we won't do that. She's to be admitted in my name." Frank drove all the way up to the entrance and from there they carried her to an examination room.

The Doc lay Lu down on a bed and called for someone to come and help undress her and prepare her for a bath. She had to be washed before they dressed her in the hospital's clean clothes.

Will and Frank felt content that they had left Lu in the right place, where she could get the right treatment.

"We'll follow this up when we return," said Frank. "We have to go up to Phonsavan tonight and spend the night there at some suitable place, so we can start the morning with all the things we were supposed to have done today."

"Okay then," said Will, although he was not happy at the prospect of staying in yet another unfamiliar hotel.

"Will, our Chinese Doc was skilled, wasn't she? She knew what she was doing," Frank asked.

"Yeah, of course. If you've been doing the same thing for thirty years, you get really good at it. If not, you're not worth anything."

"Well, I thought she was nice, anyhow," said Frank and headed towards their hotel to get the things they would need to spend the night in Phonsavan. "One thing that struck me was that no one else in the family joined in to help. There were several huts in that yard and if I understood it right, all of her family lived there. Where were the others? It was only Prim and her grandmother who took an active part in helping out," he continued.

"Well, it's probably like in most families: everybody minds their own business," Will replied.

"But Prim's got a paternal grandmother, a maternal grandfather and apparently, an enterprising paternal grandfather. But there was no sign of any of them. I'd assumed that if someone got into trouble, everyone would pitch in to help, right?" Frank said.

"With some people, perhaps," Will replied.

"Her grandfather has a car of his own so he can't be that poor. Besides, he was away on business, whatever that means," Frank decided.

Lu had been seriously affected by the rape. Even with the best care available, would she ever recover? Could she ever recover? Her fate remained in the balance.

Chapter 28

Final Stretch

Songchai continued to guide the tied-up boats down the river. They had come into an area where the river flowed less rapidly than previously. Everyone on board appeared to be sleeping, all except Kitepong, who was sitting in the fore watching out, ready for any unpleasant surprises that might emerge from the water. Even their new guide was asleep, or at least, that was what Songchai assumed. They had passed Dong and Ban Naphan during the night and now, they were bound for Ban Khien before they were due to arrive at Khemmarat which would be the end of the line for everyone apart from Songchai. He would continue down to Khao Nong Kon in order to close the deal. It was early morning and the guide opened his eyes to order people around.

"You heard me; we're to go in to Ban Khien on the Thai side. End of discussion!" he barked.

Then, he took out the gun from inside his plastic bag and held it up for everyone to see, without pointing it at anyone in particular.

"What's this all about? said Songchai. "We're going to Khemmarat."

"No, we're going to Ban Khien. Khanawat will meet us there. That's where you're to go!" he reiterated.

The others became wide awake and wondered what was going on.

"What's happening? Why is he standing there with a gun in his hand?" asked Moa.

"I'm not going to that village," said Surachai, his eyes fixed on the brute. "You can take your gun and go to hell!"

The guide lifted his weapon and held it in front of him, with his arm straight out. He stared at Surachai without blinking and said again, "You are to go in to Ban Khien, or I'll shoot you, you piece of shit!"

The bang drowned the sound of the engine, which was in a low gear. It echoed along the river and would have been heard for many kilometres in the soft breeze. Surachai fell to one side. Songchai and Kitepong threw themselves towards him and as they got to him, blood begun to run down the side of his head. Moa, Lek and the other girls in the boat screamed. Some of them began to cry and hid their faces in their hands to avoid the sight.

"You heard me! You better make bloody sure we get to Ban Khien, or I'll shoot you too, old man," said the guide, now pointing his gun at Songchai.

"I'll drive you to the village if we can continue down to Khemmarat," said Songchai.

"I don't give a shit where you're heading, just make sure to let me and the girls off at that village," he replied.

Kitepong was sitting by Surachai, who was bleeding heavily from his ear. He had been fortunate; the bullet could just as well have hit him right between the eyes and he would have been dead in an instant. Now, he was alive, but less cocky. The bullet had grazed his cheek and split his ear into two halves. He had passed out briefly but now woke up and realised he was bleeding profusely. All he could hear was a loud ringing.

"Here you are, Surachai, I'll just hold a t-shirt over your ear and then we'll bandage it up. Could you hold it for a while? Can you manage that?" asked Kitepong.

Surachai rose to a sitting position and leaned towards another seat to support his upper body while he held the t-shirt over his injured ear.

"I have a gun as well, hidden below the foredeck of my boat," Kitepong whispered into Surachai's good ear.

"You're lucky I didn't shoot you dead, you piece of shit," said the bald, tattooed thug. "But if you keep on looking for trouble, you'll end up in the river; you can count on it. You want to be fish-food?"

"Start the engine, Songchai, so we can get to that bloody village and end this," said Surachai.

"Where in the village do you want us to stop? At the main jetty or outside?" asked Kitepong.

"You're to stop at the far side of the village. You'll see a big white van without windows, standing by a jetty just past the village. You are to berth there. We'll arrive soon, so girls, be ready to get off in Thailand."

"That's nice," said one of the girls. "I've had enough of this."

"I think we should take off as soon as we get ashore," said Moa looking at Lek.

"Yes, absolutely, let's do that," Lek replied.

"But what are we to do about our IDs? They've taken them!" Moa reminded her.

"Sod them. We have no use for them in Thailand and we have some money, so it'll sort itself out one way or another," Lek said.

"I'd pay anything to be free of this," said Moa, looking at Lek. "I just want to get ashore and away from this boat."

"Let's cut loose from this shit when we've disembarked the girls," Surachai said to Songchai, "And after that, no more passengers!"

"Look over there and you'll see the jetty," said their guide. "Not even you can miss it, old man."

He would get the guy for that 'old', Songchai reflected, steering the raft toward the jetty.

"Make sure you get ashore quickly," said Kitepong. "We're not contracted to wait about."

"We'll take as much time as we need, so chill out!" said the thug.

"I'll navigate up to the jetty and push the boats up against it using the engine," said Songchai. "That way, we don't have to weigh anchor and it'll take less time. We're going in against the current, so we'll lie more steadily during the short time it'll take them to get ashore."

"Make sure to take all your belongings with you!" said Khanawat's henchman to the girls. "And be quiet as you get off the boat! We don't want people to see us stopping here and above all, we don't want to draw the attention of the police. Remember that you're entering Thailand without papers. The police will send you back via a reception camp if they discover you and it might cost you dearly. So you'd better be silent."

Songchai did exactly as he had planned. He held the boat against both the current and the jetty by using the raft's propeller.

"Come on!" said the muscled hoodlum. "Hurry up, run to the car and jump in. We'll let you off along Road 222 in the village of Nong Phu. It's just ten kilometres from here. Then, you'll be on safe ground."

All of the girls ran towards the car.

"But Moa!" said Lek. "I thought we'd decided not to go with them! We were going to split! Come on, now!"

"I've changed my mind, Lek," Moa said. "I don't think it'll be a problem. He's just said they're letting us off ten kilometres into the country, where it's safer."

Everybody was in the van now except Moa and Lek. The sliding door was still open and none of the girls knew what awaited them when it closed. Through the opening, the other girls could see the tied-up boats leaving the jetty and their tattooed guard approaching the van.

Moa and Lek looked at each other, nodded and they both stepped up into the van. They realised that they had very little choice in the matter but they also knew that they had no idea where they were going or where they would end up.

*

Surachai was in a foul mood and not just because he'd been shot. He was convinced that Songchai had not been telling the truth. When they had planned the transport of the weapons, Songchai had told them that he had the police under control. This was clearly a lie and after what had just taken place, they could all see it.

"Not far to go, now," said Songchai. "I'm looking forward to reloading to road transport on the Thai side."

"Can we really count on that?" asked Kitepong acidly. "You promised us a lot of things from the start and we've reached the point at which we are all beginning to doubt you. What do you want us to believe? Will things turn out as you said, or what?"

"I'm sorry for what's happened, but it would hardly have turned out this way had you not insisted on taking us to your so called friends. It was you who drew this upon us, not me. And look at Surachai! Just look at the state of him! We've got your 'friends' to thank for that," Songchai said.

They moved out onto the river as Supot started to separate the boats from one another. "Make sure to get the motors going, so that each of us can travel using our own engines," he said. "And Surachai, do you think you can manage to drive your boat?"

"Not a chance," whimpered Surachai. "It hurts too much. Why didn't you shoot that bastard? I have to get to a hospital. You have to drive me to Ban Na Muang. It's downstream, past Khemmarat."

"But that means you won't be able to help us unload," Kitepong observed.

"What do you need me for? Are you suggesting that I should hold one hand on my head and the other one on the cargo? No dammit! I'm going to Muang. One of you will just have to pick me up tomorrow or later tonight," he said.

Surachai's plans to snatch the cargo from Songchai had been completely abandoned after all that had happened.

"We'll have to tow him," said Songchai. "I'll drive down to Muang and arrange for him to get to a hospital. You'll have to wait for me out on the river, a little north of Khemmarat. It shouldn't add too many hours to the journey."

"Alright, stay where you are," said Kitepong to Surachai. "I'll get a line over to my boat from yours and then we'll lift you over to Songchai's boat. Are you still bleeding badly?"

"No, I don't think so, but my ear's still ringing and it hurts like hell," Surachai replied.

"Lie down on your side with your wounded ear upwards. I've got some whiskey left. It'll probably do you good to have a glass. It'll help numb the pain, I'm sure," Kitepong said.

"Give him just a little," said Songchai. "If the doctors notice that he's tipsy, they won't treat him until the alcohol leaves his body and that's not a risk we can take. He'll just have to endure the pain without the booze. It's for the best."

"Well, you didn't listen to what I said, did you? I said one glass of whiskey, not a bottle!" Surachai emphasised.

"Enough of this fuss!" said Supot. "Let's get going!"

When Surachai had been lifted onto Songchai's boat, Songchai opened her up and steered out onto the river. Songchai didn't say much during the course of the trip. But Surachai had to reveal everything he knew about the buyer, the transport and the financial transaction. He believed that there were plenty of elements of this arrangement that might have been planned better, even by himself.

Kitepong looked at Songchai's boat as it vanished quickly down the river and was engulfed by darkness.

"Should we forget about him and do this ourselves?" he asked Supot.

"No, that would probably be a mistake, even if it is tempting. We'll wait, like we agreed, a little to the north of Khemmarat. With a decent pace, we should be there in about an hour. That'll suit us just fine. It'll be daylight by then and we can stop by at a beach. We can relax, eat and rest without anyone getting suspicious. That'll be a change after this hellish night," Supot confirmed.

*

In the cool morning air, it felt liberating to be on the way again, all the more so now there were rid of Khanawat and his henchmen.

The northern part of Khemmarat revealed itself, like all other villages along the river, with a jetty. But they chose instead to berth by the beach in the shade of the trees, a hundred metres beforehand.

"This will be a good place," said Kitepong. "We'll push up onto the beach so that we'll lie with the current. The river isn't that strong here and it won't be long until Songchai returns. I wonder where he planned for us to unload."

"Well, we have to see, I guess. I just hope he's got all this sorted. As far as I understand, it was Surachai who organised the container transport and the freight company," said Supot, as he lashed down the boats with a long line around the trees that stood by the beach. Tied together, the boats laid themselves in the direction of the current. The men began to prepare breakfast, which once again, comprised cold barbecued fish and vegetables.

"I think I'll take a nap after breakfast," said Kitepong. "I've been awake all night. One can really get worked up by an idiot like that. And I never thought I'd end up in a situation like that. One thing's for sure: I'll be a lot more careful next time."

"Yeah, I can understand why Voratep opted out. He probably had an inkling that there would be trouble and it might end badly. And he wouldn't have hesitated to kill, if he'd been subjected to the same indignities as Surachai and he knew it."

"You're right, there," Kitepong said.

"By the way, couldn't we have taken Surachai to the hospital in Khemmarat?" asked Supot. "It's not far from here, is it?"

"Are you out of your mind! That's on the Thai side! If we'd gone there, you can be sure some doctor would have reported us to the police. What would've happened then? No, that would never have worked," Kitepong replied harshly.

While they talked, they ate everything they had taken out from the larder box, which was sufficiently cool, having been stored deep in the keel.

"Well," said Supot when they had finished their breakfast, "I think I'll lie down and rest too."

The two men lay silent, listening to the sounds around them, the water gurgling pleasantly beneath them, the gunwales scraping lightly against each other and the noise of boats passing by. Before long, the river had rocked them to sleep and they both descended into pleasant dreams. But their sleep was cut short by the roar of a boat motor.

"Damned rude!" shouted Supot, without bothering to look and see who had disturbed them.

Kitepong wondered what was going on, but it was just Songchai arriving. He was the same as ever.

"What the hell! Are you sleeping? Half a day has passed! Do you think I've had any sleep?" he asked them.

"No, but what would you rather have had us doing, polishing weapons, or what?" replied Supot.

"I mean, I've had neither sleep nor rest and from what I can see here you've had time to eat, too," Songchai confirmed.

"Indeed we have and if you'd stop being such a grumpy bastard, we have some food for you too. Just lash down your boat and let it swing with the current. You can rest assured that once you've eaten, you'll be as content as we are," Supot said.

Kitepong had a couple of questions for Songchai and it was best to ask them now before it was too late.

"What's your plan? We can't lie around here all day," he asked.

"We won't. I'm going up to the village as soon as I've eaten and put on some ordinary trousers. I can't possibly go there with just a sarong around my waist and nothing on under it," Songchai said.

"That would probably be appreciated by any of the women in the village who happen to be looking for fresh meat," said Kitepong, laughing.

"We've got no time for that at all for the moment," Songchai said.

"What? Do you really mean that you have no time for such things anymore?" Supot said. "I'll be damned! What's happened to you? You never used to miss a chance before, did you?"

"That's as may be, but right now we have neither time nor opportunity for that. When I've had some breakfast, I'll walk up to the haulage company, which is supposed to take the goods down to the coast. They know we're coming and they're prepared but I think we'll have to move from here," Songchai said.

"What kind of haulage company is going to help us carry a cargo like this?" asked Supot.

"Well, the name is just three letters and it's quite an established business, so it should go smoothly for them even if they have to pass roadblocks," Songchai began. "They're streetwise, these guys. I'll go and see if it's possible to walk through the shrubs and thickets here. If it's not, I'll have to get there via the beach and then up onto the road to Kong Pha Niang. It's lucky I've been here a couple of times before. One thing I'm sure about is that we shouldn't go to Arun Prasert and the village's main jetty."

Songchai wolfed down his breakfast, changed clothes quickly and vanished into the thicket, only to return a few minutes later.

"It was impenetrable, worse than the jungle we're used to back home. I'll have to go along the beach," he said.

*

He half-ran barefoot along the beach causing it to whirl about his feet, enjoying the feel of the sand. It had been a long time since he'd done anything like this. After some hundred metres, he turned off and up into the village and then, onto the road towards Niang. It proved to be a long walk, all the way to Prasert and then right to Khinrat where the haulage company's office lay in a low, scruffy building with a large backyard stacked with containers of various sizes, all of them badly worn.

Songchai stopped for a while outside and examined the containers. He wondered which would take their cargo and what journeys these containers had already completed. Then, he entered the building. Just inside the door was a small staircase with just a few steps. Songchai wasn't looking where he was going and almost immediately, he tripped and fell with a crash. None of the three people sitting in the office missed his entrance. He moaned and crawled forward on all fours as he made his way in. They looked wide-eyed upon this odd man. But when he managed to rise to his feet, they smiled in relief and asked him how they could be of assistance.

"I'd like to speak with your manager, Malcolm," Songchai replied.

"That's me," said one of the men. "What can I do for you?"

"I'm Songchai, from Tat Kuang. I understand that you have an agreement with my young relative, Surachai, to help me with a transport."

"Oh, I see," said Malcolm. "So you're the man with the goods which are to be taken to the coast and then onwards. There's no need to go into all the details. Surachai told me everything."

He looked thoughtfully at Songchai. "Where is the freight?" he asked. "And where is Surachai now?"

"Surachai had to visit a local doctor. He had an accident. The goods are just some hundred metres north of Khemmarat." Songchai replied.

"Good, then you're to do as follows. Can you stay where you are until tonight?" Malcolm asked.

"I think so," Songchai confirmed.

"Good. Later on, then, you're to go down just south of Khemmarat, to the junction with Banghing on your left, another river which flows into the Mekong. After that, you'll see a smaller river immediately to your right. It looks a bit tight but once you've covered a short stretch, it'll soon get wider. You're to head up that river to the first bridge. The road there is called Wisit Si. We'll be there tonight after dark. Under the bridge, we can unload the goods easily from your boats by hand and load them into the container lorry which will be standing by on the bridge," Malcolm explained.

"Okay, I've got it. But if it's a public road, is it really safe to stand there loading?" Songchai asked.

"It won't be public tonight. We'll make sure the police shut it down for repairs. But right now, I have to take care of a lot of things to make sure it all works," said Malcolm and gestured to Songchai that he should leave.

"Wait a minute, what about money? I have co-workers who need to be paid tonight. And according to Surachai, half is to be paid now and the rest down in the harbour," Songchai reminded him.

"Everything's been taking care of. As you say, you'll get half tonight and the rest later. Make sure you don't trip on your way out though, since there's no one to help you outside," Malcom said.

Could Malcolm be trusted? Would Songchai and the others get paid? Would they end up in prison? These were all questions on Songchai's mind as he made sure not to trip his way back outside into the sunlight.

The 'Behind the Scenes' Series
by Staffan Norstrand

Book 1
Crime and Suffering

Book 2
Bodies for Sale
(To be published in March 2025)

Book 3
Rich and Poor
(To be published in August 2025)

Book 4
Changing Identities
(To be published in November 2025)